PENGUIN BOOKS

I CAN'T BEGIN TO TELL YOU

I Can't Begin
to Tell You

E L I Z A B E T H   B U C H A N

PENGUIN BOOKS

PENGUIN BOOKS

UK | USA | Canada | Ireland | Australia
India | New Zealand | South Africa

Penguin Books is part of the Penguin Random House group of companies
whose addresses can be found at global.penguinrandomhouse.com.

First published by Michael Joseph 2014
Published in Penguin Books 2015
001

Printed in Great Britain by Clays Ltd, St Ives plc

A CIP catalogue record for this book is available from the British Library

ISBN: 978–0–718–15800–2

www.greenpenguin.co.uk

MIX
Paper from
responsible sources
FSC® C018179

Penguin Random House is committed to a
sustainable future for our business, our readers
and our planet. This book is made from Forest
Stewardship Council® certified paper.

For Elizabeth, my Copenhagen companion

From 1940 to 1946 the Special Operations Executive (SOE) was a British secret service that supported Resistance in all enemy-occupied countries.

Chapter One

Day One

Kay Eberstern was moving as unobtrusively as she could manage through the tongue-shaped wood of ash and birch which ran alongside the lake on her husband's Danish estate. It was five o'clock on an early November evening in 1942.

It was imperative not to be seen.

At this time of the evening the men working on the estate went home and they would be taken aback if they caught sight of Kay lurking here. They would ask: 'What is the master's wife doing?' If it were peacetime, they might conclude that she was meeting a lover. But it was not peacetime. It was war, Hitler's war, and British-born Kay had got herself caught up in it. If she was spotted, gossiped over, or betrayed, there could be, almost certainly would be, serious repercussions for the Eberstern family.

Her orders had been to wait for an hour every evening in the wood at Rosenlund, for up to three days. Here she was to rendezvous with 'Felix', a British-trained agent who, if all had gone to plan, would have arrived in the area in order to set up resistance operations. She had also been warned that the plans might go awry and the mission aborted. The agent was being parachuted into Jutland and faced a difficult sea journey to Zealand and a subsequent cross-country one into the Køge area.

Kay could have no illusions as to what might happen to Tanne and Nils, her children, or to Bror, her husband. Everyone knew that the Danish police weren't backward in coming forward in rounding up anyone involved in this sort of activity and handing them over to the German *Gestapomen*.

Was outraged decency a sufficiently good reason to put Tanne and Nils, and her marriage to Bror, at risk? Was her refusal to tolerate evil, cruelty and a creeping fascism worth it?

Being seriously apprehensive was a new and unwelcome sensation and Kay was struggling to master it. If her task hadn't been so crucial, and in other circumstances, she might have set about analysing its effects. Damp palms and a queasy stomach were predictable. Less so, were the upsurges of bravado followed by the slump into panic. Like a disease, fear caused weakness and debilitation.

The winter was gearing up and, at this time of the evening, it was growing cold. She pushed her gloved hands into her pockets. Tomorrow, *if* there was a tomorrow, she would take pains to kit up more warmly. It hadn't occurred to her until she was actually standing and freezing in the wood that she should think practically and prepare. For a start, she needed a torch.

Why was she here?

What was happening back at the house? Had she been missed yet? Birgit was preparing dinner and Kay had been careful to tell her that she hadn't been sleeping well – not an untruth – and would be taking a nap.

An owl hooted: a hollow, eerie sound.

Kay shifted uneasily.

Two years ago, on 9 April 1940, Hitler marched into Denmark and declared it a Protectorate with a special blood-brother relationship with the Reich, completely ignoring the non-aggression pact which he had signed with Denmark.

It looked as though the Danes had been caught napping.

Rumours of Hitler's intentions had been circulating for months. Kay had turned into an obsessive listener to the BBC while it reported what was happening in Austria, Czechoslovakia and Poland – but in Denmark, even with Germany just next door, events had seemed removed, almost remote. She and Bror took their places at the breakfast table early on that

April morning, he pale and grim, she flushed and on edge. They gazed at each other and Kay imagined she heard in her head the appalled cries of protest at this new arrangement of Europe.

It had taken all day to get a phone connection to her mother in England. Fretful, anxious hours, and lipstick-stained cigarette butts were heaped in the ashtray by the time she got through.

'Kay . . .' Her mother was on the verge of weeping, which was unlike her. 'Your sisters and I have been desperate to hear from you. We've heard the news. Are you all right?'

'Are *you* all right?'

It was baffling how such important conversations could be reduced to the basics.

Kay searched to make the verbal connection mean something. 'We're getting over the shock.'

'Darling, couldn't you come home?'

Home.

She thought of Piccadilly Circus, of the lisle stockings she used to wear, of nips of sherry in meanly sized glasses and overdone beef for Sunday lunch, and of her mother standing in the passageway of her tiny cottage at the end of a waterlogged lane clutching the telephone receiver. She thought, too, of her mother's deferential, polite widowhood lived out on the edges of a society that didn't rate widows very highly.

Coming to live in Denmark, she had left all those things behind.

'Kay, I wish you didn't live so far away. I wish . . . I wish . . . I don't want to die without seeing you again.'

'You're not going to die, Mother. Do you hear me?'

Her mother pulled herself together, as Kay knew she would. 'I've taken in two little boys, evacuees. The bombing is so bad in London and they're sending all the children into the country. They had fleas! Imagine! They don't speak the King's English. But I'm getting used to it . . .'

The timed call limped to its three-minute limit.

England was cut off.

Kay shook herself, determined not to dip into homesickness. Her life was here now, in Denmark.

How hard it had been to keep the homesickness and misery at bay when she first arrived as a nervous and badly dressed bride. Having met Bror at her friend Emily's twenty-first dance, she had married him only six months later. It had been a fast and exciting transition. Too rapid, perhaps? Although she was deeply in love and saw her new life as an opportunity to be grasped, she had been ignorant of the battle she would face in turning herself into a woman capable of running Rosenlund. The Ebersterns expected conformity and there were times when she had had to fight to subdue her rebellion. There had also been occasional clashes with Bror, whose politics were more old-fashioned than hers.

Yet in those early days her senses had been stoked and stroked by physical love, by the sights and scents and tastes of a different country, by the challenge of mastering the Danish language and customs. It had been a time of languor, of sensuality and of plenty, when the glittering mysteries of ice and fog during the long dark Danish winters offered some compensation for the occasional moments of sadness.

Inside Kay's walking shoes, her toes were cramping.

Sweat had gathered at the bottom of her spine and the waistband of her skirt was unpleasantly damp. The truth was that she was frightened. Truly terrified she had made the wrong decision.

To steady herself, Kay started counting up to ten.

One . . . two . . .

They were lucky at Rosenlund. The war had not really hit them here yet – or in Køge, the ancient fishing port just three miles to the east. Only a short train ride from the capital, Rosenlund still could, and did, function along traditional rural lines. The seasons dictated its agenda. So it had been easy, and natural perhaps, to duck away from the worst and for family life to continue, not so much blithely, but removed.

All the same. All the same . . . was a refrain that ran frequently through Kay's mind.

Elsewhere, Danes who opposed the Directorate were being rounded up. There were reports of torture and of murder in the streets and in the cells of Vestre prison in København (as Kay had learned to call it). Others were holed up in houses which they trusted to be safe, only to be betrayed by fellow Danes, the so-called *stikker*.

In the early days of their love affair, Bror told her: 'In Denmark it is a point of honour to care for our communities.'

Then, she believed him.

Anyone could see that in giving Bror possession of the eighteenth-century ochre-painted house, with its farmlands and woods occupying a fertile curve outside Køge, fate had dealt him a royal flush.

She had only to conjure the image of his tall, fair figure standing by the window in the elegantly proportioned drawing room, looking out across the lake to the fields and wooded clumps, to hear him say: 'As long as one field lies against another supporting it, there I shall be . . .' It was the voice of a man at ease with his task, caught up by an urgent, emotional, almost mystical, union with the land.

No one could accuse Bror of not caring for his inheritance.

'Three,' she muttered to herself. 'Four.'

Think of something else . . .

The early days . . .

Bror wooed Kay with stories of the Danes. Obviously. He told her of Vikings, of fishermen, artists, designers, navigators, wireless inventors, democrats. He told her of heroes and their voyages, of the Danes' ongoing tussle with the sea.

He described how the sea turned iron grey in winter and brilliant blue and amber in summer. He explained the geographical oddity which meant the Baltic froze in winter because it wasn't very salty. He singled out the pebble beaches, the pines, the wild myrtle and gorse and the tiny islands which peppered the coastline.

He told of being the small boy, then the teenager, who got up before light and went out with his father to shoot duck on the mist-shrouded marshes. The making of a crack shot.

The salt tang. The silence. The swoop of the birds. The beating of their wings.

Almost word for word, Kay remembered what he said.

Bror painted a land of cool, clean beauty and astringent winds ... all of which Kay discovered to be true when it became her home and she found happiness.

Bror Eberstern, her husband. To outsiders he was a courteous landowner, with a laconic, sometimes brusque, manner of which they could be afraid or daunted. Only a few intimates knew of his gentleness and tenderness and the reserve which masked his feelings.

No man was an island and it followed that no woman was either. Habit, children, their shared bed, their shared days, their deep feelings for each other – these created the ties which had grown thicker and tougher over the years. Yet Bror had gone and made a decision, a political one, which had the power to change her life.

Kay was angry about it. Bitterly so.

She shifted position, kicking up the undergrowth which smelled of leaf mould mixed with recent rain. So much of life had its scents and stinks: newborn babies, roasting pork, bad drains, fresh bread, the glamorous and addictive aroma of Turkish cigarettes, the tanning lorry, pink and white sweet peas. So did waking early in the morning to a world cleansed by the dark, to recently polished leather shoes, Bror's aura of tweed and tobacco ... To be conscious was to engage with sensations in which she took endless pleasure. To be alive was a gloriously tactile experience, gloriously absorbing. Any eloquence she might summon to describe what she was experiencing faltered in the face of the shimmery intensity of her feelings.

Five forty-five. Fifteen more minutes before time was up.

In wartime, the senses were assaulted in new ways. People were less clean, less well fed. Poverty and scarcity smelled different.

If poverty smelled, did fear smell too? These days fear and suspicion were everywhere. Danish police were checking every traveller on trains and on boats and ferries. *Gestapomen* patrolled the ports. Then there were the *stikker*. Nosy. Officious. Highly dangerous. And you never knew where they were.

That *stikker* were a big problem wasn't surprising. Their equivalents would be everywhere, including Britain. No society was incorruptible and no one's motives were unadulterated. When Kay's father lay dying, he let slip to his daughter a little of what he had learned amid the mud and the blood of the Great War: 'When you are cold and hungry and frightened . . . or wounded, you don't care about political philosophies or the passions which drive them. They fall away. You want to survive and you will sacrifice most things to do so . . .' Watching his features drain of life, she cried helplessly. At the time, her grief was too overwhelming for her to examine what her father had meant but the halting words must have rooted in her unconscious mind for she remembered them now.

A grey, insubstantial mist which had previously settled over the lake was shifting. The darkness folded down. There were noises which she half recognized, half not, for, in her state of heightened awareness, they appeared to be extra loud and ominous.

Time?

Five minutes to go. The knot in her chest slackened for she doubted Felix would turn up now – whoever he was. A hero? An opportunist? A non-conformist? A communist? It was common gossip that it was only the communists who demonstrated any open resistance in Denmark.

In the two years since Denmark had been occupied Kay had lived in a bubble. It had taken the lunch with Anton, Bror's cousin, for her to understand that some men and women were responding to the need to be decent and, believing their government to be supine, were taking matters into their own hands.

If that was so, what did Bror's actions make him?

Asking and answering the question made Kay feel dangerously out of kilter.

Crack.

What was that? Heartbeat accelerating, Kay whipped round. Nothing. Breathing out slowly, she refocused on the lake. The mist had now cleared and the light from the stars nipped and bobbed on the water.

Would Felix be tall, short, old, young? Was he Danish? Probably. Otherwise the language barrier would be too difficult. Even after twenty-five years in Denmark, Kay still spoke with a foreign inflection.

Time was up.

She was off the hook for today and, for all that she had resolved to be strong and resolute, she was thankful.

Glancing over her shoulder, she moved off in the direction of the house.

. . . 'Pack up your troubles in your old kit bag . . .' the ghost of her father sang in her ear in a cracked baritone. 'Can't you be quiet, dear?' said her mother . . .

Immersed in her marriage as Kay had been since she arrived here twenty-five years ago, occupied by motherhood and life at Rosenlund, she'd found that the power of England to evoke an intense response in her had diminished. Yet, since that April morning in 1940 when Hitler marched into Denmark, she had been winded at odd moments by homesickness – its jolt speeding through her body in an almost physical manner. 'Plucky little Britain is punching above its weight,' said Anton and she wanted to cry out: 'My country!' Then she remembered. No, England wasn't her country any longer. Denmark was.

Remember that.

Even so, she found herself wanting to rap people on the chest and to say: 'Do you understand Britain has gone it alone?'

Here in this wood, where Danish sphagnum moss lapped around her shoes and the smell of water pricked in her nostrils, Kay would have given much for the sight of the damp ox-eyed daisies and rose-bay willow herb growing outside her mother's cottage . . . to be sitting with friends in a dark, smoky Gaumount cinema . . . to be rattling along in a red London bus, to be dancing to the band in the Savoy in someone's arms – preferably Bror's but those of any warm, handsome male would do for that moment. It would mean being part of a nation who knew where they were. *Fighting Herr Schicklgruber.*

Breathe in. Breathe out.

Go home.

Chapter Two

A couple of weeks ago, out of the blue, Anton Eberstern, Bror's first cousin, had rung Kay at Rosenlund to invite her to lunch at one of København's most talked-about restaurants.

She went.

The restaurant was the sort of professional enterprise in whose cosmopolitan gloss was embedded the famous Danish *hygge* – a cultivated cosiness designed to shut out the world's troubles. *Hygge*, Kay reckoned, was the Danish riposte to the wear and tear of cruel winters, a fragmented territory and an often hostile sea.

Bror was going off on a ten-day fishing trip on Jutland with his cousins, the Federspiels, but he dispatched Kay to act as his eyes and ears. 'Anton must be up to something,' he said with the curious expression that she could never get to the bottom of. They occasionally discussed the antipathy between Bror and Anton – or, at least, Kay tried to discuss it, but she never got very far since Bror's response tended to be anything but rational. 'I don't think he's ever got over the fact that I have Rosenlund,' he once admitted. 'And he's rotten to women.' Kay had laughed and informed Bror that he had just made Anton seem twice as attractive. A womanizer with a slight grudge. 'Every woman in Denmark will make it her mission to heal him.'

The train had been crowded, as was usual these days, and the talk in the carriage had been of the watered-down milk which had become the norm and the difficulty of obtaining petrol. In København itself there were German soldiers in the streets, older and shabbier than might have been expected from the reputedly smart-as-paint *Wehrmacht*.

When Anton got up to greet her in the restaurant, she was startled by his neat blond moustache. 'That's new.'

'Admiring my beauty. Don't frown, darling. It's my tribute to Herr Hitler.' He smiled but not with huge amusement. 'Camouflage in war is sensible.'

She peered at Anton.

The cousins may have borne a family resemblance – the jawline, the blondness, a certain facial expression. That was deceptive. Temperamentally, they were chalk and cheese.

Anton was shorter and of slighter build than Bror. When not in his uniform, he displayed a fondness for cashmere coats, Savile Row tailoring and custom-made shoes. He loved political gossip and diplomatic intrigue and was well informed. He made the best of lunch companions.

In comparison to Rosenlund, Anton's house and land were modest – there being only a small acreage with which to enjoy a mystical relationship. If he minded – as Bror suggested – he never gave the slightest indication to Kay. A bachelor, he concentrated on love affairs, good wine, cigars and the flowers which he grew in his famed hothouses. To receive one of Anton's bouquets was said to be a signal for seduction. Life was too serious to be serious, he told Kay. She believed him until she grew wiser and more sceptical. Anton was a colonel in Danish military intelligence and, presumably, somewhere in the mix of charm and conviviality was a professional.

Anton ordered for them both.

Over the fish soup, he regarded Kay with his customary combination of overt lust and admiration. As the bride, Kay had found Anton's behaviour unsettling. These days, she found his lightness of touch attractive. Once or twice she had asked herself if his obvious admiration pandered to her vanity. Just a little? More than a little?

Anton raised a glass of Chablis. 'The hat is good, Kay. Blue on blonde hair is magnetic. Did you buy it on one of your little trips to Paris?'

The hat was royal blue with a black feather and wispy netting and nestled on Kay's piled-up hair. The effect was particularly good with the Eberstern pearls round her neck, something she knew perfectly well when she dressed for this meeting.

'Yes,' she said and sighed, remembering wet streets, perfume, garlic soup, making love with Bror in a hotel room. 'I miss Paris.'

'Did you wear it to seduce me?'

'Oh, the masculine mind.'

'Are you sure you didn't? Anything can happen after lunch, you know.' He held her gaze. 'I love you, Kay, for how quickly you stopped being British and dowdy after you came here.' There was a tiny pause. 'How are things at dear old Rosenlund?' A further pause. 'And dear old Bror? How's he taken it all?'

Bror had been angry and unsettled by the German takeover of the country. 'Think of the numbers, Kay,' he'd said in response to her frantic question as to why no one had gone out and fought. 'There are seventy-five million Germans and only four and a half million of us. Who do you expect to win? Who? Tell me . . .' He'd grasped her by the shoulders. '*Tell me.*'

She'd looked up at him. 'But not too . . .' The words were stillborn.

Geography and politics did not make up the whole story for Bror. There was also a question of kinship. The Ebersterns had German relations and knew Germany well. It was logical, Kay told herself. Inevitable. Bror wasn't British or American and part of his psyche responded to the Germanic traditions. Over the generations, German wives and husbands had come to live at Rosenlund, leaving echoes in the house and on the land. No wonder Bror's reaction to the Reich's presence was complex and, almost certainly, fraught with tensions.

Discussing Bror with Anton was tricky and she avoided it when possible. 'Making-do, like everyone else. Some of the men are trickling away to work in Germany.'

'Dear, oh dear,' said Anton.

She didn't mention that they had been forced to cut back on expenditure or, now short-handed, Bror got up earlier, held daily meetings with Arne, his foreman, and worked later to keep it all going.

The waiter topped up the glasses.

'Do you know what he has been up to?'

She sensed that this was a loaded question and instinct told her to keep her reply neutral. 'Business trips up here. Out in the fields. Talking to Arne. The usual.'

It wasn't quite true. With a touch of apprehension, she recollected Bror had – unusually – taken to closeting himself in the estate office to make phone calls. Once, she had answered the house telephone to an official-sounding voice asking to speak to her husband. That had been followed by an unexpected trip to København.

Anton chose his moment. 'Have you heard about the Declaration of Good Will?'

Something clicked. This lunch had been plotted out – a manoeuvre. More likely than not, she was being used to get at Bror for some purpose.

Anton continued: 'It's been drawn up by the Agricultural Ministry to keep the Germans quiet. Landowners have been asked to sign it. Has Bror mentioned it?'

The information came as a shock – and she was forced to take a moment before asking: 'What are you trying to tell me?'

Anton took on board her reaction. 'Have you heard about it?'

'I haven't, no.' She ran her finger around the rim of her wine glass and it gave off a tiny shriek. 'But if I had . . . ?'

He shrugged. 'If you sign a document such as the Declaration you are on the record. The Nazis are brilliant at records. I thought you should know.'

'Anton . . . ?' He was making her uneasy. 'Why should I know this?'

'Ask Bror.'

'I will.' Kay hoped her smile would mask her sudden terror that Bror had done something stupid. 'And where do *you* stand?'

She expected . . . well, what? A riff on the virtues of keeping one's head down? The impossibility of Denmark doing anything but what it was doing. Perhaps even admiration and support for the Reich? It was what many Danes believed.

His gaze shifted around the room and then focused hard on her face. 'Kay, the situation in Denmark is dismal but there are alternatives.'

She could not have been more surprised. 'Meaning?'

'This is for your ears only.' He waited for the implications to fall into place. 'Understood?'

An astonished Kay nodded. Anton poured out the last of the wine with his usual dispatch.

'Danes can't fight in the conventional way,' he said. 'But there are growing numbers of those opposed to the Nazis hiding up in Sweden and England. Some of them who've managed to reach London are being trained in undercover work. Intelligence-gathering, sabotage, mustering underground armies.'

It was as if an earthquake had shaken the restaurant and Kay was wandering, dazed, through the rubble. 'But isn't the Danish army working for the Nazis? Aren't you?'

'I'm working alongside . . .' Anton dropped his searchlight scrutiny. 'Everyone has to be very, very careful. They are not kind to what they call enemy terrorists.'

Kay dredged her memory. Not long ago, a story had done the rounds about a British-trained parachutist jumping out of a plane over Jutland and his parachute failing to open. His smashed body had been discovered by the authorities and the reprisals, once they had rounded up anyone they thought might have been involved, were very bad.

'So, in England . . . ?' she murmured.

'You miss it?' Anton must have caught her confusion and nostalgia.

'Yes. When the war began, I was horrified, of course. But since the invasion of Denmark I feel differently.' She tucked a strand of hair back into her chignon. 'Not surprising, is it?'

He was sympathetic, almost tender. 'It makes you realize what it means to you?'

'Yes. Big events do.'

Anton lowered his voice. 'Denmark is not high on the Allies' agenda. Even so, the British, including these people I was talking about, will give some support if we can get organized here. Unfortunately, this means they will interfere in ways we don't necessarily like but . . .' He shrugged. 'Can't be helped.'

Her bewilderment more or less under control, Kay strove to understand the implications. 'Surely, if there's trouble in Denmark, it will tie up the German troops here even though they are needed elsewhere.'

It was a small triumph of strategic thinking.

'So . . .' Anton gave one of his smiles. 'You do keep up.'

'Anton, look at me.' He obeyed immediately. 'You know I could betray you.'

The handsome features darkened. 'But you won't, Kay. Because you're British. Because you're no fascist.' Again, the tender note sounded. 'Because your heart beats to an English drum.'

She flinched.

Two tables away a couple blew kisses at each other. Across the room a man in a loud tweed suit was eating a solitary meal.

'These people you talk about in England . . . ?'

He got her gist. 'Who are they? A curious bunch. Bandits operating in the shadows. From what we can gather, and we are not supposed to know about it, there's an outfit based in London which trains men – and women – for undercover operations and infiltrates them into occupied countries. It has Prime Minister Churchill's backing . . . being a bit of a boy scout himself, he's very keen on it. We've seen it referred to in one report as the "SOE".' He spread his hands as if to say: *God knows what that stands for.* 'But intelligence chatter has picked up talk about "The Firm". Its existence is top secret.'

'How did you make contact?'

'Darling Kay, the first rule is to never ask questions.'

'But you're taking a risk telling me. A big one.'

'Calculated, Kay.'

She stirred in her seat. Fingered the pearls at her neck. She had the oddest notion that Anton had unearthed an element in her of which she had not been aware.

'All sorts of things are needed. For instance, if we are going to work with the British we need safe houses for agents to hide up in. I've already organized one or two in Køge.' He stared at her and she felt, suddenly, older, more experienced, more laden with knowledge than she had ever imagined. 'You get the picture?'

She glanced up at the ceiling of the restaurant, its decorative plaster work reminding her of whipped cream. God only knew how it would survive if København was bombed like London.

Sense prevailed.

'If you're asking me, I can't,' she said. 'The children. Bror.'

'Tanne is twenty-four. Nils is twenty-two. Hardly children. And Bror . . .' Anton dismissed him with a gesture.

Bror had done something. But what?

Kay collected her wits. 'No,' she said.

Anton allowed a long moment to elapse into which she read disappointment, a slight contempt.

'I understand . . .'

It was clear that he didn't.

Anton snapped his fingers at the waiter, asked Kay if she wanted anything and ordered a double brandy for himself, then launched into a description of the *fester-kinder* party recently held by his neighbours . . . the buffet, the wines, the conversations, the nightmare of transport without petrol. He was at his most brilliantly diverting and it meant nothing.

'I must go,' she said at last. 'I'm sorry.'

'Don't be.' His lids dropped over his eyes. 'There is one thing . . . Some pamphlets need delivering to Lippiman's bakery in Køge.'

'That's simple,' she said and held out a hand. 'Give them to me.'

He raised his eyes. 'I don't think you understand, darling.'

Then she did.

'The previous courier was caught,' continued Anton. 'I need someone to pick up from the contact at the station and deliver them. Lippiman does the rest.'

The hidden parallel world in which Anton dealt was beginning to piece together. 'Mr Lippiman!' She glanced down at her left hand where the ring with the Eberstern diamonds caught the light. 'How surprising people are. I thought I knew him.'

'You thought you knew me.'

Kay sat very still. 'This is really you, Anton. I had no idea.' Something was shifting in her mind . . . but what? 'Why did I have no idea?'

'No one ever knows anyone.'

'Anton, what is Bror up to?'

He sat back in his chair. Easy and amused. Malicious. 'Ask him.'

There was a silence.

'I *really* must go.'

'Of course.' He reached over and captured one of Kay's hands. 'Would you do this? Just this once? The courier will wait on the platform for the afternoon train with a basket. It's just a matter of you taking the basket and dropping it in at the bakery on the way back.'

What had Anton done to her? She felt newly connected, but also disorientated – as if she had been pushed out of the shadow into blinding sun.

'It's very simple, Kay.'

With an excitement that was almost erotic, Kay allowed her hand to remain in his. 'If I am caught?'

'Ah.' He retrieved his hand. 'Then I would deny everything and swear my undying support of the Reich. Which means I'm unreliable and you are on your own. Understood?'

The girl standing on the platform where the Køge train was waiting was roughly the same age as Tanne – far, far too young to be putting herself in danger.

Kay's excitement drained and a faint nausea replaced it.

Someone should tell her. Someone should take her in hand and explain what it would mean to be found out. Where was her mother?

A basket was parked by the girl's feet and she was wearing inadequate-looking boots which Kay feared would let in the cold and wet.

Still some distance away, Kay stopped and pressed a hand to a cheek flushed from the wine at lunch. A couple of German soldiers in their green-grey – *feldgrau* – uniforms swaggered past her. Knowing they were being watched, they talked loudly, made jokes and showed off. Halfway down the platform, they stopped to light up cigarettes.

The girl with the basket stiffened visibly.

No, Kay willed her. *Act normally*.

Grasping her handbag strap, Kay walked up the platform. The girl registered Kay's presence. Then she turned her head away.

The movement exposed a delicate neck and its pale vulnerability triggered a violent reaction in Kay. It was like the moment when she had first held Tanne in her arms and had been overwhelmed by powerful and, as she had discovered, ineradicable impulses to protect her child.

The girl could be Tanne.

And if she had been Tanne?

The image of Rosenlund took shape, with every breath growing brighter and clearer – its high windows, the terraces, the lake, the fields and woods. She heard the sound of the harvest being brought in, the squeal of the pigs herded up for slaughter, the clunk of the threshing machine. In a terrible old pair of linen trousers, Bror was climbing into the boat with a picnic basket, followed by the children. It was a sunny summer day, and the sun bounced off the water as they rowed over to Princess Sophia-Maria's island in the middle of the lake. She heard their shouts and the yell as one or other of them jumped into the always-freezing water.

Kay wasn't going to endanger them.

Denmark could hold its own. It would survive.

For God's sake.

Turning around abruptly, Kay made her way back down the platform, pushing against the tide of passengers heading for the train.

Common sense had triumphed – a powerful and protective shield which she had raised for the right reasons.

Chapter Three

Day Two

'So there you are,' said Bror. 'I wondered where you'd gone.'

Jacket in hand, Kay swivelled round. Bror was advancing down the tiled passage to the place where the family's outdoor clothing hung on labelled pegs – in Denmark it was important to keep track of warm clothing.

'Goodness, you startled me,' she said.

He observed the jacket in her hand and the brogues on her feet. 'Isn't it an odd time to be going out?'

She glanced at the pegs with the neatly stowed jackets and coats. There was Tanne's Norwegian hat, Nils's green Norfolk jacket bought on a trip back to England, Bror's hunter's jacket.

It was astonishing how, once the mind was made up, the lies slid as easily off the tongue as her breakfast *ymer*. 'The dogs seem restless and I need a bit of fresh air.'

'Do they?' Bror was surprised. 'They were out for hours with me this morning.' He pointed to the door at the end of the passage where the fanlight displayed the intensifying dusk. 'It's too dark and cold, Kay. Leave it for this evening. I'll take them out tomorrow.'

This was the Bror whom she knew so well – whose sweetness and gallantry she knew so well too.

'I don't think you understand. I want a little time to myself.'

He stuck his hands in his pockets, bent his fair head and seemed to be absorbed by the sight of his shoes. 'You can't remain angry with me, Kay. We have to be clever, both of us. Sooner or later you must accept the changes.' She was silent. Bror persisted. 'You're still very angry.'

Yes, she was.

She wanted to tell him that, since their conversation by the lake when Bror had told her the truth, something had changed between them. And something had changed in her, Kay, too. In doing what he had done, Bror had displaced the subtle balance of love and loyalty which had existed between them for so long.

She pulled on her jacket and buttoned it up, tight and hard. 'Yes. Very. Go back to your newspaper, Bror.'

In response, Bror reached behind her for his jacket. Hooking it off the peg, he said, 'I'm not letting you go out on your own. I'll come with you.'

The day after the København lunch, Kay rang Anton from the hall in Rosenlund. A fuzzy image of herself was reflected in the polished hall table while she talked – and it was as if she was watching a stranger. 'I've been thinking things over. A lot of things. Particularly what you told me about Bror.' She gathered her resolve. 'I need more chapter and verse.'

'Talk to him yourself.' Anton's voice sounded hollow down the line.

'Anton . . .'

Anton considered. 'I've got an appointment in Køge,' he said. 'Can you meet me there?'

It was done.

'Kay . . .' Before she put down the receiver, Anton sounded a warning. 'Remember what we agreed?' He was reminding her to say nothing. 'And, Kay, never talk on the phone.'

They met 'by chance' in Køge's main square.

It happened to be market day. Stalls lined the square and seethed with shoppers. Butchers were doing a good business as was the milk stall. Under a striped awning, the baker had laid out a display of Bror's favourite gingerbread which caught Kay's attention.

In uniform, Anton always presented a dapper sight. Out of it, he blossomed into elegance. Today, since he was on home territory, he had slung a cashmere coat over his suit and a red silk scarf round his neck. Beside this magnificence Kay, in her second-best grey flannel costume with a grey felt hat which dipped over one eye, felt less modish than previously. He kissed her in a more or less cousinly fashion and as he led her to a bench he remarked that the hat wasn't a patch on the Parisian one.

He watched her fiddle with her gloves and waited patiently for her to begin.

'Those pamphlets? What was in them?'

He frowned. 'Don't waste my time, Kay.'

'I wouldn't do that,' she said.

'All right. It was a list of commandments. Don't work for Germany; or if you do, work badly. Join the fight for freedom. We're trying to get the message out to the outlying rural areas.'

After the positive feelings that resulted from not accepting the pamphlets, it had come as a shock to Kay to discover how one small non-action – as small as not stretching out a hand to pick up a basket – could so profoundly unsettle her equilibrium. For it had.

She laced her gloved fingers together. 'Anton, you do understand . . . ?'

But he wasn't interested in her protestations. 'The author was a brave man. He hid the copies in a room full of deadly bacteria in the Serum Institute and risked his life.'

'And the girl? What's happened to her?'

Anton shrugged. 'Not my business. Nor is it yours.'

What was done was done. Kay looked up and over to the canvas awnings flapping in the wind. 'Tell me more about this declaration or whatever it is.'

She knew perfectly well that she had fed Anton an opportunity to indulge in a little malice. He took it. 'How peculiar. You're always at pains to tell me that you two are as thick as thieves. Don't you and Bror . . . er, discuss?'

'That's the point. I can't ask him. He's still away until next week, seeing the cousins in Jutland. Anyway, even you can appreciate it is difficult for us . . . for me.'

'*Are* you serious, Kay?'

She bit her lip and looked away. The twenty-four hours which had elapsed since her lunch with Anton had seen a crack opening in her loyalties to Bror. 'Yes,' she said.

He shifted closer to her on the bench. 'To repeat what I said at our . . . our delightful lunch . . . After the initial relief that Denmark's occupation would be relatively peaceful, unlike that in France or Poland, many Danes are increasingly questioning the situation. We don't want violence but no one can fail to notice that the British and Americans are both fighting. "Why aren't we in the fight?" these Danes will ask. And "What can we do?"'

A man in a trilby hat stopped to light a cigarette. He glanced at Kay and Anton. Anton fell silent and waited until he was out of earshot.

Touching her arm, he said, 'In your case, you might think: But I'm British and therefore I'm in the fight, but I'm not sure how. Because of the peculiar Danish situation, it isn't clear-cut.'

A woman in stout boots and carrying two milk churns clanked past.

'The British have made it clear to our contacts that they are too tight-arsed to fund an underground army here but they would, nevertheless, like us to provide intelligence and do lots of lovely sabotage. Railways, bridges, factories . . . you can imagine. Naturally, there's a problem. Intelligence and sabotage aren't always compatible because sabotage triggers reprisals and muddies the waters for the intelligence-gatherers.'

She stared at the houses on the opposite side of the square, the autumn sun illuminating the rich reds and burnt siennas of the painted facades. 'Surely it won't make any difference as it's likely there will always be reprisals?'

Anton raised an eyebrow. 'Kay, you've missed your vocation. Listen . . . German troops are constantly in transit to and from Norway. The Nazis also need to maintain garrisons here in case the Allies invade through this route.' He allowed the last point to sink in. 'Granted, it's unlikely, but the Allies will invade one day, you know. The Germans also need to patrol the shipping routes bringing in the Norwegian minerals which they badly need. Bauxite for aluminium, for example. All of which makes them vulnerable.'

Her eyes narrowed.

She could imagine lines of German troops waiting for trains. Temperatures plummeting. Snow in piles. Breath steaming. Cigarette butts raining down. Grey-green uniforms. The men talking – *Schweizerdeutsch*. Southern dialects. Prussian vowels. A babble. But maybe for those men . . . those boys . . . the Danish skies where the stars and planets burnt in the velvety black would be a reminder of home . . . ?

'You've gone quiet, Kay.'

She stirred. 'The people you're talking about . . . they are brave.'

'Yes.' For once Anton sounded completely sincere.

'Like the girl on the platform.'

'Stop thinking about her.'

She realized then that she envied these unknown people – for their commitment and their immunity to fear which, on some level, they had to have.

'Kay, I want you to think about something. I don't want you to make up your mind, just to think about it. In a few days' time there will be someone who will need a safe house in the area and a place to hide his wireless transmitter. Do you know what that is?'

'To send messages?'

'Good girl. I just want to point out that there are plenty of potential hiding places at Rosenlund.'

Yes. Yes, there were. Hundreds.

How many rooms were there? She could never remember. How many outhouses?

It was possible to spend more than a day combing through

the estate and still not be entirely sure that all of it had been covered. On first arriving at Rosenlund she had existed in a state of constant astonishment and it had taken her a couple of years to adjust to it.

Places to hide a clandestine wireless transmitter?

Kay turned to Anton. 'You love Rosenlund, don't you?'

Anton held out his cigarette case to Kay. She shook her head. He extracted one and lit up. 'Of course I love it. Wouldn't anyone?'

There were the outhouses – lots of them. There were the woods. And the workers' cottages, some of which were already empty because the men had left to work for the Reich.

She combed through the possibilities.

There was the house. Recently repainted in its customary soft ochre, its main rooms faced south towards the lake but others were tucked up under the eaves, or built along corridors infrequently used.

There was the garden. There was the avenue of limes which cast its lure to the walker: *Come down through me to the water's edge.*

There was the lake with Princess Sophia-Maria's island rising out of the winter's green-grey ice or the bright, hard clarity of the summer's blue spectrum. There was the island's summer house – a little decayed, smelling of winter mould and spring rain, rotting a little and home to spiders and their victims but, viewed from the shore, as pretty as a Fragonard fantasy.

If she brought in the bandits from the shadows . . . what then?

She glanced sideways at Anton. He was peacefully smoking his cigarette, one leg hooked over the other. Over the years, she had got him wrong. Maybe, maybe, she had got the other things wrong, too.

'I'll come with you,' Bror repeated. He was already buttoning up his jacket. 'It's too dark for you to be out on your own.'

The heat rose to her face and she turned her head away. 'Like I said, go and read your newspaper.'

But he gave her no choice and, in the end, she whistled up Sif and Thor, who hauled themselves reluctantly from their baskets.

'They don't look restless to me,' he remarked.

They left the house by the back door and walked around the kitchen garden. Kay urged that they should make for the lake. 'The moonlight on the water will make it easier to see where we're going,' she said.

Bror made no comment.

They were used to walking side by side: talking, sometimes linked together and usually with the dogs. Kay couldn't count the times she had only to turn her head and Bror would be there . . . on the cold days when their eyes and noses streamed, in the flat yellow summer sunshine, or on the midsummer nights when the sky was almost too crowded with stars.

They left the gardens behind and struck out along the rough path which was the alternative to the lime walk down to the lake. Sure-footed as ever, Bror set the pace. In the dark, he loomed large and solid.

For the first time ever, she wanted him gone.

Bror sensed her mood. 'You don't have to speak to me . . .'

She could tell from his tone that there was a hint of a smile.

When they reached the lake's edge, Kay turned east towards the tongue-shaped wood and Sif and Thor, having woken from their torpor, foraged enthusiastically up ahead. Kay walked rapidly, managing to leave Bror in her wake, and as she neared the edge of the wood she whistled and the dogs came bounding up.

Bending down, she whispered in Thor's tensed, silky ear, 'Rabbits, go.'

The effect was immediate. Thor leaped crabwise, turned and raced along the shore, barking ferociously, with Sif in hot pursuit. The noise was exactly as Kay wished: fit to raise devils.

Bror caught up. 'You're exciting them for no reason.'

No reason?

She imagined the agent who might be mounting vigil among the trees – a man trained into living a secret life, carrying with him a clandestine wireless transmitter. If he was there, and she hoped he wasn't, he was probably cold and hungry and exhausted.

There was nothing she could do about it.

Would his training kick in at the sound of the dogs? Would he conclude: *I am being warned and I'd better get out?*

'Sorry,' she said. 'What's the time, Bror?'

He squinted down at his large square watch. 'Sixish.'

Sounding more conciliatory, she said, 'Perhaps we should go back.'

He caught her by the shoulders and pulled her to him.

Then he let her go.

It was then Kay understood: Bror was desperate to convince her that what he was doing was right. He needed her on his side.

She fell into step beside him. Day Two was over.

Chapter Four

Bror had returned from the fishing trip on Jutland in the late afternoon just over a week after Kay's meeting with Anton in Køge's market place.

Halfway down the lime walk, Kay heard the sounds of his arrival. The dogs did, too, and they set up a howling before circling behind Kay and disappearing back to the house.

Kay did not follow them to greet him as she once might have done.

Instead, she continued down to the lake and stood and watched the water, which always gave her great delight. An eddy at the water's edge – stirred by the colony of eider duck which had landed further out towards the island – shook the pebbles in a frail replica of a tide.

Undecided, anxious, unsure . . . was she being sucked back and forth over the pebbles like the lake water?

The slanting autumn sun struck its surface and the ray split into shades of white and blue. Underneath, the stones were outlined with extraordinary clarity.

It wouldn't be long before Bror came to find her.

Correct. Five minutes or so later the dogs came pattering up and his figure could be seen walking down the lime walk. It was a matter of moments before he reached her, caught her up and kissed her.

'I'm back,' he said unnecessarily. 'Miss me?'

'Yes.'

Good at reading her, he took a cue from her expression. 'What's wrong?'

'I want to talk to you.'

Placing a finger under her chin, he up-tilted her face. 'Do

that. It's been a long, lonely journey. Lots of spot checks. Soldiers all over the place. Not much to eat.'

How familiar he smelled with the mix of his cologne – ordered regularly from the shop in Berlin, for nothing else would do – the rough tweed of his jacket and just the lightest tang of male sweat.

She stepped away from him, which alerted him.

'I take it this is serious.'

England, she thought. *Bandits in the shadows.* 'Did you sign the Declaration?'

The blue eyes narrowed. 'Who've you been talking to?' There was a pause. 'I see, Anton.'

'Not exactly. Why didn't you tell me?'

'Anton should be less loose-tongued. He has an axe to grind and he likes to cause trouble.'

'What axe?'

Bror said in level tone. 'He's also a womanizer.'

'Are you seriously telling me Anton thinks he'll seduce me by telling me that?' She squared up to Bror. 'Why didn't you tell me?'

'Isn't it obvious?'

'No, it isn't. Make me understand this . . . Why have you sold us to the Nazis? I understand your feeling and affections for Germany. I share many of them. I like your Munich relations. I know my children have German blood in them and I have always been proud of it . . . but Hitler is mad. And so are the idiots around him. Actually, I take that back. They can't be idiots because they seem to be quite effective. But they're evil.'

Tails at full mast, the dogs shot out from a clump of bulrushes. Bror snapped his fingers at Sif. 'Down, girl.'

Kay turned away. 'Don't put us in the wrong, too. Think about the Americans having come in with the Allies. The situation can't be that bleak for you to do this, not as bleak as it was at the beginning of the war.'

'But they are bleak,' he said. 'We can't ignore it. Communists are being rounded up –'

'And you agree with all that?'

That angered him. 'Don't treat me like a fool, Kay.' He stuffed his hands into his pockets. 'Listen to me, the Reich is a very efficient machine, perhaps the most efficient the world has seen. It will win. We Danes have an advantage because the Nazis think we share in their Aryan brotherhood rubbish. I think we have to capitalize on it to save lives.'

Up in the sky, flying low, a plane screamed across the house and lake. The noise was ear-splitting . . . and, somehow, barbaric. Furiously, she pointed at it. 'Your friends.'

Bror didn't bother to look up. 'Well, let's hope for everyone's sake it isn't a British bomber.' He paused. 'We will have to get used to the noise of planes.'

In spring, the patch of bulrushes which the dogs had taken themselves into was ring-fenced for the nesting birds, but now, in autumn, the huge spiky seed cases were stiffening in the cold. Bending down, Bror traced the outline of a seed head. 'I've signed the Declaration of Goodwill to the Occupier. The Minister of Agriculture drafted it and asked the landowners to endorse it.' He straightened up. 'I did it to protect you, the children, Rosenlund.' He was addressing her back. Almost pleading. 'It will keep us safe, Kay.'

At that, she turned and grabbed the lapels of his jacket. 'But you didn't consult me! I would never have said yes. Never.' She tugged hard. '*Why* didn't you ask me?'

'I didn't because it's difficult for you.' Kay was silent. 'Do I need to point it out? I wanted to spare you.'

She pushed him away and stamped her foot down hard. A shower of grit rose and pattered back to earth.

'Think about it, Kay. The minute war was declared we, the Danes, lost half our export market – our market with the British. How do we make it up? We have to eat and earn money. There's always the risk of social unrest if trade and production fall. People will starve. The Germans want our food, our meat, our expertise. That need will keep Denmark going until the war is over.'

'If the Nazis are beaten, your name will be on that document, Bror.' A piece of grit had fallen into her shoe and she concentrated on its sharp sting.

'Here . . .' He had noticed. 'Lean on me.' Kay unlaced the shoe, took it off and knocked out the grit. Bror continued: 'The community has to survive and I have to try to make sure it does. Not taking extreme positions will serve us better.'

She shoved her foot back into the shoe and knelt down. 'What about German morality? You can't just march about Europe invading every country that takes your fancy.' The bow wouldn't tie and she yanked at the laces.

'You British are special . . .' He was stepping carefully but not carefully enough. 'But you're islanders, Kay, and it influences how you see the rest of the world. The Germans and the British are always at each other's throats. Danes are more practical and less ambitious in that respect. We prefer to endure and put our heads down.'

The soil under her knee was brown and green, and strewn with pebbles, but they blurred with the onset of her fury. Whipping to her feet, she said: 'Do you know what you have just done?'

'You're going to tell me.'

Her voice shook. 'You've just told me I don't belong here. But I've lived here longer than I lived in England. Remember that.'

'Kay . . .'

Bror put out a hand to restrain her but she dodged out of reach. Turning on her heel, she left him gazing over the flat, shiny water.

It was easy enough to avoid him for the rest of the day. Inviting herself to supper with an artist who was currently renting a cottage in Køge and with whom she had made friends, she made sure she was out of the house until bedtime as well.

Returning home at ten-thirty or so, she went straight upstairs to their pretty yellow-and-white bedroom. There she sat at the dressing table brushing her hair with hard, determined sweeps that set her teeth on edge.

Bror entered.

She glanced up. Ignoring her protest, he prised the brush away. 'My job, I think.'

When he brushed her hair, there was no need for explanations, or even talk. She had learned the signs. Short, sharp strokes indicated Bror was agitated – probably something to do with the farms or the house. Slow, hypnotic ones told her all was well. Often, the brushing of Kay's hair was the signal he wanted her.

By the same token, if Kay held herself stiffly, or did not respond, he knew he had reparations to make. If she relaxed – easing back against the chair – he might abandon his task to kiss her neck.

These were the signals between them which made up a coded language they both understood. It contained their marital world: their jokes and teases, their angers, their desire for one another and, until recently, their mutual understanding.

She closed her eyes. Bror was so gentle – but then he always was with animals, with children, with her.

Drawing the bristles through the long, blonde strands, he said at last, 'Kay, it's war and we have Tanne and Nils to consider.'

'Oh, so it isn't Rosenlund that's your main concern?'

He slapped the brush down on the glass top of the dressing table.

'Do you mean to be so childish?'

She picked up the brush and pressed it back into his hand. 'Then don't tell me I don't belong here. Ever.'

It was Bror's turn to apologize. 'I was clumsy.'

'Thank you.' He caught up a handful of her hair and she asked in a low voice: 'Have you any idea how you hurt me?'

'Very much, I expect.' He teased the brush through a lock of hair – and the strokes seemed to replicate themselves up and down her body. He shifted closer. 'You and I must decide how to get through the war. Together.'

She got to her feet and folded back the lace-edged top sheet on the bed. The under sheet was pulled taut and inviting over the softest mattress topping that Denmark could manufacture. She looked up at him. 'Yes, we must.' She removed her dressing gown. 'But you have made it difficult.'

Bror shrugged. 'That's the burden I shall have to carry. I couldn't do otherwise.'

'Not even for me?'

'It was for you. And the children.'

She stared at him. 'But we have to think about the bigger issues.'

He sat down on the edge of the bed. 'Survival is a very big issue and I know you'll say, "But not survival at any price", and it's a good argument. We've never had to face starvation, or brutal retribution, and others do, but we have a duty to survive, too. Kay . . .' He was sad, sorry, determined, reasonable, and, suddenly, much older. 'Don't think I haven't thought about it. It's far harder to take what some might consider the coward's path.' He looked down at his clasped hands and said simply, 'I know that's what you think.'

There was a long, horrible silence.

Do I help Anton? Do I not?

Coward.

'Come here, Kay.'

After a moment, she obeyed. He stood up and began to ease off her nightdress.

'No,' she said, resisting. 'Not while we're like this.'

'Please,' he said. 'Let us try. It's a way of understanding.'

They knew so well how they both responded, and what they wanted from each other. This time, Bror was determined to make her part of who he was and what he felt for her – and she slipped into the old pleasures, as she had done so many times.

At the finish, however, Kay was no clearer on what to do.

Bror raised himself up onto an elbow. 'Kay, please remember . . .' He was searching for the right nuance. '. . . it hasn't just been me and Rosenlund. It's been you, too. You've been part of it and I couldn't have done it without you. We've been a partnership.'

'"Why aren't we in the fight?" these Danes will ask. And "What can we do?"' reiterated Anton in her ear.

She turned her head on the pillow to look at him and the lazy, sensual, miasmic aftermath of sex disappeared. To her distress, she was looking at a man she wasn't sure she recognized. 'A war changes people and things. Bror . . . you signing the Declaration has changed the situation . . . That's what I feel . . .' She twisted the sheet between her fingers. 'I won't mention it again but, if we are to be truthful, I must say.'

He rolled over and kissed her. It was a rough, hard gesture. 'And you not supporting me,' he pointed out. 'That changes things, too.'

After he fell asleep, Kay remained awake, her fingers bunched up into her palms. War had a long reach. Being innocent of what that meant did not spare anyone from its malignity. Bror had never disappointed her, never let her down . . . never let anyone down as far as she knew. Now, he had.

She must deal with it.

Her imaginings were as vivid and disturbing as they usually were in the small hours. She brooded over her weeping mother, the beatings, the violence, the Nazis' rape and pillage, the death of decency. In particular, she thought of the young girl standing on a platform on a railway station with her death warrant by her feet.

The mind could not absorb too much at once – or, at least, not hers. Picking through the pros and cons, she reminded herself that any big decision was riddled with conflict and, possibly, contradictions. When fear of being caught had to be added to the mix then . . . then the terrors and complications threatened to be overwhelming.

Early the next morning Anton telephoned and caught Kay at her most fatigued and fragile. 'I need help,' he said. 'You're my last resort. I was going to send flowers to someone but she's gone away. They are so beautiful that I don't want to waste them. Can I send them to you?'

Irresolute, she clutched the telephone receiver.

'Kay . . . ?' Anton adopted the wooing tone. 'They will go to waste.'

Bror's pragmatism wasn't enough.

Bandits operating in the shadows.

She heard herself say in a perfectly normal voice: 'How lovely.'

'I'm not quite sure when. It could be tomorrow, or one of the following two days,' he said. 'Just as soon as I can get hold of the gardener. He usually manages to deliver things between five and six p.m. But if he hasn't after three days, then he won't because the flowers will be past their best.' There was a pause. 'By the way, darling, the birches down by the lake look very fine this year, particularly those just by the oak. You know the one.' There was another pause. 'I meant to ask you the other day if you've read Steinbeck's *The Moon is Down*? You should, it's very good, even in translation. Do ask your visitors about it and see if I'm right.'

The following afternoon, a bouquet of autumn blooms in arterial reds, marmalades and the deep black-red of a dahlia arrived for Kay.

Their spicy, piquant scent hinted of soil and sun, which never failed to delight Kay. She bore them off to the vase room and, while she arranged them, she tried to make sense of the intelligence which Anton had given her over the telephone.

One agent coming in. Wait for up to three days in the birch wood by the oak tree. The password is . . .

One by one, she placed the flowers into a glass vase. Catching up the black dahlia, she rolled it between finger and thumb and realized its stem was thicker than the others.

She understood.

Her fingers shook as she unwrapped the piece of paper folded tightly round the stem and read: *Darling Freya, you have forsaken me for Felix.*

It was signed: *Odin.*

Carefully, she inserted the dahlia into the arrangement.

Her name was Freya.

By Day Three, she was better organized.

She had boots and a thick jacket, plus the torch. Letting herself out of the kitchen wing, she made her way down to the lake by the path she and Bror had taken on Day Two. It was the best route because it had the virtue of being out of sight of the house.

This time, she had made sure that Birgit served tea to Bror in the office, where he was labouring over accounts. 'Plenty of gingerbread,' she instructed Birgit. 'And make sure you refill the pot.'

Even a thicker jacket provided no real barrier to the cold snaking through her body. She tightened its belt. Soon, all too soon, the sun would disappear from the land and winter darkness would lock down over Denmark.

Then the real cold would arrive, catching Jutland, Zealand, Funen, Lolland and the hundreds of other islands in its icy grip. It would drive roots deep into buildings, into the sea, into the earth, and it would colonize water. As it intensified, ice fantasies would build, crystal by crystal, in rivers and streams and, under the freezing onslaught, even the toughest trees would stoop in homage to the cold.

Making stealthy progress through the trees, Kay kept a check on the time. Every so often she stopped to take stock. A deer startled in the undergrowth crashed away, insects scuttled over the leaf fall. Halting finally at a curve in the path where three birches grew close to an elderly oak, she settled to wait.

What was that?

Three days of vigil. Had they sapped her courage and resolve? Had they strengthened them?

Five-thirty.

In the undergrowth there was movement. A twig snapped.

Kay held her breath.

A figure wheeling a bicycle materialized out of the darkness.

She breathed out.

He was tall, as tall as Bror, and whippet thin. As he drew closer, she could see that he was young, early thirties perhaps, and dressed in worker's overalls.

The figure stopped, hands clasped tight around the handlebars. 'What are you reading?'

The voice was hoarse and tired.

She couldn't answer immediately – for she was struggling with a sense of unreality. Pulling herself into order, she managed: 'Steinbeck's *The Moon is Down.*'

'Freya.'

'Felix, welcome.'

Chapter Five

For Felix – not his real name but he almost preferred it to Kasper – this rendezvous was the culmination of a profound change of heart, of philosophy, of a way of life.

Two years ago, as a committed pacifist, he was pursuing an ordered and predictable existence. Now he couldn't even be sure that he still had a life ahead of him. No one could have any illusions: doing what he was doing dramatically shortened life expectancy.

The morning on which the Nazis invaded Denmark, he and Jette, his girlfriend, were in bed in her København flat.

A neighbour banged on the door. 'Get up, the Germans are here.'

Jette didn't stir. Hers was always the deepest of sleeps.

Padding in bare feet over to the window, Kasper, as he then was, looked out. Scattered across the pavements and the square opposite were handfuls of leaflets which had been dropped by aircraft. One of them rested on the window ledge and he grabbed it. It was German propaganda and the message was clear: *accommodate, adjust, cooperate.*

Sitting down on the edge of the bed, he observed the tousled, unconscious Jette. Reaching over, he woke her and told her the news. Later on, they listened to the wireless and heard the announcement that the Danish Government was prepared to accept and to work with the new Protectorate.

'Kasper, don't look like that.' Jette was boiling water for much-needed coffee. 'We'll survive. We'll just keep our heads down and carry on as before. You have houses to build. With your status, it doesn't matter who the government is.'

She was complimenting him, the award-winning architect he

had become after hard thinking and hard work . . . the architect who specialized in light, airy, practical social housing conceptually light years away from traditional Danish design.

'You believe that?'

She poured the water over the coffee grains. 'If you're a true democrat you can't reject the vast majority. The Danes want peace and the government has ensured that they have it.'

In her white wool blouse, pleated green skirt and a necklace of tiny glass beads, Jette looked so clean, so neat . . . so immovable. In that moment, irrationally, and certainly unfairly, for his beliefs on non-violence were as strong as hers, Kasper hated her.

'So you don't mind what has happened, Jette?'

A thoughtful person, she took time to answer. 'Of course I *mind*. But I'll live with it. So will you.'

The coffee grounds sifted through the boiling water to the bottom of the pot and Kasper reflected on Denmark's military weakness, on the geographical impossibility of fighting and on the two hundred and more Danes who lived on the border in North Schleswig, who would suffer if there was trouble.

'I'll live with it.'

The words did not sit easily on the tongue.

Later, he found they had spread like an ink stain. They were whispered in the office, on site, in his inner ear when in bed with Jette. They were repeated in other ways and in other places by those whose manner varied from the angry and resigned to the smug or subversive. Yet the unease grew.

Poor Jette. As Kasper was dragged increasingly into his preoccupation with the war, his temper shortened.

She tried to make sense of the puzzle Kasper now presented.

'I don't understand you, Kasper. I don't . . .'

Question to himself: why was he spending more and more time with the groups whose aim was to create 'a just anger' against the occupation, especially as quite a few in the groups were writing and printing underground literature? One of them – dark, Jewish and far too thin – asked Felix to help distribute them. Which he did.

'Living with the status quo,' he explained to the bewildered Jette, 'does not mean you approve.'

Question: why was he talking to those who had contacts with the tiny, still shaky, resistance in Denmark? And why was he so interested in the whispered accounts of escapes to Sweden and London?

Question: why was his vocabulary expanding to include words such as 'sabotage', 'infiltration'?

He was learning how powerful the unconscious was when it desired its own way – how it pushed and prodded. He went out of his way to seek out examples of Nazi brutality and repression. When fighting broke out in the København streets, he rushed to observe. When his friend, a communist journalist, was thrown into the Vestre prison, he bribed a guard to let him visit and came away seriously disturbed by what he had seen.

One morning in the spring of 1942, he woke up and told Jette that he was leaving.

She turned a gaze drenched in misery on Kasper. 'It's someone else.'

'No.'

She pulled together the tattered remnants of pride and her always predominant desire to be rational: 'If you go now you will never come back.'

He took in the peachy skin, the silky hair, the kind earnest expression, the anguish which lay under it. A mixture of relief that the matter had been brought to a head, guilt at the relief, affection and a giddy-making sensation of liberation, rooted in his chest. 'I understand.'

Half an hour later he let himself out of her apartment. She stood on tiptoe to kiss him goodbye. 'You've changed. You're not the man I first knew.'

Within days he had shut down the architectural practice, sold his flat and deposited the money in the bank. Instinct told him to cover his tracks, and Kasper observed it by cycling to Frederikshavn, where he bought a passage in a fishing smack over the Øresund. Once in Sweden, he made contact with 'Richard' in Stockholm, a fellow Dane to whom he had been directed by the daughter of his old professor. Richard, he was told, could put him on a plane to London to meet 'certain' people.

Richard was cautious. He wanted to know who Kasper was, what were his motives and contacts, and he forced him to kick his heels for a week while he ran a check. 'Don't speak to anyone while you're here and do your best to be unobtrusive. Spies are like rabbits in Stockholm, and it's impossible to tell which is which.' He grimaced. 'Most of them are probably double agents anyway. We'll get you out when a decision has been made.'

Then it was all systems go.

With masterly understatement, Richard warned Kasper of the rigours of the flight. 'You'll be rammed up the bum of a British Mosquito for the duration. Since the Luftwaffe also use the airport, it can be a bit tricky getting you on board but it shouldn't be too bad. It'll be bloody cramped. Use the oxygen mask. You can get brain damage at that altitude.'

'Who will I be meeting?'

'Can't answer that, old chap. You'll have to trust me, Kasper.'

That was the last time he answered to his real name.

Funny that. He didn't miss it.

As soon as the Mosquito landed he was bundled into a car and driven to London. Still groggy, he peered out of the window, sorting out impressions. His parents divorced when he was ten, and his mother fled from Odense to England, where she married an Englishman. The result was that he was shuttled between Britain and Denmark as a teenager, and he became familiar with England and London. Peacetime London, anyway: the prosperous and bourgeois one, smugly grand in places and more or less clean, if smudged with tar and smoke.

King's Cross, Marylebone Road . . .

Clearly, the war had changed the city in subtle, and not so subtle, ways. Two years into conflict, the dirty, pocked streets spilled out their innards and heaps of rubble lay all over the place. There was what he could only describe as a rot, miasmic and despairing.

The car crawled through the streets, swerving to avoid the potholes and the patches of water seeping from fractured water mains, and he longed for something reassuring, even a coffee, a good coffee. But that, as he later discovered, was nigh-on impossible in England.

Having arrived at his destination, he began the process of initiation into The Firm. 'Your name is Felix,' he was told. 'You will answer to no other.' At a series of meetings he was addressed by the heads of the intelligence, signals and Danish sections. Their briefings had been, more or less, unanimous.

Our organization specializes in the unorthodox and clandestine . . . Our approach is unusual, unconventional thinking is our point, and it is so secret that total silence is demanded of you.

He learned that there had been very little undercover activity in Denmark to date. A couple of radio operators had been smuggled in with their sets earlier in the year but both had gone silent. The worst was feared.

What we want you to do, Felix, is to light a flame of Danish resistance and stoke it into a sodding great bonfire.

He warned them of the extreme difficulties of operating under a puppet government with legions of informers on all sides.

To their credit, the section heads listened with care, then they issued their directives.

We will train you, and then you will go and do something about it.

So far, only the communists had made real efforts to resist and they paid the price by being frequently rounded up. To make headway, Felix would need to build alliances and coalitions with them.

Do deals with the Reds, make a few promises but don't offer too much . . .

Wasn't that just like normal politics? He would have to find ways of burrowing into an acquiescent population. Of course, it might prove to be easier than he estimated now the Nazis were busy draining the country of its meat and dairy, and pinching the able-bodied men to work in German factories.

After his induction in London, Felix was sent for training to a number of Special Training Schools, the STSs, run by The Firm.

One of his first tasks was to learn Morse code. That had been a pig. In The Firm's slang, Felix was not a natural 'pianist'. 'Pity you're not musical,' observed the Morse instructor. 'The musical ones do best.'

Forced to practise hard and often, tapping out the rhythms on any flat service, he found his dreams were invaded by its staccato bleeps.

'- -..,-.- -,.-' This was his call sign: ZYA. It belonged to him, and to him alone. He would use it to contact the Home Station, back at base.

ZYA.

Home Station allocated times for agents to make contact, and he'd been told that whenever his scheduled call, his 'sked', was due, the signals clerk allocated to him at Home Station would patrol the airwaves, waiting patiently for him to transmit his call sign. It would be a moment of trust, of faith that the letters oscillating through the frequencies were precise and faithful to the message.

A signals clerk would have no idea who Felix was, or where he was, and the not knowing was a requisite for this shadow existence. In fact, by the time The Firm had finished with Felix – driven its tentacles into his psyche and changed the patterns of his thoughts – he'd been hard put to know who he was as well.

Going into the field meant that an agent carried several

identities stacked one on top of the other. Felix's call sign was ZYA but his code name, the one he would use to transmit his messages, was Mayonnaise. His field name was Felix – the name he would be known by as he worked to build resistance in Denmark. He was also in possession of a couple of aliases, complete with identity papers sewn into the lining of his jacket.

There was much to take in.

Learn every detail we've given you. Your birthplace, your background, your uncles, your first woman, your pet rabbit. This is not a joke.

So it was that, as a fully trained undercover agent working for what was known as The Firm, Felix found himself being driven by a FANY to a secret airfield somewhere in England. From there he would be parachuted back home into Denmark.

His right hand beat out a tattoo on the leather armrest: - -..,-.- -,.-

The FANY had dark hair bundled up under a cap and the back of her neck was clean, pearly with youth and inviting. Who was she? One of the hand-picked girls who were trained by the undercover services to help with practical matters, to drive, courier and God knew what else. At the STSs, FANYs – the initials stood for First Aid Nursing Yeomanry, a hark back to the First World War – were everywhere. They were polite, even-tempered, necessary. Trained into absolute discretion, too. Neither she of the pearly neck, nor he, would talk on the journey other than in the barest of exchanges.

The car blinds had been pulled down but not quite far enough and, here and there, he caught flashes of buildings. Felix peered out to witness the weary and dun-looking population picking its way around the rubble in the street. Back to their homes? Out for the night? He spared a thought for the inconvenience and exhaustion of shopping, keeping clean, travelling . . . These were the topics he used to consider when he dreamed up onto paper his light and airy houses, back in the life which he had left behind.

At the final meeting with the chiefs, he had been given an unequivocal and bleak picture.

There is some activity on Jutland. We've managed a couple of arms drops there but not much else.

In the driver's seat, the FANY jabbed her foot on the brake. 'Sorry, sir,' she said as they jerked to a halt. 'Pothole.' She added, 'It wasn't there yesterday.'

Having headed north for approximately an hour the FANY turned right and drove along the road which, so pitted was it, clearly led to hell. The car axle shrieked in protest and the wheels rattled. Next, they appeared to be in an ordinary field with a farmhouse and a barn beside it. However, to their left, an aircraft taxiing down a runway suggested that this was no typical farm. The growl of its engines split the night's silence. A uniformed man emerged from the farmhouse, introduced himself as Felix's dispatching officer and ushered him inside the barn.

Inside, equipment was stacked on shelves lining the walls and a fire burned in the grate. A group of men checked over piles of stuff on the table.

'Now then,' said the dispatching officer, issuing Felix with overalls and a parachute. 'Here we go.'

There were a couple of other 'Joes' waiting to go in with Felix. Both Danish. The first was tall and sandy-haired, with the kind of flat features which Felix disliked. He gave the barest of greetings before demanding a drink and then a second, and paid no further attention to Felix. The second Joe appeared to be a different kettle of fish. Short, with thinning hair, slightly bandy-legged, he was nothing to look at. Schoolmaster or a clerk in an obscure ministry? Or something like that. Would he handle anxiety and fear well? He was not in the least heroic-looking, rather the reverse, cutting an unremarkable, almost anonymous figure. Paradoxically, despite his obvious jumpiness and a dry little cough, he looked a better bet for the undercover life than his nervy companion.

Curious. The little man with his dry cough was the kind of person whom Felix found himself wishing to protect. Security reasons forbidding them to share their field names, they exchanged code names. 'Mine is Vinegar.' He trilled an arpeggio up Felix's sleeve with his fingers.

He was telling Felix he was a pianist. Well, that was two of them, at least. The section heads had promised that they would send in more pianists as soon as they could train them, but couldn't make any promises as to when that would be possible.

They warmed their bums in front of the fire, and having been chilly on the drive this made Felix almost too hot.

'I would kill for a drink,' Vinegar confided to Felix, 'but I daren't.' They were speaking in Danish. 'Are you scared?'

'Yes. You?'

'Shitless.' Vinegar articulated the word with great precision. He pointed to the third Joe patrolling the barn entrance with an empty glass clutched in his hand. 'So's that one. But he's choosing to drink instead of owning up.'

Felix smiled. Vinegar was nice.

The dispatching officer was professionally cheerful. 'No need to worry, you've got a top-hole pilot. The best. He'll fly just above the water and Jerry won't clock you. Makes the old bus skim like a bird. Not many can do that.'

Ten minutes later they were led out to the waiting Halifax.

The dispatching officer had spoken with a forked tongue. It was a tricky journey flying low over the Skagerrak. They were crammed into the plane's fuselage. No leg room. Bodies rigid and the plane creaking and shuddering like a haunted house. Wrapped in shock-absorbent Koran fibre, the wireless sets – Felix's and Vinegar's – swung like demented pendulums from the strut to which they had been strapped.

Felix could make out Vinegar across the cramped space. As pianists, they had even more in common. To wit: their life expectancies were short. Less than short.

Both of them knew it.

He had just closed his eyes when the pilot made a ninety-degree turn and sent him crashing into Vinegar. Not a good move. Vinegar groaned, retched and vomited into a bag.

The smell was awful and it wasn't just the vomit. Petrol. Sweat. Flatulence. Stale burned-engine odours.

Sweat slid down between Felix's buttocks but his skin was as cold as ice.

Vinegar was glassy and sweating, too, like a pig. 'Sorry,' he murmured. 'Not what was ordered.'

Vinegar retained his precise inflection despite his palpable fear, which Felix judged to be of the knee-knocking, bowel-loosening variety. He cursed silently. That sort of fear was infectious and he didn't wish to catch it.

Again, without warning, the Halifax lurched upwards.

A shout through the speaker tube: 'Tracer flak. Hold on.'

A corkscrew dive.

Predictably, Vinegar was sick again. Afterwards, he pulled his knees up to his chin and bowed his head. He was a picture of wretchedness. Felix and the third Joe managed to keep sitting upright.

'For Christ's sake,' mouthed the dispatching sergeant into the speaker tube. 'Not so low. We're about to hit the water.'

Up they went again. This time in a scuddery ride across the sky towards the target drop zone.

The red light snapped on.

The dispatching sergeant hooked up the static lines of each of them in turn and jabbed Felix in the ribs to indicate what he had done. 'Ready?' Then he lined up the containers which would go in after the parachutists.

The light flared into green.

Vinegar jumped first. A small mercy, given the state of his stomach. His set was pushed out behind him.

Next out was the third Joe who disappeared into the night sky.

Don't forget what we have tried to ram into your heads . . .

The dispatching sergeant's hand pressed down onto his shoulder. 'It's a go,' was screamed into his ear.

A push.

Jumping.

My God, he was jumping . . .

The cold, heavy air slapped away the stinks of the Halifax but the shapes rearing up towards him were more menacing than he remembered from training, the slap and whine of the air in his ears was magnified to a louder roar and the tug on the parachute when he landed was tougher to control.

Moonlight splayed over the turf where he found himself, flat out and tangled up in lines, and he smelled mud and cold grass and just a whiff of brine. Raising his head, he spotted his wireless set with its parachute streaming out like a Portuguese man-of-war. The seconds spun by. Disorientated, head swimming, he thought: *I am home.*

A couple of figures pelted towards him.

Training kicked in. Felix scrabbled for the harness straps and hauled in the parachute. There was no sign of Vinegar or the third Joe.

'Welcome,' the first figure said as he loped up. 'I'm "Jorgen".' He grabbed at the parachute and helped Felix to roll it up. 'We have to get going. The police are moving in. A *stikker* has tipped them off.'

No time for passwords. No time for thinking. Felix was hustled towards the van parked at the edge of the field.

'The others?'

'Wind got them. We think they've landed a mile or so back. A couple of the men have gone to pick them up.'

At the very least, he needed to know if Vinegar and his set were safe. 'Can we check on them?'

'No,' said Jorgen. 'Don't you understand?'

Two other men loaded the wireless set into the van, hoisted in the containers with the guns and explosives which had come down safely with it, and shoved Felix inside. His legs and torso smarted from the hard landing. The engine choked into life.

He leaned out and said to Jorgen, 'Let me know about the other two. It's important.'

Jorgen ignored him. 'Hurry,' he said to the driver. Then he turned to Felix. 'You've been away too long, *ven*. Can't hang around. Everywhere is riddled with *stikker*. You can't trust anyone.' He added with menace: 'The fuckers.'

Chapter Six

The A Mark II* wireless set. Three compartments – receiver, transmitter and power supply – complete with headset, the crystal plus a spare, eight fuses, a screwdriver and sixty feet of antenna wire. The total weight when packed into a suitcase was approximately twenty pounds.

Felix looked at it. What had The Firm's boffins been thinking when they constructed this one? Not only was it cumbersome, but there was nothing quite as obvious as a man in wartime carrying a heavy-looking case.

But he had to deal with it. Having landed in the south of Funen, he was aiming to make for a safe house in Køge run by 'Jacob'. From there he would make contact with 'Freya'.

Making his way east, he needed his wits and his training as he was passed down the resistance line – men and women who fed him, sheltered him and handed him onwards – always heading towards Køge and the rendezvous. It took over a week. Days when he experienced fear and distrust – how could he not? – and became reacquainted with profound loneliness. It would be, The Firm's instructors promised him, an education in the ways of the self.

Do you trust yourself, sonny? Do you believe in yourself?

They knew what they were talking about.

He reached Køge in one piece. A skim of porridge ice was shuffling over the sluggish sea around the port, creaking and groaning with the currents. A thicket of masts poked up inside the harbour. Berthed boats thudded and clinked with the ebb and flow of the water. Apart from a solitary tanker out on the horizon, the sea was empty of vessels.

He permitted himself a moment to gaze up the coast towards

København, only a short train journey away. Once he had established the Køge network, he would dig in there.

Back in London, Felix had been briefed on Jacob, who would be his main contact in the area. Jacob was unmarried and lived alone, which sounded ideal. But you could never be sure.

'Give me a percentage of how trustworthy Jacob is?' he demanded of the briefing officer.

'Reports are good. But you can only go so far with reports. Up to you to judge.'

The question of trust – how much, how little, where, was it plentiful or in short supply, had it run out? – had become everyday currency. It added a depth and provocation to the thought processes.

Located on the western outskirts of Køge, Jacob's cottage was a traditional building of the type Felix knew so well from his upbringing in Odense, with a slate roof and a large gable. On entering a small downstairs room, he was hit by a familiar stew of smells: tobacco, old rope, wet wool, a hint of sealing wax, wood smoke. In the rudimentary kitchen there were whiffs of salt fish, grease and rancid oil for the lamps – the things necessary for survival. But over and above these was the stink of what he knew so well from his work: grinding poverty, the elements of which he had striven to eradicate in his modern designs. The only thing from that childhood home which was missing in this cottage was the primitive odour of his own fear of his father, who had beaten Felix regularly as he grew up.

Jacob turned out to be in his early twenties: a fair-skinned acne sufferer, thin to the point of emaciation. Over a rough and ready meal of herring and bread, he brought Felix up to date. German and British aircraft had been busy in the skies, propaganda was being dropped by the British, Køge was riddled with *stikker*, local bus services were pretty much suspended and only the rich could afford petrol.

Felix got the message. Jacob was a communist who wanted

to make it clear that Felix was the outsider. Still, he had courage and principle and gratitude was due to him.

Later, Jacob showed him the bicycle Felix could use. 'Do you know where you're going?'

Before he left the final training school, Felix had studied the map and the briefing notes.

Rosenlund. Three miles west of Køge. An estate of approximately 3,000 acres with the house at its centre, plus lake with wood.

Further intelligence revealed that lack of public transport ensured it was pretty much isolated, which made it ideal for Felix's purposes.

'Don't get caught with a map,' Jacob said, opening the chest under the window. 'Maps are hard to find, and if you do get caught with one the police will assume you're a terrorist and hand you over to the *Gestapomen*.' He shoved over an oilskin, a jacket and overalls. 'Take these.'

'Thanks.' The overalls were too short and smelled of sweat and God-knew-what. But they would do.

When Jacob went to fetch something else, Felix shrugged off his jacket and whipped out his penknife. Slitting open the cuff of the right-hand sleeve, he extracted a leather pouch and checked the contents. Ten diamonds.

Bloody guard with your life. They're White Africans and a couple are four carat.

The Danish section chief had been precise in his instructions. Again and again, Felix had been made to run through the names of contacts in København to whom he could sell them, then bank the money and use it to fund operations.

He readied himself. It was then Jacob sprang a surprise. Emerging from the lean-to by the cottage's back door, he thrust at Felix a leather box into which air vents had been cut. 'Pigeons. They were dropped a day ago.'

'What the — ?' Felix eyed the box. 'I wasn't told anything about pigeons.'

Jacob wasn't having any of that. 'Apparently your contact is expecting them. I can't deal with them. The drop yesterday has stirred everything up locally so you would be wise to use them for messages until things have settled down again.'

The bicycle was a boneshaker. With the pigeons stowed in the basket under some carrots and cabbage leaves and the wireless set strapped onto the back he felt conspicuous in a bad way. 'Poor devils,' he informed the pigeons. 'Your life isn't your own. Neither is mine.'

A wind sliced into his cheek. Even the oilskin offered no real protection against the chill and he was taking time to warm up. Above him Mars was making its early evening debut. The ash trees, the larches, the wind in the pines, the flat fields and the shrieks of the birds . . . these elemental pieces of Denmark were seeded into the workings of his body and spirit. Without question, this was his country, and with every step, with every rattling cold breath he took into his lungs he was repossessing it.

He was beginning to feel better.

The journey to Rosenlund took longer than expected. His bloody fault. At a crucial junction, he forked right instead of left and was forced to retrace his route. So much for the map study. Half an hour into the agreed waiting period, he slipped into the Rosenlund estate via the gate and pedalled alongside the wood. When the lake came into sight, he dismounted and wheeled the bicycle into the tree cover. The pigeons protested at the jolting. 'Shut up,' he told them. All the same, he took pity, slinging the box around his neck to give them a softer ride.

He knew from the map that the wood formed a tongue-shaped clump which ran parallel to the lake. Cautiously — checking, always checking, to the right, to the left, over his shoulder — he manoeuvred through the trees.

Contact: Freya.

London told him that she had been set up by 'Odin' but nothing much more was known. She had to be taken on trust.

A glint of water through the trees rewarded him. So, too, did the figure of a woman waiting between three birches and the solid block of an oak. He clasped the handlebars tight. 'What are you reading?'

She didn't reply at once and Felix had a bad moment. Then she said: 'Steinbeck's *The Moon is Down.*' The answer sounded unpractised and there was a hint of a foreign inflection.

He breathed out a long breath. *Thank God.*

They sized each other up. She, awkward and, clearly, feeling her way.

'I'm sorry I took so long.'

'My instructions were to wait for three days.' She was sounding more confident. 'Then abandon it. I had almost given you up.'

He detected a note of regret. 'I've just made it, then.'

'We'll have to wait until the estate workers have finished their work and gone home . . .'

Again, he detected hesitancy. He propped the bicycle against a tree and settled the birds against his chest. 'It's cold.'

Unusually for him, a veteran of the Odense winters, the cold was bothering Felix. Perhaps it was tiredness? The instructors had warned of how low temperatures and too little sleep cranked the body down into second gear and sapped morale.

She glanced upwards. 'The snow is on its way. I hate to think it won't be warm again until spring. That's the worst thing. Not like –' She didn't finish the sentence.

He suddenly realized that she wasn't Danish. The foreign inflection had given her away, and he took a bet with himself that she had been going to say: *Not like England.*

He squinted down at her. Tall, forty-three, possibly forty-five, wearing woollen trousers, a belted suede jacket plus fur-lined boots. It crossed his mind that it wasn't fair that Freya looked fit and healthy while English women were battling with rationing. It kept them slender enough, but the lack of cream and butter meant that their hair didn't shine nor their skin glow. Plus, those battling English women had to make do with skimpy and badly fitting clothes.

'The pigeons . . .' He directed his thoughts on to the business in hand. 'Were you expecting them?'

'Ant –' She corrected herself. 'Odin sent me a second message after I got the one about you, warning me about them.' She didn't elaborate but glanced at her watch. 'Not long now. Leave the bicycle.' She crept forward to the point where the trees gave way to a stony shore.

Felix checked his Browning pistol in his jacket pocket, unloaded the wireless set, laid the bicycle down flat between two tree trunks and adjusted the strap of the pigeon box over his shoulder.

He edged forward.

Freya's hand shot out and stopped him in his tracks. 'Don't move.'

No need to be told twice.

For someone starved of feminine company, the voice in his ear was liquid honey. 'It's one of our farm workers taking the short cut home.'

Who was she?

Don't ask. That was the rule.

It hadn't taken more than a day undercover for Felix to discover that some of the rules talked up by Home Station were useless, and others hadn't been thought of. They needed thinking about. He would suggest them when . . . when he returned. Far more useful probably was the advice given by his instructor who taught him about enemy organizations.

The country you knew before the war will have changed. Spare a thought, too, for what's going to happen to it when the war is over. It will change again.

The breeze was strengthening and a strand of Freya's hair

whipped across Felix's cheek. She brushed it away and, catching a hint of perfume, he felt a stab in his guts. Lust? They had been warned about that, too. Those tough, gifted instructors at The Firm's STSs had thought about most things.

The body has no discrimination. It muddles responses and very often equates desire with danger.

They moved forward. Felix strained to make out the terrain. He knew from his briefings that there was a large lake with an island more or less at its centre. This had a jetty and some sort of summer house on it. In the distance there were arable fields and cottages and, a mile or so away, a house perched above lawns which sloped down to the edge of the water.

Silence. Felix shifted from foot to foot.

Again, she whispered in his ear. 'I'm taking you to the pigeon loft. It hasn't been used in years but it's out of sight of the house and I've readied the cages for the birds. I'll go first.'

The path which she led him down wound away out of sight of the house and felt rough and little used under foot. After five minutes, they came to a row of outhouses, a couple of which were not in good condition. Freya ignored them, slipped past rusting machinery housed under a lean-to and halted by a barn-like structure at the end of the row. Picking up a bucket, she tussled with the door and disappeared.

Felix checked to the right, to the left and over his shoulder.

Keep checking. Checking should be like breathing. Trust no one, sonny.

He followed her.

Inside, a bare bulb hung from a crossbeam and struggled to illuminate hay bales and a litter of farm equipment. Ancient pigeon dung smeared the mud floor below a couple of pigeon cages.

With her back to the door, Freya was scrubbing the top of the wooden bench. He sized her up. With delicate features and with a faint air of command, Freya did not look the kind of woman who did much scrubbing, rather the reverse. Felix set down the case. 'You know, you must always keep a watch on the door.'

She glanced round. 'Is that spy-speak?'

'Elementary security.'

'Listen –' she scrubbed harder '– I'm just helping out a friend. I'm not like you.' A sliver of soap dropped onto the floor and she bent down to deal with it. 'I'm just doing him a favour.' There was a pause. 'This is the only time.'

He was tempted to say that it didn't work like that. Once in, once you had stepped into the shadow, you were in it. It was a state of mind.

'I meant to do this earlier,' she said. 'If we are to have the birds, it has to be clean.'

The door was damp and took some forcing shut. He leaned back on it and observed Freya at work. In the end, he had gone into this war for a principle that had proved stronger than his pacifism. The need to fight evil, to save Europe and for the honour of Denmark. These were the big concepts which would, he hoped, offer something to cling to when things got bad – when faced with pain, gut-loosening fear or extinction. Even so, if he ever got back to London he would tell them that the big concepts weren't the whole story. It was small things that got you through long, lonely uncomfortable hours. The warmth of the sun after hiding for hours in the dark, the small kindness of a bag of heated cherry stones handed up to him while freezing in an attic, a bed with a mattress. For a man in his thirties, watching a good-looking woman such as Freya would also be high on that list.

Her movements were graceful and a pleasure to watch and gave him a sort of solace. Wasn't the relish he took in them proof that, if he was to die here in his torn-up homeland, at least he would not do so desensitized by war and violence?

'The birds could get ill, you know. I've looked it up,' she said.

Her Danish was excellent and the hint of foreign inflection distractingly attractive.

'I borrowed a book from Arne, my husband's foreman. I told him that I was thinking of breeding pigeons for their meat.

You know that the Nazis are pinching all our pork and beef?'
She took the pigeon box from Felix and lifted it onto the bench.
'It's all right, boys,' she said in English. 'You're safe.'

A pigeon's protest reverberated around the barn.

'In the old days, there was a thriving pigeon colony here. It's
in my husband's records. It was the sign of a gentleman's residence, apparently.'

The information dropped easily from her lips.

'Don't tell me any more,' he said. 'It's best.'

She shot him a look. 'I see.'

He helped her to undo the buckles and ease off the lid.
The interior was divided into two sections, each one containing a bird with bottled water and grain pressed into a hard
block.

After the initial flurry, the birds went quiet. Freya reached in
and lifted out a big, buff male. The label on his section read:
Hector. The second, a darker bird, was Achilles. 'Hello, Hector,'
she said softly. The bird's eyes were bright and watchful. 'Easy
now, boy.' She walked over to the cage and placed Hector inside.
'The books said they might be panicky and restless so we'll
have to be nice to them and talk to them in English.' She went
to lift out Achilles.

'Wait a minute,' said Felix. Extracting a box of cigarette
papers, he teased out the one on which he had written a message in code.

Arrived safe. All agencies up and running. Please confirm Vinegar is operational and in place. Mayonnaise

Folding it up, he slipped it into the tiny tube to be fastened
onto the pigeon's leg. 'It needs to go soon.'

'They need rest,' Freya said cheerfully. 'But I'll send Achilles
off tomorrow morning.'

'What exactly have you been told?'

Her eyelids lifted revealing misty-grey eyes. 'Nothing much.'

'Right.' He took a decision. 'I have to hide something.'

There was a tiny pause, but one he knew was significant – as if she was gathering herself up to step into the shadow.

'If you mean the wireless transmitter . . .' Her gaze held his. 'I know about that.' She pointed to the floor. 'It's all arranged.'

Dropping onto one knee, she pulled back a tarpaulin. It was so old it was rigid. Underneath, a couple of boards had been slung over a hole in the dirt floor. 'It's not brilliant but it will have to do for the time being.' She assessed the case. 'It's not so easy to hide.'

He shrugged. 'I will be moving it about. But I will have to use it here very soon and, after that, from time to time.' He touched her arm. 'That *is* all right?'

She sat back on her heels. 'Yes.'

'Sure?'

She nodded and her hair swung against her cheek.

He stowed the case in the hole and, together, they manhandled the boards and tarpaulin back into place. Seizing a broom waiting in the corner, Freya swept dust over the hiding place.

She was breathing hard, her breath audible, nervy.

'A warning,' she said, pushing a heap of dirt across the furthest corner. 'Apparently the Nazis disguise the direction-finding vehicles as delivery vans. They give themselves away because they are always petrol-driven. Many people round here have to make do with gaz. So watch out.'

Again, he gave himself the pleasure of watching her. 'Is there anything else I should know?'

She considered. 'Did they tell you in London about the King and Hitler?'

Felix nodded. He had been briefed in as much detail as The Firm could muster. There had been much collective amusement when it was discovered that Hitler had sent the Danish King a fulsome telegram to congratulate him on his birthday in September and the king's reply had been terse to the point of insult. However, it hadn't been so amusing when a furious Hitler suspended diplomatic relations as a result and sent in

General Werner Best, an SS man to his last shiny button, to take overall charge of his favoured Protectorate.

Freya propped the broom against the wall and produced a packet of cigarettes from her pocket. 'Best's nickname is "Hitler's Revenge" and he's not a nice man. But for the consequences, someone ought to kill him.'

Her physical beauty was in sharp contrast to the notion of murder and assassination . . . her skin, the blondeness, the softness belonged to the mother smiling at a baby. It belonged to the lover. Beauty belonged to the deep, sweet ecstasies of the flesh and to the feelings which promoted life, not death.

She held out the packet of Escorts. 'Want one?'

Actually he did, more than anything, but he pushed the packet away. 'Not here. Smoke is a giveaway.'

Her gaze flew up to meet his.

Again, he felt that she was positioning herself. Pushing her mind towards acceptance? Readying herself for something which, she sensed, was inevitable?

Finally, she said, 'It seems I have a lot to learn.'

Was she telling him she was in?

Her gaze veered towards the door and the moment passed.

'I'll be back,' he said. 'Tomorrow.'

The bicycle ride back to Køge took it out of Felix. His body ceased to pump adrenalin, and the stiffness in his muscles slowed him down.

The priorities. Contact London. Check Vinegar and other Joe in place . . . He hoped to God that Vinegar had made it and was safe. Check safe houses. Hide weapons. Begin recruiting.

The list was a long one and the cold nearly bested him.

Doubt was a condition of life – his life at any rate. But he had learned to deal with it. Doubt was a spur. It made action leaner and fitter. More effective. Even so, on that hard journey back, Felix found himself asking: *Am I up to this?*

Chapter Seven

Hidden in the back of Jacob's cottage, and almost felled by some hefty slugs of schnapps, Felix dozed on and off.

He was back in training at The Firm.

'My name is Major Martin . . .'

Major Martin, or DYC/MB, as he signed himself on his messages, welcomed Felix into a stuffy, cramped room, not much more than a cupboard really, in the building used by The Firm's Danish section, somewhere near London's Marylebone Road.

Felix was not a natural observer of human beings – he preferred buildings – but Major Martin's very dark brown, almost black, eyes made an instant impact. These rested on Felix thoughtfully. 'You are probably not going to love me much.'

During his training, Felix had become better acquainted with English humour, which took getting used to. 'Probably not,' he answered.

Major Martin indicated a chair. 'So why have we met? Because, as an agent in the field, you will need to send messages back here. In code, obviously. These will be picked up by our signals clerks in one location, decoded by our decoders in another and then analysed in yet another. For security reasons, none of the departments are allowed to communicate with each other. So we have to try to make it all work. I am responsible, along with others, for the coding part and I am going to teach you how to do it.'

'Black days,' said Felix.

Major Martin tapped his finger on the table as if to say: *Steady on.*

'We use the poem-code system here,' he said, and Felix picked up an undercurrent, a reservation in the tone. A scepticism? 'Put simply, the code sender selects words from a previously agreed poem, numbers the letters of those words as the key and buries the message in a grid that combines the numbered code letters with a lot of useless letters.'

Felix was relieved. 'That sounds reasonably straightforward.'

The major then went on to give a detailed explanation of the system, describing the encryption, the transpositions, the indicator groups, the laying of traps in case the message was intercepted, the feints to fool the enemy, the counter-feints . . .

'Christ,' said Felix.

'Sending messages also requires you to include two security checks. A bluff one which you can use to fool the enemy and the real one which . . .' the major's voice held steady, 'we hope the enemy never get hold of. No one else will have yours.'

Rummaging in his briefcase, Major Martin produced a piece of paper. 'First off, I'm going to give you a poem.'

'I thought agents chose their own poems.'

Major Martin glanced up at Felix. 'Let's see . . . If you asked me to predict your choice I would plump for something from your Danish national poet. Failing that, Kipling's "If", because it's likely to be a British poem that you've heard of.' He sounded ultra dry. 'Good thinking. But if you have heard of it, so will the enemy.'

At this point, both of them lit up cigarettes.

Major Martin balanced his on the ashtray. Smoke rose between them. 'Why is it the intelligence services, not so aptly named, refuse to understand that the enemy reads poetry too? In fact, more than we do.' He sent Felix a wintry smile. 'But we are getting around this with our very own Ditty Box.' He pushed the paper across to Felix. 'We have fine minds working on them. Some of the ditties can be read by a maiden aunt without a blush. Most of them can't. Sad but true. It's easier to remember a filthy poem.'

Felix read aloud.

> Do you wish for a silver fish
> To leap through the stream?
> Do you wish for the light
> To shine on yours and mine?
> Do you wish for the peace of my kiss?

He grinned. 'Can't I have a dirty ditty?'

'They're all in use. But I'll get the FANYs on to it. They're ace.' Major Martin glanced at the ditty. 'Sorry, not one of our finest. But it was composed in the small hours. Could you memorize it?'

Felix was warming to Major Martin. 'I may be cold, hungry, in the dark and surrounded by the flower of the Gestapo closing in, but I promise to remember The Firm's second-best poem. But I have to say, it's not even a second best . . .'

'I apologize, I really do, but the enemy won't know it. Bonus?'

Felix dragged on the cigarette. The major watched him.

'Does it help to know that we will keep your test coding exercises? If you make a muddle and we can't decode the message – we call those the indecipherables – we will crawl all over your test coding exercises. They reveal your weaknesses, your lapses of speech, so to speak. We will use them to help us work out what has gone wrong.'

'Even if they've captured me and are making me send messages?'

A small silence.

Major Martin was wise enough not to comment. 'I'm here to persuade you that you possess the skill and competence to send these messages. In return, you must allow me to understand how you work.' He pushed another piece of paper in Felix's direction. 'Being Danish you might know about ice hockey.'

'A little.'

'I want you to tackle the exercise I am about to set you as if you were assembling an ice hockey team.'

'Major Martin, this gets better and better.'

Major Martin smiled. Again, there was a suggestion of deep anxiety behind the easy manner. He worries about us, Felix thought. Major Martin is responsible for sending us lot out into the darkness armed with not much more than doggerel, and he knows it.

'You have twenty minutes,' he said. 'Choose your words from the poem and encode: "Send explosives, guns, chocolate *stop*".'

It was hard work and Felix found himself sweating. Some idiot had suggested to him that there was poetry in encryption, in the silent stalking down of words, in transforming them, but for the life of him he couldn't see it.

Major Martin assessed the result. 'I detect a case of coding paralysis,' he commented. 'A word of advice. Always go back to the beginning.'

The session was proving to be a humiliating one.

'Stubborn is the word,' said Major Martin.

'Stubborn it is . . .' The words issued through Felix's gritted teeth.

Major Martin eventually wrapped it up. 'Good. But you have forgotten something vital.'

'The security checks.'

'Correct,' said Major Martin. 'If I, or one of my formidable team, read this message we would assume you and the set *had* been captured.'

'What about the decoding?' asked Felix.

'Decoding will be for another session. Coding and encoding are different animals. It's rare to be good at both. Odd that, isn't it? But I'm going to make you practise until you beg for mercy. A few tips: free your language, vary your transposition keys. *Don't* fall into set patterns. Code as if you are . . . er . . . making love.'

Felix was shaken awake by Jacob shouting in his ear. 'Go, go. Police in the street.'

For precisely that reason, Felix had not undressed. It took

only seconds to snatch up his boots, jacket and peaked hat and let himself out of the back of Jacob's cottage.

He wheeled the bicycle into the street, jammed on the cap and set off in the direction of the town centre, keeping the pace deliberately leisurely. At Sankt Nicolai Kirke he pushed the bicycle behind a bush, went inside, selected a pew at the back and bowed his head. For twenty minutes or so, he would sit it out in the church.

What he wouldn't give for a hot bath. For clean and basic things. For water washing between his legs and toes. For the smell of a good soap. This thought surprised him, for when had he ever cared about scented soap?

Jacob's overalls were too short in the crotch and, for all that he had extended the shoulder straps, they bit into his balls. Felix grinned. His first task in the service of Denmark? Save his balls.

Early morning light streamed in through the arched window above the high altar, glossing the circular altar rail. He noted how the arch was there to support the breadth of the wall, the keystone taking the strain while the Gothic line was meant to express the human aspiration to reach heaven . . .

Architectural vocabulary was second nature to him. Less so, the architecture of resistance. At the STS they taught the structures of an underground army and explained how it was modelled on the interlocking cells of a bee colony, which was the strongest and most efficient exemplar in nature. There would be one overall leader – himself – and three or four group leaders who knew nothing of each other. Their task would be to move around this area of Zealand, recruiting and training, but no action was to be taken without the overall leader's permission.

His ruff a startling white above his billowing black robe, the pastor walked down the aisle. His gaze rested on Felix. *Hostile?*

It was an error to assume that religious men would be on the side of the angels.

Get the hell out.

He abandoned the bicycle and made for the street running behind the *Torvet* – the main square. Here, the half-timbered houses, painted ochre or bull's-blood red, and the grey paving stones looked as serene as they must have done in peacetime. He bought a newspaper, found the café which Jacob had told him was a rendezvous, and settled at a window table with a coffee and a *kringle* pastry. Both were of bad quality but, his body craving fuel, he got them down.

Automatically, he kept a watch on the street. Automatically, he checked that there was a back entrance to the café.

Second nature, now.

A fishmonger pushed his cart heaped with herring and pink roe past the window. The sight reminded him powerfully of the time when his parents were still together and they still had a family life of sorts.

Remember Anders, Pastor Neuman's son and his best friend? What games they had played. Lanky pests, the pair of them, running alongside the fish carts, imitating the cries of the mussel vendors – and frequently having to scarper, hiding up in warehouses, watching the fishing boats go in and out of the harbour and taking bets on which one would get stuck on the sand bank. One sun-flecked summer's day they had built a fleet of Viking long ships with mussel shells and corks and sent it over the sea to Valhalla.

Sometimes, in the spring, he and Anders cycled past the hanging birches at the end of the street, past the red church and into the countryside. In the rye fields the larks sang, the cherry trees at their edges foamed white and blush-pink and the pair of them talked themselves hoarse. When the cold returned, they switched operations and went searching for treasure on the shoreline, the sea painting white salt hems on to their boots and, above them, gulls wheeling in big, watery skies.

Enough.

Felix read the paper thoroughly. There was news of the curfew in København, complaints about the lack of merchandise in the shops and the scarcity of cigarette papers. An editorial argued for keeping the peace. 'We don't want, or need, uprisings or sabotage.'

When Felix next looked up, Jacob was seated at the next table. Through dry, bitten lips, he said: 'Police everywhere. My neighbour, Lars, was found trying to make a gun in his house. They shot his daughter.'

'Dead?'

'She'll survive but minus her leg. Don't come back to me. They're watching.'

The waitress placed coffee and a pastry in front of Jacob and Jacob fell on them, licking his finger to scoop up every crumb and draining every drop of coffee like a man who was famished.

Some hours later Felix wheeled the bicycle into the Rosenlund estate, pushed it into some bushes and waited under the cover of the trees for dusk to fall. Out here, the silence was almost disconcerting, and the ground under his feet, layered with leaf mould, was heavy going.

The initial exhilaration at being back in his homeland had leached away. He ached all over. He was tired and he wasn't sure where he was going to hide up for the night.

Having made it to the pigeon loft, he found Freya was already waiting for him. This time, she wore a jacket with a fur-lined collar which framed her face. Like Anna Karenina, he thought.

Her greeting was friendly, and she touched him on the arm. 'Achilles went this morning.' She sounded a touch wistful. 'He seemed glad to go.'

Watched by a beady-eyed Hector, they dragged back the tarpaulin where the wireless set was hidden. 'Time's a bit tight,' he warned.

'Then I'll help you.'

'You should go. It's dangerous.'

'I know,' she said, calmly and without fuss. Even so, when she raised her eyes to his he caught a hint of turmoil.

Together, they set up the equipment on the bench and, on Felix's instruction, Freya looped the antenna wire over a rafter. 'You're a natural,' he said.

She gave a short laugh. 'Someone else said that to me.'

Felix plugged in the valves and headset, selected the correct crystal and connected the power pack. Using the calibration curve pasted into the lid of the case as a guide, he feathered the dial. 'Got it.' He had hit the correct frequency and a neon light glowed. He looked up at Freya. 'Last chance to leave. The German listening stations will be fixing on us this very moment. Somewhere in Berlin, or Augsburg or Nuremburg or –'

'Stop, Felix.'

She appeared to be torn between wanting to flee . . . and something else. What? A curiosity and an excitement which kept her rooted to the spot?

'You are about to talk to England,' she said. 'God only knows how it's possible but it's so good to know. A miracle of science.'

With the arrowhead pointing to 'Transmit', he waited until the bulbs glowed ever brighter and tapped out his call sign.

Immediately, scything through the ether, came the response: QVR. *Ready to receive.*

Home Station was there. Back in England, someone was listening out for him.

QTC1, he tapped. *I have one message for you.*

MESSAGE NUMBER 4 *stop* SITUATION QUIET *stop* RESISTANCE MINIMAL *stop* REQUEST WIRE-LESS SETS, SMALL ARMS, EXPLOSIVES *stop* PLEASE CONFIRM VINEGAR SAFE AND OPER-ATIONAL *stop* REPEAT CONFIRM VINEGAR OPERATIONAL . . .

Twenty minutes later he signed off: QRU. *I have nothing further for you.*

'Quickly,' he said, shutting everything down.

Working in silence, they packed up the equipment in the case and Felix snapped the locks into place. He looked across to her. She was tense and absorbed in the task. What unexpected collusions this work had got him into. Apart from a few facts, he knew nothing about Freya – except for one thing. She held his life in her hands.

'Can I stay here tonight? The safe house has turned out to be unsafe for the time being.'

Freya was dusting down her jacket and he detected a hesitation.

'*Gestapomen* shot a young girl this morning in the neighbouring house. She'll lose her leg.'

A flare of anger. 'Poor girl.' She was silent for a moment – clearly battling with the decision. 'All right. I'll bring . . . As soon as it's properly dark I'll organize food and a quilt. Otherwise you'll freeze.'

'Sorry to ask you.'

She gave him a straight look. 'Don't be.' Again, he sensed she was gathering the resolve to drive herself further along a road. 'You must ask if you need anything else done.' She sounded husky with strain. 'With the work . . .'

He showed his surprise. 'I thought this was a one-off?''

'One gets sucked in,' she said.

'Not good enough, Freya.'

She breathed in sharply. 'I've – I've changed my mind. I don't think one can stand back any longer. I thought I should. I thought I *could* . . .'

'Let me think about it.'

She nodded.

Freya left to fetch the food. Alone again, Felix inspected Hector's cage.

The men and women who can do this work are not necessarily the obvious ones.

What did he knew about her. Enough to trust?

The case for . . . He ran over it. The case against . . . ditto.

Fatigue seemed to wrap his mind in wet felt. He dropped down onto the floor, propped himself up against the wall by the bench and set about decoding the incoming message. The task ate up the last of his current stock of energy. Checking his knife was still strapped in place round his leg and his Browning pistol was in his right hand, he allowed his head to drop onto his chest.

The footsteps invaded the safe and warm silence of his sleep. Light, purposeful, cunning. *Wake up.* Rolling silently to his feet, he took a grip on the pistol.

Where am I?

This wouldn't do. He had to be sharper, quicker, more on the case than this.

Her voice sounded through the gloom. 'It's Freya.'

She proffered a bundle in both hands – rather as she might hold an offering in a temple. 'Food and a quilt.' She was wearing a scarf and strands of silky, blonde hair tumbled onto her shoulders under it.

He took the bundle and set it down.

She seemed to be waiting.

'About what you said earlier . . .' He couldn't be sure because the light was bad but she seemed to pale and, again, she gave a sharp intake of breath. 'I need a courier.'

She went very still.

'You can retract the offer,' he said.

'No . . .' she replied after a pause. '*No.* I mean, it's clear to me . . . I can't not act. I can't retract. I have to come in with you. I *have* to.'

Her vulnerability was almost painful to observe and Felix abandoned every rule about not asking questions. 'What about your husband? Children? You realize what danger you will be putting them in –'

'Stop . . . I know.'

He was tempted to shake her to make her see sense. 'You could just stay safe.'

'Safe? Yes, I suppose that is correct . . .' Her voice was strengthening. 'But not safe from conscience. Not safe from knowing for the rest of your life that you failed to act. Where does the family fit into this? I don't know, Felix, but I believe in decency, the sort where a young girl doesn't have her leg blown off for no reason.' She shrugged and the fur edging on her jacket rippled with the movement. 'Selfish? Perhaps it is but I've also discovered lately that I'm proud of what Britain is doing.' She gave a quick, nervous smile. 'Does that answer the question?'

Poking a finger through the bars of the bird cage, Felix experimented with a waggle. The bird observed him with a complete lack of interest. 'I would have to inform London.' He glanced at her. 'Obviously you couldn't go to England to train, which would be the best . . . the safest . . . thing to do. But I can teach you some of what I know.' He fell silent for a moment. 'Do you understand how dirty this business is? It's danger-ous . . . very dangerous. It will involve lying and almost certainly having to commit crimes. We have to eavesdrop and spy on people we know and sometimes love.'

'I'm not stupid.'

'Sorry.'

Extracting a scarf from her pocket, she handed it over to him. 'You'll need this.' She sounded collected and businesslike. 'And I do understand.'

'Then I'll do one more sked here. Any more and it'll be too dangerous. The big problem is there're not enough sets in the country. Pitifully few, in fact. I plan to ask London to drop in several. We'll hide them in various places and I can move between them. Much better than using couriers to transport the sets. But until London obliges we have to –'

She anticipated him. 'You want me to take this one somewhere.'

No one knew better than Felix what he was asking of Freya. 'Yes. I am. You're a woman and the Nazis aren't, as yet, so suspicious of women. They're stopped and searched less often. You would be a good cover. I imagine you visit København from time to time? Frequently?' She nodded. 'Good.' He wound the scarf round his neck – and it felt like a noose. 'When I give the word, get on the midday train to København and find the newspaper vendor by platform five. A contact will meet you there and tell you where to take it.'

She gave a half smile. 'Any tips for the job?'

He glanced over to the spot where the set was hidden. His brain, starved of sleep and food, projected a pinkish-red aura over it.

'Behave absolutely naturally – and that can take some doing. You must work out, too, how to react if you're challenged.'

'I'll manage. You're not the only one with a cool head.'

If that was a tease, it wasn't funny, he found himself thinking. Sourly. Then, he felt ashamed and imparted a piece of news which he suspected would please her. 'Apparently Achilles made it.'

Her face lit up. 'I told him about the green fields and berries in the hedges, and the nice warm loft which was waiting for him. He got the message.' She laughed rather delightfully at her own joke. 'But Arne – I mean someone – told me that the Germans have orders to shoot anything that might be thought a homing pigeon.' She placed a hand on the door latch. 'You must eat your bread and cheese.'

'Is there butter by any chance?'

'There is.'

'I'm in paradise.'

He came and stood beside her. Freya was a reasonably tall woman but, since he topped her by a couple of inches at least, he was forced to look down. Her face was half in the shadow. She shifted a little and he caught sight of a long neck framed by strands of fur.

Outside, there was a noise. A crack of ice, or hardened wood? Freya froze. He bent over and whispered, 'Go.'

She didn't argue but vanished through the door.

Felix backed up against the wall and waited, pistol in hand, for a good twenty minutes.

Nothing.

So far, his war was playing out with alternating episodes of fear and pulsing adrenalin, then long cold stretches of boredom and – almost – dissatisfaction.

Not to mention the lack of a hot bath.

Chapter Eight

The Firm had commandeered Henfold House, which was a couple of miles from the small town of Henfold in the Midlands. Inviting its owners to take up residence elsewhere for the duration, they turned it into Listening Station 53d. It was promptly named Gloom Towers by its disrespectful staff.

That much Mary Voss knew. But not much else about the outfit for which she found herself working. No one did – certainly not Nancy or Beryl, who were the two girls to whom she mostly talked. The others, her fellow FANYs who worked alongside Mary on the shifts, tended to ignore her. At forty-one, Mary was considered far too old to bother with. Mary got that. But Nancy and Beryl were less blinkered by their youth and Mary often shared a cup of tea with them in the canteen. Their odd friendship, which had developed as the months went on, was, for Mary, one of the unexpected pluses of a war.

As usual, the signals room where they worked – the former laundry in the Victorian kitchen wing – managed to be both cold and stuffy. The small radiator fixed to the wall was worse than useless and the windows let in the gusty draughts.

'They'll be fixed. I swear by my mother's milk.' The corporal in charge of maintenance said that so often that no one listened any more.

'We dream on,' said Nancy. Even on the night shift, Nancy habitually wore bright lipstick and her hair in a complicated roll because 'we need to keep cheery'. Mary admired that battle spirit.

She located Number 33, her station, and sat down. No one acknowledged her, nor did she expect them to. Right from the beginning, they had been taught total concentration on the job in hand. The training had been hard. Sometimes she dreamed of the room filled with long wooden tables at which they practised Morse on the dummy keys. As a girl's speed got better, she was shunted up to the next table, ever closer to the instructor. Most of them got stuck on one letter or another. Funny that. Her particular stumbling block had been the letter R, but she had fought to smooth out every last jag and imperfection.

Anyway, here she was with Morse flowing in her bloodstream – so much so that she found herself automatically tapping out odd words when they caught her eye. 'Exit' and 'railway station' being among the most frequent. It was, she often reflected, quite extraordinary how she could translate everyday objects into a dot and a dash.

Mary looked up. On the wall opposite was a large poster with the words 'Remember the Enemy is Listening'. As if they didn't think about it morning, noon and night.

The wooden chairs had been designed to torment the signals clerks, so uncomfortable were they – and so roughly finished off that the girls' precious stockings snagged on them.

She embarked on her routines.

Check the clock.

Check the board on which had been written up the agents' call signs, their code names, the frequencies on which they transmitted and their skeds.

In the next hour, she had two skeds. Shifting around on the unforgiving chair to find a more comfortable position, she put on the headphones. Immediately, she was immersed in a clicking, hissing, gurgling world.

Close eyes to let hearing adjust. This was one of the golden rules.

Tune the dial to find the frequency.

If only, Mary thought, and not for the first time, if only they had the bang-up-to-the-minute American HRO receivers with their pinpoint accuracy instead of the old dinosaurs the Brits were lumbered with . . . Then she would be there on the button waiting for her agents. Instead, she was forced to keep one hand on the dial because the frequencies had a trick of melting away.

Easy now. Swivel the needle ever so slowly back and forth through the spectrum until the whole sweep had been covered.

'I think . . . what do I think? It's like searching the wireless for dance music on those foreign stations after the parents have gone to bed and Auntie BBC has shut up shop for the night,' said Nancy. Maybe. Mary wasn't sure she wished to consider something as serious as their work in Nancy's light-hearted way.

Final time check.

Who the agents were she had no idea. The signals clerks were not given even a hint. They were told nothing apart from the bare operational facts of the call signs and the skeds, and they were instructed not to speculate.

That she found hard.

All the girls agreed this was misguided policy. It showed that the bigwigs did not trust them and, considering how hard and exhausting the work was, the lack of trust made the signals clerks indignant. The long hard slog during the nights, when they were forbidden to break, even for a cup of tea, was especially taxing. 'If they didn't have us,' said Beryl. 'What would they do?'

Mary concentrated. Often the signals were weak but she had trained herself to be receptive to the merest drift of sound.

A bubble bursting.

Atmospheric music . . . the waltz of the wave bands.

Time?

Pencil poised in her right hand, she made another foray into the frequencies with her left.

It was forbidden to get close to their agents. Those vulnerable, quixotic, brave pianists. The instructors had been precise. No little wireless exchanges. No sneaky transmission of the number 73, which meant 'best wishes' in any radio language and could be taken to mean 'keep your chin up' or 'we are thinking of you'. Mary wondered indignantly what difference it would make. What harm could there be in making a tiny human gesture across the ether?

When she had got to know them better, Mary talked it over one day with Nancy and Beryl as they sat drinking their tea in the canteen. The other two girls exchanged glances. Complicit.

'Can you keep a secret?' Nancy's red mouth curled at the corners. 'Sometimes me and Beryl slip in this . . .' She knocked out the letters on the table.

'My goodness!' Mary was taken aback. The letters spelled out the word 'shit' – but, in a flash, she understood why. They were the fastest letters to transmit.

Over the teacups, which sported scummy rims because the water was hard, Nancy and Beryl were regarding her in the way that was now familiar to Mary: cut the old girl some slack.

'We've shocked you,' said Nancy.

'No,' Mary replied hastily. 'No. Please don't think that. It's just rather a strange message of comfort.'

Beryl giggled. 'Too right.'

What they were expected to do was to learn their agent's individual style of transmitting. 'Think of it as handwriting,' the instructor said. 'We call it the agent's "fist".' During the training, it was drummed into them that they must listen out for even the tiniest variants. Oh, the pleasure, both visceral and deep, it gave Mary to know that she turned out to be particularly good at it.

'Is your agent on the run? Surrounded by the enemy? Transmitting in fear, cold and darkness? Is he or she who they said they are?'

In her bones . . . *in her bones* Mary knew she could answer all those questions, and the more she considered and observed, the more she realized that the authorities didn't possess her expertise. They didn't have a clue. She and the girls *knew* their agents and understood. If asked, she could have told the authorities a thing or two about themselves which they hadn't dreamed of.

In some respects, she and the girls were operating just as subversively as the agents.

In the signals room, the intensity of the work had upped the humidity but it was still freezing. Mary's feet were turning numb but it was of no matter. Goodness knew what conditions were like for the men and women for whom she was straining every ounce of concentration. Where were they transmitting from? Deepest France? Poland, perhaps? Surely not Germany? Some were hesitant, some impetuous, some sloppy. Only that last shift, for instance, the agent had been frightened. Don't ask Mary how she knew. She just *did*. Anxiety burned over the airwaves and she had the oddest notion that it seeped into her bone marrow. His or her distress affected her, and she had been forced to marshal all her reserves to transmit Home Station's message back.

Hang on . . . She had willed her faith, her support, her care to pour through her fingertips.

On schedule a high-pitched sound drilled into her ears and she snapped to needle-sharp attention.

ZYA

The agent would continue to transmit the call sign at one-minute intervals until she answered.

What power Mary possessed between that moment of receiving the signal and the moment when she placed her finger on the transmitter key and responded to it. Yes, it was a brief interregnum, but during it she held total sway – which was quite a thought for someone who had never had significant control over her hitherto unremarkable life.

Her finger pushed down the transmitter key. QRK. *What is my intelligibility?*

QSA4. Her signal readability was apparently four.

QTC1, tapped the agent. *I have one message for you.*

Mary's pencil travelled over the log paper.

QRU. *I have nothing further for you.*

After adding the sign-off from ZYA, Mary placed the paper in the basket from which it would be collected and taken to the decoders, and then, uncaring that the signalmaster might bawl at her, she slumped back against the chair.

What are you doing, Mary Voss?

I'm listening.

To the cries and whispers.

Of those I am forbidden to know.

Those in the dark.

Out there.

Hours later – and the end of the shift was in sight.

Her energies burned up, Mary was woozy and depleted, which meant she would need to take extra care not to make mistakes. All too aware that the present shift pattern was wreaking havoc with her constitution and her sleep, she felt permanently askew, as if she was sailing with a broken compass. Her dreams were particularly bad – vividly disruptive and alarming – and she awoke battered and exhausted.

The dreams were almost certainly her mind registering its protest at the upheaval to her body. Seven days on days. Seven days on nights. But she wasn't about to repeat the mistake of discussing the problem of sleeplessness to the others. When she had mentioned it to Beryl some months ago, Beryl had shrugged as if to say that working nights didn't bother her, which made Mary feel even older than she was.

Yet the fun she had in the canteen made up for a lot. To be united in camaraderie was a novel experience for Mary. In her previous job as supervisor at her local telephone exchange, she had had to respect the boundaries and keep herself to herself. But here she couldn't help overhearing the chat and the free exchange of opinions. Oh, how they disliked the bosses, the predatory men, the rotten conveniences and the endless spam, but their collective admiration and loyalty for Mr Churchill gave them a nice warm glow. Before they went on shift there tended to be lots of jokes and chat at the tables. Post-shifts were more subdued occasions and the girls regarded each other through glazed eyes or stared at the exhortations pinned up on the canteen walls.

YOUR SILENCE IS VITAL
WALLS HAVE EARS
IF THE ENEMY DISCOVERS US THEY WILL
    BOMB US

Mary often wondered who it had been at the telephone exchange who picked up that she knew Morse. Whoever it was must have had connections and Mary found herself being interviewed by a woman in a severely cut suit in a vicarage in Kensington, who asked her all sorts of questions, including how she had learned Morse. The answer was simple: her father, who had been in Signals during the Great War, had taught it to her to help Mary out before she joined the Girl Guides.

The woman in the suit had looked very grave. 'Miss Voss, if you were instructed to keep a secret, and to keep it for the rest of your life, could you do it?'

Her answer must have been convincing because, before she knew it, Mary had joined the FANYs and signed the Official Secrets Act.

The shift ended and Mary fetched her coat from the room which in a previous life had had been designated for the house's vases – *an entire room for vases!* – and now did service as a cloak-room. She glanced in the meanly dimensioned mirror propped up on the windowsill. Hair still neatly rolled up. Tie straight.

It was eight o'clock in the morning and her day was ending.

When she stepped outside, figures were drifting up and down the drive, their faces pallid and ghostly in the quasi light of a December day – probably, like her, suffering from too little sleep. There were a couple of WRAAFs, an army sergeant and a stream of cipher and signals clerks.

Nancy came out behind her. 'Lucky sods,' she said. 'At least they can get to the pub when they come off duty.'

The sergeant from provisions, the one with a ridiculous handlebar moustache, passed them on the steps and gave a thumbs-up.

'I think he fancies me . . .' Nancy took her time to smooth her gloves over her hand. 'He can think again.'

A car drew up in front of the main door. A chauffeur sprang into action and a uniformed figure with many pips and braids emerged from its interior.

'Bigwig,' said Nancy. 'I could put up with him for the car.'

Mary focused on the bigwig, who was ruddy and portly with a mean little moustache. 'No, you couldn't.'

Mary's digs in Locarno Avenue were at number eight. Letting herself in, she placed the key on 'Lodger's Hook' and went into the best parlour, where Mrs Cotton left out a cold meal and a thermos.

The tiny room was unlived-in and felt it. Of symbolic status, it was rarely used and kept in aspic, while Clan Cotton huddled around the stove in the back kitchen and kept themselves to themselves. Mary knew that Mrs Cotton took enormous pride in the room's overstuffed furniture and starched antimacassars. Taking care, as always, not to drop a crumb, she ate her sliver of Woolton Pie and half a sliced carrot and drank the tea in the Thermos. Having finished, she stacked her used crockery on the tray and left it on the table. As soon as Mrs Cotton heard Mary go upstairs, she would dart out and deal with it.

Station 53d personnel were allocated only basic rent. Mrs Cotton's back bedroom contained a narrow bed, a chest and a chair. The single wall adornment was a grim picture of the martyrdom of a saint called Sebastian, about whom Mary knew little, but his death looked nasty. However taxing it must have been, Mrs Cotton kept the house spotless. 'It was what I was put on earth for,' she said when Mary complimented her. Hers was a life dominated by scruple and scrubbing, a life in which she fought against the odds to produce fresh laundry and provisions. Mary admired the stoicism.

Fatigue had beaten her and Mary sat down with a thump on the bed. Reaching under her skirt, she unhooked a suspender. The evenings were mornings and the mornings, like this one, were midnight. She had never been an early riser at the best of times. She had been a girl who rebelliously drowsed and dreamed until her mother told her off. How many lie-ins had she enjoyed in her life? She could count them on the fingers of one hand. Once – Mary fumbled for the second suspender as she recalled the sweet and funny memory – once she and her cousin, Mabel, saved up and took themselves off for a night (in separate rooms, of course) in the splendours of a hotel in West Wittering. They had hung the 'Do Not Disturb' signs outside their rooms. From time to time Mary thought wistfully of that deep, unbroken slumber and the long, luxurious return to consciousness.

Her stockings were not glamorous ones, but precious even if the darn rubbed on the right big toe. She rolled them down and her flesh shrank from exposure. Experimentally, she pinched a bit of inner thigh, the area which rarely saw light of day. Still soft and silky.

Oh, Mary.

No one had ever felt its softness and silkiness.

'Your fate is in the stars, dear,' her mother had had a habit of saying whenever the vexed subject of marriage came up. 'It's no use wishing otherwise.'

As time went by, Mary knew her chances of marriage and physical fulfilment grew fewer and, worse, with each passing year she felt elements in her spirit wither and deplete. She strove valiantly not to allow that atrophy.

'You can tell the difference between a woman who's been

loved . . . and one who hasn't.' Her mother again, her beady eyes invariably fixed on her daughter as she spoke.

Wriggle out of suspender belt. Remove her one good vest on which – unfortunately – Mrs Cotton had launched some kind of military offensive, shrinking it into a felted garment of torture. Unfasten brassière.

Pour water from the ewer into the enamel basin. Wash face. Wash all over. 'Strive for cleanliness, inner and outer,' the vicar at their local parish had preached. 'It's marvellous, my brethren.'

Was it?

She glanced at the clock, a cheap buy from Woolworth's. Housed in red tin it was the brightest object in the room. *Hurry, Mary.* It wouldn't be long before she had to get up again.

Throwing back the sparsely feathered eiderdown and ancient blankets, she slid into bed. The cold sheets always gave her a bit of a shock but, forcing herself to relax, she lay back and closed her eyes. She had to be rested for the next shift.

No mistakes. Ever.

She began to drift.

In another life, Mary would be warm. Her underwear would be made from silk and the finest cotton and she would be able to buy books whenever she wished. Currently, her budget permitted only one a year. What else? Good white bread every day. A proper dentist, because her teeth were a problem, always had been, and her mouth housed a catalogue of aches, some dull, some excruciating . . .

There was half an hour to the end of the shift.

Mary and Nancy exchanged looks and, under the bench, Nancy tapped out a Morse rhythm with a foot.

'Shut it,' hissed Beryl.

Mary realized that, increasingly, and however tired she might be, she dreaded signing off. It was true. Because in that fizzing, gurgling world to which she listened bubbled a wellspring from which she drank.

Check the clock.

There was one more sked to go. XRT, code name Vinegar.

Along with ZYA, code name Mayonnaise, he was one of her new agents, and therefore to be especially cosseted and nurtured and protected. She was the only one to know that Vinegar had been a bit iffy with his first transmission back to Home Station. In fact, more than iffy. Plain out of control. He had used the wrong sign-off and muddled up a frequency. But he had got the hang of it. Actually, she was surprised at how quickly Vinegar had turned into an excellent keyer. By his fourth transmission Vinegar had got the hang of it and *she* had got the hang of him by then, too – his Cs (pointed, regular mountain peaks), and his Ms (a tiny dunce's cap).

It had bothered her a bit, that rapid transition. 'He's settled down very quickly,' she confided in Nancy. 'On those first transmissions he was so nervous. Next thing, he's as smooth and confident as you could wish.'

Nancy shrugged. 'Why are you so bothered about it? He just needed a bit of time, that's all.'

Nancy was right. Even so, Mary brooded over Vinegar. Eventually, she brought up the subject with Signalmaster Noble, who told her that she was being fanciful and over-cautious. 'Go and do your job, Voss,' he said. *Get out of my sight.*

Vinegar. How did he manage, out there in the darker areas of the war?

She was sure Vinegar was a 'he'.

She imagined him dark-haired, tall and perhaps very clever. Brave, anyway. Yes, heroic.

Was he alone?

Where in the many possible countries was he?

She pictured him keying in from, say, a barn, the wireless transmitter propped on a hay bale and the aerial threaded up into the rafters. Again and again, the signals clerks were warned not to speculate, and they weren't supposed to know the ins and outs of clandestine transmitting. But none of them were stupid. They all knew one end of a wireless transmitter from another, and if the powers that be didn't trust them, that was their look out.

She had never experienced extreme fear, only the dull thud of a vague but persistent anxiety about the future, and of how life would pan out for a forty-one-year-old spinster. Anxiety was trying enough, and sometimes in the past it had made her take to her bed with one of her headaches. But crippling, paralysing fear? She couldn't, and didn't, pretend to know about that.

The noise in her ears stuttered and faltered. She adjusted the dial and watched the needle swing.

This ugly, ungainly machine wove a secret network of sound. To use it was to risk death, and, worse, the demolition of body and spirit by torture. Yet maybe . . . maybe Vinegar knew that Mary was listening out for him, guarding him, pouring her reassurance down the airwaves. Maybe it made him feel better.

Foolish?

BRSTU XOSAR VOPYI . . .

She took down the message, basketed it and watched it being taken by the dispatch clerk in the direction of the cipher room.

Chapter Nine

They had been summoned up from the bowels of Gloom Hall for yet another endless lecture on security.

Did the powers that be never let up?

It was ten a.m. on a winter's morning and the place was bloody freezing because no one, not even in the nineteen hundred and forty-two years since Christ was born, could work out how to keep a place warm, which, you might have thought, would not have been beyond the wit of man.

So reflected Ruby Ingram as, with a group of her fellow cipher clerks – not to be confused with the signals clerks with whom they were not allowed to fraternize – she trooped into the lecture room to which they had been ordered. There were forty of them. Girls with brains. Girls without brains. Girls from the Shires. Girls from the tenements. Some pretty, others not, some hiding behind the terrible spectacles which was all that seemed to be on offer these days. Average age: twenty-one.

Not surprisingly the noise was ear-splitting.

Ruby didn't blame them. Talking at full volume helped the girls to ignore the calculated insult by the men in charge of failing to provide them with chairs.

'Who do they think they are?' said Frances.

Ruby eyed her. Along with salt-of-the-earth Janet, Frances had turned out to be a friend but she could sound as haughty as a duchess.

'They think they're men.' Ruby was at her most wry.

'They *are* men,' Janet pointed out.

This was the Janet who, late one night, had posed the question: 'Why should possessing a visible organ between your legs mean you rule the world?'

The lecture room, which had probably been a dining room or, possibly, a small ballroom before the war, smelled of damp and chalk, and reminded Ruby of the bathrooms at Newnham College.

No, she mustn't think about Newnham. Mustn't think about Cambridge. Mustn't think about the fact that, having achieved a brilliant Double First in Maths, she was not granted her rightful degree. Because? The answer beat out wearily in her brain. Because Cambridge University did not grant degrees to women.

Janet waved a hand in front of Ruby. 'You with us?'

Ruby bestowed a rare smile on Janet, who was an oft-time saviour. On the bad days when Ruby was crippled with pain from migraine, Janet was always there. Somehow she obtained hot-water bottles and aspirin and told her to shut up when Ruby railed at her affliction.

Ruby's chilblains itched. Frances shivered visibly.

'Why are we waiting?' sang Janet in her strong, confident soprano.

'Because,' a male voice announced from the door, 'you are waiting for me.'

Silence fell as swiftly as a tropical night.

Flanked by a sergeant, a uniformed man walked the length of the room to the lectern. Placing papers on it, he faced the girls. 'My name is Major Martin. Peter Martin. I'm sorry I've kept you waiting, but I did so on purpose. I had every intention of making you uncomfortable.'

That was one way of getting their attention. Ruby nudged Janet.

Major Martin was just above average height and slight. Late twenties? Possibly thirty? Dark hair. Dark eyes. Well-shaped hands. His uniform was pressed, his Sam Browne belt shone but, curiously, his shoes needed attention.

Balancing lightly on the neglected shoes, he leaned on the lectern. 'I was having you recorded.'

A collective gasp greeted this information and Ruby thought she saw a gleam of satisfaction light up the dark gaze.

'Sergeant Walker here is going to play it back to you.'

The silence turned into an embarrassed one as a babble of voices was released. It took a moment for Ruby to unscramble the sounds issuing through the speakers on the ceiling.

Janet's voice sang out: 'Why are we stuck in this piss house?'

That was plain enough.

Beside Ruby, Frances coloured violently at the replay of her plummy tones lambasting – in terms no lady should utter – the sergeant who had ushered them into the lecture room.

It didn't take much for Ruby to be prodded into objecting and she spoke up. 'That's not fair, sir.'

Major Martin shifted. 'No, it isn't fair, Ensign . . . ?'

Didn't he know that FANYs were only ever addressed by their surnames?

'Ingram.'

He held up a hand for silence and got it. Forty pairs of eyes focused on him. 'Thank you all for coming to see me in this . . . er, piss house. Your colleague here questions the fairness of the little trick that has just been played on you. A good challenge, but I'm going to demonstrate to you how fairness has nothing to do with it.' His gaze, thoughtful and professionally sceptical, raked over his audience. 'You lot have trained on pretty average material. The sort of stuff that streams in and out of base stations and embassies and is coded and decoded in relative safety. But you have a chance to progress.' Again, he held up a hand. 'Have I got your total attention? I hope so, otherwise you will be returning to your former, and almost certainly duller, lives. With one difference. Your tongues will have been cut out.'

Major Martin clearly enjoyed the stir *that* created.

A joke. Ruby closed her eyes for one . . . two . . . three seconds. Well, it was something positive in their dull lives.

When she opened them, Major Martin sent her a look which suggested he was amused by her reaction.

He continued: 'We now know that you have all complained of the cold and discomfort in no uncertain terms. Let's take a look at this pitiful situation. You have been made to stand up for . . . twenty minutes, give or take? Very annoying, I grant you. The room is unheated and we didn't allow you to put on your greatcoats. Torture, you might agree.'

Frances muttered. 'Get on with it, man.'

'I want all of you to think about a different situation. You are hungry, cold and, worse, shaking with fear. You are on the run, and you have to get a message back to London. It's dark. You have no light and no shelter. And the message you have to get back to London is one that *you have already transmitted*. Why?'

He looked around his audience. Frances's handsome mouth had dropped open and a faint pink remained in her cheeks.

Audience enslaved, mission accomplished, Ruby concluded.

'I'll give you the answer. You are retransmitting the same message because we here at Home Station *have not got our act together*. So, I'm going to ask you the question: What is fair about being tormented by fear, sleeplessness, hunger and discomfort, and by being on the run, when you are required to retransmit a message that you have already risked your life sending previously? The joke being that with every transmission Jerry gets a better fix on you.'

He suddenly switched tack and threw a question at Janet. 'Where were you before you fetched up here?'

'Typing pool, sir.'

'Well, I think I'd rather be in this piss house than a typing pool. And I'll tell you why. You have a chance to do something. Instead of running around making cups of tea for your male superiors, you can be on the front line of, admittedly, a secret theatre of war, so you can't boast about it, but what you do will make a difference. This is what I'm offering you.'

Now, why is he looking at me? Ruby returned Major Martin's scrutiny. No bashful avoidance.

'Women in particular should take their chance. They probably won't be thanked for it but that's beside the point.'

He can hold an audience, she thought. *I'll give him that. He can pull a stunt, too. I'll give him that as well.*

The FANY tribe stood as acquiescent as anyone could have wished. Ruby knew that under many of the uniform-covered chests surged various difficult, even disobedient, emotions but they knew when not to misbehave.

Peter Martin checked his watch and held up a piece of the paper used for incoming signals. 'Since ten o'clock last night we have received two indecipherables. The first is from an agent in France, code name Abel. His cover is blown, the Gestapo are after him and he needs to be picked up fast, but we need to know the map coordinates. However, they are trapped inside the indecipherable. The second indecipherable is from an agent in Denmark. Denmark, as you will all know, is small and flat. If you are an agent, it is even smaller and flatter. It's easy to be spotted, particularly if you are walking around with a clandestine radio. In fact, you are about as inconspicuous as a lit-up Christmas tree. More radios are needed, therefore, to be dropped in and kept in hiding places so the agents can move unencumbered between them. Why? Because it is dangerous to transmit from one place only. The message contains details of a drop zone scheduled for tomorrow. Unfortunately, the agent was either bone tired, frightened or, possibly, under the influence of too much Danish beer and we can't read it. I can't go into any further details, but we can't miss the slot.' Major Martin paused. 'Let me remind you, an extra radio could make the difference between a dead agent and a live one.'

Ruby put up her hand. 'You want us to crack these two?' She allowed a beat to elapse before adding: 'Sir.'

Twelve hours later Ruby missed the bus from her digs, where she had snatched four hours' sleep, which meant she had to kick her heels for a good twenty minutes.

She was paying for the five extra minutes in bed. But her sleep had been fretful, filled with the noise of teleprinters and jumbled letters and snippets of random information . . .

She'd woken exhausted, with a dry mouth and an incipient headache, knowing full well the duty sergeant would enjoy the tongue-lashing he would hand out. She'd fumbled for the remaining aspirin in the bottle and swallowed it down with a glass of water.

Now she was stuck here, in Henfold's town centre. Such as it was. Apart from an unremarkable market square, there was a W. H. Smith, a chemist, a jeweller (fat lot of good in a war), plus a butcher with the inevitable queue outside it. At each end of the shopping parade there was a pub and, miracle of miracles, a library housed in confident, high-Victorian municipal architecture.

Head still faintly throbbing, she walked towards it.

'Come on in . . .' The pale, male, malnourished-looking librarian at the desk dug into his limited energy reserves to welcome her. 'Please use us, but if you want to take out a book you will have to join.'

Ruby couldn't say to him, 'Can't do that. Top secret.' Instead, she gave him one of her smiles, designed to make the recipient's day. Crossing over to the reference section, she hauled out the *D* volume of the Encyclopaedia Britannica.

'Denmark is a tiny country with a population of under 5 million . . .' she read. For reference, she checked the publication date of the encyclopaedia: 1929. 'It is spread over some one hundred islands . . .'

She skimmed through descriptions of 'Northern Smorgasbord' and 'Southern Hideaways' where it was possible to feel 'you're far away from civilization'.

On further inspection, the pages, foxed and musty, offered a grand tour through Danish geography – gentle inclines, neat, bright-coloured houses, barns and woodpiles, the glint of a pale sea – and a little of its history.

Who exactly were the Danes?

Perhaps nothing encapsulates the essence of Danishness better than the idea of *hygge*, the companionship experienced by Danes when they gather together. To experience a sense of *hygge* is to retreat into a peaceful and cosy world . . .

The volume was heavy but she knew exactly how to balance it, an expertise acquired during the hours spent in the library at Cambridge.

She had learned wonderful things in that library.

Binary numbers make it possible to represent all computable numbers as infinite sequences of 0s and 1s alone . . .

How excited she had been on first reading the theory. She'd been like a girl with her nose pressed against a window pane through which she could make out the sweet and glistening enticements of the new mathematics, a girl who thought she could bring the world to her feet.

She could safely say that interested her far more than any human being.

Back to the encyclopaedia.

Denmark was 'very small and flat'. Given their work and what was going on there, the agents in place wouldn't have much in the way of camouflage. She recalled Major Martin's softly spoken and urgent injunctions. What a stunt he had pulled. He minded very much about those undercover men and women and was going to make the cipher clerks mind, too. Ruby liked that. There was none of that stiff upper lip, British-men-don't-display-feelings kind of approach to the situation but, rather, passionate engagement. Nor had there been any of that barely concealed patronage and the run-along-and-leave-the-grown-up-stuff-to-us attitude displayed to women by the majority of men she had encountered.

As Major Martin said, agents over there were trying to get the wireless sets from London delivered safely. They needed all the help they could get. Help which she, Ruby, knew she could give them because she was clever enough to do so. Granted, her contribution would be small but it would matter.

Think.

She stared at the books on the shelves and rehearsed the principles of encryption to refresh herself. Adding on and sub-stituting letters were the simplest of the principles employed, the latter becoming more complex when a single letter was substituted with letter pair – but it was a process subject to mistakes.

Think, Ruby.

'In practical cryptography,' she had been told in her early training, 'part of the message transmitted does not make up the message itself but conveys instructions on how to decipher that message. The non-message letters are called indicators.'

All the basic stuff. Too basic for what was needed for the problem in hand? Perhaps she should consider the refinements and additional complications to encoding and decoding which had been thought up by fiendishly clever people.

Ruby corrected herself. Don't go too fast. Agents in the field were not necessarily fiendishly clever mathematicians. They functioned on the basic applications and possibly a level above, but not that much above.

Ruby replaced the encyclopaedia, wrote down the word *hygge*, which she liked the sound of, and went to catch the bus.

In the cipher room, the girls had divided themselves up into teams and were continuing to work flat out on the two indeci-pherables. You could feel, measure almost, the tension.

So far they had made five thousand attempts.

'The crack teams haven't cracked it,' said Ruby taking her seat alongside the others.

'Shut up,' said Janet.

'If you say so.' Ruby reapplied herself. She checked the indi-cators, which would tell her which words of the poem had been chosen by the agent when he encoded the message, and focused on them. There were three immediate possibilities. One: the indicator groups were mutilated by transmitting conditions and taken down incorrectly because poor reception meant the signals clerk had not been able to make head or tail of them. Two: the agent had been badly trained and was muddled. Three: the agent had been captured and the radio was being played by the enemy, who did not know to include the indicator groups. Yet. An ominous word. Ruby knew little enough about what was going on but enough to know that if a radio operator fell into enemy hands, it was probably only a matter of time before the indicators and codes were tortured out of him or her.

The first assault on the indecipherable proved useless.

Ruby massaged her fingers and settled down to the coding version of a long plod through the foothills before base camp even came into sight.

Depressingly quickly, she knew that this was going to be the equivalent of climbing the Himalayas without ropes.

Four hours later, shaky and exhausted, she waited by the bench of the duty officer in order to inform him that it was still a no-show. He was on the phone. 'This is not the five loaves and two fishes affair, you know,' he barked and put down the receiver. 'We don't have enough people.' He glared at Ruby. 'You're to report to office thirteen,' he said. 'Third floor.'

Ruby didn't move. Blimey, what was she wanted for?

'*Now*, Ingram.'

The third floor was reserved for Higher Beings, where the lucky buggers benefited from the light. Generally speaking Ruby nourished a healthy scepticism about the Higher Beings. All the same, she wouldn't have been human if she hadn't been curious to see what was up. More than curious.

However, it was Major Martin who waited by the window – and that did surprise her.

At her entrance, he turned round and she was shocked to see he had black circles under his eyes.

'Sir, are you all right?'

He raised one dark eyebrow. 'I could do with more sleep.'

'Sorry, sir. I didn't mean . . .'

The eyebrow returned to base. 'It's all right, Ingram. You are allowed to demonstrate normal human responses.' He smiled grimly. 'Even if they remind us how awful we look.'

'I didn't mean that.'

'Yes, you did.'

She smothered a smile. Major Martin was nice. 'Yes, I did.'

'Good. Now we can exchange views without pretence. Sit down. We have twenty minutes precisely, and I want to talk to you about something.'

She was genuinely startled. 'You want to talk to *me*?'

'What's so extraordinary about that? Don't people talk to you, Ingram?'

She stifled a smile. 'Sorry, sir. We are used to being treated like pond life.'

'You shouldn't accept that,' he said.

What did he mean? Her? The girls? Had he singled her out? To Ruby's astonishment, she felt a faint flush steal over her face.

He continued: 'I don't want you to think like that any more. I want you on side and I want some proper work and hard thought from you.'

A tiny flutter of triumph went through her breast. *At last.*

He had noticed her. He knew she had brains.

Office 13 was at the corner of the house and enjoyed the advantage of two windows, the clear light exposing the tiredness etched into their faces. Perhaps the murk of the cipher room had its uses after all?

Martin regarded her thoughtfully before pushing a piece of paper over the desk. 'On this, there's a message in code and another *en clair*. I'm going to give you ten minutes to decode and encode.' He glanced at his watch. 'Ready.'

She decided not to be annoyed by this lapse into the schoolmaster. 'I need something to write with, sir.'

He rootled around in his briefcase. 'Why don't you have a pen on you?'

'Because ...'

A pencil now balanced on the flat of his hand. She looked up into his face: a nice face, an exhausted face.

'Come *on*,' he said.

Ruby accepted it. 'You're right, sir. I should be carrying a pencil.'

She didn't often back down but she could tell that he was a fair-minded person and fairness and a chance to prove herself was all she asked.

First off: take the frequency count. Think of it as feeling a pulse. The cryptographer's pulse.

She sensed his eyes were on her lowered head but refused to be hurried or flurried. After a while, she forgot about Major Martin. Ten minutes later she put down the pencil. Silently, she pushed the paper back over the table to him.

He barely glanced at it. 'Too simple?'

'One should never underestimate the task,' she said. 'But, yes.'

'How would you describe what you have just done?'

'I suppose you could say that I corralled the letters and brought them to heel. Then I applied some intuition.'

'How very female.'

'From time to time it works, sir. So do educated guesses.'

'That wasn't main-line traffic,' he said. 'That was an agent's message. It's baffled quite a few.'

She nodded. 'The first transposition had gone wrong.'

The light in the room had grown even more dazzling.

'Agents' coding and decoding require different aptitudes and casts of mind to the main-line coding activities. Wouldn't you say?' He smiled a smile which signalled one colleague's acknowledgement of another.

She felt a visceral thrill. Major Martin had unearthed what she longed for – to be in on the discussion. He had spotted that this was her territory. Wrestling with problems was her meat and drink, and just as necessary.

'Sir . . . can I say something? I know it's not my place but I think you should hear it. The indecipherables. I've been thinking around the problem. Why not dedicate a section of the cipher clerks to work solely on the indecipherables? Train us in the specifics.'

Major Martin sat back and interlocked his nice-looking fingers.

Had she gone too far? Had she been too quick to push her luck? Well, hell, Ruby didn't care. He needed to know that people like her were not just ciphers themselves.

'Actually, we're on the same page,' he said. He sent her a half smile of approval and she wondered what lay behind all this. Because something did. 'Which doesn't surprise me,' he added.

Ruby took a deep breath. Something – the dark, expressive eyes, the sympathy reflected in them – told her that Major Martin was a man with whom she could take a risk. 'Sir, can I ask something else?'

He looked at her long and hard. *Was he going to take a risk?*

Yes, he was. 'Go on, Ingram.'

She shut her eyes for a second. This might be the end of the not-so-glowing career. 'The poem codes? Are they the most secure system?'

She had hit the nail.

For a moment, his expression was stripped naked, exposing a deep, harrowing anxiety. 'And why would you think that, Ingram?'

Ruby held out both hands. 'Even a fool, even . . .' He raised an eyebrow. 'Even a fool,' she rushed out, 'can see that a poem, particularly a well-known one, can be got out of someone. The method isn't – it can't be – foolproof.' *Idiot*, she thought. *Shut your mouth.* But shutting her mouth was not Ruby's way. 'It's wrong to send the agents off with something . . . so flimsy.'

She had trespassed. No one was supposed to discuss these things. Especially not the pond life that she was.

She held her breath.

Major Martin leaned back in the chair. He was about to say something, checked himself and then decided to go ahead anyway. 'As I see it, we have no greater duty laid on us than to give the agents a secure coding system. Not just for the sake of our country but to give them a chance of survival.'

He spoke passionately.

I knew it. I knew it. He's worried sick.

So that was it. Agents were dying alone in that darkness out there, hunted, cornered and tortured, and he minded if the reason was Home Station's carelessness or stupidity. Major Martin minded very much – and so did Ruby.

There was a click. A connection. Emotional . . . intellectual . . . mathematical? She couldn't say what precisely but it was there.

They were on dangerous territory and she knew perfectly well that they should not be discussing this subject.

Peter Martin beat a retreat. He got to his feet and said: 'Shall I tell you what I think? You can't wait to be running a show. Am I right? So, I would like you to take charge of the indecipherable team. Pick out the brightest, or rather the best, girls, train them and keep tabs.'

Disappointed that that was it, Ruby decided to make do with what she had been offered. Making a rough computation, she said, 'We'll need rotating groups of at least twelve.'

He whistled softly. 'Fine. Personnel will go mad. Top brass will shout.' His mouth twitched. 'We're due a little well-earned entertainment.'

Again, he checked his watch. 'I've got you on board?'

She nodded.

'About coding security . . . Keep thinking, as I will at my end. Say nothing. I don't know what will happen. However, I think you have the kind of mind and aptitude which might be useful.' He picked up his briefcase. 'We'd have to sort out a promotion and you would have to come to London.'

'Wonderful,' she said.

Major Martin's smile was a wintry one. 'Some people might not like it but I imagine you could more than deal with office politics. This is not a good time for the Allies . . . and we just have to put up with that sort of stuff.'

Ruby liked the 'we'.

Chapter Ten

On København's Bredgade a van shuddered to a halt and four Danish policemen threw themselves out of it.

They were armed.

Neither Tanne Eberstern nor her brother, Nils, paid it much attention.

Muffled up against the cold, the two of them were heading to a bar for a beer before Tanne went on to meet her friend, Grete, at the ballet.

A cigarette butt in the gutter caught Tanne's eye and she bent down and hoiked it up. A scavenger. But, these days, tobacco was like gold dust and, oh joy, she had discovered a stationer on the Bredgade who kept a stock of Bible paper which doubled up nicely for the roll-your-owns.

'Disgusting,' said Nils, his hand slapping in brotherly fashion onto her back. 'Stop it.'

Then she felt Nils's hand ball into a fist.

'Tanne . . . look up. Trouble.'

He shoved her against a shop window as policemen scythed through the pedestrians in the street.

'Stop.'

A youth in a navy-blue cap and worker's overalls had been heading towards Tanne and Nils but, at the sight of the police, he spun round and beat a retreat. Too late. A couple of the police seized him from behind and shoved him against the wall.

The majority of the onlookers shrank back – an animal reaction. None of them protested.

The youth looked wildly from side to side. *Help me? Patriots?* Tanne caught his expression: determined, full of hatred, on the brink. One of the police shouted at him. He shouted back. A second policeman, big and burly, stepped forward and hit him on the jaw with the butt of his gun.

There was a low mutter, a collective groan, from the onlookers.

Blood streamed.

His cry of pain was also one of protest.

Shameful. The thought tore through her.

The policemen squared up to their victim. Breathing heavily, some flecked with sweat.

'Name?'

'*Fuck off!*'

'Your papers?'

One of the policemen dug into the pocket of the youth's overalls.

It was then she noticed the *Gestapoman* sitting in the front of the policemen's van, watching events. He was smoking.

My God. Tanne realized with a flash of comprehension that the police were enjoying their new licence to unleash violence. The presence of a *Gestapoman* whipped them up. The victim's arms were now spread out in crucifixion, the tendons in his wrists stretched like string under the pale skin. Blood dripped onto his collarless shirt.

Here was an especial shame. Danes were perpetrating war on fellow Danes.

'Let him go,' she shouted and Nils's hand clapped like a trap across her lower face.

'Shut up, Tanne.'

An alley ran down to the left of the shop they were standing outside. A cyclist emerged from it at speed. Poising at the junction, he readjusted his balance, put his head down and rode directly towards the knot of police. Wham! His wheel slammed into the legs of one policeman. The man bellowed and slumped to the ground.

The diversion gave the youth a chance. He wrested himself from their grip and took to his heels.

Run, run, Tanne willed him.

Weaving in and out of the shoppers and pedestrians, he pelted down the street and out of sight. One of the police gave chase. A second yelled at the onlookers to stand back while he attended to his fallen colleague.

The fourth?

The cyclist swung the bicycle round and pedalled furiously towards Tanne and Nils. Oh God, she thought. He was aiming to go back the way he'd come.

No.

In horror, she watched as the fourth policeman drew his gun, dropped to his knees. The gun jerked. There was a whistle – almost musical – and a tearing sound.

Tanne was standing a little in front of Nils and the blood spray hit her first, pattering over her feet, pooling onto the road. It was then she smelled it. Hot. Rank.

His head smashed in by a bullet, the cyclist hit the ground. Wheels spinning, his bicycle fell on top of him.

Inside her leather shoes, Tanne's feet were slippery, and a red stain oozed over her stockings. A single rivulet of blood ran down her left leg.

The scene burned into her vision.

The onlookers seemed frozen. Terror? Outraged and disgusted at the behaviour of their own police?

Shock made her incoherent. *His blood is on my legs. His blood is on my legs.*

The felled policeman cried out and cursed as his colleagues tried to move him.

'Don't get involved,' hissed the woman who was standing beside Tanne. She was clutching her shopping basket to her chest.

The injured policeman was manoeuvred into the back of the van, where they laid him flat, and the body of the cyclist was thrown in beside him. The van drove off in the direction of the hospital.

The street looked normal. *No, it didn't.* People moved in slow motion. The cobbles were hemmed with blood, which was trickling into the gutter. An echo of the bullet's whistle, and the crump as it hit the skull, remained in the air. A life had been snuffed out.

She spoke through lips that didn't want to obey her. 'I must wash my legs.'

They were standing outside a well-known sausage bar. Nils hustled her inside it and they found a table. He asked for a bowl of water and helped Tanne to clean herself up.

A waitress, pale and on the verge of tears, slapped a menu on their table. There was a nervous clatter of cutlery. The phone by the till rang and was answered. The last rays of sun slanted in at the window, seeking out the shock and shadows on the diners' faces. The massy block of the Dagmuhaus building across the square was as ever, and the traffic in the street had returned to normal. Yet all was different. Witnessing that scene had changed her.

Nils nudged over a glass of beer. 'Drink.'

She steadied her hand. 'Do you think he was a communist?'

He shrugged. 'Possibly.'

'He was someone's son, brother.' The beer was good and she sucked in a second mouthful, then searched her bag for her tobacco stash and cigarette papers.

'I know.'

'Terrible things are happening in Denmark.'

'Yes, they are.' Nils was calm and matter-of-fact. 'But we have to carry on as best we can.'

Tanne shrugged. How come Nils was so . . . untouched? Clumsily, she resumed the task of rolling the cigarette and lighting it. 'Here, want one?'

'No.' Reaching over, he stilled the fingers that seemed to have lost their control. 'Don't take on. Don't let it get to you. Don't let anyone get to you.'

Blood. Brains on the road. Death.

'Aren't you upset about what we've just seen?'

'Of course. But you mustn't think about it. Otherwise it weakens you.'

'But we have to think about it. Nils, you can't not have an opinion.'

'I disagree.' Nils was his customary, infuriating, detached self. Her brother had a hide inches thicker than most and she could never make out if this was genuine or, for some psychological reason, he had cultivated imperviousness, and very successfully, too.

She and he were chalk and cheese. Nils was considered something of a mathematical genius, and his strengths, such as they were, could not be more different from Tanne's talents. He had taken his first degree at eighteen. Since then he had been sequestered at the university, adding a master's in symbolic logic, plus a PhD, to his academic achievements. So highly did the university rate him that they had given him a set of rooms overlooking the main quad and told him he could occupy them for as long as he wished.

The alcohol was working its way through Tanne's system – soothing and steadying. 'What's the latest project?'

Normally Nils brushed aside questions about his work because he knew most people didn't begin to understand. On this occasion, he was prepared to humour her. 'Electronic communications,' he said. 'We are working on a small revolution. Actually, a big one.' He grinned.

She flicked a shred of tobacco from her finger. 'Do your new German masters at the university know about it?'

Very soon after the Nazi takeover of the country, German academics from Heidelberg and Munich arrived at Nils's department at the university and muscled in on the research.

Nils glanced around. 'You mean my new *esteemed* colleagues?' He lowered his voice. 'Even I know you must watch what you say.'

Squinting at him through the cigarette smoke, she murmured, 'Your new and esteemed colleagues, then.'

'My brilliant German colleagues know all about me. They made it their business.'

Looking at Nils, she was struck by his innocence – his mad faith that everything could carry on regardless – and shivered. 'Nils, you will be careful?'

'Why wouldn't I be? I intend to stay in my rooms doing my work for the duration of the war, and I won't be prised out.'

She sent him a quizzical look. 'You really, really are not going to take sides? You are not going to say the Germans are right or wrong?'

'No.'

'Not even after –' She stubbed out the cigarette. 'Not even – ?'

'No.'

There it was: the shutter rattling down and cutting Nils off from the rest of humanity. It was an excellent tactic, giving him freedom to pursue his thoughts without the muddle and fuss of other considerations. It never occurred to him, nor would it have mattered to Nils, that others had to carry the can for a lot of things as a result.

The stains on Tanne's stockings seemed to her as bright as burning beacons. 'One day I might begin to understand what symbolic logic is.'

He looked at her with that contemptuous but affectionate look that she knew so well. 'There's no need.'

'I'm supposed to be at the ballet,' she said, after a pause. 'Grete will be waiting.'

Before they parted Tanne insisted that Nils returned with her the following day to Rosenlund, for dinner and to stay over for a night. 'The parents fret about you. You don't see enough of them. Let them check that you are all right.' She added, 'We are a family.'

Nils had a way of pushing Tanne into sounding so much older than was necessary. A hundred years older.

'The condition of being a parent is to fret. It doesn't mean anything. Anyway, I don't want *Far* going on at me.'

'Nils, he doesn't. You choose to see it like that.'

The contemptuous but affectionate Nils was back. '*Far* and I don't understand each other, never have. I think he's blinkered. He thinks I am a peculiar species who has the misfortune to be his son.'

Aha, thought Tanne, picking up a touch of regret and resentment in Nils's tone. It wasn't all as cut and dried in her brother's mind as he would have her think.

'No need to look like that, Tanne. As the inheritor of his sacred Rosenlund, you get the special treatment.'

She frowned.

'And *don't* tell me that you find it a burden. You love the idea.'

Did she?

Despite all this, Nils allowed Tanne to persuade him and, the following day, they caught an early afternoon train to Køge.

Thick with cigarette smoke, the carriage was crowded but they managed to commandeer the last two seats. '*Mor . . . Mor . . .*' wailed a child, wanting the attention of its exhausted-looking mother, who couldn't rouse herself to respond. She wore a hand-knitted jersey in bright green which had been patched and re-patched. Her husband ate his way stolidly through a meat pie wrapped in greaseproof paper. Every so often the mother's gaze rested on the diminishing meat pie but her husband did not offer her even a crumb.

The train eased out of the station and, almost immediately, came to a halt. Tanne glanced at her watch. Stop-go. Stop-go. This was the way trains functioned in the war. Thank God, the child cried itself into exhaustion.

Yesterday's street scene had played, and replayed, in her head a thousand times – every small detail starkly etched. The blood-splattered cobbles. The splintering of bone. The tense huddle of spectators.

Horrible.

Wrong.

Nils dozed. Tanne diverted herself by looking out of the carriage window. She thought about the dress she had ordered from *Fru* Nielsen. Powder blue: designed to complement the ashy tones of her hair.

Bloodstains.

She concentrated on *Sleeping Beauty*, a ballet she knew inside out. A fragile Princess Rose, whose ankles looked as though they might snap at any minute, had been kissed passionately awake in a scene which usually evoked shivery, warm feelings. Not this time. Death in a street had shaken Tanne's assumptions and she was now beginning to understand that she had been living in ignorance of the realities – gulled by an upbringing in the innocent wilderness of Rosenlund.

As arranged, Arne was waiting at Køge station with Loki harnessed into the pony trap. Nils seized Arne's hand and shook it. Arne was the one person to whom he showed obvious affection. 'How are you, Master Nils?'

'All the better for seeing you, Arne.'

Each ran a check on the other – her slight brother and big, burly Arne. They were friends: the sort who went fishing together and sat in contented silence for hours, firm in that friendship. Nils climbed up beside Arne. 'I'll take the reins.'

At Rosenlund, Tanne stopped in the hall to admire an arrangement of hothouse flowers. She checked the card beside the vase: 'To Kay, with love from Cousin Anton'.

Running up to her bedroom, it was impossible to miss the family tree placed at the turn of the stairs. No inhabitant of Rosenlund, no visitor, could ever be in doubt as to the Eberstern pedigree.

In 1777, Bertel Eberstern had been granted a patent of

nobility. In 1798, his son, Carsten Eberstern, married Princess Sophia-Maria of Westphalia. And so it went on.

Those dead forebears, many of them German, still had the power to mould her existence. As the elder child she would one day step onto the estate and kneel to accept her future. Being the younger, Nils would not inherit, and from time to time he needled her about it. 'I can choose my own life,' he pointed out. Flatly. Unsympathetically.

Could Tanne?

When she inherited, it would be to care for the land, the house, the farms, for the duration. A curious position to be in, but she enjoyed it and resented it, sometimes with the same breath. Adults of her parents' generation regarded her with approval, for she possessed future status. Yet if she confessed to her friends what her future entailed her words were met with indifference and, occasionally, contempt.

Nils was correct. She wasn't free.

But she could be. She could be.

Sometimes she lay in bed and plotted escaping to Rome or Paris. To live in an attic and behave disgracefully.

'Most women in the world don't even have the vote,' her mother had pointed out, more than once, when Tanne voiced her misgivings. 'Let alone the right to take possession of their inheritance. Denmark is ahead of the world.'

And I should be grateful?

At those moments she hated her mother, who was so settled, so in the mould. Had her mother ever rebelled? Or ever considered that there was another kind of life, that no one should be in thrall to bricks and mortar? Did she ever get angry, as Tanne so often did?

Who knew? Her daughter didn't.

Then, in the aftermath of strong emotion, stole the calm of passions spent, the familiar image of the beautiful house and land lodging uppermost in her mind. She remembered the times riding out with her father, rising at dawn for the duck shoot, the boating parties, the family eating and talking together. It was, she told herself, a Platonic ideal of rural life – a utopia, a benign autocracy – where it was possible to live the good fulfilling existence.

Pausing to look through the large window at the turn of the stairs, she saw the knife-sharp, frozen lines of winter had formed like the first exploratory strokes of a drawing. Where the late sun hit the lake there was an explosion of light and icy dazzle. She grimaced. Those summer vistas, the radiance of trees and lawn, were now only memories.

As usual, tea was served in the small sitting room overlooking the garden and lake. Nils was already installed in a chair by the window doing a crossword.

Tanne sat on the arm of the chair. 'Am I annoying you?'

He did not bother to look up. 'Yes.'

'Did you ring for tea?'

'No idea.'

'You probably did.'

The door opened and, in rubber boots over her bare legs, as was her wont, Arne's wife, Birgit, appeared with the tea tray. Nils leaped to his feet – he could be quick when he wished to be – and captured the tray. 'It seems I did.'

He put the tray down on the table, and flicked Birgit's plait. 'You're going grey, Birgit. It suits you.'

As she left the room, Birgit smiled at him over her shoulder and said: 'Go on, be as rude as you like.'

The habit of taking tea had been imported into the family by her mother. A silver teapot. Bone china so fine you could see your fingers through it. A plate of cake. Kay always specified Victoria sponges and boiled fruit cakes. So English. If Tanne had anything to do with it, Danish favourites such as *kekstorte* and Napoleon's Hats sneaked onto the cake stand and, of course, their father's favourite gingerbread. It was civilization, tricked out with lace napkins. A small ritual knitted up into the greater one of Rosenlund's daily existence.

Their father arrived. He had been out for hours riding the boundaries to check on the winter arrangements, which meant endless checking up on fodder, silage, fuel and cattle shelter.

He was still in his riding clothes and was moving a little stiffly. He went straight over to Nils and dropped a hand on his shoulder. 'Nice to see you, Nils. Are you staying long?'

Nils was not as tall as his father. The family joked about a distant troll ancestry sneaking into the warrior Ebersterns. Nils pretended he thought it was funny, too. The joke had rippled along through the years until the day their mother said, 'Have any of you considered that it might be my ancestry?' shocking them all into silence because their mother's background never seemed to come into it. 'Whoever it was,' said Nils, who minded about his lack of height, 'was no friend of mine.'

'Until tomorrow,' he answered. 'I've things to do.'

Translated, this meant Nils yearned to quit the beauty and elegance of Rosenlund and return to his hermetic, dusty, comfortless set of rooms.

'Don't you want to know what's going on here?' her father asked.

'To be honest, not particularly.'

He was disappointed. 'It would be nice if you stayed,' he said. 'Won't you?'

Nils got up and wandered over to the window. 'No,' he said flatly.

'No interest at all in what's going on?'

'Why should I?' Nils turned round to face him. 'You and Tanne have it all sewn up.'

'But there's a war on.'

'I know,' said Nils in a very deliberate manner. 'I know.'

Nils may have been shorter than his father, but they shared the same colouring and cast of features and, when they were angry, similar expressions. There comparisons stopped and contrasts began, for their characters could not have been more dissimilar. Difficult people, both of them; difficult to gauge and, Tanne suspected, a mystery to most.

But she loved them.

She stepped into the breach. 'Nils, some of the stock died last winter because of the cold. We don't want that to happen again.'

'So? You've stocked up. Simple.'

'But the milk yields are down,' said her father.

Nils shrugged.

Don't push too hard, Far, Tanne told him silently.

He gave up. 'What's going in København?'

'The usual,' Tanne replied. 'Shopping, theatre, eating.' A man was shot dead. 'I went to the ballet. *Sleeping Beauty*. It's on all the time.'

'Of course it is,' said Nils. 'Denmark kissed awake by Prince Charming. The question is: who is Prince Charming?'

Something went click in Tanne's head. So? The arch of the ballerina's foot . . . she had been balancing not on an aesthetic pin but a political one. How stupid Tanne had been not to have seen that the ballet was being used as a coded message of defiance. No wonder *Sleeping Beauty* was being performed all the time, and how irritating that it was Nils who had pointed it out.

'København is stuffed with Danes eavesdropping on other Danes,' continued Nils. 'The *stikker* who report things to the Germans. The atmosphere is most peculiar and jumpy.'

'Surprised you notice.' Tanne was a little sour.

He flashed her a look as if to say: *That was not worthy of you.* 'No one feels safe to speak their mind. Even I've noticed.'

No, it wasn't worthy of her, and she was annoyed with herself for allowing point-scoring habits from their childhood to resurface. Tanne made a face at him. It was so unlike Nils to comment on anything other than his immediate concerns. These, he once informed her, were formulae, theories of computable numbers, academic papers.

Her father snapped his gingerbread in two. A fine dust fell to his plate. 'Be careful what you say about the Germans.'

'We know what side you're on,' said Nils, goading. 'It must be increasingly difficult to square it with Mother.'

It wasn't like Nils to be malicious. Amused, disdainful, removed . . . yes, but malice did not often figure. It was the war, she thought, with increasing desperation.

Her father elected not to notice. 'Perhaps the *stikker* are necessary. Order must be maintained. Rebellion and resistance make life impossible.'

Tanne heard herself exclaim. '*Inform* on your fellow citizens?'

'We have to consider Denmark's position,' he said, not unreasonably.

She stared at him. 'But that's it, *Far*. We do have to consider.'

It was true – and she had not done so. Not properly. Not in depth. Worse, she did not possess the political vocabulary to describe what she felt.

'We have to deal with Germany,' her father was saying. 'It's not what Denmark asked for but we've done it. You must consider that the communists could be as much of a threat.'

'Overdoing it, *Far*,' said Nils from his perch by the window.

Her father swung round to face him and Tanne read in his expression both disappointment and a baffled irritation.

'Do you two understand anything? Have you seen what Stalin is up to? First he joins in with Hitler and overruns Poland. Why? Answer: because he reckoned he could snaffle a piece of it. Now he's fighting on the side of the Allies, but it isn't for love of peace and democracy. It's because he has his own plans for expansion. Denmark might well be among them. Do you want to live in a communist country? Better the devil you know . . . And there is Rosenlund.'

'Oh, Rosenlund,' said Nils in a sarcastic voice. 'Rosenlund . . .'

There was a long awkward pause. Her father pushed his cup

and saucer away and lit a cigarette. 'Whatever you think, Nils, it is worth saving. And I will.'

Why, oh why, did he say such things? He wasn't a fool and he certainly wasn't a bad man.

Her gaze sifted over familiar things: the secretaire with the bowed legs, the chair with the curling back, the long pier glass painted bronze and decorated with a lotus-plant design, the china pots under the window patterned with blue agapanthus and fiery geraniums, the bone china on the tray, the fine Danish landscape over the fireplace of a clearing in a birch wood covered by spring anemones.

'Hello, darlings.'

Their mother stood in the doorway, dressed in one of her pretty woollen afternoon frocks. She had a heightened colour and looked younger than Tanne had seen her for a long time.

'Sorry. I was out walking and I had to change.'

All three stared at her.

'What is it?' she asked. 'I can feel the atmosphere.' She snapped her fingers and the noise sounded like a gun shot.

'The war, of course.' Nils resumed his seat.

Tanne glanced down at her teacup and noticed that the saucer had a chip on its rim.

Her mother sat down in her usual seat behind the tea tray. With a deliberate movement, she lifted up the teapot. 'I think you were discussing politics.' She poured herself a cup of tea. 'Not a good idea.' She picked up the milk jug and the colour deepened in her cheeks. 'It's a subject we should leave well alone.'

Tanne's gaze shifted from her mother to her father. Neither of them was looking at the other. 'We can't,' she said flatly. 'The war is happening.'

To her surprise, her mother's hand whitened with tension as it grasped the milk jug. 'That's why we have to make sure we don't quarrel.'

'*Never forget . . .*' her mother used to say.

'*Never forget what?*'

'*We are a family.*'

It was possible to both love and hate at the same time. Yes, yes, it was. When Tanne hated her mother, she hated her more than she loved her. Sometimes it was vice versa. Her mother was her mirror image – all mothers and daughters were. Whereas her feelings for her father were fixed and constant, like the planets, and driven by the need to protect him, her feelings for her mother shifted like the tide.

Early-ish the following morning, Nils went back to København.

A year ago, the decision had been taken to train Tanne in the running of Rosenlund and she had been summoned to a session in the estate office, which was lined from floor to ceiling with the ledgers. The ledgers went back to the early nineteenth century, and contained a switchback narrative of bumper yields, harsh winters, golden summers and barren harvests but none, apparently, as bad as the past twelve months.

Checking over the accounts with him, she was shocked to hear her father swear under his breath. Dairy yields were down, plus the order had come through from the Town Hall to requisition a number of their precious pigs.

'What right do they have?' Tanne demanded.

Her father moved over to the window. A troubled silence followed before he explained that the German Reich and the Danish Protectorate were now one family. Families shared.

'*Sharing*, yes,' said Tanne.

This was a new world with new realities and again, Tanne felt ashamed that it had taken so much time for her to realize what was going on.

'If this winter is like the last one . . .' He turned to face her. 'Tanne, darling, promise me that you will never get involved in anything stupid.'

'Why?'

He looked at her as if she was mad. 'Why? Because –' He gestured at the ledgers. 'You know why.'

'I understand.'

He turned back to the window. 'More important . . . is your safety.'

Badly bruised from a tussle with a gate in the north field a couple of days ago, his hand rested on the blind. The flesh was green and yellow, the nail blackened. It must be hurting him. It was a reminder that her father could be wounded and her heart squeezed in her chest.

At university, she had talked politics endlessly and, she now acknowledged, carelessly. With Aage, Grete, Hannah, Gooda, all close friends, she had debated the overthrow of the monarchy, putting students into Parliament and turning pacifist. 'We are articulating Denmark's future,' they told each other and thrived on the noisy clash of viewpoints. She remembered Aage leaping up onto a table and managing to look both magnificent and ridiculous.

How pleasurable the long beach walks dodging salt-bleached driftwood had been, and the demanding summer bicycle rides and, when back at university for the autumn and winter, the exciting and messy sessions with printing machines and duplicators.

None of them had understood how their ideas would work in practice. Still less what a war meant. Certainly not the *realpolitik* of guns and greed and killing.

She joined her father at the window and he reached out, put an arm round her shoulders and pulled her to him. Together, they looked out onto the winter landscape.

Very often at this time of year, a light, pretty snow was the first to fall. Then the winds arrived, the sky lowered, more snow fell, packing down the pretty and sparkling surface into a sullen, greyish layer over which could be seen the spoor of desperate deer weaving this way and that.

Arne had taught Nils and Tanne how to spot the signs of winter starvation. 'A hungry deer scratches up patches of snow to try to get at the leaves below. Watch for the scatters of urine in the snow that mean they are dying.'

'Promise me you won't get involved, Tanne?' her father repeated.

She sneaked a sideways look at him. Her father's fair hair was silvering up. Definitely, he was older, more careworn, slightly haunted. She had always felt that she knew him best of all, and considered him as 'hers'. She understood his handsome, slightly remote exterior hid passionate feelings. Perhaps a vulnerability? Her friends knew better than to criticize him in her presence because Tanne protected him, sometimes against her mother.

'I promise.'

Chapter Eleven

The snow fell for a day.

Kay received a message from Felix which had been tucked between stones in the wall that ran around the back of the estate. 'Please bring Aunt Agatha's present up on Thursday.'

So it begins, she thought.

How do I do it?

It was no use being indulgent, or weak. Having opted to walk this particular path, walk it she must. She was doing it for decency in the largest, widest sense, but that was not to say she didn't feel frightened, because she did.

She worked out her tactics.

On the Wednesday evening, she put on her black lace dress – a favourite with Bror – and made sure they ate a good dinner. Afterwards, they retired to the small sitting room. Birgit had lit the fire and the card table was pulled up in front of it.

Tanne was staying with a friend in Køge and they had the house to themselves.

'A game of Snap?' she suggested.

'The best of five.'

Bror played ferociously but not ferociously enough. Kay beat him three games to two. Good.

'Darling . . .'

Bror smiled his slow, rather sleepy smile which had so enchanted Kay on first meeting him. 'I know that tone. You want something.'

'Could I have the car tomorrow? I want to go and see Nils. I'll park it at the station and be back on the evening train.'

'But you don't like driving in the snow.'

'It wasn't that heavy a snowfall so the roads should be passable.'

Bror laid down his cards and made for the whisky decanter. She felt a chill. 'Bad loser, darling?'

Glass in hand, he turned round and looked at her. Her smile faded.

'You're not going to København to meet Anton, are you?'

The breath seemed stuck in her lungs. Getting up from the card table, she said, 'I'll have one, too.'

Bror handed her a measure in a cut-glass tumbler. It tasted of Scottish peat bogs, of wild berries and mountain water – which she remembered from holidays in Argyll before marrying Bror. 'You haven't answered my question, Kay.'

Relief.

It was the wrong question and she could deal with it. Kay cradled the glass against her stomach. 'No. I'm not going to see Anton.' It occurred to her that she should be more indignant and she added sharply: 'It's a ridiculous question.'

Bror considered the contents of his glass. 'You don't need me to tell you that Anton wants you, Kay. I notice he's been sending you flowers . . .'

'Look at me, Bror,' she said angrily.

'You see, I think . . .' He came over and placed a hand under her chin.

She was conscious of his energy – his strong, focused energy – flowing through his fingertips into her. 'Perhaps *you* should be thinking more clearly, Bror.'

He turned away.

'Look at me, Bror.'

He shrugged and took up a position by the fireplace. 'I think that you're still angry with me about signing the Declaration. Am I right?' Kay was silent while she worked out her next step. He continued: 'You forget how well I know you.'

'The Declaration's nothing to do with Anton. You're mixing up the two.'

'Anton would absolutely make the Declaration his business. It's a way of needling me. Anyway, he told me once that if there was a war it was best to be on the side which America was likely to support. Which I'm sure will be your position.'

'So?'

Bror dropped the subject of Anton. 'You and I have to be careful that we don't let all this divide us.'

She bit her lip – and the guilt which was becoming a companion settled over her.

'Nothing to say, darling?'

'This *is* ridiculous, Bror. You know how I feel about the Declaration and I am certainly not going to sleep with your cousin. Can we talk about something else?'

'Better we talk about it, than brood,' said Bror.

Clutching her whisky, Kay walked up and down, and the heavy material of her skirts swished in the uneasy silence. 'Haven't we enough to deal with at the moment?'

'Kay . . .'

It was the voice which had wooed her so many times.

The old feelings kicked in – and they also provided a solution to this particular conversation. 'Darling Bror . . .' Kay went over to him and pushed the glass against his chest. 'Sorry, I'm so sorry . . . this bloody war.'

He took her glass, set it down and pulled her to him. His hands slid over her shoulder blades. 'I'm sorry, too.'

When Bror apologized he meant it and she knew how difficult it was for him to do so. Within her armour of black lace, she was as tense as a coiled spring and she longed for the impossible – to return to the beginning. With a sigh, she pressed her face against his chest.

His grip tightened. 'Kay . . . ?' He placed a finger at the base of her neck – precisely at the point where the pulse beat. 'Why do you want to see Nils? Is there anything wrong?'

'He's my son. Why wouldn't I want to see him?'

Nothing was normal any longer. The lie took shape as easily

as the truth. It was then Kay understood that part of her had already broken away. Part of her was already on that train with the wireless transmitter, working out what to do, how to proceed.

He kissed the place on her neck where his finger had rested.

She murmured, 'You should want to see him, too. You must try to be closer to him, Bror. Promise me. You never know with a war . . .'

Her voice trailed away. Had she overdone it? Nils was always a slightly tricky subject.

He flinched. 'Nils has left home.' Bror allowed himself a note of regret. 'Which makes it easier as I don't have to think about him all the time.' He laid a hand on her breast and his touch set up familiar sensations in her pelvis. 'Kay . . .' Gently, he pushed her towards the sofa.

She looked up at him. 'Here?'

'Yes, here.'

'Goodness . . .' She laughed and dropped back onto the sofa.

Between them they fought with the folds of black lace, which they wadded around her hips. She undid his trousers. He engaged expertly with the button of her French lace knickers.

It was fierce, hot and relatively brief. At one point he turned her over, at another she rose uninhibited above him. The moment appeared to satisfy a need in both of them, and reminded them of an element in their life together which was in danger of being lost. It was, Kay thought, a stirring, salty reminder of the early days when lust preoccupied them, and nothing was political.

Afterwards, they lay jammed together on the sofa like a pair of teenagers.

'My dress! My poor dress,' said Kay.

They smiled at each other, broken and uneasy smiles.

What next?

'Go to København,' Bror said. 'But if the weather is bad, I insist you get Arne to drive you.'

The snowfalls had freshly iced the countryside, and thrown soiled, sleety sheets over the towns and villages.

On the journey from Køge, Kay rubbed a circle out of the ice crystals on the train window. Then she peered out across a white, shrouded landscape. Was she prepared to die for this land?

Retrieved from the pigeon loft, the case was on the rack above her.

Please. She sent a prayer up into the ether. *Please. Let me do this properly.*

As instructed, she waited by the newspaper vendor at the main station in København. A youth in a peaked cap brushed up against her, slipped a key into her hand and whispered the address, adding: 'The flat has been checked out. No children. No maids.'

That was important. Children and maids posed a risk

On the pavements, the snow was piled six feet deep but, unusually, the authorities had made no move to clear it away. Carrying the case, Kay emerged from the station. A bitter wind blew from the north which bit into her exposed skin and swirled up her skirt. More than thankful for her boots and gloves, she adjusted her hat and headed for the tram stop.

The city was eerily silent. Cold always dulled her brain and, as Kay grew older, her aversion to it deepened. It crept into her bones and she dreaded the prospect of another vile winter like the previous one.

There were two other passengers at the tram stop, both of them bundled up into coats and scarves. Kay pulled off a glove and checked the key zipped into a compartment in her brown crocodile handbag.

The tram was only half full. Kay chose a seat in the middle of the carriage and tucked the case under her legs. Two German officers got on and sat down in the seats in front her. 'Thank you, thank you,' one of them said politely in bad Danish.

They were dressed in the *feldgrau* soldier's uniform but, at a pinch, they could have been taken for tourists. Kay was forced to study the back of their heads. One of them had a mole at his hairline, the other had fair acned skin. Their ordinariness made it difficult to feel anything stronger than mild distaste.

The tram hissed along the tracks.

The young girl in a threadbare brown coat seated beside Kay stood up and pushed her way to the standing area at the back.

A few seconds later an elderly man heaved himself to his feet and joined the girl. It wasn't long before the majority of the passengers followed suit and jammed the standing area, which meant Kay and the German soldiers were the only ones still seated.

More clacking of wheels, plus muffled conversation from the standing platform filtered towards Kay.

A cool head, Felix had instructed. *Act normally*.

Despite the tuition, Kay's foot anchoring the case trembled and a numbness crept up her right leg.

If she remained seated, she would be marked out. If she got up, it would be obvious that the case was heavy. Split-second decision. She concentrated on steadying her foot.

Get off the tram.

The next stop was in sight. She picked up the case. One of the soldiers looked round. He had a pleasant, unassuming face. 'Let me help you,' he said.

What was normal? What was normal? Certainly not the cocktail of terror and disbelief flowing through her veins.

But this nice, ordinary-looking soldier had read the manual: 'Be polite to the natives of whichever country you are occupying.'

He held out his hand.

She thought rapidly, running through her experiences of

fraternizing with Bror's German cousins and connections over the years.

What got the best response from them?

In a flash, she remembered sitting in a plush Munich café, the women at one end of the table, the men at the other and a violinist hard at work on a Strauss waltz. Plates of choux pastry larded with cream were piled high between them. The men smoked cigarettes and kept a close eye on their wives, Kay among them. Play the little woman, she thought. Like the English, German men liked to think that they held all the cards.

'Thank you,' she said and followed him to the back of the tram. 'You're so kind.'

As she pushed past a knot of passengers, a finger jabbed into her back. She flinched. Another drove painfully into her side.

'Nazi lover.'

The words were uttered softly but loud enough. Turning her head, she encountered blank faces.

The soldier deposited the case on the pavement and wished her a good day in bad Danish before getting back onto the tram.

The tram drew away. Shivering, Kay looked up at the group of hostile faces, ashamed that she minded what they thought of her.

A feeble sun emerged from the grey cloud but didn't do anything to raise the temperature. The case handle bit into her fingers and her feet were blocks of ice.

At a junction with Østergarde, she peered into a shop window in which was reflected a blurry, moving collage of other pedestrians checking for tails.

Her own face looked back at her.

Always, she had considered her features too non-descript, except for her chin, which Anton, in one of his flirtatious moments, insisted was a stubborn one. 'You look as soft as butter, darling, but your chin tells me you're a fraud dressed up in pearls.' She was wearing the substantial Eberstern pearls and an exquisitely cut suit under her coat which, along with the blue hat, was the fruit of one of her pre-war Parisian trips.

How was she managing the transition from well-to-do Danish matron into a secret operator who could be hunted and shot, along with her family?

Nothing will have prepared you for it . . . Felix again, instructing and cautioning.

Once more, she checked for a tail in a shop window. It was then she realized that the pearls were unwise. If anyone saw them under her coat, they would mark her out. Impatient with herself, she undid the clasp and dropped them into her bag. Lesson learned.

She quickened her pace, walking as fast as she could manage with the heavy case and without drawing attention to herself.

The safe house was reached through a courtyard at the centre of which the last of the hawthorn berries still clung to the trees. Looking neither right nor left, she skirted round the courtyard. Her nervousness intensified, driving acid into her stomach. God only knew how many pairs of eyes might be watching.

Inserting the key into the door, she pushed it open and stepped onto a pile of letters.

It was apparent at once that no one had been in the stale and unaired flat for some time. Setting the case down, she went on the prowl. In a room leading off the hall there was a vase of mummified flowers. Dead flies littered the windowsill. The floor-length drapes at the windows were coated in dust. The cushions on the sofa still bore the imprints of the people who last sat in them.

Back in the hall, she picked up the post addressed to Mr, Mrs and Master Frederick Mueller and stacked it in piles on the hall table, ready for the addressees to read the contents.

She knew in her heart that it was a useless gesture and something rotten had happened to the Muellers. All the same, she felt obliged to make it. Otherwise, it was to give up.

In the kitchen, a recipe book lay open on the sideboard. 'How to make a garlic sausage,' Kay read. In the sink, dirty cutlery rested in scummy, stagnant water, but the shelves around the room were neatly arranged, the storage jars labelled in a clear hand. The family who had lived here had been proud of the place.

Something – and it wasn't difficult to figure out what it might have been – had gone wrong for the family.

Light the gas. Fill the kettle. Place it on the ring.

Exactly what had happened to the Muellers?

The net curtains at the windows were good quality. Parting them a fraction, Kay checked out the courtyard. Scarlet pinpricks of the hawthorn berries caught her eye in the gloom.

All clear. Except that it wasn't. Nothing was.

The gas popped, making her jump. Since there was no milk, Kay made herself sit down with a few leaves of tea floating in the hot water and smoked a cigarette to steady herself. Not having anticipated a nervous reaction to her new role, she had been surprised by the disruption to her sleeping and eating patterns.

The front door was opening. In a flash, she was on her feet and, for the first time in her life, she wished she had one of Bror's guns.

Dead on time, it was Felix. The overalls had been replaced by a thick coat, smart trousers and a jacket, with a Fedora pulled down over his face. He tossed the hat onto the table. 'Any tea spare?'

The cupboard was well stocked with china and Kay found a second mug. 'How are you?'

They were speaking in low voices.

'Fine.'

Felix wasn't fine but tense and preoccupied. Kay pointed to the case and he placed it on the table.

'Any trouble?' he asked.

'No.'

'Followed?'

'No.'

He snapped open the locks and eased up the lid. 'How's Hector, by the way?'

'Hector? He and I have become friends. But I think he's homesick.'

'He'll be home soon enough.' He surveyed the case's contents. 'I'm sorry I had to ask you to bring it here.'

'I thought London was supposed to train the sentiment out of you.'

He pointed a finger at his chest. 'Observe, I am still human.'

The flash of humour was reassuring. 'Felix, look at me.'

His lips twitched. 'Gladly. Very nice, too.'

'No one is going to suspect the British wife of Bror Eberstern.'

He turned on her. 'That's stupid, Freya. Don't be.'

It had been a long time since she had been addressed so tartly and her hands tightened round the mug. 'The Nazis know that I'm aware they will be watching me because I am British. Therefore it's likely they'll conclude that, because I know they're watching, I won't dare to do anything.'

'The key word is "likely". Unreliable at best.'

It was then she realized that she was not the cause of his anger but bearing the brunt of it. 'Trouble?'

He was checking out the Send/Receive switch. 'Perhaps.'

She knew that he should not go into detail. But he did.

'The word is that . . . Well, reports have it that an agent up in Jutland is out of control.' He grimaced. 'Drinking heavily . . . Apparently, when he drinks, he talks. He's been warned. Many times.'

They were standing very close to each other, whispering.

'What will you all do?'

'Christ. Don't ask.'

In the heat of the moment, he had raised his voice.

'Shush.' She laid a finger on his lips.

He brushed her hand aside, but checked himself. 'There's been no word of Vinegar either at this end of proceedings. London tells me that he's up and running when I ask them to confirm. But I'm uneasy and I don't know why. My contacts on Jutland have not set eyes on him. They just leave the messages in the drop boxes and vice versa.'

'He could be being ultra cautious,' she said.

'Maybe.'

She imagined the resolution which needed to be scraped together before abandoning oneself to the unknown and the moment of terror before the opening of the parachute. 'He may have been injured and is lying low.'

'He's picking up the messages and sending them.' He wrapped a length of the aerial round his finger and stared at it. 'You can't be in this game without considering the possibilities. We have only London's word that he's not dead. But what do they know? Is Vinegar a traitor? Are the Germans playing back the wireless set? Or am I delusional?'

'If Vinegar was taken what could happen?'

Felix was playing with the handle of the case. 'Probaby tortured. The Jutland network would be compromised and there's a good chance we would be, too. If that was the case . . .' He looked up. 'If that was the case, dear Freya, we would have to take to the hills.'

'Not many hills in Denmark,' she pointed out.

Felix stared at her. Then he gave a short laugh. 'A lot depends on who's got him, if anyone has. Gestapo or the military. Whoever, they might run him until they want to pull us in. They could be using Vinegar to transmit to London . . .'

Kay was curious. 'What's he like?'

'No hero to look at, but I liked what I saw.'

Time was going slowly. Her jangled, snapping nerves, perhaps? 'More tea?'

Felix wasn't interested in the tea. 'We're underfunded and need people. London is clueless and, for all the protests to the contrary, doesn't care that much about Denmark. We need more sets and more pianists. London sent in a couple before me, but according to my contacts one of the sets was smashed up on landing, the other pianist was caught transmitting in a block of flats.'

She didn't need to ask what had happened to him. She didn't want to ask.

'Unless we have more back-up,' said Felix, 'I'm hindered from running the network because I'm always trying to reach the set, wherever it is.'

Clasping the mug, her hands sought to absorb the final vestiges of warmth from the hot water, and she heard herself say, 'I'll train.'

'Not in the mood for jokes.' Felix set down his mug on the table and, peering at her, realized it wasn't a joke. 'No.'

'Yes,' she countered.

There were things to be done and men were dying and girls were having their legs shot off. And here she was in a flat made terrible by its owners' enforced absence. And her husband . . . ? Her husband could be considered a traitor.

'You don't know what you're doing.'

'Agreed, I can't go to London to train, but there must be someone over here who can teach me Morse?' She pushed for the *coup de grâce*. 'You can't afford not to take me up.'

'It's dangerous.'

'Self-evidently. Give me a proper reason.'

'You are more valuable as a courier.'

'The two aren't mutually exclusive.'

'Almost.'

'But not quite.' She was making headway. 'Get another wireless set sent in. Teach me Morse. We'll keep one set at Rosenlund and the other in safe houses here.' She thought of her recent journey and her travelling companions of anxiety and acid stomach. 'Get thee behind me,' her father used to say of his longing for brandy. It never worked but it was worth trying. 'Between us, we can keep up the skeds but ensure we never fall into a pattern. We just have to work out a system of communication and message drops.'

What was she doing? The voice she was hearing belonged to someone else.

Felix ran a finger along the edge of the case. 'You may be right. There's a push to develop new wireless sets over here. We're good at radio technology. London might be persuaded to allow us to train our own operators.'

He fished a cigarette stub out of his pocket. 'Do you know how long the average life expectancy of a wireless operator is?'

What was she doing?

'No point in asking, Felix, or in answering.'

'Six weeks.'

She looked away towards the window.

'*Why* would you do this, Freya?'

She thought – rapidly, longingly – of the place which had become her home . . .

Summer sun – how she loved it. Rosenlund's long windows thrown open to expel the cold winter air trapped in its corners and to invite in the fresh, warm day. Clean bed linen. A book by the fire. The lake at Rosenlund frozen into a spectrum of exquisite colours. Good food . . .

She thought of her family.

Bror. Tanne. Nils.

Felix lit a match. As it flared into the gloom, she understood an odd truth: once you had committed, the urge was to commit further. Deeper.

He dragged at the stub of his cigarette and sucked in smoke. 'Freya, I'm trying to put you off.'

Smoke drifted between them. She wanted to remind him of his own rules. *Smoke is a giveaway.* But the sight of his tired, drained face shut her up.

'Someone has to do it. If it isn't me, perhaps someone with a young family will and that would be worse.' Her reasoning was taking shape, urgent and imperative. 'London wants and needs intelligence. Yes? It wants things to happen in Denmark. Yes? They haven't much to depend on except people like us. Denmark has not had a chance to prove . . . Well, what? That it can fight?' She leaned against the table. 'If we don't do our best, Denmark *will* go under.'

He clapped softly.

'I'm curious, Freya. You're not Danish.'

'Shut up, Felix. I'm as Danish as anyone. And British. And someone who is saying that action is necessary.'

Felix took a decision. 'Come with me to the bookshop on the Strøget in half an hour.'

It was a yes.

She glanced at her watch. 'Sked time?'

Felix snapped to attention and parted the net drapes at the window just a fraction. 'The lookouts should be in place by now.' The drapes dropped back into place. 'If you can, before you go on air make sure you have lookouts. They may save your life.'

He sat down, put on the headphones and flexed his right hand. 'Ready.'

She watched him, willing her heartbeat to return to normal.

ZYA. *The call sign.*

QRK. *What is my intelligibility?*

QVR. *Ready to receive.*

A good ten paces behind him, Kay trailed Felix through Tivoli Gardens. Like the other parks, it was crowded with people snatching some fresh air and daylight before the long night closed in.

Felix left Tivoli by the south gate and Kay followed him.

He had done his chameleon routine: hat pulled down over his face; wool scarf wrapped round his neck. Looking straight ahead and walking briskly, he managed to mimic most of the men in the city.

Crossing the street, he doubled back on his tracks and they

retraced their route through the shoppers until they reached the fashionable and popular bookstore in the Strøget. Felix came to a halt and was apparently absorbed by the display in the front of the window. Kay walked past him and entered a boutique selling women's underwear. She spent ten minutes discussing the dearth of lace trimming and bought a couple of sweat pads for under the arms.

She went back to the bookshop.

Check the window, Felix had briefed. *If there's a Tolstoy on display, it's safe. If there is a copy of Homer's* Iliad, *it isn't.*

She peered through the window where frost patterns were gathering. Copies of the Bible, an illustrated volume of Norse Myths and a pre-war novel were arranged in the front of the display. Tucked into the back there was a luridly jacketed copy of *Anna Karenina* beside the latest edition of *Mein Kampf*. Someone had a sense of humour.

Kay went in.

A man with a prophet's beard was serving at the counter, and she asked him the name of the translator of the *Anna Karenina*. 'If you follow me,' he said, 'we can look it up.' He ushered her into the back of the shop.

The furiously untidy and stuffy room into which she was ushered stank of smoke and the white paintwork was tinged yellow from nicotine. Running across one wall were bookshelves, stacked from floor to ceiling with books and periodicals.

Felix already sat at a round table whose surface was pitted and stained with cigarette burns and water marks. Two other men sat opposite him.

The first was a raw-looking youth with a shaved head, in blue overalls. The second, attired in a business suit, was Anton.

It wasn't hard to pick up the tension in the room and, as Kay entered, Anton sent her look which she interpreted as a warning to shut up about knowing him.

She wished he wasn't there. Anton's presence added an unwanted complication.

Felix introduced the youth. 'Freya, this is Jacob.'

'*Hej*, Jacob,' she said.

Jacob didn't bother with niceties. He ran a hand over his head. 'Any chance you were followed?'

'No.'

Kay sat down and Felix surveyed the faces at the table. 'Last Monday, Jacob's friends in the Køge cell were rounded up. We've had reports from a contact working in the laundry who said she heard screams from the cells. Jacob's here because he needs to lie low for a few days.'

Jacob's pale features creased in anger. 'I want to try to get them out.'

'No,' said Felix. 'We can't.'

Jacob rounded on him. 'You don't give all the orders.'

'Yes, I do,' said Felix – and Kay saw a new side to him.

Anton held up a hand. 'Shush.'

Jacob rose to his feet, moved over to the door and listened. He looked awkward and ungainly but, Kay noted, he could move like a cat.

Jacob gave a thumbs-up and leaned back against the door. 'So you won't help?' His frown was now so deep it looked permanent. 'My mother would do more than you lot.'

Anton steepled his hands, pressing the tips of his fingers together. Kay could tell he was regretting this meeting, and disliking Jacob. 'Action cannot be taken in isolation,' he offered. 'Your communist friends are admirable, but not equipped. What would your mother prefer? Her son alive or dead? Or would she like to listen to your screams?'

'Listen, Jacob . . .' Felix listed a pitifully sparse inventory. Guns: ten Sten guns, ten Colt pistols. Ammunition: approximately two hundred rounds. A quantity of plastic explosive. 'But it's not enough.'

'So you won't do anything?'

'*Can't* . . .' said Felix. 'But if we could we would.'

Felix's obvious sympathy succeeded in calming Jacob down.

Kay liked him the better for being patient with the younger man.

They discussed the position from all angles. The resistance could recruit an underground army, and would do so, but, without help, they could not lay hands on much in the way of weapons. London would have to send in regular drops by plane and the group would have to locate drop zones and weapons dumps.

'London holds the purse strings,' said Jacob. 'And Denmark has to obey.'

Jacob's resentments and prejudices were openly worn and Kay wondered if London knew how much it was resented?

Anton did not contribute much, which struck Kay as odd. Was it policy? Or was Anton sitting on the fence for some reason?

'We are agreed. London is the only way to get our hands dirty.' Felix touched Kay lightly on the shoulder and Anton frowned. 'Any thoughts?'

'I agree that we should work with London as much as possible.'

Felix glanced at Anton for confirmation. 'Any objections?'

'Only the old one,' replied Anton. 'My contacts don't want any trouble. They want everything quiet so they can pass on intelligence unobtrusively. Wrecking railway lines and factories stirs up the enemy who, of course, react badly. That makes it difficult for them.'

'Why are we here, then?' demanded Jacob.

It was a rhetorical question.

'At the moment, we only have British-made wireless sets in the country,' said Felix. 'We hope this will change. But one is mine and there is a second one in Jutland. They're pigs to carry around, plus they operate on alternate currents.' He gave a wry smile. 'In Denmark we operate mostly on a direct one, so it is sometimes difficult to use them.'

'Trust the British not to check.' Anton snapped open his cigarette case.

'Our engineers are secretly working on a new prototype radio transmitter. It will be able to switch currents, and also transmit at high speed which means the message is virtually undetectable. But they need time and places to set up secret labs. And they will need the crystals from London.'

'Any idea when they will be ready?' asked Anton.

'Who knows?' said Felix. 'It's highly dangerous for them.'

Guns. Ammunition. Radio communication. Recruitment.

Kay had wandered into a mad, fractured universe.

Felix and Jacob left, and Anton and Kay remained seated at the table.

Kay picked up her bag. 'Do you agree with what has been decided?'

He shrugged. 'It's the best we can do.'

Kay took her lipstick and powder compact out of her bag. 'Are you serving several masters, Anton?'

'Don't you trust me?'

She applied lipstick to her bottom lip, angling the compact so that the mirror reflected Anton's face, but she couldn't read his expression. 'Should I?'

His hand snapped round her wrist. Startled, she almost dropped the lipstick. 'Never doubt me.'

She removed his hand and, slotting the lipstick and compact back into her bag, snapped shut the clasp. 'Why should I?' she said. 'Unless you give me reason.'

Anton took hold of one of Kay's hands, this time gently. 'How pretty and elegant.' Turning it over, he raised it to his lips and kissed it. His mouth was warm on her cool skin. 'The British secret services have their own jealousies and factions. Our information is that the British senior intelligence services consider the outfit which trained Felix to be filled with upstarts and amateurs, and they go out of their way to obstruct them.' He gave her back her hand. 'Enjoy the ironies, darling. The Brits are at war with Germany but fight each other.'

'Isn't that what people do in organizations? The Nazis fight each other like rats in a sack and Jacob and his communists have no love for us. Nothing's new.'

'I had no idea how wise you were, Kay.' He picked up his hat. 'We'll leave separately. Where are you going?'

'To see my son.'

Chapter Twelve

Ruby wrestled the word 'København' from the encrypted message, but that was more from an inspired guess than the result of her persuading the text to yield up its secrets logically.

It was a bugger, this one. A double-dyed, double-decker bugger.

It had been well over a month since her meeting with Major Martin and the dismal Christmas of 1942 had come and gone and nobody much rejoiced either at the arrival of the new year. It was bloody cold, too, her digs increasingly horrible and, even though she enjoyed heading up the teams, the work on the indecipherables was grinding and headache-inducing.

Sometimes she thought about Major Martin. Actually, if she was truthful, it was more than sometimes. What was it about him that so intrigued her? It didn't take long before she cottoned onto the fact that she liked him because he had asked her opinion.

Seated at their benches Attila Team shifted, sighed, muttered and scraped their chairs along the floor. Apart from the professional saints, most were jumpy and short-tempered. No doubt it was that time of the month – it was for her, and bugger that, too, because it hurt.

Curiously, Attila Team seemed to suffer it at the same time. Was this biological quirk worth examining? When a group of women gathered together on a regular basis, why did this synchronization happen? Was this another plank in the argument that, far from being an expression of divine will, humans were merely a collection of cells which obeyed only the laws governing physics and biology?

However, unless she was prepared to ask everyone, which

she wasn't, or conduct a scientific sampling, her theory would, of course, remain just that.

But the notion of being suspended in primal space, without moral purpose, was intriguing, liberating.

It was important to concentrate on the text. To seek. To think.

After a bit, Ruby cheered up. She could feel her mind strengthening and improving. In this war, the scientists and mathematicians were proving to be the magicians, and she was one of them.

It had taken some weeks to get this unit up and running. With the patterns imposed by the work, the girls hadn't gelled instantly. There was some grumbling, some bad temper and one or two incipient rebellions which Ruby had nipped in the bud.

'A right bloody tyrant,' said Janet.

Then, without explanation, gears shifted. The unit fell into shape and had been operating beautifully ever since.

She was proud of herself.

She reapplied herself to the message. What could she tease from it?

She ticked off the list. Pair C and T was number 1 in the code groups. Pair N and B was number 2.

It was painstaking, exhausting work. Dull . . . dull . . . beyond dullness, but oh so important. The letter pairs were refusing to acknowledge one other. Each one of them had declared divorce and no amount of her counselling was bringing them together.

Ah, maybe that was it? She spotted and pounced on a hole below the water. During the numbering phase of constructing the code, the agent had made a mistake which meant the lettered phase, which depended on the accuracy of the numbered phase, was sailing merrily out to sea without the lifebelt of its indicators.

Letters netted in, corralled and tamed.

She pencilled 'Bluff check present' in the top left-hand corner and 'True check present' in the right-hand one, and placed the text in the relevant out-tray for Intelligence to weave their spells over.

The door opened. A rustle went through the room. Ruby looked up.

Major Martin.

'Surprise,' murmured Janet.

First off, his uniform could have done with a press and his belt a polish. Not that she cared. Second, the dark eyes were troubled.

The last, she did care about marginally. Only marginally.

'Can't keep him away, can we?' Frances directed a look at Ruby. 'Can we?'

Major Martin took up a position by the window for which the indecipherable teams gave daily thanks. Having a window reminded them that the world still existed.

Ruby speculated as to what was going through his head. What would she be thinking if she was in charge? Was this new set-up going to work? Was he wasting precious, precious resources? Had he got it right?

She was increasingly certain that it wasn't all straightforward for the chiefs – all men, naturally – in this war. It was a conclusion that would have pleased her mightily if the situation hadn't been so serious. Still, from time to time it was fun to indulge in a touch of *Schadenfreude* before calling herself to order.

'The chairs don't look too comfortable,' Major Martin said eventually.

This was astonishing. It was unheard of for anyone senior, or male, to consider their comfort.

'They aren't comfortable, sir,' said Frances in the confident plummy tones of her class. 'Could you get us some decent ones?'

Ruby hid a smile. Major Martin would live to regret his overture. They all knew there was nothing he could do about the bum-numbing chairs. Requisitions for equipment were nigh-on impossible. Like petrol, butter, pretty clothes and, oh, most things.

Still, he had a captive audience. Maybe that pleased him? 'I wanted to thank you all.' Was there a tinge of melancholy in his tone? 'The system seems to be up and running . . .'

Was it? Had she thought of every last detail? Had she thought through the systems?

'How many indecipherables?' Peter Martin was asking.

She snapped to attention and answered, 'Six last week. They were dealt with within twenty-four hours. Two yesterday.'

'Have you cracked these last two?'

'A minute ago. It was . . .' She pointed in the direction of the out-tray and rolled her eyes.

'She means it was a bugger, sir.' Janet wore her best smirk.

Ruby gave her the have-you-gone-off-your-tiny-head glare. 'It was.'

'How long did it take?'

'We launched a blanket attack on it for a day, sir,' she said, realizing she was sucking in more and more of the jargon every day. 'Then I spent two shifts on it.'

He frowned. Again, Ruby picked up a deep anxiety and knew what caused it. It would be the acidic, creeping worry that, cryptographically speaking, they were not solving the problems quickly enough for the men and women out there who were relying on them.

'Carry on,' he said and left the room. A second after the door shut behind him, Janet sniggered.

'Shut up,' said Ruby.

Yet when the sergeant poked his head round the door half an hour later with a summons, she wasn't surprised.

Peter was waiting for her in an airless cubby hole by the main entrance to the building. It had a tiny table and one chair.

He held up a warning finger. 'Top secret, Ingram, never to be talked about now, or in the foreseeable future.'

'I understand perfectly.'

Peter tucked a file into his briefcase. 'Goodness!' His lips cradled a smile. 'I'm not sure "meek" suits you.' Ruby frowned and then thought better of it. 'We had a conversation about your considerable underused abilities. I also suggested that I want you transferred to London.'

'The London bit hadn't escaped my notice.'

'Patience is a virtue.'

'Not in a war.'

'No.' He leaned back against the table and pointed at the chair. She shook her head. She wasn't going to sit while he lounged above her.

He gazed thoughtfully at her. Assessing? 'Until recently all agents' messages were received and distributed back to us by the so-called senior intelligence services, who do not like The Firm one little bit. But that's another story. Our top brass don't like SIS either and they went to work lobbying the powers in Whitehall. The result is . . .' At this point, Major Martin sat down, leaving Ruby hovering. 'Well, The Firm has been allowed to form a new Signals Office in London. It has to be staffed twenty-four hours a day and will form a clearing house for agent traffic. The country sections will be told to maintain contact. Attached to it will be a newly formed Security and Planning Office whose function is to monitor the security of the agents' traffic, to identify any problems and to think strategically. That's where you would fit in. But I also need you to keep working on the indecipherables. I can't waste your talents.' He paused for emphasis. 'You will be busy. Fiendishly so. '

She said softly: 'Halleluiah.'

'Halleluiah, indeed,' he said, wry, dry and amused.

Nothing happened for a couple weeks until one morning when Ruby clocked onto her shift and was presented with her transfer orders.

She rushed to pack and to organize transport to the station. Slow train. Filthy train. But a train going to London.

'Unheard of,' Frances had said when Ruby broke the news to her and Janet. 'You're sleeping with him.'

'Lucky sod,' said Janet. 'Is he good?'

'He's good,' replied Ruby. 'I trust him.'

'I meant in the sack, you fool.'

She was surprised that she minded about leaving the girls.

She glanced up at the netting luggage rack. What little clothing she possessed was packed into brown paper parcels and tied with string.

'For God's sake,' she heard Frances say in her ear. 'Don't you possess a suitcase?'

Her reply had been brief. 'No, my parents' house was bombed, and we lost everything.'

Barely any light managed to struggle through the gloom of the winter afternoon, a frost was closing in and, by the time the train steamed into the station, dark had fallen. The platform was dirty, the air was smutty and it was no warmer here than in Henfold. Welcome to London, she thought, feeling her spirits dip.

To her immense surprise she was met by a car and driven off to the Ritz, where she was told that a gentleman was waiting for her in the dining room. Without being told, Ruby knew who it would be.

She was right, which was brilliant and flattering and all that. Not so brilliant was the fact that she had no time to do her hair or to pull the seams of her stockings straight.

Heigh-ho.

'This is very good of you,' Peter Martin said to Ruby. 'To come, I mean.'

'Yes, isn't it?'

That obviously took him aback, and he peered at her to see if she was joking or not.

She allowed herself a smile.

'Oh, good.' He relaxed. 'I thought for a moment . . .'

'That I was a humourless man-eater, or something?'

He did not confirm. He did not deny.

'Tell me about Cambridge, Miss –'

He was about to say Miss Ingram. She didn't want that.

'Just Ingram, don't you think?'

'I do think. Or perhaps I don't. Perhaps Ingram suits you better?'

She surveyed the piece of fish that had been placed in front of her. God forbid it was snoek. Thank goodness the candles in the centre of the table threw a kindly light over her plate. 'Cambridge was interesting but a disgrace.'

'I'm sure you've let them know how you feel.'

Ruby hoped that she was managing to convey just how deep her anger was. 'When the war is over, I shall lobby for a woman's rights and I shall fight for my degree.'

Had she gone too far? Not that she cared. She was used to the anger which she carried around with her. Anger, plus the disinclination to be nice, or rather, to be feminine.

'I agree,' he said. Without irony, and seriously.

His response was not one that she was used to.

She pressed on. 'Women should fight more. We've been bred to be passive and accepting. We have to put up with the same as men . . . bombs, war, the lot, but the difference is we are second class. The war might change attitudes.' Her lips tightened. 'But I'm not holding my breath.'

He really was looking at her. 'Change will come.' To her surprise – or was it outrage? – he touched her hand as it rested on the table. 'But don't count on it happening overnight. Things will change because change is part of our human condition, but it takes time.'

'That's the sort of argument men employ when they know they're on the defensive.'

'I thought we were having a proper discussion,' Peter said. 'In which we consider the propositions and debate them.'

Ruby pulled herself together.

He continued. 'All revolutionaries want results now. Be careful. True change takes patience. But instant upheaval often results in things returning to the status quo. Think of the French Revolution.' He spread out his hands, palms upwards. 'Maybe you won't see it until your daughter grows up.'

Exasperated, she exclaimed, 'How have we ever evolved?'

Peter Martin laughed and poked at the food on his plate. 'By eating fish. It helps the brain.'

The fish had proved not too bad and, a while later, they left the Ritz to stroll towards Piccadilly Circus. It was dark, but in a few shops there was frantic last-minute blacking-out activity. As they strolled, not saying much, a large moon rose above the city throwing a gorgeous, hopeful light over it and doing its best to mask the dust and rubble, and the stink of coal, gas and rotting rubbish stirred up by a bombing raid two nights previously.

'The moon is lovely,' she said, 'but I can't help thinking its beauty is such a contrast with the anxiety and fear which most people are experiencing that it's almost cruel.'

He was silent.

'Don't you think?'

'I think it is better to have beauty at some cost than no beauty.'

Someone jostled against them and their hands brushed each other's.

'Ingram, how did they find you?' Major Martin sounded more relaxed.

'I won a crossword competition. Best time on record, apparently. The next thing I knew, I received a letter ordering me to an interview in London with a pompous man who told me precisely nothing except I would be bound to secrecy, even in the grave. And would I accept?'

'Why did you accept?'

By now they had reached Piccadilly Circus.

'It's funny being here with no Eros,' she said.

'You haven't answered the question.'

She turned to him. 'Everyone has to take a chance in life. It was the pompous man and whatever he was offering, or a terrible secretarial job.'

'I see.'

'No, you don't. You're male. Anyway, one life isn't enough. You have to try several.'

'Good God, I wonder if they know what they've taken on?'

His obvious amusement stung and she felt patronized. 'And I wonder why you've taken me out?'

'Because . . . we have to continue our discussion.' He steered her away from the other pedestrians. 'Keep your voice low.'

They continued towards Leicester Square and while they walked Major Martin kept a wary eye on passers-by and explained that the poem-code method had come about because the intelligence powers that be considered it better security for the agent to carry the code in his head. 'But you and I,' he said, 'and some others know better.' It was a bad system for two reasons. One, the slightest mistake in the coding – 'and Ingram, just imagine some of the difficulties and dangers most agents will be operating under' – resulted in indecipherable messages. Two, the poem could be tortured out of the agent.

During the past few weeks, Ruby had had time to think over the implications. Even so, she was horrified. 'We can't let agents go into . . . into wherever they go with a flimsy set of tools.'

'That's my point.'

'Do we have any idea how many are being captured and giving away their codes?'

'Classified,' he said.

But she could tell from his tone that the numbers were significant. 'Can you tell me anything about what's happening?'

'No.'

She felt that omnipresent anger tie up her voice. 'Why would you bother with me, then? Why are you telling me this?'

Abruptly, he stopped and she almost collided with him. 'Because I'm offering you something to consider other than your anger, which is, I grant you, justifiable.' The moonlight brought the lines of his face into relief. 'But this is a war and you are a clever and gifted woman. Anything I manage to do will take persuasion and it will be inch-by-inch progression. We need unorthodox minds to get round these problems and I want to use you to help me get there. I can't reach the end of this war   I can't die – knowing I didn't try to help these agents. So, you see, it's your cleverness which I'm interested in, not your anger, or anything else. And the same should go for you.'

For a revelatory second, Ruby felt an acute . . . well, disappointment. About what, exactly? That he thought her clever? Wasn't that what she was always wanting? Needing? Demanding? He was giving her what she wanted. 'I apologize,' she said. Apologies never came easily to her and she repeated it.

He was amused. 'Did that hurt?'

She grinned. 'Almost.'

His hand rested on her shoulder for a couple of seconds. 'Not easy, is it?'

'No,' she admitted.

'But we agree?'

Yes, they agreed. And that was something.

Speaking in a low voice, he moved closer. But not too close. 'We don't live in a vacuum even in a war, when most things go by the board. Here on the Home Front we also have to think about how we fight and, if we can, square it with our conscience if the methods are not always the obvious ones.'

'Again, I agree.'

'Then how can we live with ourselves if we give those agents a coding system which can be tortured so easily out of them? Where is the morality in what we are doing? Why should we ask them to give their lives for nothing? Particularly as we don't witness the results of our complacency. The broken-up bodies. The blood. We only read about it in some bland report. If that.

Agents will be tortured. We know that and there is no way to prevent that happening. But, if it is to happen, let's make it impossible for them to give up any information – by not giving it to them. Then, at least, they are . . . suffering for some purpose. It will have meaning.'

Would it? Did suffering ever have a purpose? Ruby found herself raising her face to look at him and an unfamiliar emotion tugged in her throat, in her chest, deep in her guts. The moonlight falling over their features played its tricks, too.

Chapter Thirteen

When Ruby checked into the office the following morning, she was allocated a space squeezed into the far end of a corridor alongside Peter Martin's secretary, a shapely blonde.

'I'm Gussie,' the latter informed Ruby as she sorted piles of paper into buff folders with TOP SECRET stamped on them. 'I expected you earlier.'

'I got lost.'

'From Waterloo?' The idea seemed to astonish Gussie.

Ruby edged into the space between the second desk and the wall and sat down. Gussie's pile of folders grew.

'How are the digs? Took me a bit of string-pulling but I got them in the end.' She looked up and Ruby found herself being assessed by a pair of very green eyes. 'They're much sought after.'

The 'sought after' bit must be the view of the river, not the grimy sheets and unappetizing breakfast provided by a surly landlady. 'I'm very grateful.'

Gussie transferred her attention back to the job in hand. 'I've been here since the off, and know the ropes. Anything you need, ask my permission and I'm sure I'll give it to you. If you need to talk to Major Martin, check with me first.'

Definitely not that friendly.

Gussie continued, 'I should warn you there's been some comment about your showing up here. Not everyone likes it.'

'Normal rules don't apply in wartime,' said Ruby.

Gussie took on board the message. Ruby didn't intend to be intimidated. 'No, they don't.'

Ruby shrugged. She pointed to an in-tray on her desk. It was already overflowing. 'These are for me, I take it.'

'They are.'

She glanced through the papers which included one on tightening up security procedures and an indecipherable marked 'Top Priority'. She hauled a couple of pencils out of her bag, plus her notebook. On the first page she had inscribed: 'Mathematics knows no races.'

Underneath she had written out a quotation from the great G. H. Hardy:

> Three hundred and seventeen is a prime number not because we think so, or because our minds are shaped in one way or another, but because it is so, because mathematical reality is built that way.

Yet the point about encryption and decryption was precisely because minds did shape them. They did not float in a mathematical ether. Someone decided on the message, and worked out how its components were connected. The circumstance in which it was composed mattered very much. Mathematical detachment, in the true sense, was not possible.

Questions needed to be asked of each message. Did this man or woman truly understand the system? Did they have a good memory? Were they careless? Did these agents have absolute confidence in the system? If captured, God forbid, had the wireless operator the sort of personality that could outwit and resist the Gestapo?

Ruby picked up her pencil.

As the days wore on, she found it lonely work. She missed the rudeness, the bottomless well of bad language and the humour of the girls. She marshalled the facts – as sparse as hen's teeth – which she knew about her employer. Not that anyone ever talked but, if asked, she reckoned most of those in its service would be hard pressed to tell you what The Firm was exactly, or what it did. Everyone knew about their little area within it but had no clue how to piece together the whole.

Everyone tiptoed around hugging their secrets. If this behaviour wasn't vital, it would be funny.

Carry on, Ingram.

A couple of weeks later Gussie took a phone call. 'Get your skates on, Ingram. You're wanted at the Other Place.'

'Where?'

'You will be taken,' said Gussie.

It turned out to be a flat off Portman Square used by The Firm's French section. It was a top-secret location and, officially, Ruby didn't know about it.

As part of their induction, and before they moved on to one of the training schools, two French agents had come for a coding lesson. Major Martin wished Ruby to be there as an observer.

Was this going to be a waste of time? Far better that she got on with developing the ideas, the theory, the practice.

Major Martin caught her eye as the two agents filed into the room. *This is the human dimension,* he seemed to be telling Ruby. They were introduced by their current aliases, but not their code names.

On his previous mission, Augustine had been caught and tortured. Having managed to escape, he had been picked up by a Lysander from a field near Poitiers. He was pale, haunted-looking and had a wracking cough. Eloise was slender, with short dark hair and pale skin. Ruby judged her to be not much older than she was. Wearing a buttercup-yellow jersey, she seemed intelligent and spoke fluent, if accented, English.

They settled down to business. 'Augustine, I want to pick your brains,' said Major Martin. 'You've been operating in the field for some time. What can we do to make coding and sending messages more secure?'

'*Tuez tous les Boches.*' Augustine's little aside was accompanied by a phlegmy cough.

Eloise touched him on the arm. '*Du calme.*'

'Here's what I think,' said Augustine when he had his breath back. 'Having to keep to regular and predictable skeds adds to the danger. The Boches have direction-finding units all over the place. Once they have a sounding and they know the timing of the skeds, they surround the area. *Alors . . .* they sit and wait for the agent to come on air. *Voilà. C'est fini.* The skeds should be varied so they won't know when we come on air. It will also give us more time to move the sets about.'

'Agreed,' said Major Martin. 'I'll speak to Signals.'

Eloise fixed large eyes on Augustine.

She's sucking in every piece of information, stifling her nerves, Ruby thought, and her own jangled in sympathy.

'Anything else?'

Augustine shook his head. Then he tossed into the room: 'Sending messages is a joke. Except instead of laughing, you lose your life.'

There was a short heavy silence.

'It was bad out there,' said Major Martin. 'I know, and I'm sorry.'

Ruby swallowed.

Major Martin produced a set of coding exercises and handed them to Augustine. 'For you, these are more a matter of brushing up. Don't worry if you're rusty. You can relearn quite easily. We can schedule several sessions before you go back in.' He focused on Eloise. 'This is the first session for you.'

Eloise plucked at the wrist of her yellow jersey with nervy fingers.

'First rule: you must never send a message of less than one hundred and forty letters. If you do, it will be to tell us that you are caught.'

How intense these two were . . . in the way they held themselves and how they spoke. Augustine already knew about cold and hunger, flight, distrust and betrayal. Eloise was anticipating them, and yet was still willing to go in.

Augustine began his exercise but was promptly poleaxed by a coughing bout. He started over again.

Eloise licked her pencil and got on with it, her jaw set. But her hand was unsteady.

Ruby's gaze collided with Major Martin's. *We are the lucky ones.*

Eventually, they were done. Ruby cast an eye over the results and it was obvious that Eloise's attempt was clumsy and riddled with mistakes.

'Could you take Eloise outside while I go over security checks?' Major Martin was asking.

There wasn't much room. The flat was stuffed with people and a spiral staircase took up a lot of hallway. Agents were presumably coming in and out and, for security reasons, Park, a butler-like figure, hustled Eloise and Ruby into a room which turned out to be a bathroom with an exotic black marble bath.

'Don't you come out of here,' said Parks, shutting the door on them. In the corridor outside, masculine feet clattered up and down. There was a burst of Polish and a woman asked, '*À quelle heure, à quelle heure?*'

Ruby gaped at the bath. She had never in her life seen such a thing.

They perched on its edge. Eloise fiddled with the cuff of her yellow jersey again. '*Merde,*' she said as a piece of wool unravelled.

'Is there anything I can do to set your mind at rest about the coding?' Ruby asked her.

Eloise clutched the side of the bath, her knuckles almost bursting through the skin.

'It's not natural to me. I worry that if I'm under stress I'll forget how to operate.' She looked at Ruby. 'I *worry* . . . so much depends . . .'

'Practise. Every moment you have spare, practise. But, if you really don't think you can cope with this side of things you must say so.' She tapped the marble to emphasize the point. 'Please. It's not a failure.'

The advice seemed to calm Eloise. If you can give an agent an escape route, Ruby realized, coping with a situation was easier.

'Eloise, do you mind if I ask you a few questions?'

She shook her head.

'I am trying to understand how the codes we give you work for you. We need to know how you cope under different circumstances. For instance, when you're in a hurry, or in the dark, or frightened.'

'Oh that . . .' Eloise got to her feet. 'Forgive me, but I must use the lavatory.'

'I'm so sorry but I can't give you any privacy.'

Eloise shrugged. 'Do you think we care about privacy any more?' She raised her skirt and sat down on the lavatory. 'That is the least of the worries.' There was a modest rush of liquid into the pan and Eloise had finished. She washed her hands.

'The five words you chose from your poem when you did the exercise,' Ruby checked through the file, 'the ones which indicate your transposition key – can you tell me why you chose them? For instance, why did you choose "book"?'

'It's easier to spell than some of the other words in the poem. I know it. I won't forget it.'

'And "red"?'

'It was short. And when there is no time . . .'

'And "sunshine"?'

She brushed the feathery fringe away from her forehead. 'An indulgence. It reminds me of home.'

Ruby took notes.

'What if . . .' Eloise gave a shuddering sigh. 'What if I can't – I can't manage when I'm out there? What if I fail?' She held out her hands and Ruby dropped her notes and seized them and held them tight.

'You won't fail. I promise.'

The words were inadequate, so inadequate, and the promise an empty one.

Soon afterwards, Major Martin called in Eloise, and Augustine joined Ruby in the bathroom. He lowered himself gingerly onto the edge of the bath.

'I know you had a bad time,' she said. 'Have you recovered?'

He turned a haunted gaze on her. 'I won't be forgetting, if that's what you mean. But, I was lucky. Fine people took care of me and I got away. Others weren't so lucky.' Now he looked anywhere but at Ruby. 'In prison one of ours was brought in with a broken leg. The Gestapo took great delight in twisting it at regular intervals. It was part of the torture . . .'

'*Part* of his torture?'

Ruby's hands clenched.

'Someone else had their eye taken out by a fork.'

There was nothing to be said.

'May I ask you something?' It was too difficult to dwell on the details and Augustine changed the subject. 'If an agent needs extra help with codes can they ask for it?'

'In theory, yes.' She eyed him thoughtfully, wondering if he was thinking about Eloise. 'Please, you realize you must not involve yourself with other agents?'

He shrugged as if to say: *You know nothing of what it's like. You know nothing of how it works. We need each other. We need each other to be strong and confident.*

True. How could Ruby know what it was like? All she could say, all she could give in the way of comfort was: 'If you talk to Major Martin, I am sure something can be done.'

'*Merci.*'

'No. We should be thanking you.'

Never in her life had she felt so useless.

She ate and drank encryption. She dreamed it. She breathed it. She struggled with it.

But after the interviews with Eloise and Augustine, she had worked out something. The more they knew about how agents might work – dived into the recesses of their minds, mapped the nooks and crannies of human emotion – the better they would serve the men and women who went out, regardless, into the field.

A couple of days later Ruby came on shift and found Major Martin in the office. He was holding one of her decrypts.

He turned to Gussie. 'Would you mind?'

With exaggerated effort, Gussie got to her feet. 'I'll give you ten minutes.'

Major Martin cocked an eyebrow. 'Gussie is without price. Have you killed each other yet?'

'She's a good woman,' said Ruby.

He pushed the paper towards her. 'There's a query on the last grouping but one.'

'Sure.' She unlocked the drawer containing her working papers and spread them out on the desk. Together they bent over them and she pointed to a numbered pair. 'There . . . that was the departure on this one.' She took him through the process. 'See, the agent made a mistake here and I traced it back. I can't make sense of the word. It's a foreign one. "Dan_k". There is one letter missing.'

'S,' he said.

'Dansk?'

'Danish.'

He did not elaborate and she did not ask.

Major Martin placed his hands on the desk and leaned towards Ruby. 'Any thoughts, Ingram?'

She was tempted to say that it was impossible to conclude anything useful unless one knew the whole story – but thought better of it.

'Ingram, don't waste time.'

Eloise's words flashed across her mind: 'What if I fail?'

'I want to say that I am completely behind the idea that the poem-code system should be dropped and replaced by one which the agents could not possibly remember.'

'Good. I agree. Others agree. That's why we want you to think about it.'

'If we are in agreement, why can't we do something?' She shut and locked her papers in her drawer. 'Hasn't The Firm co-opted the most dextrous and flexible minds around? Aren't we supposed to be unorthodox in our thinking?'

'That's the theory.' He sounded tarter than a slice of lemon. 'Bear in mind we still have some chiefs whose mind-sets were formed when the Empire thrived. They take persuasion.'

This was funny, and not funny. 'Could you provide the agents with a print-out which has worked-out keys already on it? The agents would use this once and then destroy it. For the following sked they use a second set . . .'

Major Martin seemed genuinely pleased. 'That's been thought of, too.'

She sent him a look. 'I'm curious about why you need me? If it's all been thought of.'

'I wanted more than one mind on the problem. So, write me a report.'

'Will it happen?'

'I bloody hope so. There are problems. The top brass and their mind-sets . . . Another question: could you use paper? Or should it be some other material which would be easier to hide? Paper is bulky and detectable. But the far more serious consideration is –'

Ruby was ahead of him. 'If the enemy discovers we are using this one-use method, they will copy it and *we* won't be able to read their traffic.'

'That's it,' he said. 'That's the problem.'

'So giving the agents extra security means we shoot ourselves in the foot.'

'Isn't that like life?'

Huddled into her space at the end of the corridor, Ruby began work on a security dossier. By this time she had wised up to the system, had snaffled a typewriter from Stationery and hunted down spare typewriter ribbon.

She read extracts from a secret manual written by instructors who trained recruits at Beaulieu in the arts of covert warfare.

Do not deceive yourselves about enemy objectives. The orders are that enemies of the Reich should die, but not before everything possible has been squeezed out of them. They want your codes. They want information. Who trained you? And where? Coding practices. In some instances, they might try to talk you into becoming double agents or stool pigeons for a time, but it depends on who is holding you. We gather from debriefs that the German military intelligence, the Abwehr, have a softer approach. They begin friendly, then progress to greater threats and then torture. The Gestapo, however, will start with torture but they will keep you alive until they get what they want. In those circumstances we ask you to try to hold out for forty-eight hours, which should give your networks time to disperse.

No one is expected to withstand prolonged torture. Therefore a better strategy is to try to avoid third-degree interrogation during which you would almost certainly tell them most things. Feed them information in a controlled manner. If necessary, surrender your codes reluctantly; offering some cooperation in playing back the sets would give you temporary credit. This means you have a chance of keeping your security checks secret which, when they do play back the sets, will alert Home Station because the security checks won't have been included in the message.

'Where is the morality in what we are doing?' Peter's voice echoed in her head. Then it occurred to her: in this game morality is not enough. You had to be practical, inventive and bold.

Perhaps Peter was wrong in his emphasis?

She thought hard and long over the problem of coding security, forcing her mind down strange pathways. How do humans behave? What are their priorities in certain circumstances? Are the Germans so different? If so, in what ways?

Her typewriter clacked in tandem with Gussie's.

1. Agents are under huge pressure. Ergo, it is to be expected that at least one of their messages over a period of time would be classed 'indecipherable'.
2. Therefore, their messages must be regularly tallied and inspected.
3. Home Station must always insist on the Security Checks.
4. Training records should be kept and always available.

How high in German priorities would enemy agents be? Had the Germans been putting their top cryptographers on captured material? The questions were endless, the answers fewer, but she was always led to the same conclusion: The Firm's coding needed to be more secure.

The phone went on Gussie's desk. The typewriter cacophony diminished as Gussie answered it. When the call finished, she turned to Ruby. 'You're wanted on the fourth floor.'

'Sod it,' said Ruby.

'Yup, sod it,' said Gussie. 'On the other hand, I'm pleased because, for a few minutes at least, you won't be cluttering up my precious office space.'

'I love you, too, Gussie,' said Ruby.

In the stuffy office up on the fourth floor, two men hunched at the desk over a large flow chart annotated in green ink. A third, Peter, was seated opposite them. At Ruby's entrance, three pairs of eyes looked up. Two of them were unwelcoming. Cigarettes burned in the ashtray. Peter introduced his colleagues.

'This is Lieutenant-Colonel Nettlesham from Intelligence . . .'

The younger of the two men ran a professional eye over Ruby and nodded. He was smart, she decided, probably thoughtful.

'And this is Major Charleston from the Signals Directorate.

Gentlemen, this is Ingram, whose work on the ciphers has been so useful.'

Pale and overweight, Major Charleston sighed audibly.

Ruby braced herself. Unorthodox minds ... *Unorthodox minds?* Looking at the major, she thought not.

'I want Ingram to outline to you both the ideas I asked her to work on.'

Major Martin had not warned her he was going to do this.

Ruby muttered 'Hell' under her breath, opened her mouth and began. 'First, we should consider the context,' she said. 'We have to ask whether our traffic is considered important enough for the top German cryptographers to be unleashed on it.'

Major Charleston's mouth folded into a peevish line.

Ruby continued. 'Presumably, all the top code crackers are employed on military intelligence, so the odds are our traffic doesn't as yet receive priority attention from the enemy. But as soon as expert cryptographers are put on the case they will easily decode much of it. Perhaps they already have?' She shot a look at the men – tight-lipped and uneasy. 'I know I can't ask these questions or get any answers. But even with less expert enemy cryptographers working on intercepts, the system we currently use is dangerously insecure, and it is only a matter of time before they crack them.' There was a pause. 'Not only that, but once agents are captured it is a near certainty that they will be able to get the coding information out of them.'

Major Martin asked: 'Are you all right, Charleston?'

The major, who looked as though he was in the throes of a minor heart attack, threw him a look designed to slaughter at three paces.

'Sirs,' Ruby's mouth was drying up. 'The poem code should be abandoned.' Peter was looking at her approvingly. 'As soon as possible.'

Major Charleston recovered his powers of speech. 'The poem code is used by many other organizations. Our *sister* organizations. They manage perfectly well.'

'May I remind you, this isn't about protocol . . .' Peter intervened. 'This is a matter of the highest urgency and also our duty.'

'And may I remind you, Martin, that we are fighting a war with no time or resources to fiddle about with half-proven theories.'

Colonel Nettlesham cleared his throat. 'We're not taking any decisions until we have debated the pros and cons.'

'The pros are that obviously our agents can use this system reasonably easily.' Peter said it coolly enough but she had an instinct that he was angry. 'The cons are that, almost certainly, any intercepted messages are being read. I hardly need remind you that the Germans read poetry, and write it. Rather well, as it happens.'

The colonel was rolling a bulldog clip over in his fingers. 'The possibilities exist. Of course they do. Logic tells us that, but what I have to do is to assess the balance of probabilities.'

'Sir,' said Ruby, 'doesn't logic also suggest that if an agent is caught his or her poem code can be tortured out of them?'

Major Charleston stood up and turned to the colonel. 'I don't think we require Ingram's thoughts any longer.'

She appealed to the colonel. 'Sir, would you like a report?'

'Yes,' he said curtly. 'You will write it within the next two days. It will be top secret and sent to me, and only me. That is an order.'

All of which meant the report would land on his desk and stay there. Stuck.

'I'm going to resign from this place,' she informed Gussie on returning to their office space. 'They need maths teachers out there. Schools are crying out for them.'

Gussie was highly amused. 'Ingram, you've no idea. No one ever resigns from The Firm. It can't be done. Either they dismiss you, which means they cut out your tongue. Or they lock you in chains for the duration.'

'Ah,' said Ruby. 'That clears things up.'

Chains of command. Stupidities. Ingrained bureaucracy and turf wars, even in an organization such as this one where the clever were given full rein. Closed minds. Towers built of paperwork. Dead ends.

In the academic world there were infinite numbers and letter combinations fighting to be freed up. The numbers created patterns, glorious patterns, which linked into an as-yet-imperfect understanding of the universe. She could be there, unlocking doors and windows.

She pulled herself up short. This was a war, not a hothouse for theories. Somehow she had to extract the humanity that was secreted in the selfish bits of her and use it.

'It's a man's world.' Gussie patted the unfortunate perm which had reduced her normally glossy hair to a frizz.

'Not for ever,' said Ruby. Pointing to the stack of paperwork Gussie had already dealt with that morning, she added, 'Furthermore, you run the place.'

'We'll keep that a secret, shall we?' Again, the pat on the damaged hair. 'Sit down and get on with it.'

Ruby translated this to mean: *We understand each other very well.*

Chapter Fourteen

Kay picked up Felix's latest message: 'Could you bring my hat home on Tuesday? I left it in København.'

A sked was due and Felix was probably operating in the Køge area and couldn't make København in time. Checking the trains, Kay realized it meant an overnight stay.

As predicted, Bror didn't like it. Irritated and more than a little rattled, he asked: 'Why do you have to see Nils so much suddenly?'

'I like to see him. *You* should see him more often.'

Bror frowned. 'Is that the truth?'

She felt rotten. Bror was suspicious that she had an assignation with Anton and she was causing him pain.

Yet if Bror was disturbed, so was Kay. Deception was far more demanding than she had imagined and she found it hard to handle. Guilt weighed her down. It was omnipresent. She felt it in everything she did and she couldn't shake it off. As a result she was avoiding Bror, which did nothing to help matters between them.

Eventually, she said: 'I'll send Nils your love.'

Whenever she was in København on her own, Kay stayed at the Damehotellet, which was clean, convenient and for women only. The walls were painted in soft, pale colours, there were flowers everywhere, and it had good linen. Unlike Rosenlund, no country mice or rat dared to poke its nose in there.

Planning for this particular stay involved thought. She had packed her overnight things into a shopping bag and taken good care that Bror didn't see her leave otherwise he might have questioned the lack of a suitcase.

She arrived at Damehotellet with the wireless set, which she had picked up without trouble, plus a bundle of *Frit Danmark* for distribution in Køge. With the set and leaflets hidden in the wardrobe of her room, she prepared for her dinner with Nils. This involved dressing up the carefully chosen black suit she had been wearing all day with the Eberstern pearls and earrings.

Observing her image in the mirror, Kay was reassured. She looked what she hoped. A smart wife and mother. Better still, under control.

She returned to the hotel soon after ten-thirty. The maid had plumped up the quilt on the bed, laid out her satin nightgown and drawn the brocade curtains. The room was warm and comfortable and, for once, the war retreated into the background.

The phone rang.

'Kay,' said Bror.

'Darling . . .' Kay sat down on the edge of the bed and pleated the hem of the nightgown between her fingers. 'It's very late. Are you all right?'

At times like this she envied Felix his solitariness in his undercover life. His lack of family. The advantage he possessed in not having to account to anyone.

'Good dinner?'

She caught the undercurrent: *Do I trust my wife?* That hurt. It really hurt that her decisions were eroding a marriage which had been built up over so many years. But this was what happened. What did she expect?

'Nils took me to his favourite restaurant. He's working hard and I came back here. I was practically asleep when you rang.'

At his end, Bror cleared his throat. 'Nils told me you were having an early supper.'

'As it turned out we couldn't get a table until later.'

Be careful when lying, Felix had cautioned. *It's the small ones that catch you out.*

'Are you checking up on me, darling?'

He cleared his throat. 'I think I am.'

He sounded odd, troubled.

'Bror, this is not like you . . .' The words were clammy with her deceit. 'Something's happened. What?'

'Ove Poulsen has given in notice. He's going to work in Germany.'

'Ove!' Ove's family had been at Rosenlund for generations.

'A slap in the face for me,' said Bror.

Ah. Again, guilt raised its dark head. 'You mustn't take it personally.'

But Bror would take it personally. Of course he would. Rosenlund was his Arcadia, a tangible expression of a life philosophy, and he took pains to ensure the men were comfortably housed and their work arrangements were fair.

'I told him never to come back.' She heard him take a sharp breath. 'Kay, it's going to leave us very short-handed.'

'We'll manage,' said Kay.

He asked what train she intended to catch in the morning. Kay told him. 'I'll make sure Arne meets you,' he said, adding, 'Curious thing, Kay, when I took the dogs out – we found a pigeon in the old pigeon loft. Arne tells me that he found it and put it in there. He never mentioned it.'

Arne?

A finger ran down Kay's spine. 'Poor thing. It must be lost. I hope Arne took pity and tucked it up with some food.'

'We're not a care home for pigeons.'

'It's not in anyone's way, is it? Besides, if food gets short we could always eat it.' Bror laughed. At a beat, the atmosphere changed. Greedily, she grabbed the few seconds when it could be said that all was well between them. 'Couldn't we?'

'So you are turning into a good Danish wife. It's taken twenty-five years.'

Her handbag and shopping bag over one arm, carrying the wireless set in the case in the other hand, Kay made for the Left Luggage at the station. Having deposited the case, she bought a magazine at the newsstand and went to inspect the platform where the Køge train was waiting.

If there were security checks or soldiers, she would leave the case in Left Luggage. But the platform was clear and, in due course, she retrieved it and boarded the train.

The journey was straightforward but not comfortable. Sitting quietly in her seat, her coat draped over her shoulders, Kay hid a thumping heart and sweaty palms and tried to remember anything she had ever read about the art of relaxation. Fear of being frightened was worse than being frightened. Wasn't it?

Arne was waiting at the station with the car parked alongside a couple of grocery vans. A snow flurry was casting a fresh white layer over the grey-black slush.

Lifting the case into the boot, Arne's eyes widened as he registered the weight. 'Shall I cover this with a rug?'

Snapping to attention, she nodded.

Arne. One of them?

The snow was coating them both in ghostly feathers. 'I gather you found Hector – I've named him Hector – in the old pigeon loft. Isn't he superb? I've grown fond of him but I suppose I ought to send him on his way one of these days. Except that it's so cold.'

'He's a nice bird, *Fru* Eberstern. I would say he came from a good home.'

'Oh dear, they're probably mourning him.'

Arne tucked in the rug. 'I hope you know what you are doing.'

'Looking after a stray bird, Arne. That's all.'

The lock on the boot always required an effort and Arne gave it a good shove. 'That's very kind of you, *Fru* Eberstern.'

The train sounded its whistle and shunted out of the station, leaving the snowy platforms abandoned under a grey sky.

'Best to get going,' said Arne.

Even in Køge the roads were slippery. Arne nosed the car

down the street and headed for the turn-off to Rosenlund. Kay leaned back in the seat and closed her eyes.

Suddenly, Arne swung the car off the road to the left and Kay was thrown against the door.

'What are you doing?'

'Roadblock ahead,' said Arne. '*Feldgendarmerie*. Lots of them.' He pressed the accelerator and the speedometer needle swung upwards.

'There was no need to do that.'

Arne's mouth set in a grim line.

There was no time to speculate. Either Arne was with her or not, and she took the calculated risk. 'Did they see us?'

'Can't say.'

They found themselves in a side street – where the car was conspicuous by being the only one amongst a scattering of pedestrians who were plodding through the snow. The grey light dulled the yellows, ochres and bull's-blood red of the buildings. Steam seeped up from a grating. Kay tapped his shoulder. 'Arne, slow down. We're drawing attention to ourselves.'

At the end of the street, Arne turned left into the road that led up to the market place. 'We should go around the back of the town,' he said.

Kay squinted up ahead. 'We can't. There's a second roadblock.' She shrank back – and, to her shame, felt a moment of debilitating terror. *What have I done?*

She forced herself to think.

'We're going to have to bluff it.' Mercifully, her mind began to work clearly. 'Arne, get the case out of the boot and put it on the back seat. I'm going to sit with it and pull the rugs over me. And I'm going to be ill.' She unwrapped the scarf round her neck and tied it over her hair, pulling it well down. 'Have you got a knife, something sharp?'

Arne didn't waste time on questions, but hunted in the dashboard compartment and handed her a penknife. Kay ripped off a glove and slashed the plump part of her thumb.

Blood bloomed like a pretty little pimpernel flower and grew obligingly into a small peony. She blotted it with her handkerchief.

Arne slid the case into the back and Kay climbed in, wedging it behind her legs. He threw two rugs over her. She rammed her glove back on, sat back against the leather upholstery and held her handkerchief up to her mouth.

They drove at a moderate speed towards the roadblock.

A young and blond *feldgendarme* stepped out into the road and indicated they should stop.

Arne obliged and rolled down the window. The *feldgendarme* stuck his head in and said, '*Raus*,' followed by some sentences in German.

'We don't understand,' said Arne in Danish.

Kay coughed. Inside her glove, her thumb smarted. The *feldgendarme* beckoned to a Danish policeman who was also manning the roadblock. Thank God she didn't recognize him.

The policeman was instructed to translate. Wooden-faced, he explained, 'You must get out. We wish to search the car.'

'What's happening?'

'There are reports that terrorists are operating in the area.'

Arne heaved himself out of the driver's seat. 'Of course.' He walked around to the boot and clicked it open. 'Please.'

The *feldgendarme* turned his attention to Kay and she sagged back against the upholstery. The Danish policeman opened the passenger door. 'Please get out.'

Kay murmured, made an effort to do so, coughed huskily and made a play with the bloodstained handkerchief at her mouth. 'I'm sorry . . .' She drew the words out. 'I don't feel well.'

The *feldgendarme* demanded of the policeman: 'Find out what's wrong with the woman.'

She spread out the handkerchief and pressed it to her mouth. The blood on the linen was a fresh scarlet.

The policeman looked horrified. 'TB?' He didn't have to translate it for the German.

Arne shrugged.

Sweat sprang onto her upper lip and spread under her arms. Her legs, clamped round the case, threatened to cramp.

The blond *feldgendarme* stepped backwards. 'Stay away. The woman should receive immediate medical attention.'

'Drive on,' the policeman instructed Arne.

Snow was beginning to fall in earnest. As they drove through the roadblock, great flakes of it settled on the policemen and soldiers. Handkerchief still pressed to her lips, Kay regarded them over it. These were men she had outwitted.

Once out of Køge, Arne was forced to drop his speed in order to negotiate the now treacherous roads. White spears of larger plants poked up through the snow blanket and the smaller branches on the trees were already sagging under the weight.

Did one talk?

'How did you know, Arne?' she asked eventually.

He shrugged.

'You haven't mentioned it to anyone?'

'No.' Arne shook his head. 'How did you know what to do, *Fru* Eberstern?'

She glanced down at the stained handkerchief. The blood had made the cotton stiffen. Is that what happened when people were shot? 'The Germans are terrified of TB. Well, everyone is, aren't they?' As Arne turned the car into Rosenlund's drive she added, 'I don't want to involve you in anything further. Arne, you can, and must, forget this incident.'

'I'll do that, *Fru* Eberstern.'

'It must not come between you and *Hr* Eberstern.'

She regarded her hands as they rested in her lap. 'I really am sorry.'

'I know what I am doing, *Fru* Eberstern.'

They exchanged wintry smiles.

'Arne, can you take the back entrance and drop me by the outhouses? I want to say hello to Hector.'

As soon as the car drove away, Kay slipped into the pigeon loft and slid the case into its hiding place.

Back in her bedroom, she was in her underwear and changing her stockings when Bror came in.

'Good trip?'

'Interesting.' Kay sat down and rolled one of her treasured sheer stockings up her leg. Bror watched her. She heard her voice rising a little higher than normal as she reported a mish-mash of gossip and hearsay, some of it diverting. There was the anecdote of the German officers who, having hung up their holsters and belts in a restaurant cloakroom, discovered at the end of the meal that they had vanished. There was the boy in Aalborg who had stolen six grenades but didn't know what to do with them and returned them.

She inserted her foot into the second stocking. 'It's almost funny.'

'I suppose it is.' He bent over and, keeping his eyes trained on her face, hooked the suspender into the stocking welt. In that past life together it would have been an erotic, intimate moment, probably resulting in the stocking being removed.

But that wasn't possible now. Bror jerked at the suspender, catching her flesh in the fastening.

She laid a hand over his. 'You're hurting me.'

'Sorry.'

She removed her hand.

'Kay, don't repeat those stories in public, will you?'

'If that's what you wish.'

It was anguish to realize that she no longer felt safe with him and he was no longer her refuge. And vice versa. And equally harsh was the understanding that total estrangement would be easier than stringing him along.

She stood upright. 'What are you angry about?'

'There's something going on, Kay. You're acting oddly. You . . . look different.' His eyes were as dark a blue as she had ever seen them. Moving over to the door, he made to leave, checked himself and swung round. 'You know there's nothing more important to me than you and the children?'

'Yes, yes. I do.'

'But I don't know whether you know that, any more. I don't know what you're thinking. Or whether I can rely on you.'

'Is this about Anton? Or politics?'

'You tell me.'

'Don't you trust me?'

Her discarded blouse on the chair with one of its shell buttons hanging by a thread . . . a tiny drift of powder on the dressing table . . . the jewellery case with the Eberstern pearls on the bed . . . How curious that, at this moment, she would notice these things.

'I think Anton means something to you and you are . . . well, seeing him.'

Bror had handed her a solution on a plate. She trembled at the implications. How pernicious would it turn out to be if she took it? Enough to cause them profound pain. Possibly tear up their lives?

Nevertheless, a point had been reached.

'Is that what you think?'

'I do.'

She shifted her gaze to the floor – a guilty gesture. 'I refuse to answer.'

'I want to know.'

'Please get out of here, Bror.' Her hands were placed defensively on her chest. 'And don't come back. Not tonight.' She paused. 'Not for many nights. Go and sleep somewhere else. Until we sort this out. But, the way I feel, it won't be soon.'

His lips went white. 'It *is* Anton.' Kay was silent. 'Isn't it?'

She made herself look up into his face. 'It's true I like Anton very much.'

Without another word, he turned on his heel and left the bedroom.

Kay's knees gave way and as she sank onto the bed her

bandaged thumb snagged on the coverlet. She had cut it deeper than she intended and the wound stung.

So did the internal wound.

The following morning, an exhausted Kay waited with twenty or so others outside Lippiman's bakery in Køge.

A queue for Lippiman's bread had become a feature of the war. If it was raining, it made for misery – and played havoc with the women's hair. Sometimes, however, unless it was bitterly cold, standing outside for a few minutes and enjoying the aroma of freshly baked bread was pleasant enough.

She thought of Tanne's birth. That had been another bitter winter's day. During her labouring, she had taken comfort from the sight of the ash tree, its branches rimed by a deep frost, outside the bedroom window at Rosenlund. Just before the moment of the baby's arrival, the setting sun tipped it with fire. Weeping from pain, she watched the light change and wondered if she would live to see the next day.

She recalled, too, a memory from the early days with Bror, when he drove her triumphantly into Køge for the first time. 'But it's old,' she had exclaimed, then blushed when Bror teased her back: 'Darling, it's not only the English who have a history. We have a history. A distinct one.'

When they were small, Nils and Tanne badgered Arne to tell them the local stories. 'Let me see,' he would say. 'Do you mean the one about the naval battle in Køge harbour during which Sweden was trounced?' He had a chest-load of yarns: of monster fishing catches, of midsummer celebrations and, of course, of the Køge ghost that sailed a ghostly boat out to sea. In summer the boat was said to skim over the water. In winter it broke through the creaking, shape-shifting ice.

The queue shuffled forward. A couple of women with plaits pinned round their heads had forgone the customary headscarf, and they must have been regretting the cold. There was an elderly man in a coat too big for him and a girl with a shawl and no coat, who shivered visibly.

In the past, the queue would undulate with gossip but a wartime bread queue was different. There was no ongoing conversational murmur, and no jokes. Voices were hushed and muted and, as Kay observed, there were several in the queue who were keeping a sharp eye on the others.

Inside the bakery, the morning's bake of rye loaves had been set out on the shelves by the door, displaying a spectrum of browns, from light tan to burnished ebony.

'Good morning, *Hr* Lippiman.' She handed over to him her basket containing the bundle of *Frit Danmark* wrapped up in a napkin. 'Birgit asked me to buy four loaves.'

Lippiman placed the basket containing the bundle on the shelf below the counter. He appeared calm and focused. As she watched, he whipped out the package and dropped it into an empty bag of flour which he pushed with his foot further under the counter.

He put three loaves into the basket and held up the fourth one. 'It's a little soft,' he explained, packing it in. Only now did he look directly at Kay. 'I hope you have a good day, *Fru* Eberstern. My regards to *Frøken* Eberstern. Tell her I'll have her favourite gingerbread tomorrow.'

Kay laughed. 'If I know my daughter she'll be down.'

The roads had seemed clear and she had driven to Køge in the trap. Loki was bored and fidgety and Kay took extra care guiding him across the marketplace. Loki trotted past the Town Hall – built in 1552, as Bror informed her all those years ago – and the Monument on the harbour. She always forgot in whose honour it had been erected but, bearing a similarity to Cleopatra's Needle in London, it reminded her of home. As they passed the circular Water Tower genially presiding over the town, Kay looked up.

Why, oh why, did there have to be a war?

Arne's street fronted onto the canal. His house was one of the older ones. A modest building with dimpled glass in the windows, painted the blue of a sunlit sea. Bror regularly urged Arne and Birgit to take up his offer to live on the Rosenlund estate. To no avail. The cottage having been in Arne's family for generations, the couple were not budging.

Kay brought Loki to a halt. Maintaining a tight hand on the reins, she knocked on the door with her whip. 'Arne, are you there?'

While she waited, a man and woman walked past. He was in a navy-blue pea jacket, she in a dun-coloured raincoat and a home-knitted wool hat. They seemed hurried. Awkward.

'Do you know them?' She pointed out the couple to Arne when he emerged from the cottage.

'I don't ask, *Fru* Eberstern. Nor should you. People come and go here these days. Spying for the Germans, or trying to escape from the Germans . . . who knows?' He swung himself up and kidnapped the reins from Kay. 'Shall we go?'

Kay fastened her jacket up tight and arranged the rug over them both. 'The roadblocks have been taken down.'

Loki wound himself up to a trot and, avoiding the main thoroughfares, Arne drove them through the side streets and onto the Rosenlund road.

They talked together comfortably in a conversation ranging over repairs to the house and farm matters and, because the Germans were taking as much of it as they could lay their hands on, how pork was at a premium. Arne let slip that pigs were being smuggled into the butcher for slaughter, and the wives of the workers on the estate were secretly making hams and salamis to be hidden away.

Eventually, he asked, 'Your thumb, *Fru* Eberstern?'

Kay stripped off her glove and poked under the dressing. 'Looks as though it will take time to heal.'

Arne peered down at the oozing scab. 'Don't let it become poisoned.'

At Rosenlund, the day was punctuated by Kay's usual commitments but, when it began to grow dark, she slipped away to the pigeon loft.

Hector fixed her with bright eyes. 'Hello, boy.' Kay checked over his water and feed. 'Don't you look sleek and rested? But you won't be put in danger if I have anything to do with it.' Her voice sounded ghostly in the cold loft. 'Just remember, you don't speak English.'

England.

Don't think about England. But she did. She did and it hurt. It hurt. And she thought how strange it was to be reminded so viscerally that the umbilical still stretched between her and her mother country.

On her return to the house, she paused for a moment to look at it. The light from the windows cast pathways across the lawn and gardens and, out on the lake, the winter ice was as thick as it could be. She knew it so well. The beads of air trapped in the frozen water created a white palette which sparkled on sunny days but turned grey and melancholy on the bleak ones.

It would be a long time until, once again, they heard the shuffle and roar of ice melt which heralded spring . . . until white anemones and snowdrops flowered under the maples and the smell of wild garlic sifted through the air.

She bit her lip.

Sif and Thor hoved into sight. Behind them came a familiar figure.

'Tanne!' Kay smiled. 'You gave me a fright.'

Tanne was wearing one of her father's heavy tweed jackets and a woollen hat with ear-flaps which, years ago, Kay had bought her on a trip to Norway. She was flushed with cold.

'Giving the dogs a run. What are *you* doing?'

'Walking.'

'You do a lot of walking these days.' Tanne fell into step. 'I'm curious.'

The wind was getting up and Kay shivered. 'Let's go in.'

Inside the house, Kay pushed Tanne towards the porcelain stove in the hall. 'Darling . . . quick, warm yourself up.'

The dogs clicked over the black and white marble tiles and made for their baskets.

The damp had made Tanne's fair hair curl round her ears in a way which always delighted Kay and annoyed Tanne. She looked gorgeous and healthy and very alive.

Grinning broadly, Tanne pulled Kay to her and dug her hands into her mother's pockets. 'You're a warmer option.' There was a second or two of silence. '*Mor*, what's this?'

Too late.

Before Kay could stop her, Tanne opened up the folded copy of *Frit Danmark* she had extracted from Kay's pocket. 'What on earth have you got here?'

'Nothing. Give it back.'

But Tanne snatched it out of reach. Then she read out: '"The caterpillar of the pale tussock moth *dasychira pudibunda* is destroying the beautiful Vallo beech woods."' She frowned. '"Slowly but surely, the caterpillars are feeding on the body of the beech and sucking it dry."'

'*Mor!* Where did you get this?'

'I picked it up from the street in Køge. It's not worth reading.'

'So why pick it up?' Tanne ran her finger over it. 'It's not damp.'

'Some time ago. I forgot it was in my pocket.'

Tanne raised an eyebrow. 'Even I can see that this is political satire.' She folded the paper over. 'What are you going to do with it?'

'Burn it.'

Tanne ignored her. '"Denmark must retrieve its honour." So that's what you have been thinking about during the *walking*?'

Kay took the pamphlet out of Tanne's hand, opened the grill and dropped it into the stove. 'Most of us have to consider the war and how we feel,' she said as reasonably as she could manage. She brushed back the mass of Tanne's hair, and added: 'But we have to be careful.'

'Don't fob me off, *Mor*.' Tanne allowed Kay to fuss over the hair. 'Are you going to tell me about it?'

'Nothing to tell.'

Tanne stepped back.

It seemed that, in Kay's war, the people she had to trust were strangers, not her dearest and most loved. The conclusion was unsettling, queasy making.

Tanne changed the subject. 'You must be worried about Gran and the aunts.'

'Yes.' Kay took off her jacket. 'Yes, yes. I keep telling myself that they'll be safer in countryside. It's London and the cities that are being bombed.'

'But do you approve of what your country is doing?'

'Tanne! It's half your country, too.'

'So it is. I forget.' Tanne picked up her discarded hat and drifted towards the staircase. 'See you at dinner.'

Most people would imagine that the subject was closed but Kay was an expert in reading her daughter. She knew Tanne. It would not be the last that she heard on *Frit Danmark* and she knew that she would have to consider carefully how to handle Tanne's questions. Knowing that she must lie to her daughter gave her a desolate feeling.

She went in search of Birgit and discovered her in the kitchen putting the finishing touches to the chicken pie. 'Arne is waiting for you,' she told her. 'Go home. I'll manage in the kitchen.'

Birgit looked scandalized. Kay realized that her instruction ran counter to the other woman's notions of order, and of how things should be done.

She prised the knife away from Birgit, saying, 'Arne needs you back in your own house.' She glanced at the window where the frost patterns were forming. 'It's getting colder. I've arranged for Frau Nielsen's Else to come in to serve.'

'Little Else?' Birgit sounded puzzled. 'She's better than me?'

'Birgit, I was trying to save you trouble.'

'*Fru* Eberstern, trouble is my job.'

'I know, Birgit. But this wretched war means we have to adapt.'

'The war, *Fru* Eberstern, means we must not let things go.'

'Go home, Birgit. Arne is waiting and you are tired. I know you are.'

For a moment Birgit was stilled in her perpetual bustle. Pink suffused her cheeks. 'Maybe. Just this once.' She took off her apron. 'But it is not good to let things go.'

On first arriving at Rosenlund, Kay had been introduced to a staff of twelve, including two housemaids, and instructed in all aspects of running a house, from the storeroom to the laundry to the menus. Every morning fires were laid, and the gravel in the drive outside was raked smooth.

These days the gravel remained churned up for long periods. The staff had been whittled down to Birgit and two of the wives from the estate who came in part-time, plus little Else.

That other life, predictable, ordered, innocent – above all the innocence – was now a long time ago.

Bror and Tanne had spent the morning together combing over the estate accounts and they talked dairy yields all through dinner that night.

Thank God, thought Kay, and she tackled Birgit's chicken pie in silence.

Sorting out the meat from the pastry on her plate, she made herself eat as much as possible. It wasn't easy. She chewed away and told herself that she was committed. She had to be. With its violence and retribution, the war threatened to invade Rosenlund's boundaries. No more pastoral idylls. In the light of events, Bror's Arcadia would prove to be only a dream, and as fragile.

Collapsed by the stove, the dogs snorted and snuffled in

sleep. Then a vehicle crunched over the gravel. Thor shifted to his feet and Sif raised her head and barked.

'Are we expecting anyone?' Bror looked up from his slice of cherry flan.

Else appeared in the doorway. 'Sir —'

Before she could finish, she was pushed aside and two uniformed Danish policemen entered the dining room.

'Sergeant Wulf?' Kay exclaimed, recognizing the older of the two. 'Is everything all right?'

'*Fru* Eberstern, *Hr* Eberstern, I apologize.'

'I think you should.' Bror had remained seated – an unusual discourtesy which meant he was angry.

Sergeant Wulf tugged at his belt. It was a gesture well known to many in his jurisdiction. He had been in charge of the Køge police station for the last decade and the joke ran that his belt had to be let out a notch each year. By report, Kay knew him to be a kindly man and more or less effectual.

'This is Constable Juncker from København. He is here to act as liaison between us and our German colleagues.'

Juncker was still youthful enough to be at the gangly stage. His uniform was new and well pressed and, having hitched his career to the Nazi bandwagon, he looked eager to toe the line.

What had she done? What had she done to her family?

There was no time for regret. Nor for panic.

Shut up, Kay.

Bror was brusque and unwelcoming. 'Why are you here?'

'Sir . . .' Sergeant Wulf was not a happy man. 'Forbidden literature has been found in a baker's van. *Hr* Lippiman's. Constable Juncker and I are following up leads. *Fru* Eberstern was seen at the bakery this morning.'

This was her fault – for she had brought the war right into their dining room.

Fear. Guilt.

The air crackled with suspicion. But, all of a sudden, she was cool and focussed.

Think of the details. When, where, how? Get them right.

'Gentlemen, some coffee?'

Turning to Kay, Bror asked, 'Do you know anything about forbidden literature?'

'No,' she said.

'There's your answer,' Bror addressed the men. 'Now go.'

Constable Juncker ignored him. His young, righteous gaze drilled into Kay. 'You do know the baker?'

'I do. I've used the bakery for many years.'

'Is it normal for you to do the shopping? Doesn't your housekeeper buy the bread?'

Kay directed her answer to Sergeant Wulf. 'We've lost staff and I like to help out by doing some of the shopping.'

Sergeant Wulf was clearly reluctant to be involved, but he said, 'You handed the baker a basket.'

'Did I?' She smiled at him. 'Perhaps I did.'

He scrabbled at his belt again. 'According to our witnesses you did. Was the basket empty?'

'I think so. It may have had my scarf in it.'

The details. Which scarf? Do not look at Tanne.

Tanne interjected. 'What has happened to *Hr* Lippiman?'

Constable Juncker got in first. 'He's been arrested and will be taken to København.'

At that, Tanne took Kay completely by surprise, her words cutting through the atmosphere: 'You're going to hand over a *Dane* to the Germans? A fellow Dane?'

Chapter Fifteen

Tanne spat out the words.

Sergeant Wulf looked like an animal that lacked the guts for the kill.

'A Dane!' Tanne repeated, her thoughts scurrying through a moral and patriotic maze. 'A fellow Dane?'

'Tanne, *quiet.*'

She had never seen her father so angry.

But she was past caring. 'Why?'

Constable Juncker said simply, 'Denmark needs to be healed.'

Tanne was speechless. On hearing this idiotic remark, the fragments of thought which had been swirling around in her head for months cohered and became clear. Herr Hitler was not only mad and bad, but capable of infecting the whole world with his madness and badness. She opened her mouth to object, then caught her mother's eye. *Don't.*

She heard Aage's voice replaying in her head their old university rhetoric. *Democracy. Freedom. New dawn.* What would Aage be making of the war? Tanne knew the answer. Aage would declare he was sickened to his guts and the country, supine and spineless, was damned. (Once upon a time, she had been a little in love with Aage until she realized that his passionate demagoguery disguised a bully.)

When the men first burst in on their dinner, Tanne reckoned that Constable Juncker might be stupid, an impression she held until she encountered his cunning, calculating gaze and revised her opinion. Juncker was unembarrassed and on the make. Very much on the make. Unabashed, he moved around the room – taking in the fine prints, the gilt pier glass, the Sèvres china on the shelves. At one point, he reached over to touch an antique Chinese *famille rose* plate. She nearly cried out: 'Don't you dare.' It was such a pretty plate, decorated with delicately painted roses and daisies, and one of her favourites. Then it occurred to her that it was possible he had never been so close to such a valuable object. Who wouldn't wish to touch a *famille rose* plate?

She heard herself asking, 'What will happen to *Hr* Lippiman now?'

'He will be taken to København and handed over to the German authorities.' Constable Juncker returned to his perusal of the plate.

Her mother's expression gave nothing away. She fixed her eyes on Sergeant Wulf. 'I assume you're holding him at the police station?' Without drawing breath she continued, 'I'm sure whatever *Hr* Lippiman has, or has not, done can be dealt with much more competently by you. Do you need to bother your German colleagues with something so insignificant?'

Denmark needs to be healed. Constable Juncker was checking his reflection in the pier glass which hung between the windows overlooking the garden. The spanking new uniform, the slicked-back hair, the prominent lower lip, the intelligent gleam: what he saw appeared to satisfy him.

'Sergeant Wulf!' Her father was icy. 'You will both leave. *Now.*'

Her mother placed a restraining hand on his arm. 'Darling,' she said. '*Darling*, I am sure Constable Juncker would like a brandy before they go out into the cold. Why don't we all go into the drawing room?'

Her father's protests were stilled. Deflected, he gestured to the door and he and Constable Juncker vanished in the direction of the drawing room.

Her mother spoke to Wulf in a low, urgent voice. 'Sergeant Wulf, Troels Lippiman is a friend of yours. Aren't I right in thinking you stood as a godparent for his son, and you serve together in the church?'

'Yes,' replied Sergeant Wulf, his hand shoring up his belt.

Something else was going on, but Tanne couldn't work out what.

Her mother turned the full force of her charm on Wulf. 'Whatever you decide, you must make sure that *Hr* Lippiman is permitted to visit the pastor in the church. He would want to pray. I know you will allow this because you're his friend. A visit to the church would be important to him. Help him, Sergeant. Now –' she smiled at him '– what about that brandy?'

Sergeant Wulf said: 'Constable Juncker has already informed København that the baker will be coming in for questioning.'

'All the more reason for prayer,' said her mother.

When they had left, Tanne returned to the dining room and her unfinished *delikatesse*.

Because of the war . . . because of the bloody war, Birgit had been forced to be sparing with the dried cherries embedded in the almond sponge. Still, it meant Tanne could pay special attention to each one and she made herself relish every chew of the bitter-sweet, tough-skinned fruit.

The first-floor passage outside the bedrooms was nearly impossible to negotiate noiselessly but Tanne had a long familiarity with its creaks and groans as she sped along it to the bedroom which she thought of as her parents'.

Yet only the other morning she had caught Else ferrying her father's things down the corridor to the blue bedroom. 'What's going on?' she demanded of her mother, who explained that neither she nor her father had been sleeping well and they both needed a bit of peace and quiet. It was all very confusing, and Tanne had a nagging feeling that she was missing something but could not put her finger on it.

Always, her special love in her parents' bedroom was the summer lace curtains but they were changed every October for thickly-lined blue damask ones and these had been drawn across the window embrasures. The lamp beside the bed threw a tactful glow over the room. Earlier, Else had been into the bedroom to turn down the satin coverlet and to lay out her mother's nightgown. Pearl crêpe de Chine with a touch of lace: it spoke to her of married life, a sexual life and a day-to-day intimacy she had yet to experience.

She plumped down onto the bed and picked up a book. The curtain at the window overlooking the lawn moved a fraction. Leaping to her feet, she pulled it aside. '*Mor?*'

Dressed in corduroy trousers and a thick jacket, her mother was directing a torch beam onto the lawns outside.

'What on earth?'

'Shush.'

'But what are you *doing?*'

Her mother snapped off the torch and let the curtain fall back into place. 'You shouldn't be here.' She put her hands on Tanne's shoulders and pressed her down onto the bed. 'Tanne, darling. I don't ask you to do much for me but I'm asking you . . . no, ordering you to go to bed.'

She struggled to understand. 'Is this to do with Lippiman and the pamphlets?'

Her mother kept up the pressure on her shoulders. 'Whatever it is to do with, *you* are not involved.'

On another day, at another time, lured by the prospect of a warm bed, Tanne might have been persuaded.

'Tanne, for once in your life, *obey* me.'

Was her mother turning into a shape-shifter of the old Danish tales? This wasn't the *Fru* Eberstern who had charmed Sergeant Wulf, or the occasionally dull and overprotective parent. Or the sweet and funny mother she could be. This was a woman Tanne didn't entirely recognize.

'*Mor*, what's happening?'

'There's no time to talk now, Tanne. Just go.'

Had she ever heard her mother issue an order with such force? Tanne dug in her heels. 'Whatever you're doing, I'm coming with you.'

'Don't be stupid, Tanne.' Her mother knotted a scarf under her chin.

Then she understood. Or, some of it.

'*I'm* stupid?' Tanne twitched the curtain back and peered at the garden. 'What happens if *you* run into trouble?'

Their eyes collided. 'Then you can look after your father.'

She spat back: 'Good thinking. Someone has to.'

Her mother picked up her gloves.

Tanne caught her arm. 'If you're going out to help Lippiman, I can be your alibi.'

'The Germans don't bother with alibis, Tanne.'

'Lippiman is my friend, too.'

It worked.

'God forgive me . . .' Her mother was both sharp and fierce. 'But there's no time to argue.' Wrenching open the wardrobe, she thrust a pair of trousers at Tanne. 'Put these on. Leave your shoes off.' She fished out a sweater and pulled it down over Tanne's head, pressing her hands to Tanne's cheeks. 'This is secret, Tanne. Completely secret. Understand?'

Mesmerized by this new, strange mother, Tanne agreed.

Rosenlund's front door was locked and bolted at night and they avoided it, padding instead down the pantry passage to the back door, where they kitted up in thick jackets and boots. The dogs whimpered and whined. Tanne threw them a couple of biscuits to shut them up.

Her mother eased back the bolts. 'We're going by bicycle.'

Outside, the cold scoured Tanne's throat. But she was used to that. Even so, the going was fairly hard and, in places, treacherous and they were both panting by the time they had wheeled their bicycles down the drive.

On reaching the road, they mounted. A large moon aided visibility, but it was hard to keep up a good speed. The snow, which was heaped in unexpected and powdery drifts, was laced with ice, pockets of mist loomed up at them without warning and at times it was too dark to see.

'Where are we going?' Tanne's whisper was amplified in the brutal stillness.

'Arne's.'

'Why?'

'Juncker wasn't as clever as he thought he was. He told us what was going to happen, which means we have an advantage. Arne will take the message.'

'But Lippiman is in the prison.'

'Sergeant Wulf will take him to the church.'

'How do you know?'

'Because I told him to.'

Save for the crunch of the wheels over the road surface, silence coated them. Ghostly whiteness and patches of moonlight. Fear prickled down Tanne's spine. She was aware that she had a shaky hold on the situation and she felt ashamed of her ignorance. What, exactly, was her mother involved in?

How much did her father know?

Avoiding the main street, they detoured around the back ones which, since they were icier, brought their own dangers. But they got there. Unsurprisingly at this late hour, Arne's cottage was dark. Tanne held the bicycles as her mother knocked softly on the window. Eventually, it was eased open.

A whispered exchange followed.

She heard Arne say, 'Leave it with me.'

'Hide him in Ove's cottage if you have to,' said her mother.

Arne's window shut noiselessly.

The way back was colder and harder. Tanne's energies dwindled, and the exhilaration of the earlier journey vanished. She felt weary to the bone. 'Wouldn't it have been easier to phone?' she asked when they were back in Rosenlund and rubbing themselves down.

'Arne doesn't have a phone and I don't trust anyone else. The exchange might listen in.'

'But *Mor*, even if they did, they wouldn't say anything.'

Her mother hung up her damp jacket. Her silence was eloquent.

'But we *know* them.' Tanne was bewildered.

'I warned you not to come. But you did. You must know *nothing* and you must be clever. Lives depend on it.'

'Do you know what you're doing?'

'Yes.' Her mother sat down as if her legs wouldn't hold her up any longer. 'It took me a little time, but I do know what I'm doing.' She tackled her boots. 'I was never going to talk about it, and I didn't want you involved.'

Both of them wrestled with the laces which had been rendered uncooperative by the damp and cold.

Tanne tugged at hers. To her horror, tears of rage and frustration gathered behind her lids.

'Lippiman is a good man,' continued her mother, 'and I'm not going to let him be taken. Others agree. So we are doing something about it.'

'And *Far*?'

Her mother shook her head.

'So you are all . . . against *Far* and –'

'Not against *Far* but against *them*.'

A vision of a future came into Tanne's mind. One where they would be juggling lies, watching their backs (even with friends), and moving words carefully around like counters on the draughts board.

'What about *Fru* Lippiman?'

Her mother pushed back Tanne's damp hair. 'She'll have to go into hiding, too. The Danish police have instructions to hand over anyone who might be involved. You can see Sergeant Wulf's position.'

'Where can they go?'

Her mother shook her head. 'I've no idea and you won't ask.'

'And *Far*?'

'Tanne.' Kay pulled Tanne to her feet and held her close. Just like she used to when Tanne was a child. But the words which she hissed into her ear were neither gentle nor loving. 'You will say nothing. He has enough to deal with.'

She smelled faintly of sweat, a basic human odour that Tanne never normally associated with her elegant, feminine mother – and that small dissonance was almost the strangest thing about the evening.

In bed, Tanne took a long time to warm up and she slept badly. When she woke, she lay and looked around her room. She had imagined that she knew everything there was to know about her parents, about Rosenlund. About Køge.

But she didn't.

In the afternoon of the following day, Tanne went in search of her mother and discovered her in the storeroom.

She was faced by a familiar sight. Notebook in hand, Kay was shouting across the passage to Birgit, who was in the kitchen beating eggs. Every so often Birgit shouted back.

Rosenlund's large and airy storeroom was an important place – almost the heart of the house, supervised by her mother and Birgit. Between them, they kept the shelves stacked with canned meats and beans and bottles of fruit and tomatoes. The bottles always gave Tanne particular pleasure – the yellows, ochres, russets and purples creating an autumnal patchwork against the whitewashed walls.

Tanne leaned on the door frame and waited for the shouting to stop. 'I've been in Køge.'

Her mother bent over the record book. 'Roads bad?'

'Pretty bad.' Tanne picked up a jar of tomatoes and held it up to the light. As red as blood? '*Mor*, you might like to know there was a raid on the church while a prisoner was there. He escaped.' She handed the jar over to her mother.

Her mother slotted it onto a shelf and wrote in the notebook. 'That's good.'

Tanne whispered, 'We're deceiving *Far*. It's not right.'

'We can discuss whether it's right or not after the war.'

'But *Far —*'

Her mother raised her head and glared at Tanne. 'Don't you understand, it's dangerous for him?'

Tanne digested the reproof. Looking up at the shelves glowing with colour, she said, '*Mor*, this won't happen again, will it? I mean . . . you . . . doing things?'

'No, darling. No. But we had to do something for Lippiman.' She wrote a note in the book. 'Are you here to help?'

At university, any analysis of war had been along conventional lines. As far as Tanne had thought about it, war was a male affair. Politicians sent soldiers to the slaughter. There was marching, men hunkered over campfires, supply lines and latrines. Afterwards, the politicians took over and everybody forgot about the men who died.

She had never imagined that women were fighting in this war discreetly and, she was beginning to understand, ruthlessly.

'Tanne, darling.' Her mother was back to her normal sweet and loving self. 'Do me a favour and pass me that tin of beans.'

The strange, bewildering episode was over.

Chapter Sixteen

Mary Voss was on a bus to Northampton – which was a bit of a triumph. If Signalmaster Cripps had had his way she wouldn't be taking this twelve-hour leave at all, despite Mary reminding him she had worked over Christmas.

Signalmaster Cripps was not unkind, merely overworked, and the situation wasn't helped by the fact that he currently had a cold. No one was at their best with a beacon nose, a painful crack in their bottom lip and stuffed sinuses. In the end, he had conceded reluctantly that Mary must take what was due to her.

'I will, sir.'

She had enjoyed the manner in which she had emphasized the words. Not too forceful, but sufficiently firm.

Having fought for them, she was determined to make her hours of freedom noteworthy and decided to go shopping for a new dress. Henfold did not have any of the right shops. To buy clothes therefore meant taking a bus to Northampton.

The bus was chilly and smelled of cigarettes and sweat. Avoiding the seats which were stained, Mary secured herself a window seat and it was pleasant enough rumbling along, letting her mind drift this way and that.

A couple of men in the row behind discussed the progress of 'our boys' and the German defeat at Stalingrad – which came as something of a shock. It made her realize that she had been too immured in her own corner of the war and had neglected to keep an eye on the bigger picture.

In fact she hadn't kept up with events outside of work at all since the last time she had visited her mother in Brixton, when she had been shaken to discover that the terrace where she had grown up had been bombed. Houses gaped like open mouths with so many broken, blackened teeth. Like a hot knife slicing through butter, the bomb had cut through the terrace exposing drunken staircases and cross sections of bathrooms with all their private arrangements for everyone to gawp at. One of the ruins still smoked.

She had prayed that no bodies were still in the wreckage, that no limbs were scattered about, and made herself concentrate on things she liked. A frilly blouse – a fanciful thought since no clothes were made with frills these days. A bunch of lavender. A pat of butter all to herself.

Mary had grieved. Tossed so casually out of a bomb bay, the bomb had pulverized coal scuttles, wooden spoons, rose-patterned china tea services and an array of life's pots and kettles, each with its accumulated memories. Objects which the women who slaved away in these houses would have treasured and by which they measured out their lives.

The dust . . . the dust had nearly choked her. The bombing had released so much of it. It was everywhere – on surfaces, between the sheets, on window frames, sifting into everyone's clothes, hair, nose and ears. When would they ever be properly clean again? When they came to write a history of wartime, historians must write about the dust, she thought. London was buried in the stuff and it hung in the air – minute particles of brick, stone, wood . . . and other more terrible things she wasn't going to think about.

Altogether, that last trip had been a sobering one. Her mother was growing more immobile, her temper ever sharper. Undressing her for bed had taken all Mary's powers of persuasion and of restraint. Wrestling with the buttons on the ancient liberty bodice, a 'Whiteley's best'. Much to-ing and fro-ing with hot water. Her mother criticizing its temperature. Boiling up a kettle and watching the steam paint out the vista outside the tiny kitchen window. The soft pop of gas under the kettle. Watching an expansive yellow moon shine over the roofs while she waited for it to boil, Mary was reminded of the illustrations from a childhood book of fairy tales.

The smell of an elderly body was unmistakable. So, too, was the decay and neglect enforced by decrepitude . . . the creeping indignities of stiffening limbs, of toenails thickening and yellowing with age.

Mary dreaded the ageing process overtaking her. But it would, and in her case there would be no daughter to help her at the end.

What was she doing with her life? What purpose did she have on this earth? The questions slid under the defences of her common sense and unsettled Mary. And it was no use saying God would provide because, plainly, He didn't.

Once in Northampton, it quickly became obvious that she didn't possess enough coupons for a dress. However, the shop assistant informed Mary she could buy a pair of stockings with a single one so she invested in a couple of pairs, knowing they would have to last the year. Emerging from the haberdasher's, she spotted a restaurant across the road and she treated herself to the one-and-sixpenny lunch menu and a cup of tea.

Afterwards, she walked back in the direction of the bookshop she had spotted close to the bus station.

Flunn's Bookshop was enjoying a brisk trade. Stacked on a table in the centre of the shop were copies of a Penguin paperback entitled *Aircraft Recognition* and a cheap atlas. The piles of both were diminishing at a steady rate.

But it was the travel section to which she gravitated. Increasingly, that sort of book interested her because, even if it was a little late in the day, she craved to know more about the world. She knew so little, and regretted her ignorance. For all she knew, Europe might be shrouded in darkness – which, in a manner of speaking, it now was – and its natives went around with horns on their heads. Mary wouldn't know if they did or they didn't.

Her browsing yielded a couple of nuggets. Mary learned there were Baroque churches in Germany and a pope's palace in France. Back home from the Great War and his signals unit, her father had dropped hints here and there about his time in France. The natives were strange, he told Mary and her mother. They put garlic in stews and smoked strong tobacco. What is garlic? Mary had wanted to know. She wished now that she had made him tell her more. It would have been lovely, too, to have sat down with him and, as professionals, to have mulled over the more complex intricacies of Morse and of signalling. It would have been a companionship. Of course, she could never have let her father into the secrets of her work but there would have been a good chance that he would have guessed.

An hour passed and, soothed and stimulated at the same time, Mary was completely content. Finally, she drifted towards the poetry section and took down a volume of Wordsworth.

Its pages were particularly crisp and white and the words on them appeared very black. She rifled between the Preludes and shorter poems and then . . . and then Mary read:

> Her voice was like a hidden bird that sang;
> The thought of her was like a flash of light
> Or an unseen companionship . . .

She knew of Wordsworth, of course, but not in depth. Yet that small piece of his verse told her that the poet, that grand old man, understood what she was, and what she was doing. It was a moment of pure epiphany, of excitement, of a kind of transcendence which, for a few seconds, lifted Mary above her life – her dull, obedient life – into an elemental being.

Unseen. The description chimed in so many ways with her. For Mary regarded herself as unseen. From bitter experience, she had discovered she was the sort of person who was overlooked. At first, she had chaffed against being unremarkable, and there *had* been occasions when she had quivered with the injustice of being neither pretty, nor clever nor educated. By her late twenties, she had accepted her lot and rescinded on the notion of making a big splash in life. Not that she complained, but there had been bad times when she imagined that it wouldn't take much for the ties that bound her to life to snap.

Yet, as the years passed, Mary grew stronger and took pride in her expertise at 'putting up with things'. It made sense to be a realist. The world was organized for men's convenience. 'Endurance' and 'submission' were important words in the female vocabulary – she could transmit them in Morse in a flash. There were plenty of others in her position. Plenty were worse off, and she was fed and clothed and, from time to time, had a laugh with her friends and could, more or less, cope with her mother. She grew to understand that hope and anticipation were painful emotions. Unreliable, too, and she was better off without them.

Unseen companionship . . .

A radiance seemed to be flowing through Mary.

She would never know Mayonnaise and Vinegar and the others in the obvious way but, as she now perceived in this moment of revelation, the obvious was not the only way. Not the only way at all.

How ridiculous – she realized she was crying!

Mrs Cotton forgot to check up on Mary – 'Sorry, dear, I was busy getting Mr C's tea' – and the alarm clock from Woolworth's had never kept good time.

It meant that Mary was late for her shift.

'One more transgression and you're for it, Voss,' said Signalmaster Cripps. But he didn't mean it. Not in the way Signalmaster Noble, the bully of the station, would have done. Noble he is not, ran the joke.

'Sorry,' she said. 'But I am here and ready and willing.'

'What are you waiting for, Voss? Get on shift.' She turned to go but he called after her: 'Voss, you're a good worker. But don't let it go to your head.'

Tonight up at Station 53d, an urgency surged through the ether. Mary couldn't explain how she knew, but she did. Someone was on the run. Or there was a big operation on the go.

Whatever it was they, the listeners, got wind of something momentous happening in the shadowy areas of the war.

The frequencies were jumpy tonight, too. The call signs came and went. In between her skeds, she kept her earphones on, which helped the concentration.

ZYA calling. Mayonnaise.

Mary's heart lifted.

QVR. *Ready to receive.*

Write the message down.

Don't think about anything else.

The 'handwriting' was as ever. The dashing T, the emphatic M. Yet it was strange how Mayonnaise never spoke to her in the same way as Vinegar. Apart from those early, stumbling transmissions, Vinegar's keying was so smooth and assured. Unflappable. She admired it very much. It was stoic in the face of the enemy and, in Mary's opinion, stoicism encompassed everything: heroism, courage and, yes, imagination, too.

She sat back on the wooden chair to wait out the minutes until Vinegar was due.

Half dead with fatigue, Nancy slumped over her station and the sight of Nancy's exhausted shoulders and mussed hair troubled Mary. One second's inattention and a message could be garbled. In her old life as supervisor at the telephone exchange Mary would have told Nancy off. Looking back at her time there, she concluded she might have been harsh occasionally, but she would have defended herself by saying she expected no less from herself than from others.

Very gently, she nudged Nancy with her foot.

'Go and sneak a cup of tea,' she whispered. 'Tell the Führer you have to, you know, *go.*'

They weren't supposed to 'go', but sometimes they had to and the signalmasters had to put up with it.

Nancy sat bolt upright and sent Mary a feeble grin. 'Good thinking, Voss.' She heaved herself to her feet. 'I'll have his balls for dumplings if he tries to stop me.'

The frequencies were weak. Storms were fouling the atmosphere. Yet the calls sang sweetly in her ear. Wherever they were coming from, she was there to listen to a steady stream of birdsong freighted with hurry or anguish, or with love and terror.

Tonight, Vinegar was late.

Where are you?

Bent over your set? In a field? In a church? Have you lost faith?

Are you sorry? Are you afraid? Are you lonely?

She thought of a future without the agents, *her* agents, of an existence shorn of the intensity of waiting and hoping. And dreaming . . . One day it would happen.

She would have to make do as she had always had to make do. And a little humour about it wouldn't come amiss, she reminded herself.

The needle wavered. She adjusted the dial.

Liquid sounds.

Keep calm.

Outer darkness.

Unseen companionship.

Then . . . yes. Yes, here was XRT. Vinegar. Pulsing through the interference and static.

His was a strong signal tonight

Mary began to write.

Twenty minutes later the call finished. Mary glanced up at the clock. Twenty minutes almost to the second. One moment longer and Vinegar might have been in trouble.

Her finger hovered over the transmitter key. Could she break through the barrier of her natural reticence? Could she break through the upbringing which frowned on words such as this and send 'shit' . . . as a token of her feelings, of her empathy, of her *unseen companionship*?

She didn't.

At the finish, she placed the paper into the basket. In a flash, Signalmaster Cripps was onto her. 'All right, Voss? Anything to report?'

'Nothing, sir. The fist seemed normal.'

'Right, I'll get it to the cipher room.'

She watched his retreating figure. She would have given much to follow 'her' message and to know what was in it. Just a couple of words would do. But that would never happen. It would never, ever be permitted. Secrecy between the departments was absolute.

At the end of the shift, she went to put on her coat. The other girls often complained how bulky their uniform was, but she was grateful for its warmth and relative smartness.

The lavatories were backing up again in what was laughingly called the Ladies Rest Room. They can't cope with all the traffic, was the joke. Someone had filled a bowl with water and disinfectant to make the room more pleasant, but it wasn't a place to linger.

A shoelace was flapping and she bent down to retie it – but her foot appeared to vanish down a dark tunnel at the end of which was a pinprick of light.

Fatigue. One of the effects of her constant exhaustion was to make objects appear insubstantial, or even hallucinatory, and for the hundredth time she resolved that she had to sort out her sleeping. Maybe a doctor could help? Otherwise she was going to be no good on shift.

Outside in the drive, Mary stood for a moment and closed her eyes. The incipient dizziness which occasionally attacked her at the end of a shift swirled at the back of her skull. This was the moment she always questioned herself. Had she made mistakes?

Had she failed in any way?

Was she missing anything?

Chapter Seventeen

It wasn't to her credit, but Tanne took to watching her mother and found herself questioning why she kept her bedroom light on so late. Why did she insist on going for walks at dusk? Why was she growing so thin?

On one of the harshest of February days she bumped into Arne on the back stairs. He was carrying a paint pot and brushes. Tanne followed him up to the room which, years ago, had been occupied by the English nanny. Since then, too far from the main family area and difficult to heat, it had remained empty. Besides, it was considered that the steps leading up to it from the garden posed a security risk. Its one advantage was its magnificent view of the lake.

'*Herregud!*' she exclaimed, then repeated herself in English: 'Good heavens.'

The room was freshly painted. Its woodwork gleamed, chintz curtains were at the windows and a larger curtain had been hung by the door that opened on to the garden steps.

This door had been propped open and the unforgiving cold chased the smell of the paint out into the frozen landscape.

'Arne . . . what's going on?'

Arne kept his back to her. 'Ask your mother.'

The refusal to meet her eye was indicative. She knew Arne and evasiveness was not in his nature. Arne, therefore, had been drawn into a conspiracy – or an understanding – which had something to do with her mother's uncharacteristic behaviour.

Hovering in the bright, cold room, she felt impatient, bewildered and more than a little lost.

Returning to her room, she threw clothes into her case ready for a trip to København and the ballet. Suitcase in hand, she emerged, only to overhear her parents engaged in heated argument in the hall.

'How could you, Kay?' said her father.

A mutual bitterness and distrust rose like smoky breath . . . Tanne had never heard or witnessed the like before.

Turning away, she took herself down the back staircase. Elation and high spirits were things which now belonged to the past. The war was exposing weaknesses, drawing lines, pushing people into different camps.

As usual, she was welcomed in København by Grete and the others. But it didn't take five minutes for Tanne to see that the group was subdued and anxious, especially Hannah, who looked frighteningly gaunt and jumpy. Many of them had taken to smoking furiously, and drinking whatever they could lay their hands on.

They told her the latest news. The Hotel d'Angleterre had been requisitioned by the German military and the German flag hung over it. The previous October, the King had fallen from his horse and no longer rode out daily from the palace through the city. Instead, Grete told Tanne, there was a song now doing the rounds: 'Der rider en Konge'. 'If you hear it . . .' She tapped her nose. 'It means you don't agree with putting up with the Germans.'

Worse, far worse, Hannah's brother had been arrested and she was in a bad way about it. 'You should have told me,' Tanne said. 'What was he doing?'

Hannah gestured with both hands. 'Can't say. Not safe.'

The lack of confidence stung. 'Hannah, are there things going on I don't know about? Please tell me.'

'Well,' said Hannah – and the implication was that Tanne's ignorance was shameful. 'There are people who are working for Denmark's freedom.'

'Who are they? What don't I know?'

Again the hand gesture.

Hannah also reported that there was to be a new German unit, the Waffen SS Division Nordland, which was to be recruited from the Danish people. 'They don't like Jews,' she whispered. Ministers were being sacked because their faces didn't fit. Danish laws were being meddled with and Danish dairy products whisked out of the country.

Predictably, the ballet was *Sleeping Beauty*. To the accompaniment of Tchaikovsky's ravishing legato strings and harp glissandos, and poised on a superbly arched pointe, Princess Aurora made her choice in the Rose Adagio by refusing to select any one suitor before pricking her finger and falling asleep.

How differently Tanne interpreted it this time. It was quite clear to her now that Princess Rose's romantic confusion could be interpreted as resistance. Had Tchaikovsky understood this? Didn't his music reverberate with sadness and longing for a better life?

Returning to Rosenlund in the early evening and finding no one around, she mounted the back stairs to the nanny's old room to discover her mother on her hands and knees in front of a cupboard, stowing bandages and disinfectant in it. The curtains were drawn and the room had been made very attractive, with comfortable armchairs, a desk and a chair, a lamp, and a fire burning in the grate.

'I thought I'd find you here,' Tanne said from the doorway.

Her mother started.

'I don't often see you doing any housework, *Mor*.'

'Don't sound so suspicious, darling.' Her mother sat back on her heels. 'I've been meaning to organize myself an office for some time. I need somewhere to do my accounts.' She smoothed down her skirt. 'We talked about this before, but in future we're going to have to do a lot more for ourselves. And I need a bit of peace. You know how your father fusses.'

'Peace, yes. But bandages?'

'There's a war on, darling. You never know.'

Tanne held out a hand to help her up. 'You mustn't lose any more weight,' she remarked.

'My appetite's not so good these days.' She gave one of her little smiles. 'Perhaps I'm not so greedy?'

Tanne tried to analyse her mother's expression. Intense? Alive? Perhaps 'intense' was inaccurate. Perhaps 'excited' was a better term. Whatever . . . Kay appeared to be lit up by an inner conviction.

Was she jealous of her mother? Tanne hoped not.

Later, when they were drinking tisane after dinner, her father said, 'I wish we still had Lippiman's gingerbread.'

He fixed a cold eye on her mother.

'I do hope he's safe,' said her mother. 'No more apricot pastries.' There was a silence. 'Someone must take over the bakery.'

'No one made *brunkager* like Lippiman,' said her father.

Her mother addressed her father directly. 'Bror, I'm sorry about the gingerbread. I'll ask Birgit to find it somewhere else.'

Her failure to call her father 'darling' was very apparent. Rosenlund was a house from which endearments had been banished.

'You know the parents are sleeping apart and have been for a while?' Tanne had informed Nils when she visited him one afternoon in his unkempt, cluttered set of rooms at the university.

'Wouldn't you? You get a better night's sleep.'

'They don't talk to each other either.'

He wasn't that interested. 'A change is as good as a rest.'

That night, Tanne dreamed of her father eating the spicy, brittle gingerbread which he and she so favoured. Snap, it went. *Snap.* In her dream, she was trying to decide if she was becoming more like her mother, or not.

She woke hungry but not for food. Her body was crying out for something she could not name. Was it physical satisfaction? Emotional satisfaction? A sense of belonging? Overriding these confusing urges was the one which Tanne understood perfectly:

the need to go out to walk the land which one day she would inherit. After breakfast, she pulled on her leather boots with the thick-ridged soles and a padded jacket, and went in search of Sif and Thor. But they were already out with her father.

It was chilly heading for the lake and she pulled her hat down over her ears.

A faint spring sunshine was beginning to penetrate the perpetual grey. The thaw was making inroads into the lake ice, which cracked and hissed, shuffled and shifted. On the island, the place Sophia-Maria had favoured for her summer picnics, all the vegetation had been fossilized with frost but Tanne could just make out emergent patches of brown. Ice puddles on the path were growing liquid hems.

Tanne liked to think that she knew everything there was to know about the estate . . . where the first tiny yellow flowers of spring were to be found, or where the birds nested and the deer rutted, where the winter ice was likely to be at its most treacherous.

Rounding the western point of the lake, she turned to head back up to the house. The seldom-used path that led up to the outhouses was slippery, forcing her to concentrate on where she was going. When she next looked up, it was to see a man with a cap pulled down over his face letting himself into the pigeon loft.

Strangers were not unknown at Rosenlund, particularly these days. From time to time a tramp or someone out of work pitched up, spent a night in an outhouse and everyone turned a blind eye. She made a note to tell Arne.

It was then that she spotted her mother. She was also heading for the pigeon loft. Every so often she stopped and looked around. On reaching it, she ducked inside.

There were . . . there could be . . . several explanations as to what her mother was doing with a strange man, but only one made sense.

The teenage emotions which, years ago, Tanne had so often

battled to master now resurfaced. Rage, real rage, and disgust, and astonishment.

It was none of her business what her mother did.

Yes, it was.

Neglected for so long, the door to the pigeon loft was swollen and didn't want to budge but she pushed hard and it yielded.

Her mother and the stranger were crouched over some sort of instrument. He had exchanged his cap for a pair of headphones.

The scene was disconcerting enough. More frightening was the pistol the man snatched up and pointed at her chest.

Her mother interposed herself between Tanne and the gun. 'It's all right, Felix.'

'Who is she?'

To her astonishment, her mother, instead of revealing who Tanne was, said: 'I can vouch for her. I know her.'

'But who is she?'

This was ridiculous. Tanne said, 'She's my mother.' Turning to her, she demanded: 'What *are* you doing?'

'What are *you* doing, Tanne?'

Her mother's hostility shocked Tanne. 'I saw this man, and then you.' She shrugged. 'I thought you must be meeting him.'

'It could be put like that.' Sounding more like her normal self, her mother prised the gun away from her companion. 'You're to get out of here.' She snapped on the safety catch of the pistol, put it into her pocket and hustled Tanne over to the door. '*Go.*' There was real fear and distress in her voice. '*Go.*'

A pigeon called from the cage. Tanne shook herself free and swung round. A bird, its bright eyes gleaming in the shadow behind the bars, looked back at her. 'Whose is this?'

'Quiet.' The stranger held up a hand for silence and with the other adjusted a knob on the machine. A light glowed. He pulled the headphones over his ears and began writing on the paper in front of him.

A curious noise sifted through the loft. High-pitched.

Her mother looked from him to Tanne and Tanne thought she saw tears in her eyes. 'God forgive me, Tanne, you'll have to stay here for the moment.'

Tanne watched as the man, rigid with concentration, took down groups of letters.

'What –' she began but her mother put her finger to her lips, crossed over to the door and peered out.

Was it five hours later, or only ten minutes, when the stranger tossed aside the headphones and stood up? Older than Tanne – she guessed – he was dressed in overalls, unshaven and obviously angry.

'Who's this?' Tanne asked.

'Felix,' replied her mother, who seemed more composed.

She addressed him: 'Is that your real name?'

'The only one I answer to.' He was concentrating on the piece of paper in his hand. 'You'll have to deal with her, Freya.'

Freya?

'You must be quiet,' ordered her mother.

Tanne asked herself if it was because an essential element of her brain had gone missing that she was failing to understand what was going on.

There was a whiff of ancient bird dung . . . there were tins of creosote and lime whitewash stacked under the bench, an abandoned rake . . .

Time shifted and she and Nils were back playing in the pigeon loft. Tanne pelting Nils from above with pebbles. Nils vowing instant death. The hay fight from which they had both ended up catching fleas.

Felix began to pack the equipment into the case.

'Freya, get her out.' He did not look at Tanne as he coiled a length of wire.

'I have every right to be here.' As soon as the words were uttered, Tanne regretted how childish she sounded.

He gestured to the instrument that she had – finally – realized was some sort of wireless set. 'Are you being deliberately stupid? You're putting yourself in danger. Think of your mother, if not yourself.'

Her brain was moving slowly, ponderously. She was trying to make connections, and trying to make sense.

'Are you sending messages?'

His eyes reflected irritation and impatience at her and her questions, but what did he expect?

'Felix,' her mother's voice held a warning.

Felix shut the case and snapped down the locks.

Her mother was checking the door. 'Someone's coming.'

Without warning, Felix grabbed Tanne and covered her eyes and mouth with his hands. He was strong, very strong. 'Not a word,' he breathed in her ear.

His feet braced, he held Tanne hard against his chest in a grip impossible to escape. She was both hot and cold with outrage, with fear and . . . with a strange excitement.

Inside the pigeon loft, she could hear her mother moving around. Then footsteps could be heard padding along the tamped-down mud path outside and the pressure on her mouth increased. No one moved.

Eventually, Felix released her and gave her a little push. She blinked and found her balance. He went to the door and peered through a crack. A little out of breath, her mother leaned on the broom.

Tanne scrubbed at her mouth. 'That was unnecessary.'

'No, it wasn't.' He did not bother to look round. 'Don't make the mistake of imagining anything is unnecessary if it keeps one safe.'

'What have you done with the . . . whatever . . . that thing . . . the set?'

'You don't know,' said Felix. 'Understand?' He turned his head. 'Freya, will the coast be clear?'

Freya.

'I'm pretty sure it was Arne. I recognized his coat. He will have gone.'

'I'm not moving until you explain,' said Tanne.

'Go, Felix,' said . . . Freya.

The light from the door illuminated unshaven features that were grey with fatigue. All the same, Tanne acknowledged, he was a good-looking man.

A nod. Then, without another word, he picked up his cap, stuck it on his head and disappeared.

She gazed after him. '*Mor*, have you gone mad? No, scrub that. Have *I* gone mad?'

Her mother took Tanne's arm, hustled her outside and fastened the door.

'Answer me.'

'Don't argue. Go back to the house and wait.'

In her bedroom, Tanne found herself peering into the mirror. Did she recognize herself? She backed away to the bed, sat down on its edge and went over what had happened. Her mother, her infuriating mother, was clearly caught up in resistance work.

How blind could you be? Why hadn't she considered what was going on out of sight months ago? The war was more than two years old and she should have been sharper and wiser. It wouldn't have taken much wit to realize that resistance must be there. From her mother's action over Lippiman, from what Hannah had told her last night, from what she had just witnessed, she now knew without a doubt that it *was* there.

She had been blind.

Tanne looked down at her hands. It was dawning on her that every person had to make up their own mind about where they stood.

It was then Tanne was assaulted by an unwelcome thought. Even worse than her political and moral myopia was the knowledge she had been outdone by her mother.

She dismissed that one as unworthy.

What was she to do?

Change out of her walking trousers, for a start.

Punctuated by long pauses during which she found herself staring glassily out of the window, she hunted out a wool blouse and serge skirt.

My mother is a liar?

Again, she consulted the mirror, then picked up her hair-brush and tackled the snarls in her hair.

She was attempting to fasten the buttons at her wrist when her mother came into the bedroom and shut the door quietly behind her.

Tanne didn't look up. 'Don't bother to lie to me, *Mor.*'

'I'm not going to lie.' Kay sat down in the antique chair uphol-stered in a blue-and-white stripe that had been given to Tanne by her Swedish godmother. 'I want you to listen carefully.'

Tanne slipped on her shoes. 'How long have you being doing this, *Mor?* This isn't just rescuing Lippiman or distributing a few underground pamplets, is it? This is bigger, something organized.'

'I can't go into detail, Tanne, except to say that what you saw affects your safety and it won't happen again. But you must understand that absolute secrecy and discretion are imperative. *Do* you understand?'

'Last time I checked, I had a brain.'

'Don't joke, Tanne.'

'Where did you get the equipment? Where are these mes-sages going?' She bent over to adjust her shoe. 'Why are they being sent?'

Her mother was twisting her wedding ring round and round her finger. 'The less you know, the less you can reveal under duress.'

'Duress?' Tanne's heart gave a massive thump. 'What are you talking about? Are you in trouble?'

'I thought you said you had a brain?'

Tanne shrugged.

'Use it, Tanne. What do you think men like Juncker are capable of? Or the *Gestapomen*. Or –' her mouth was set '– the SS? You've seen and heard what's happening on our streets, in the prisons and . . .' She sighed. 'You know what's being said.'

'I'm not blind or deaf.' Tanne was struggling with the cuff again. 'But are *you* playing politics to annoy *Far*?'

Her mother got up and took possession of Tanne's wrist to deal with the rogue button. Her hand was perfectly steady. 'You don't *play* politics in war.' It was a quiet, but deadly, rebuke.

Angry with her mother, but angrier with herself for being so slow, so uninformed, so out of control, Tanne couldn't resist saying, 'Have you thought that you are putting *Far* and Rosenlund in danger?'

'I think of nothing else.'

'So why do it? Just because you crave a bit of adventure with a stranger?'

'Take that back.'

There was a pause.

'Sorry, *Mor*.' Tanne swallowed. 'I'm being stupid. It's the shock of finding you . . . But why you?'

'Do you want the truth? I wasn't bold or brave or decisive. I was asked to help out once. I said yes but only the once. But it doesn't work like that. Let that be a lesson, Tanne. One tiny step and you are sucked in.' The grey eyes were troubled. 'In the end, I had gone too far to turn back. But I've had my life. You haven't and you *mustn't* get involved.' Raising Tanne's hand to her mouth, she kissed it and pressed it to her cheek. 'Listen to me, *min elskede*. Please.'

The gossip in København. Shootings. Killings. Prison. Torture. Death. Belief. Principle . . . All these were closing in on Tanne and she had to make sense of them.

Her mother was still talking: '. . . But I do believe the Nazis have to be stopped. I want to be able to say that I went to the aid of my country.'

It irritated Tanne. '*Your* country?'

Silence.

'I suppose I should have known that would be your reaction.' Her mother made for the door.

'Stop!' Tanne was beginning to feel desperate. 'Please. Let's start again. I am involved, *Mor*. I've seen what I shouldn't have done. That makes me so.'

'No, it doesn't.'

With a snap, she opened the door and almost collided with Bror. Having returned from his morning inspection of the grounds, he had washed and changed. His hair was damp, his eyes bright from the exercise and Tanne knew he would smell of his special Berlin cologne.

'Raised voices. Are you two quarrelling?'

He looked only at Tanne.

Tanne's eyes encountered her mother's. Her mother's secrets were bad enough. The danger was frightening. Worse, was the destruction of the perfect candour between herself and her father.

From now on, Tanne could not say anything. She had to be silent.

The strain told on Tanne. Her head pounded incessantly, her eyes were inflamed from interrupted sleep and she found it an effort to concentrate on even the simplest tasks.

A few days later she drew her father aside after breakfast.

'*Far*, the Germans are demanding a percentage of what we produce on the farms. What if we don't declare the total dairy yields?'

They happened to be by the stairs, standing almost directly under the family tree.

Unusually, a lock of hair had fallen over her father's face which made him look younger. 'Are you turning militant?'

'No, only practical. Why should they take our hard-won yields?'

'I'm not going to discuss it.' His silver cigarette case was never far away, and he took it out of his pocket. 'Tanne, I'm planning a duck shoot. Do you want to come?'

Childhood memories springing up from the time when she craved nothing more than to be with her father, tucked up in a hide, or wading through the marsh. Riding across the fields, wind stippling the water, the ever-changing cloud shapes. Their whispered asides. Mud, salty marsh, sappy, whippy grass. At the end of a hard session, the exhaustion which flooded, sweet and lovely, through the body.

'No, thank you, *Far*.'

'Not shoot?'

She bit down on her lower lip. 'With everything that's going on, I don't see duck-shooting in the same way.'

He shrugged but she knew that he was offended. 'No discussion? Shooting duck is over? Just like that?' He turned away. 'If that is what you wish.'

She wasn't going to let this go. Calculating that, in the end, her father would not ignore anything which affected Rosenlund, she said, '*Far*, you haven't answered my question. The dairy yields?'

Tanne was right. He took a moment and then refused to answer the question directly: 'There're more ways of skinning a cat than the obvious. I was thinking of ploughing up the south meadow to try for extra crops next year to make up the shortfall.'

He smiled down at her. 'The Protectorate is not going away and, whatever the bad history between Danes and Germans, we remain cousins.' He pointed to the family tree. 'Think of Sophia-Maria.'

'Even if the Nazis are wrong, *Far*?'

'Ah, so . . . I can see what you are thinking. The wind is changing. Am I right?' He extracted a cigarette from the case and a fleck of tobacco drifted to the floor. 'Tanne, I could support your idea by falsifying the figures, but I would be putting Rosenlund at risk.'

Tanne forced herself to look at him but her thoughts were elsewhere.

Messages needed to be sent . . . to whom and when?

He continued, with a touch of impatience. 'It wasn't possible for Denmark to defend itself. We didn't have the troops and the border is easy to cross. Why not save lives and negotiate? Why not ensure that Rosenlund survives. For you.'

Perhaps her father was right and life could continue as normal? Practicality. Pragmatism. Wasn't the first duty of life to survive it? Planted in the human spirit was an ineradicable will to live. The images which now haunted Tanne rose in her mind . . . Hannah's pale contorted face as she described how her brother had fled from the police, the dead cyclist, his blood on her legs and trickling between the cobblestones . . .

'What if I don't want it?'

'Tanne. Please.'

'What if the price isn't worth it?'

'Because you're young, my darling daughter, you can't see it. When I die, you will be thankful for this.'

Tanne watched him take the stairs two at a time. At the top he turned round. 'But don't worry, I've got plenty of years left in me yet.'

For a moment, his hand rested on the rail.

How lonely he seemed. Even with her mother by his side, he had always been a bit of a stoic.

But it didn't make him right.

Tanne fled back to København for a few days, calculating that different faces, different places would give her breathing space.

Arriving in the afternoon, she discovered that Grete and Hannah were tied up until the evening. No matter. She made her way to a favoured spot: the gardens of the Rosenborg Palace.

Fireworks, bonfires and any midsummer celebrations had all been banned for the coming year, but the Københavners didn't appear to be too depressed about these restrictions on their national life. In fact, they appeared to enjoy flouting the regulations and had come out in droves to enjoy a pale spring sunshine and to mill about in large groups. Well wrapped up, Tanne settled herself on a sunny seat to watch one particular group drinking beer and singing songs of an increasingly patriotic nature, while elsewhere there were deals being done, arguments taking place, lovers meeting and families taking pleasure in being together.

She spotted a German soldier exchange a packet of cigarettes for shaving soap with a man in a brown suit, and a youth in a *HitlerJugend* shirt helping a mother with a screaming toddler.

Ordinary things. Ordinary life. Yet, not.

'Look at this . . .' cried a blonde girl in a green overcoat, clapping a beanie hat with British RAF colours onto her head.

Within seconds, a couple of Danish police surrounded the girl. One of the policemen grabbed her wrist. She tried to wrest it out of his grasp.

Tanne got up.

Move away, Tanne. Survive.

Not honourable. Pragmatic, though, if . . . if . . . she was to work for Denmark's freedom.

The girl's friend froze with a biscuit held halfway to her mouth, watching as a German *feldgendarme* materialized out of the crowd and ordered the blonde girl to her feet.

She was now sobbing.

The *feldgendarme* gestured towards the exit and the Danish police dragged the girl away, leaving an upended bottle of beer to soak into the grass where, only a moment ago, she had been happily chatting with her friend.

A veil dropped over the promise of the day. In its place was a sourness. Those closest to the incident were rattled and anxious. A woman in a headscarf hustled away her two children. Others headed out of the gardens.

Tanne edged her way towards the exit. At the Kron-prinsessegade gate, a man stood aside to let her through. He was wearing horn-rimmed spectacles and his skin looked an unhealthy greyish colour. Even so, she recognized him.

'Felix.'

He turned on his heel and walked swiftly away but she ran after him. 'You were with my mother.' That brought him to a halt. 'Who are you? Tell me.'

His gaze shifted up and down the street. 'Shut up, please.'

'Tell me, then.'

Felix came to a decision. 'Turn down Dronningens Tvær-gade and at the junction with Bredgade there is the Café Amadeus. Order a coffee.'

This was a dream. This was real. She had strayed into a Hans Christian Andersen's fantasy. A bubble lodged itself in her chest. Excitement? Laughter? No, surely not laughter. More a sense that she was arriving at a place which she hadn't known existed.

The coffee was in front of her when Felix arrived and slid in beside her on the banquette. She circled it with her hands. 'You look different.'

'It's amazing what glasses and a bit of dust on the skin can do.' His eyes moved restlessly around the room. 'Don't make it obvious but the man who has just come in . . . what's he doing?'

'What?'

Gathering her wits, Tanne bent down to adjust her shoe and sneaked a look. The man? Elderly, almost befuddled-looking, with a wispy beard. He had ordered a beer. He was watching them. She fiddled again with her shoe and straightened up. 'He's watching us.'

Felix leaned towards her. 'Kiss me.'

Not for one second did she hesitate. His mouth was alien and not at all passionate. Up close, his skin under the dust was smooth and fresh and she breathed in an unfamiliar scent.

She forgot her wavering, confused politics, the fears for her mother, her *anger* with her mother, the plans for the future. *What future?* Just for those moments nothing mattered except this stranger's lips on hers. Nothing at all.

She could tell that he was taken aback.

For the first time, his smile was genuine. 'Sorry about this but you'll have to kiss me again.'

Better. Much better. When it was over, she murmured: 'Who are you and why are you seeing my mother?'

'Do you imagine I am going to tell you?' His mouth rested by her ear.

She drew back in order to look into his eyes – as intently as a true lover.

Felix locked his gaze with hers. 'Not bad.' He kissed the base of her neck – and a sweet and wild music struck up in Tanne's head. 'We have to get out of here. Put your arm round me.'

Tanne got to her feet, pulled Felix upright and said gaily: 'Let's go, *elskede.*'

Entwined, they left the café and walked down the street. At the junction, Felix halted. 'Sorry about that. I thought I had shaken off the tails.'

She kept her arm round Felix. 'I don't know anything about you, or where you come from. Certainly not your name. But please tell me what's happening.'

He placed his hands on her shoulders. 'Listen to me. Do not get tangled in this. Do not.'

How strange. Her mother had talked of the step by step. The tiny incremental changes. Of the waters washing over the head.

Recklessness, a wanton exhilarated recklessness, had Tanne in its grip. She reached up and kissed Felix again on the lips. 'But I am.'

Chapter Eighteen

The dentist's surgery off the Strøget, København's main pedestrian street, had the advantage of a basement room, plus a door opening into the garden where a couple of scrubby laurel bushes offered sanctuary to the birds recovering from the winter.

Wearing headphones, Kay crouched over a dummy transmitter key, her finger tensed so tightly that the joint had whitened. With her was 'Johan', an employee of Bang & Olufsen, who was instructing her in the mysteries of Morse. A burly, balding, middle-aged man, with an unhealthy mottled complexion and customarily wearing a jacket and frayed bow tie which had seen better days, he was a good, patient teacher.

She had been at it for several weeks. It was now April and the learning process hadn't been easy.

The room was crammed with dentist materials: small boxes of cement, a discarded hand drill, mouthwash and, arranged on the shelves, row on row of plaster-of-Paris denture moulds. Every so often Kay looked up and encountered their macabre grins.

Upstairs, the dentist's drill stopped and started.

Dot dash dash, Freya tapped: W.

The drill fell silent. Johan held up his hand. They had agreed it was safer to wait for its whining cover.

Kay slipped the headphones round her neck. 'I'm sorry I'm not a natural, Johan.'

'I've had worse, my dear.'

The flutter and whirr of the birds busying themselves in the laurels was, she decided, delightfully reassuring.

The gnat-like whine recommenced. 'Go,' said Johan.

Replacing the headphones, Kay reapplied herself to the transmitter key. With a grinding effort, she translated another letter into dash dot dot dash: X. This was followed by dash dot dash dash.

'Y . . . good,' said Johan, 'and now Z.'

Dash dash dot dot.

'Not so bad,' was the verdict.

She felt as exhausted as if she had run a race. 'It was dreadful.'

Being versed and skilled, Johan could have been superior about Kay's stumbling progress. But, natural teacher as he was, he offered up useful pointers instead. 'Listen to the sound combinations, as you would do to music.'

'And I thought I was musical.'

Kay tried to stand up but Johan pushed her down. 'The only way forward is to keep going.'

She laughed and reapplied herself.

'Listen for the melody of the letter rather than counting the dits and dahs,' he said, tapping out air-rhythms. 'The human brain learns a language much more easily when meaning is attached to the sounds. Without it, the brain has no handles to make that attachment. So . . . if you take the letter D in Morse, it might be more readily remembered as "dog did it" instead of "dash dot dot". Imagine a picture of your favourite dog and, hey presto, the symbol becomes part of the mental furniture.'

A figure slipped through the garden and let itself into the room.

'Felix.'

'Johan.'

Kay did not look up.

He observed Kay's halting efforts. 'Progress?' he asked.

Johan leaned over Freya and adjusted her keying finger into a more natural arc. 'By and large, yes.'

Kay finally met Felix's eyes. 'I'm trying,' she said.

Despite looking grim, Felix flashed a smile. 'We got you the best instructor in the country.'

Kay redoubled her efforts while Felix and Johan exchanged the latest information on the progress of the new, portable wireless sets which were being secretly developed.

'It's risky, really risky,' said Johan. 'We are forced to keep moving locations and it's difficult to transport and hide the components. But when we're done,' he said, with justifiable pride, 'you'll be able to carry a set in something as small as a briefcase.'

'Any idea when?' Felix eased into a chair. 'God, I'm stiff.'

Johan shrugged. 'Who knows? Tell the Nazis to go home and I could do it tomorrow.'

'I'll have to give London some sort of steer.'

'Oh, London . . .' Johan's tone was becoming familiar to Kay – that of the Dane who didn't much care for British interference. 'Word has it they're hostile to us training our own radio operators here. Tell them from me to stuff it, and tell them we need the crystals. Soon.' He sighed. 'Before soon.'

Oh, London. Kay's instinct was to spring to its defence, but she kept quiet.

Johan picked up a briefcase which was stuffed with papers. At the door, he turned and said to Felix, 'We do *need* the crystals.'

After he had gone, Felix slumped back in the chair and closed his eyes.

'Are you all right?' Kay touched his shoulder.

His eyes flicked open. 'We need guns, we need explosives, we need money and recruits . . .' He grabbed her arm. 'And getting them depends on this fragile wrist tapping out the messages.' He ran a finger over the junction where the veins rose over the swell of the thumb. 'And mine.'

Felix's guard was down. Kay rubbed her keying finger, which had swollen. 'Is it something in particular?'

Various expressions chased over his features, mostly caustic. 'It's a piece of cake to run an underground network.'

Kay had never seen this side of Felix. Was he frightened? Exhausted? Or, God forbid, ill? 'Talk to me. I'm here.'

He stared out into the garden. 'Sweet of you, Freya. But I can't tell you anything you don't need to know.'

'They must have discussed with you in London that the mind can only take so much stress?' She was sounding very maternal. 'You're under appalling strain.'

'I'll manage, but thank you.'

How much could one person cope with on his own? It was a question which, no doubt, she would explore.

'Actually,' she said. 'I want to ask a favour. Would it be possible to get a letter out to Sweden, where it could be posted on?'

'Probably.'

'It's my mother. She'll be worrying and I want to reassure her. She's quite elderly and not in good health. If she died . . . What I mean is that I don't want her to die without hearing that I'm fine.'

'What will you say?'

Would she tell her secrets to her mother . . . about Bror? Felix? Bloody Morse code?

My Darling Mother,

I hope above everything that you and the sisters are well. I have no idea where you are but I imagine you are at home.

This is to tell you that we are all well. Would you believe it, life is almost normal and the war has hardly touched us? In fact, we have had parliamentary elections so democracy is alive and well here. Bror is busy with the house and the estate. I help him as much as I can. Tanne is here with us, but goes to and from Copenhagen to see her friends. Nils is busy with his research at the university. So, you see, our life under the Germans is boring and uneventful . . .

I think of you often . . .

'You won't mention that the Germans have imposed the death sentence for sabotage?'

'No.'

'Or the suicide of a wireless operator, one of ours, when *Danish* police tried to capture him?'

'No.'

'Or that the election was a complete farce and we now have a puppet government?'

'Isn't truth the first casualty of war?'

He raised an eyebrow. 'I'll do what I can.'

Kay picked up her bag. It was happening slowly but their minds were beginning to mesh. She had become better at anticipating what was needed, at understanding the disciplines and demands of deceiving on a grand level. It was a question of perception, and the way her mind worked these days was changing. For one thing, she knew lies were necessary. So was questioning every move. Whom did one trust? Where were the safety nets and the escape routes?

Reaching for her lipstick, she made up her lips. 'Have I smeared any?'

'It's perfect.' Felix barely glanced at her, and mooched over to the door. 'Did I ever tell you I saw a photograph of you in the paper when I was hiding? After I first came in.'

'That must have cheered you.'

'You were wearing a lot of jewels at some function.'

'Ah, the jewels.' She put the lid back on the lipstick and dropped it into her bag. 'I'll be wearing those tomorrow. It's the dinner for the Knights of the Silver Sword.'

'Grown men dressing up?'

'The women are dressed up, too.' His reaction amused Kay. 'A lot of people who matter will be there. Also some Germans. What should I be listening out for?'

'Troop movements.' Felix snapped to attention and explained that intelligence was revealing the Germans had a big problem. Hydro-electric power sites were being sabotaged daily by the

Resistance all over the Reich, so they were forced to rely on aluminium batteries. 'But they need bauxite to make aluminium and guess where that comes from?'

Kay knew that. 'Norway.'

'So, anything about ship and troop movements which would indicate where it might be coming in,' he said. 'You never know, Jacob might get lucky and be allowed to blow it all sky high.' He laughed – but not with any humour.

The sound shivered down her spine. It was getting to Felix: the anxiety, the paranoia, the simple fact that you stood a good chance of not being there the next day.

'Something *is* wrong. I'm not leaving until we have it out.' She pointed to the grinning plaster casts. 'Deaf as posts.'

Her new assertiveness was pleasing to Kay but she also cared about Felix. Caring would make her vulnerable but there were limits to an agent's detachment.

'The agent on Jutland. The drinking one. We talked about him before.'

'It's still going on?'

Felix looked grim. 'He promised his leader that he would reform. He did for a while. But he's back on the booze and it's got the better of him. Reports have come in that the stupid bugger was overheard boasting about his training.'

'It must be so hard,' she said. 'To know yourself.'

'You watch them –' Felix spoke more to himself than to Kay '– they watch you. Day after day, week after week, it's cat and mouse. At first the body takes the brunt of the strain . . . aches, indigestion, stiffness, the need for a drink. Then the mind begins to play tricks. Holed up, you think you're safe. There is a knock on the door, a bullet's crack. They take someone else and your nerves snap with terror and . . . a terrible thankfulness. It isn't you this time. But next time?'

There was a silence and her thoughts went this way and that. *The need for a drink* . . .

'How did London miss it?' she asked.

He shrugged. 'It happens. No one can predict what life in the field will do to you.'

'Get him out to Sweden.'

He looked at her as if she didn't know what she was talking about – which she didn't. 'Try persuading a full-grown recalcitrant drunk to do what he doesn't want to do. So . . .'

What exactly?

Reading what was written on his face, she felt a hard, sharp shock. 'We can't do that . . .' She noted she used 'we'. 'That's not justice. I mean due process.'

Before the words left her lips, she knew they were redundant.

Therein lay another, less specified, kind of danger.

'We're not in the playground, Freya.'

'We are fighting this war so we don't end up like the murderers and thugs, too. You can't put us on the same level.'

He cut through. 'This is war, Freya. You want to live. I want to live . . . and we could all end up dead. The point is that we might have to do things that put us on a level with them. It's debatable, morally speaking, but simple in practical terms. Who do you want to survive? Them? Or us?'

She thought about London and the little she knew about Felix's organization. Putting together a bunch of tricks, training agents, parachuting in weapons, planning sabotage, recruiting an army to create a resistance with bite. Was it possible for London to understand what it entailed? Not really. It was Felix, she and the others who were the here-and-now . . . the watchers, the doers. Yes, even she, grafted-on Dane – Tanne's words – as she was.

'Did you think like this before . . . in the other life?'

'Of course not. Stupid question.'

He sounded sad.

'Then we can't do what I think you're thinking,' Kay said.

'It's him or us. Probably. You want to survive, don't you?'

Yes, *yes*.

It was as if she was physically stepping over a line. And she knew she could never go back. 'What can I do?'

He barely moved a muscle but she knew he was relieved.

'Contact Jacob. Tell him Holger Danske must act. That's all you need say.'

She had one last stab. 'And if I don't?'

'Then . . .' He was almost tender. 'You're no use to me, Freya.'

She turned away and encountered a grinning plaster-of-Paris upper and lower jaw that was out of alignment.

'I'd have to kill you, too.'

Joke.

Footsteps could be heard clattering down the stairwell. In a flash, Kay had packed the dummy transmitter key into a box labelled Periodontal Extractor. She pushed Felix into a chair. 'Open your mouth,' she whispered. 'Pretend you're a patient.'

But it was Lars, the dentist. He put his head round the door and said, 'The lookouts are signalling trouble. Get out the back.'

They fled.

The Knights of the Silver Sword held two dinners a year, in spring and autumn. The order dated from the Middle Ages and the reasons for its founding had almost certainly been forgotten by the influential guests who were there solely to promote their own interests. Some years back, Bror had been elected onto the committee, pleasing him greatly. He never missed a dinner and Kay was expected to be on his arm.

It involved dressing up, which – however democratically minded they were – the Danes liked to do. White tie, medals, long gowns, jewels . . . the lot.

A couple of days previously, Bror had cornered Kay at Rosenlund. 'I need to talk to you.'

'Of course.'

They hadn't spoken properly for weeks – only the necessary exchanges of information and detail for day-to-day arrangements. Bror remained in the spare room. A great silence lay between them.

'The dinner,' he said.

She scanned his face. Blue, stormy eyes. 'I'd rather not come this year,' she said.

'You will, Kay.' She raised an eyebrow and he modulated his tone. 'Please. Whatever is happening, whatever you decide, I ask you to be there.'

She settled on the pale blue chiffon dress thrown over a silk shift that she had worn to a pre-war wedding. On putting it on, she discovered that she was thinner in the waist, with a flatter stomach and slightly bulkier shoulders. In the past, before their estrangement, Bror used to tease her about her *weiner-brød*, and she was delighted with her sleeker body.

Seated at the dressing table in the bedroom at the hotel, Kay dusted powder over her shoulders. There was a knock on the door.

It was Bror, resplendent in white tie and medals. 'Ready?'

'Just my earrings to fasten.'

Her hands trembled with nerves and she fumbled the process.

He was watching her – but there was no tenderness, nor indulgence in the regard.

'Let me.'

He bent over her and she smelled the familiar cologne and the starch he favoured for his boiled shirts. Deftly, he hooked the earrings into place.

'There.'

No extra loving, sexy touch.

She missed it. How she missed it.

Letting go was always hard, but this was the hardest thing Kay would ever ask of herself – the letting go of mutual delight, mutual trust, anticipation and intimacy.

She rose to her feet.

'You look beautiful.'

Why did Bror bother? The exchange was formal and under-pinned with distrust and distance.

Last year, in this hotel room, it had been very different.

Then, she had looked at Bror and said, 'You've hardly changed since I met you.'

Bror had touched her bared flesh just above the cleavage. 'Will you marry me?'

She had given a soft laugh. 'Of course. But I should point out we are married.'

'But I like asking you, over and over.' He'd slid a tender finger into her cleavage. Do you remember that first time?'

She did.

It had been before their wedding but they couldn't wait. Bror undressed her and she trembled with the daring of what she was about to do. With each garment he dispatched to the floor, he paused to look. 'You're beautiful, Kay.'

So was he.

He'd drawn her close. 'I never thought I would say this to anyone but I can't live without you.'

Calling on memories was exhausting and a bad habit.

She looked around the comfortable hotel room, her eyes resting on the bedspread, puckered where she had sat on it, the half-open drawer of the dressing table and the sliver of the bathroom, with the towel thrown over the side of the bath, just visible through the door.

The coiffured, bejewelled and assured *Fru* Eberstern was still there. But she was only part of the story. The wife, mother and chatelaine now hid the woman who was more than a little in love with the idea of being someone else. That had consequences.

Flicking up his tails, Bror sat down on the edge of the bed. 'We haven't talked, Kay.'

Kay eased a kid glove over her wrist and pulled it up her arm. 'You mean about Anton.'

'You more or less told me you were having an affair. Are you?'

'I'm not going to answer that.' The blood thudded in Kay's chest.

There was a silence.

'I haven't slept for weeks,' he said at last.

That hurt. Inflicting pain on someone you loved did hurt. Of course. And this was to destroy their customary kindness to each other, their intimacy and the automatic assumption that the other was *there*.

'But Anton's only part of it, isn't he? We should be clearer about how we deal with this war.'

'You know what I feel about Hitler.' She reached for the second glove and plaited the fingers. 'Look, I'm here to support you tonight.'

'You've made that clear.' Bror's hands dropped between his knees. 'When we go home we must . . . we must sort out our lives. But I'm too weary and tonight let there be peace between us.'

The last tiny kid-clad button was wrestled through its buttonhole. 'Oh Bror . . .'

Her sadness almost overpowered her. In all probability, she had lost a lover, a friend and a husband.

And the life they had made together.

He looked down at his shoes, polished to brightness. 'It's only going to get worse. Isn't it? So tonight shall we be united?'

He rose to his feet.

She picked up her silk stole and draped it round her shoulders, contemplating the worst.

'You haven't said yes. Do we have a deal?'

She nodded. 'Agreed.'

He bent down and kissed her on the cheek – a perfunctory, businesslike gesture.

Could a heart break? The way she felt, she supposed it could.

On entering the reception, she was cornered by an old friend, Clara Ramussen.

'Kay! You look wonderful. And you've lost weight.' She sent Kay a look that asked: *Have you acquired a lover?* 'Tell me the secret.'

'It's all the walking, Clara. Petrol being so scarce.'

'Goodness, I shall have to take it up,' replied Clara. 'I might get myself a new husband.'

The reception was crowded. There was the usual collection of Danes, and some German and Swedish businessmen. But, this year, the number of uniformed German guests had swelled noticeably.

Dashing in his dress uniform, Anton spotted Kay. Picking up two glasses of champagne, he came over and gave her one. 'How are you?'

Kay accepted the glass. 'For once, I'm really pleased to see you. I need your knowledge.'

'Nonsense, you're always pleased to see me.'

The odds were that Bror was watching and Kay raised her glass to Anton's. 'Tell me what I should know.'

'Good idea,' he said, without shifting his gaze from her face. 'Most of the Germans are run-of-the-mill and probably of not much interest.' He gave her some details. 'But there is one, General Gottfried. I've arranged for you to sit next to him . . .'

The ballroom where dinner was served was impressively mirrored and panelled. The pennants and flags of the Knights of the Silver Sword, celebrating ancient battles and feats, had been brought in for the evening and hung up on poles. The effect was magnificent.

On Kay's left was Aksel Fog, one of the stuffier knights whom she had known for years and just about tolerated. On her right, as Anton had promised, was the Abwehr general, General Gottfried.

General commanding Abwehr Signals Unit. Anton had briefed her under his breath. *Almost certainly dealing with intelligence, too. Make friends. You know what to do, darling.*

Anton was sitting further down the table and sent her a little smile.

The general proved to be charming. He had a long clever face, a dress uniform stiff with medals and ribbons, and excellent manners. He told her that he was commanding the København unit. He lived in Koblenz and, although he could not admire København more, he missed his home town very much. 'I am very proud of its architecture and its fines wines. Both are essential for the civilized life, don't you think?'

He spoke without irony which, given his obvious intelligence, surprised Kay.

Judging her silence correctly, he said, 'You consider that invading other countries is uncivilized, but all empires come about because of invasion, including the British one.'

He went on to talk about the Romans, of whom he approved. 'Their discipline and military ethos were vital elements in a highly organized operation. Without them, there would have been no empire.' He raised his glass to her. 'The British Empire is less a product of discipline and more the fruit of inspired amateurism, wouldn't you say?'

This was his second reference to the British, which she took to mean the general had done his homework on her.

A cramp shot through her stomach.

'I genuinely admire the British Empire,' he added.

What could she say? Suddenly, the room felt sickeningly claustrophobic, the set-up very unsafe.

She managed to collect her wits. 'I'm sure the British would be delighted by your compliment.' She touched her own glass. 'General, do you approve this Riesling? It has obviously been chosen with you in mind.'

He nodded. 'This is very agreeable company. If I said it's a privilege to be part of it would you believe me?'

Kay was startled but hid it. If her instincts were correct, the general spoke as the outsider wishing to join the inner circle – and that was a psychological position about which she knew something.

After coffee, Kay rose to her feet and said, 'Please excuse me for a moment or two.' She made her way towards the ladies' powder room.

But Anton ambushed her before she reached it. Tucking his hand under her elbow he pushed her into a small salon off the hotel foyer. 'Come.'

'Are you mad, Anton?'

He shut the door. 'Have you learned anything?'

'You're right. He's in Intelligence.'

'Any proof?'

'He's done his homework. Knows who I am.'

They were facing each other, whispering.

Anton was facing the door. Suddenly, he reached out and pulled her to him.

'What are you doing?'

He said very softly into her ear, 'Someone is at the door.' He raised his voice. 'You know that kiss I have waited for?'

Who?

She slid into the role.

'The kiss that would mean nothing?'

'That one.' He leaned over. His mouth on hers was confident and accomplished and quite, quite different from Bror's.

'Who was it?' she murmured eventually, disentangling herself.

Anton shrugged. 'No idea.' His eyes reflected amusement, malice – and surprise. 'Was it nice?'

'Nicer than a cold bath. Not as nice as good champagne.'

Anton changed tack. 'We've been in contact with London. They want more action and have sent over suggestions.'

'Does Felix know?'

'Probably.'

'He won't like it. He likes to do things his way.'

'None of us are in a position to have our own way. Regrettably.'

She laid a finger on his arm. 'But you do, Anton.'

That amused Anton. 'Not quite.'

She had barely set aside her breakfast tray the following morning when Bror appeared. He sat down on the bed. 'The general has telephoned and invited us to the theatre.'

How should she play this? As the British-born wife? Given her anti-German stance, appearing too eager to meet the general might make Bror suspicious. Calculating her next move, Kay got out of bed and reached for her dressing gown.

'You said no, I hope. You said that we're going home.'

'Didn't you like the general?'

'He's a cultured man.'

'You're angry about the idea, though. Kay, I don't often ask anything of you . . .'

She tied the dressing-gown belt tight round her waist. 'True. But I performed for you last night. I don't think I can do it again today. I'll arrange to go home on my own.'

Bror made for the door. 'Oh, go to hell, Kay,' he said angrily, and vanished.

She dressed carefully. Rolling up the precious silk stockings and attaching them with the suspender, dropping the skirt of her navy-blue costume over her head, and fastening an Eberstern diamond onto the jacket lapel. Last, but not least, she tipped the Parisian hat over one eye. Before her eyes, *Fru* Eberstern of Rosenlund was reassembled.

She gave Bror half an hour to stew. After that, she went downstairs to the lounge where he was reading the morning papers.

He didn't notice her and she was free to observe him for a moment. She loved him. There was no doubt about that, but the man whom she loved had signed the Declaration and was friendly with German intelligence officers.

He looked up. A light came into the blue eyes and she knew that her efforts to look nice had paid off.

'I'm sorry, Bror. I was over-hasty.'

That evening, the Ebersterns were ushered into a box at the theatre where the general waited with an elegant blonde woman. He kissed Kay's hand and said: 'May I introduce my wife, Ingrid, who arrived this morning?'

Ingrid was delightful and, in normal circumstances, Kay would have enjoyed meeting her. Speaking in German, they exchanged information. Ingrid was the mother of two boys, and her other passion was the local amateur opera company. 'In the summer we give performances on the river,' she said. 'Last year I took the main role in *Grafin Mariza*.'

They chatted on.

Kay revealed that she went to the theatre and opera as much as possible but her responsibilities kept her at Rosenlund more often than she would like. She told Ingrid about the estate and its history.

'We have much in common,' said Ingrid at last. She glanced at her husband. 'I often think that our insistence on being different nationalities is nonsense. In Europe at any rate we are one big family.'

Ingrid spoke sense.

'I agree with you,' Kay replied, before changing the subject. 'Will you be staying in Denmark?'

Touching her husband on the arm, Ingrid replied, 'For some time, I think.'

In the interval, champagne was served and the general turned to Kay.

'*Fru* Eberstern, you've told me about your delightful daughter. What does your son do?'

Kay explained that Nils was an academic who was developing advanced mathematical theories. 'He can read numbers as fluently as you or I might read a book.' She couldn't stifle the pride. 'He's quite celebrated in his way.'

Never offer details. Be drab. Be unremarkable.

'I can't tell you,' he said a little later, 'how pleasant this is.'

She felt a flicker of unease.

'I'm glad you feel comfortable here, General. Are you going to travel in Denmark? For pleasure, perhaps? Some of the towns are very pretty and the scenery on Lolland is especially praised.'

The general's gaze rested on Kay. There was a great deal of sharp and analytical intelligence and a trace of humour – which she hadn't expected. 'You know, and I know, that not everyone loves us, *Fru* Eberstern, and I won't be welcome everywhere. But I will be visiting Jutland.' He looked down his handsome nose. 'If it's safe. My friends in the SS tell me they're fully occupied with terrorists and spies. I imagine you know what I'm talking about.'

How best to use this encounter? Very gently, she set down her champagne glass on the table. 'I've often wondered what happens to spies if you capture them.'

'Depends. If our friends in the SS are involved, they can be brutal. Personally, I'm against waste and I think that if you've a highly trained operative in your hands, you should make use of them.'

She smiled at the general.

Back at the hotel, Kay threw her handbag onto the bed. 'Thank God that's over.'

Bror took out his silver cigarette case. 'It wasn't so bad.'

'I'll have one of those, too.' She stretched over and pinched one.

He opened the French windows and stepped out onto the balcony. Grabbing her stole, she joined him. He lit her cigarette and she inhaled gratefully.

'Bror, do you know how many people must have seen us having our cosy theatre party with the enemy?'

'You charmed them both.'

She looked down over the hotel garden. Beyond it the lights of the capital were spread out.

'The general asked if he and Ingrid could visit Rosenlund.

Apparently, you were encouraging him to see something of Denmark. He also wants to meet Nils.'

'No,' she said. 'To both.'

'I've arranged it for next week.'

Message to Felix: *Avoid Rosenlund.*

Bror smoked in silence.

Keep tight hold of what matters.

Chapter Nineteen

Ruby and Major Martin were drinking ersatz coffee in a café in Baker Street that was a favourite of The Firm's personnel. The windows fronted onto the street and were partly covered by net curtains which had seen better days. Every time the door opened or shut, the bell above it rattled.

But the café had a pleasant enough atmosphere — almost relaxed, gossipy, cosily steamed up on wet days.

As usual, he commandeered a table at the back of the café, saying that it was essential in their line of work because it gave them a good view of the comings and goings at the door.

She liked that — for, at her ripe old age of twenty-four, Ruby had discovered an interest in people. How they looked, what they were saying . . . and what they *really* meant. It was ironic, wasn't it? As a result of her work, which consisted of codes, letters and numbers, she had discovered courage and suffering in the most unexpected places, and this affected her. Plus, on a more simple level, she also took pleasure in knowing that, although she looked exactly like everyone else in uniform, she was nurturing secrets. Was keeping secrets and enjoying them a misuse of power? A road to fascism? If so, she didn't care.

No one seated at the tables acknowledged anyone else even though, as Ruby was now aware, they might know each other well. It was good, basic security practice which would not be understood by those not in the know.

Good security was the reason Major Martin and Ruby arranged their meetings: they needed to go over the procedures again and again. This was the latest of several encounters during the past few weeks, and, if Ruby was as precise about her personal life as she was with her work, she would have to admit to enjoying them all. Two of them had even been conducted over dinner – snatched but fun – before they headed back for night sessions at the office.

Had any other elements crept into the meetings? Well, yes, and Ruby was in two minds as to how to deal with it. In her previous dealings with it, lust had been a straightforward matter. Either you slaked it or you didn't.

Major Martin briefed her on the latest in the turf wars. Perhaps it was the arrival of spring that made him look less haggard and more optimistic, but he still hadn't managed to polish his shoes. Funny, but that little dereliction made Ruby like him all the more.

'I've been thinking,' she said.

He transferred his total attention onto Ruby. 'Should I be afraid?'

She liked his humour, too, the way his joke or wry comment was often delivered with the straightest of faces.

'Out with it, Ingram.'

She stirred the coffee. 'We have the practice papers of the agents, which tell us if they have any little coding tics and habits. But that doesn't tell us what they sound like or what their Morse 'handwriting' is like. What if, at the end of their training, we ask the pianists to key in every letter and number, at varying speeds, and we record them doing this? We wouldn't let on to them why we're asking them to do it, or they'd become self-conscious. But if we then transferred the results onto graph paper, the signalmasters would have a record that could be easily read and referred to if a signals clerk questions the fist.'

From under her lashes, she watched him process the idea. In so many ways, they thought alike. Just like she would do – *had done* – he would be turning the idea around and examining it from all angles. Drawing a mental diagram. Constructing a hypothesis. Was the idea possible to achieve? What were the likely unintended consequences – for everything had unintended consequences? Security problems?

'Yes,' he pronounced. 'That makes sense. Good sense. We should have thought of it earlier.'

'If you're too close, you sometimes don't see things until you see them,' she said.

He grinned. 'Is that a principle for life?'

'How are we doing, do you think?'

How were they doing? The answer was that they were doing the best they could under the circumstances. Battling the dearth of intelligence from a war-enshrouded Europe, they found themselves shuffling forward one step, falling back two as they struggled to piece together a picture of what was going on.

Major Martin drained his coffee. 'I want to ask you something.'

Ruby experienced a flash of excitement, followed by doubt. Did he want her to go away and head up some dreary team somewhere else? After all, they agreed it was her cleverness that he wanted.

'Go on.'

'I want to know if you'll call me Peter.'

She looked up. 'If you like.'

He gave one of his smiles and it was an almost unbearably intimate moment. Ruby looked anywhere but at him.

'And . . .' He called her back to attention.

He meant what should he call her?

'Shall we stick to Ingram?'

'Right.' He signalled to the waitress and, if he was disappointed, it didn't register. 'I've been trying to work out why you're different.'

'Most women are taught to hide their feelings. They are conditioned not to be read *en clair*.' Ruby wasn't entirely joking.

The dark eyes rested on her face and she had the uncomfortable feeling that he was seeing right into her. 'From this moment on, you're sworn to tell me what you're thinking and feeling. Plain text.'

Did he want sex? Probably. That she understood far better

than intimacy *and* it was easier to deal with. Taking her boss into her bed would be part and parcel of her strange new existence.

Peter raised an eyebrow, a tiny movement but one that made her, despite herself, very happy. 'I don't want to rush things.'

Ruby was touched by the old-fashioned gallantry. She took a deep breath. 'Bombs are falling. We could be dead tomorrow.'

'I know.'

'The bombs are a reason for rushing things, don't you think?' She paused. 'I think about death a lot . . . I imagine everyone does. The idea of it makes me angry because I can't bear to think I might miss out on something important.'

'I thought we agreed plain text?'

There was a silence.

'We did.'

'All right . . . er . . . how do you feel about us finding a room?'

She smiled. 'I could blush. I could look away. I could refuse to answer. I could say that I've no idea what you're talking about. I could be shocked and angry.'

'Presumably at some point you'll let me know which.'

They could be dead tomorrow. That is what many thought and some said.

'Actually, I was hoping you would ask.'

Ruby and Peter were in bed, tangled together.

The hotel in which they had taken a room last night was dingy and run-down, a survivor in a terrace that had been bombed twice, one of them a serious 'incident' – as the idiom had it. The proprietor appeared to be past caring about any proprieties, and signed them in without a second glance.

'Mr and Mrs Smith,' Peter wrote.

Funnily enough, Peter's lack of originality over the name had triggered a moment of doubt in Ruby. How banal, she thought. The brilliant code master was not so brilliant at the logistics of the tryst. But even she, for all her boldness, had found some of the arrangements embarrassing – explaining to her surly land-lady that she would be away for the night, among them.

In the end, their mutual uncertainties unlocked new feelings in Ruby and touched her deeply. Peter's uninspired choice of 'Smith' may have been unpractised but it was a telling indica-tion of who he was.

As soon as they'd reached their room Peter kicked the door shut and threw his greatcoat onto the chair. 'Sure about this?'

She stood with her hands by her sides. 'Yes.'

He came and stood very close to her. 'Sure enough to tell me your name?'

The naked light bulb hanging from the centre of the ceiling shed an unflattering light over both of them.

'I'm not going to bed with a surname.'

She looked down at her khaki skirt and lace-up shoes. 'It's Ruby,' she said.

'Ruby.' His hands rested lightly on her shoulders. 'Ruby . . .'

Now, morning light showed between the blackout and the window frame. Ruby hadn't slept much, but she hadn't expected to. The sex and the unfamiliar person beside her in the unfamil-iar bed saw to that.

Ruby turned her head to look at him. One arm thrown out, he was breathing quietly.

The sheets felt gritty.

'What are you thinking?'

Peter had woken with a sigh, and a slight snort which she would have fun teasing him about.

She turned her head. 'About dust. About how you can't get rid of it.'

'So glad your mind is on the job.'

'I was also thinking about how people must feel when they wake up in France or Poland or Denmark. They must despair. I wonder if they know we think about them.'

'They won't have much energy to spare.'

'Do they know that we're trying to help?'

He didn't reply. Instead, he placed his hand on her naked stomach, his fingers straddling her hip bones in a possessive gesture. 'Rumours . . .' he began. 'Rumours are . . . are trickling in of round-ups and death camps in Eastern Europe. And in France.'

His words erased the joy and the vivid sensations of the night. They emphasized the flatness of the early morning and the prospect of a long day ahead.

Propping herself on an elbow, she said, 'Can you tell me more?'

The corners of his mouth turned down.

'I see. Secret.'

Swinging her legs over the side of the bed, she hauled herself up. It wasn't that warm and her arms were covered in gooseflesh. She looked down at her body. From that unflattering angle, her breasts appeared more meagre than usual and the line of pubic hair very marked against her white skin.

'You're so delicate, Ruby.'

Delicate? She had never thought of herself in that way. It pleased her. 'If you mean thin, I suppose that's because of the war.'

'I mean delicate, like porcelain.'

'Fragile and breakable.'

He reached over and touched her thigh. 'I wasn't talking about your mind.'

They were still awkward together, which was normal for new lovers. What's more, they were at a disadvantage because they knew so little about each other, and couldn't ask. She imagined that he might well have a fiancée or a wife tucked away somewhere, but decided that she didn't wish to know.

Ruby wrapped herself in the chenille counterpane, praying that it wasn't too grubby. 'Have you ever thought about secrecy? What it does and what it will do? For us? We can never tell our lovers, our children, our parents. Not even when we're dying.'

'Come back to bed.'

She ignored his summons and moved over to the window. 'Isn't it a little disturbing that the state can command total obedience?'

'Yes, it is. But, given so much depends on it, I willingly agree to it.'

'Even so.'

Peter stuffed the pillow behind his head. 'We probably don't know the half of it.'

She was taking down the blackout. 'I think . . . I think official silence can be like an infection. You don't know how dangerous it is until you have it.'

'Not at all,' he said. 'Infection can kill. Silence saves lives.'

'Perhaps.'

Her foot encountered the stained and chipped china pot that had been thoughtfully stowed in the corner beside the window. The sight of it made her a little queasy.

'*Are* you coming back?'

She cast aside the counterpane and climbed into bed beside him, slotting her body alongside his. 'Two spoons in a drawer,' she murmured.

Shivering a little, he wrapped the covers round them both. 'One day I'll make love to you somewhere truly hot.'

Ruby closed her eyes.

We're lucky. We're alive. We're free.

She turned round and encountered his gaze.

'You *are* different. But wonderful, bloody wonderful, Ruby.'

Was she going to bat the compliment back? Something stopped her: a grudging anger in her heart that she had nurtured since childhood, when everything – love, attention and encouragement – had been given to her brother. She wasn't proud of it, but there it was.

'You must let me compliment you, Ruby.'

'I thought you said that I was different from other women?'

He rolled over and placed a hand between her thighs. 'But

that's not different . . .' he pointed out. 'This still happens to you . . .' There was a silence. 'And this . . .'

Two hours later they arrived separately at headquarters. Ruby opted to go in first and was settled at her desk by the time Peter walked past into his office and shut the door.

Gussie could read the signs quicker than most.

'Heard the one about utility knickers?'

'No.'

'One Yank and they're off. Did you have a good evening?'

'Wonderful.'

Gussie's gaze was perfectly neutral. 'I keep a spare blouse, etcetera, in my drawer for the times when I have a good evening.'

Ruby did not blink. 'Good advice, Gussie.'

Gussie redirected her considerable energies onto the pile of paper in front of her. 'You're wanted at the briefing session this morning. It was decided before your "wonderful" evening. Otherwise I might have been tempted to think the worst.'

'Remind me after the war to make friends with you, Gussie.'

When they next checked into the dismal hotel, Peter was a man on edge.

Ruby was exhausted, too. In the office, traffic was piling up. No sooner had she decoded one incoming message than four more arrived.

They were too tired to make love. Instead, hands loosely clasped, they lay side by side in bed.

'The ceiling's cracked since we were last here,' she said.

'So it has.'

'Do you think the place is safe?'

'Good question.'

She kissed his shoulder and the pulse at his temple.

'It's very odd,' she murmured into his cheek, 'not being able to ask each other anything about our real lives.'

'When the war's over there will be plenty of time.'

She was startled. 'So this isn't just a fleeting thing?'

'No,' he said. 'Not.'

She wasn't sure about this development. The idea of being tied down was one she instinctively rejected. Sex was one thing – she thought of what had taken place in this room and the pleasure she took in Peter's company – but the issue of personal liberty was something to be considered long and hard.

'I imagined that, after the war, you would go home to a family.'

'I have no family,' he replied.

'Oh, I got that wrong.'

'You did. And it was the one question you could have asked.'

'I wasn't sure I wanted to.'

'I see.'

'No, you don't. It was a matter of . . . honour.'

'Is that what they call it?' he said. 'Isn't it that, despite your views on personal liberty and sexual freedom, you didn't want to sleep with a married man?'

She managed a tired smile.

They slept for most of the night. Ruby woke early to find Peter already awake. He was lying on his back and looking up at the ceiling.

'I'm not making headway,' he addressed it. 'How do you solve these turf wars?'

'Even in an outfit dedicated to the unorthodox?'

'Even in an outfit dedicated to the unorthodox.'

'Peter, have you considered you – we – may not be right?'

He turned his head and she read the gnawing doubts in his expression. 'All the time. But I always return to the same conclusion.' He gave an exhausted smile. 'So do you. I know you do.'

Considering someone else in a serious way did not come easily to Ruby. She had been too busy making her own way with mathematics, those sweet, non-temperamental mathematics, to expend much thought on others.

Now she was obliged to open up areas within herself – to delve into her mental boxes. Those tightly fastened boxes. Peter was making her see differently. 'Tell me.' She fumbled for the right words. '*If* it helps.'

'Ruby, Ruby . . .' What was he saying? That he needed her to listen to get it all crystal clear? 'One, we agree the poem code is insecure because it can be tortured out of agents. Two, we agree the alternative of worked-out keys is better. They can be printed onto silk squares, hidden in the agents' clothing and destroyed after use. Even though we agree – three – it would be disastrous if the Nazis begin using the same system.'

'And the idea isn't being taken up?'

Peter sighed. 'In any organization, in any group, there are always people who set their shoulder against change. In this case, our boss is the chief defender of the poem code.'

'He should be shot.' Ruby rolled over towards him. 'Listen, it beggars belief that this man won't see the benefit to agents. So, isn't the next step to make him see it would be to his own benefit? Convince him that there is something in it for him?'

'Go on thinking.'

'Is there any country you're particularly worried about whose traffic we could study?'

'Can't go into that.'

She caught a hesitation. There *was* somewhere.

'Why don't you organize production of the worked-out keys anyway?' she suggested. 'If the chiefs can't, or won't, deal with the turf wars, then we can. Because, as we have discussed, we know we're sending the agents off with faulty tools. And that's –'

'Criminal,' Peter finished the sentence for her.

For a while, there was silence in the cheap hotel bedroom. Ruby closed her eyes, opening them only when he added: 'I need proof, Ruby.'

'Let's get it, then.'

No reply.

She tried again. 'Why can't we analyse a country's traffic?

It might tell us something. I don't know quite what, but something.'

'Not a prayer. Each country's traffic is top secret, guarded with dragons and classified.'

'Which country has the least traffic? You can answer me that. Surely?'

'Denmark.' He touched her breast. 'Don't even think of it, Ruby.'

'Who are we fighting? The enemy? Or idiots on our own side?'

After a moment, he answered, 'I'm exhausted.'

Ruby joined him in staring up at the crack in the ceiling. 'To produce the worked-out keys you would need a team of girls to shuffle the numbers, a place for them to work, a supply of silk and a photographer to photograph the numbers onto the silk.' She grinned feebly. 'Not much.'

'Have you ever tried to get silk in wartime?'

'Bet Gussie knows someone in a ministry somewhere.'

Propelled by an unvoiced desire, they turned to each other.

'Peter, would we get the go-ahead if we obtain proof that the worked-out key system works?'

He touched the corner of her mouth with a fingertip. 'If there's proof, I promise . . . I promise I will drive the change through.'

The day hadn't even begun and Ruby craved nothing but sleep. Instead, she lay with gritty eyes and growling stomach and thought about Augustine and Eloise.

How could she begin to understand the inner world of the agent, a world in which, with each breath, they would be thinking: *They'll be coming to get me soon*?

Chapter Twenty

Around midnight, as Felix and the team waited at the drop zone, a night wind sprang up and blew coldly across it. He cursed and, with his torch, looked at his watch. There was a chance the plane and its precious cargo could be blown off course. Equally, clouds could blow across the moon and bugger up the navigation.

He did some warm-up exercises, blew on his hands and fingered the Browning pistol slotted into his belt.

They were six miles south-west of Køge in the direction of Haslev. One advantage of this drop zone was that there was only one serviceable route from Køge but plenty of back roads criss-crossing the terrain. Felix had taken enormous care encoding and transmitting the map coordinates, and prayed that the signals clerk at Home Station possessed sharp ears and fingers faster than Freya's.

He? She? What if the listener at Home Station hadn't had their mind on the job? What if they had been bored? Anticipating their day off? He thought about the web of connection, so delicately constructed in sound. If that bored listener at Home Station but knew it, the Morse which bounced between them bound them together tighter than any embrace.

Second time check.

Responsibility for the operation was huge. In fact, it was the biggest thing Felix had ever undertaken. The make-up of the Resistance was too changeable to categorize easily and he wasn't going to try. Instead, he concentrated every ounce of his diplomacy on manipulating the undercurrents, the clashing factions, into working cooperatively.

What had happened to the pacifist architect? For sure, the

Jette of the 'keep quiet and don't do anything' school wouldn't recognize him. What he did know was that the principles from that previous life didn't get you far in this one. Stealing, lying and killing did.

'*We are fighting this war so we don't end up like the murderers and thugs, too,*' Freya said. '*You can't put us on the same level.*'

The irony had not been lost on him. But ironies were for safe, peaceable times.

He shifted position. Underfoot, the soil was layered with slippery leaf mould that had accumulated over the winter.

His diet hadn't been so good lately and he had developed a mouth ulcer at the back of his cheek. Unwisely, he poked it with his tongue.

The minutes were passing.

Did she do her stuff? That listener at the listening station. He was now fantasizing that it was a pretty blonde. Slender and thoughtful, stooped over her wireless transmitter. That made him think of Jette again.

To think about the past was bad practice. It weakened you.

The instructors at The Firm had known what they were talking about.

He closed his eyes.

'Thou shalt not kill . . .' went the Commandment.

As instructed, Freya had passed the message concerning the drunken, loose-tongued agent onto Jacob. A couple of weeks later the message filtered back down the line: *The mustard has been wiped off the plate.*

Now, when he and Freya met, or spoke, there was a shadow cast over their dealings: *We are murderers. Long-distance ones, but murderers.* They never discussed it, but it brought them closer, and yet at the same time, paradoxically, it made each of them wary of the other.

The last time they met, Freya informed him she wanted to be part of the group at the drop zone.

'You're a security risk,' he'd replied bluntly. 'If anyone spots you, the well-known *Fru* Eberstern, it will act as a light bulb. God forbid if you were captured.'

No fool, Freya understood the argument. 'I want to see a plane from England. I want to look up into the sky and think: *This plane has come for me. It's come from my country.*'

Her eyes were wet.

'That's sentimental.'

'Yes, yes, it is.'

'Sentimentality is no use to me, Freya. And you're no use to me if you indulge in it.'

She'd uttered a rude Danish word before turning away.

Time?

As planned, his men, including Jacob, were taking up their positions and fanning out along the perimeter of the field, which was fringed with woodland. The instructions had been to leave home at staggered intervals, to make their way along a back road out of Køge, and to rendezvous by the line of larches that ran between the road and the stretch of scrubby grassland.

It had taken months to reach this point. Getting a drop organized was a miracle of painstaking piecing together of intelligence and planning. Anyway, Felix had taken the decision to avoid the worst of the Danish winter. There had been a couple of drops in the new year on Jutland and Funen which he had known about, one of which had gone wrong when the material had been lost in snowdrifts – all of which hardened his determination not to go operational until everything was as watertight as he could make it.

Casting his net as wide as was practicable, Felix had pulled in the men. One step forward, one step back, observing security procedures to the letter. Each recruit had been interviewed, either by him or by Jacob, but they did not share any names. All he knew for certain was that they represented a mixed bunch of allegiances and vested interests: communists, members of the newly formed Danish Unity Party, loners, almost certainly a criminal or two. He had had to trust his instincts, which were pretty sharp by now, but it was impossible to be absolutely sure.

Further discreet surveillance had been mounted to find out who in the Haslev police force was loyal and who had gone over to the Reich. 'Some of those bastards,' reported Jacob, 'are serving up patriots to the *Gestapomen* like hot meals.' He swiped a finger across his throat. 'We'll be waiting for them.'

The men were jumpy. Nervous. One of them urinated into the bushes and farted copiously. Knud lit a cigarette, keeping his hand cupped over the tip as he smoked it. Felix decided to let him. In the field, the cattle were spooked by the unaccustomed activity and had gathered in a restless group.

The chill wind knifed through Felix's clothing.

ETA of plane: five minutes. Miraculously, the sky had cleared, revealing a gibbous moon.

'What do you think?' whispered Jacob in his ear.

'The pilot will probably use the river to navigate and turn left at the bend.' He glanced up. 'It would be the best approach with the wind.'

One of the men materialized out of the cover of the trees and hissed: 'Something's coming.'

The trees threw shadows too dark to make out exactly what was moving along the road but the clunk of metal as the vehicle hit the winter potholes travelled through the night silence. The men melted into the trees. Felix snapped off the safety catch of the Browning. What a pitifully small weapon it was. He thought lustfully of the guns that were coming in with the drop.

Crouched down, breath held, he and Jacob watched as a bicycle with a trailer came into sight. Thickset and well wrapped up, the rider parked and flashed his torch twice. Felix relaxed. 'It's "Erik".' He signalled back, but as the torch beam hit the trailer it illuminated a cartoon pig painted on the side. He swore under his breath. If the police spotted pigs on vehicles, painted or otherwise, they asked questions.

He rose to his feet and loped over to Erik. 'Don't you know transporting pigs is forbidden?'

'It's a joke.' Erik was out of breath and reeked of herring cut with beer. 'Nazis got your sense of humour?'

'Nazis don't get jokes painted on trailers,' Felix commented sourly. 'When they don't get things, they shoot.'

Erik's hand shot out and grabbed Felix's arm. 'Remember our bargain.'

It wasn't for nothing that the motley bunch of instructors at STS, Old Tiny Tim in particular, had insisted on parachute discipline. Hands like hams, complexion the colour of claret, with a couple of black Labradors at his heels, Tiny Tim had been emphatic.

Destroy parachutes. Parachute silk is your ticket to hell.

But Erik, who had three marriageable daughters all clamouring for wedding dresses, insisted that keeping the parachute was part of the deal. 'Do you want me, or don't you?'

A van pulled up in the road, followed by a horse-drawn covered cart and both of them parked in the shadows. Leaving its owner to deal with the horse, the men spread out.

Felix counted the shadowy figures. Eight. Good. Further down the road, two others were on lookout. He had the full compliment.

As he looked around the drop zone he recalled another piece of STS advice.

Adapt to the terrain.

Ja. Ja.

Other agents in other countries had mountains and valleys, which were kind to them and made it difficult for the enemy. But Denmark? Denmark was as flat as . . . as a piece of paper.

The wind freshened.

One of the men coughed and spat before being shushed by his companion.

For the past few weeks, messages had streamed back and forth over the ether. Felix had begged London for more of everything: guns, wireless sets, money. Begged them. Gone down on his radio knees.

IMPERATIVE WE BEGIN ACTION *stop* MAYON-NAISE

Later messages spelled out the situation on the ground more clearly.

DANISH ARMY REMOVED FROM JUTLAND *stop* GERMANS TAKEN OVER ARMS DEPOTS *stop* MAYONNAISE
REPORTS OF ALUMINIUM PLANT UNDER CONSTRUCTION AT HEROYA *stop* ENEMY WILL SHIP IT THROUGH DENMARK *stop* MAYONNAISE

Plus the request.

DEVELOPMENT OF RADIO SETS PROGRESSING *stop* URGENT NEED FOR CRYSTALS *stop* MAYON-NAISE

Finally, there was the one which was written, so to speak, in blood.

MUSTARD HAS BEEN WIPED OFF PLATE *stop* MAYONNAISE

Did they understand what he was trying to tell them? *God Almighty, did they understand?*

He imagined the conversations taking place at the London headquarters. *Is Felix a firebrand? Has he read the situation correctly? Has he proved able? Is he the right leader? Should we replace him?* The bigger question: *Do we need Denmark on board?*

Smug bastards. Tucked up in London, they couldn't begin to understand how potent the mixture of rage and patriotism could be.

Were they as sleepless as he was? Did they function almost

entirely on adrenalin? Did their confidence dip? He pictured them in their smoky offices littered with paper and army-issue pencils. With the blackboards and the chalk dust and the anti-shatter tape on the window panes.

Did he trust *them*?

And yet, of course, there should be a healthy gulf between the eminences at headquarters and the Joes in the field. Asking questions ensured survival.

The moon seemed to grow brighter.

ETA: minus three minutes.

There was a faint rumble, and Felix spun round. A mutter went up from the men.

The noise grew. The throb of engines sounded above them like an echoing drumbeat.

He had forgotten how much noise an aircraft made and, for a shameful second, he was stricken with panic and an urge to flee. Responsibility for the men's lives rested with him and, if anything went wrong, he couldn't bring himself to think of the women and children who might curse him into the future.

The area vibrated with sound. Where are you? *Where are you?* In answer, a Whitley lumbered into view: nose down, Rolls-Royce Merlin engines throttled back. It gave the horse the jitters so the owner had his work cut out controlling it.

In reflex action, three torches flashed: the letter S.

'What's he playing at?' growled Jacob as the pilot failed to acknowledge the signal, flew straight across the drop zone and swooped out of sight, leaving trails of sound.

'Taking a fix,' said Felix.

Correct. The Whitley returned and circled. Once. Twice.

The torches flashed in a concerto of light.

'Go,' ordered Felix. '*Go.*'

Two parachutes bucked and jerked down towards the drop zone. Two more followed. Dandelion seeds tumbling, shaking, falling through the moonlit sky.

The noise was fit to waken the dead.

The wind slapped at Felix's face as, along with the men, he ran over the tussocky grass towards this descending manna. One by one, the containers landed with a slap and crack.

The Whitley returned for its final run. It approached, throttled back but anyone could see that it was off target. A fifth and sixth parachute tumbled out of its belly and went sailing way past the drop zone in the direction of Haslev.

But there was nothing they could do about it.

Laboriously, noisily, the plane wheeled. Then it dipped its wings in a signal from pilot to agent, homage from warrior to warrior, before flying away into a glimmering velvet sky.

'Go, go,' shouted Felix.

The men got to work, untangling the webbing, rolling up the parachutes. Weighing up to two hundred kilos each, the containers were buggers to move. But he had thought out the problem ahead of time and had instructed the men to bring wooden battens. These were now strapped onto the containers so that they could be hoisted shoulder high. In places, the turf was wet and unstable and it was touch and go to keep the load aloft.

The men poured with sweat.

Two containers were loaded into the van but proved much too long. One of the men climbed into the back and fastened the doors from the inside with his belt.

'Go!' Jacob banged on the driver's partition.

The van's engines ground into life. Felix ran back to the field. The wireless set? The precious additional wireless set which was so badly needed to supplement the one now hidden in the city. It had landed in the centre of the drop zone – a bulky thing with its own defenders and careful padding. Felix tugged and ripped at the wrappings to reveal the familiar case.

The men lifted the final container onto the cart but it was too heavy and the cart's wheels sank down into the soft ground. The horse baulked.

'*Bare rolig.*' Its owner talked to it softly.

Swearing, slipping, sliding, the men hauled the container back off the cart.

Having quietened, the horse was persuaded to wheel round to face the road while the men unpacked the container at top speed and stowed the contents in the back: guns, ammunition, plastic explosives, cigarettes.

Erik helped himself to a couple of cartons of cigarettes and threw them on top of the promised parachute which he had stuffed into his trailer. 'I've got to go.'

Upending a couple of bags of turnips, the men spread them out over the haul in the cart. The farmer swung himself onto his seat and snatched up the reins. He urged the horse into a trot and headed off towards the farm outside Haslev. There, for the time being, the arsenal would be hidden under bins of animal feed.

Felix helped to drag the abandoned container under the larches and dumped it in a patch of undergrowth – which was the best they could do for the moment.

A shout made him look up. One of the men sprinted towards Erik.

Trailer rattling, Erik was pedalling away. Far too fast. One hand rested on the handlebars while the other held aloft a flashing torch.

The hairs stood up on the back of Felix's neck. 'What the – ?'

Jacob grabbed a fistful of Felix's jacket. 'He's a *stikker*,' he shouted into Felix's ear.

Without a second's hesitation, Felix whipped out the Browning. '*Stop* him.'

Erik turned round . . . a vital second, and his mistake. The bicycle slowed. There was no time for Felix to consider, no time for due diligence, only time to react as he had been taught. He grasped the pistol in two hands, aimed and squeezed the trigger. The bullet pulsed out of the barrel. He fired a second time.

Double tap. One to fell. One to finish.

Erik toppled to the ground. The bicycle and its trailer crashed beside him, the wheels spinning madly.

Jacob ran over, knelt down beside Felix, felt for Erik's pulse and gave a thumbs-down. He scooped up the cigarettes, leaped to his feet and ran back into the trees.

The lookout posted on the Haslev road hared towards them. 'Cars!' he shouted.

A posse of headlights was moving along the road from Køge fast enough to suggest the vehicles were petrol-fuelled.

'Go!' Felix snatched up the case containing the wireless set. 'All of you. Enemy.'

One or two of the men panicked and ran this way and that.

The final container was dumped in the wood. The remainder of the team melted away between the tree trunks from where they would make for the back roads.

Erik's body lay where it had fallen.

Felix assessed his options – he had worked out escape routes earlier from the map. The lie of the land was straightforward but his problem was the moonlight which flooded the drop zone. If he could get across without being picked off, there was an irrigation channel on the other side which would provide cover.

He ran, the case tugging his arm down, banging his legs hard.

Felix was lean and hardened physically. Nevertheless, by the time he arrived at the north edge of the drop zone and rolled down into a drainage ditch, he was near blown. Crouching, he fought for breath.

Short pants. Breathe only in the upper chest.

They had joked with the instructors that that kind of breathing was practised by women in childbirth.

A convoy of vehicles, some armoured, raced down the road and slewed to a stop. Their doors were flung open, equipment extracted and guns set up. Dogs sprang onto the road.

He rested for five more seconds. A searchlight was already arcing across the drop zone. The dogs bayed. The firing began.

He assessed what he was up against: small arms, machine

guns, small pieces of artillery – textbook German tactics to throw the whole bloody lot into the melee.

He raised his head above the lip of ditch. The firing emanated from the road but he knew that it was only a matter of moments before the sharpshooters fanned out in a circle.

Haslev was the obvious place to make for and, therefore, not an option. Felix dropped his head, turned west and moved cautiously along the ditch. The searchlight moved onwards. Using the dark as cover he upped his pace. Maybe he'd be lucky.

Something punched him in the arm so hard that his vision blackened.

He had been hit.

Clutching his arm, he staggered on a few paces. The strength in his legs drained away. His head buzzed. Death eyeballed him as he fought to stay sensible.

Adrenalin punched in. Thank God. Thank God.

Think, Felix. Keep feet submerged to lose the scent.

The heavy case dragged him down. The ditch water was thick with mud. On he went, one step after another, reckoning his odds. Against him: a traitor who had given them away; two containers lost; the area crawling with *Gestapomen* and Danish police; a gunshot wound. As yet, thanks to the adrenalin, he couldn't feel much.

Think.

The dogs wouldn't know which scent to pick up first at the drop zone. That gave him one advantage.

Make for Rosenlund.

How many miles?

Far too many.

The adrenalin was thinning and pain was beginning to fan out from a red-hot centre in his arm.

His breath coming and going in agonizing bursts, his heartbeat louder in his head than the Whitley's engines had been, his arm stiffening, tightening, losing blood, he stumbled on.

*

At daybreak, case clutched in his good hand, he slid through the entrance in the north wall of the Rosenlund estate and wove unsteadily beneath the tree cover towards the pigeon loft. Once there, he moved a white feed bucket from the left-hand side of the door over to the right.

He didn't have to wait too long – but long enough – before Freya discovered him slumped against the wall.

She dropped to her knees beside him. 'Where are you hurt?'

Felix squinted at her, the pain making it difficult to control his eyelids. Lo and behold, in a tweed suit shot through with soft blues, Freya was transformed into an angel of mercy.

Already she was rolling up his shirt sleeve to expose entry and exit wounds in his right arm. They were blackened at the rim, and the surrounding flesh had puffed up.

'Where?'

'At the drop.'

She bent over to inspect the wounds more closely. 'You've caused quite a stir. Apparently, some of the containers came down in a field belonging to a farmer called Nyeman, to the north of Haslev,' she said. 'He and his wife tried to hide them but they've been arrested. Does this hurt?' She touched the area above the entry wound and he flinched. 'What happened? There's uproar. A man was killed.'

'I shot him. A *stikker*.' He pushed out the word with difficulty. 'There was no choice. Did the other men get back?'

'I don't know any more details.' She was patting and probing, and it hurt like hell. 'I don't think the bone's broken. You should see a doctor.' Freya got to her feet. 'Listen, Felix. I'm going to get some things. You have to stay conscious. Do you understand?'

He couldn't keep his eyes open.

Silence in the pigeon loft.

Where was Hector? Had he flown, his small body battling wind and German potshots?

The flickering images came and went.

Erik with his pig-painted trailer. How had he failed to spot that Erik had been a *stikker*? Or had Erik been just a brainless idiot only after what he could get? But Felix should have sniffed that out, too.

He had taken another life without due process. How many would be necessary to beat the murderers and thugs?

One of the instructors was bending over him.

Felix! Felix! If you think our methods are not cricket, remember Hitler does not play this game.

He groaned.

Freya was back, holding a basket. She lifted a bottle of water to his mouth and he drank thirstily. Then she poured antiseptic onto a handkerchief. 'Are you ready for this?'

He nodded. She dabbed at the wounds and he felt the scream bubble in his throat.

'I'm being as gentle as I can.'

'You smell so good, and I smell vile,' he managed to croak.

'Well, *I* don't mind, so be quiet.'

Freya bound up his arm with a piece of white cloth. He eased himself into a more comfortable position. 'We need to inform London.'

'Not safe at the moment,' she said. 'The place is crawling with police.'

He was unable to think . . . pain and exhaustion inched through him. The odour of ancient ammonia from long-gone pigeons combined with his own stink was making him nauseous.

'Send Hector,' Freya said. 'It's time he went. Give me a message, I'll take it down.'

Felix searched for the last drops of energy. 'Paper?'

Freya produced paper and pencil. 'I've taken to carrying these around.'

Felix dictated: 'Drop partial success *stop* lying low *stop* injured *stop* non life threatening *stop* have wireless *stop* Mayonnaise.'

The coding took more energy. Light-headed from blood loss, he struggled with the first transposition. What was he trying to say? What did he mean? *Partial success equalled bungle.*

Freya copied the letter groups onto the smallest piece of paper they could manage. Then she unlocked the cage. 'You're going home, Hector. It's been a long stay, but you must go.'

The bird's eyes were bright with apprehension. Somehow, she managed to slot the message into the carrier case and strap it round Hector's foot.

'Is he fed and watered?' he asked.

'It's a first-class hotel here.' With Hector cupped in her hands, she moved over to the door. 'Do you think he knows, Felix? Do you think he can sense England after all this time?' Her voice was hushed.

She slipped outside.

Felix rolled to his good side and peered through a crack in the slats.

It was still morning and the light was . . . he searched for the word . . . tender. Freya bent over Hector, and they seemed to be talking to each other. She touched the bird's glossy head, stroked his plumage, her finger coming to rest on the ruff at the base of the neck.

What was she saying to him?

Go well.

She tossed up her hands. For a second, Hector was in Felix's line of sight. Then, he had vanished.

Perfectly framed, Freya gazed after him and dashed a hand across her eyes.

She slipped back into the pigeon loft. 'You must stay here for the moment.' The tears had vanished and she was collected and practical. 'But you can't stay here like this.' She cupped his face between her hands. 'Listen to me, Felix. Are you taking this in? Wait here until nine o'clock tonight. Then make your way around the side of the house that overlooks the lake. The steps there lead up to my office. I'll be waiting. There's an attic above it which I've had cleared out. You can hide in there until I can make arrangements to take you over to one of our cottages on the other side of the lake.'

'I can't miss a second sked,' he said. 'Do you understand?'

'Transmit from the house?' Her voice faltered and she interlocked her fingers together tightly. 'Do you know what you're asking?'

'A lot.'

'No,' she contradicted. 'You're asking *everything . . .*'

The day passed. The pain came and went. Then it returned and stayed.

Felix tried to sort out the situation but his mind wouldn't work. He knew only three things. One: the drop hadn't gone well. Two: his arm was useless for the present. Three: he had killed a man.

When nine o'clock came, he hauled himself to his feet and began the long journey.

Spring sunlight filtered lightly through the attic window. Felix turned his head and focused on the flowered quilt that covered him. Poppies in every shade of red. The scarlet splodges floated across his vision.

How had he got here?

Concentrate.

He closed his eyes.

What could he remember?

Freya hiding the case in a chest under the window and tucking the quilt around him as he drops exhausted onto the floor.

'You must sleep.' She tilts back his head and gives him brandy from a glass. 'Drink as much as you can. I will fetch you in the morning.'

He is already a little drunk, and her touch soothes him. A little.

The image of Erik toppling over onto the road returns.

'Felix, the wireless set is in the chest. Do you understand?'

'Yes.'

Save for the pinpoint of torchlight, it is dark in the attic and Freya moves cautiously.

She bends over him. 'Felix?'

'Yes.'

'What was it like? The plane. Did it look – English?'

Opening his eyes again Felix looked at his watch: eleven o'clock. Avoiding putting pressure on his arm, he manoeuvred himself into a sitting position and propped himself against the wall.

Even in this state, the reflexes kicked in.

Never enter anywhere unless there is an escape route.

Low-ceilinged, narrow and, except for a window under the eaves, no obvious alternative route out. Sweating, he got to his feet, shuffled over to the chest under the window and stepped up onto it in order to see out of the window. A man could haul himself out onto the roof. Just. But its steep slope offered little cover.

He slumped back.

Eat. He must eat and he reached for the bread and cheese which Freya had left. At first, he retched but, after a couple of mouthfuls, his stomach quietened.

He wanted to weep. He wanted to laugh. Yesterday, he had killed. How easy it was to take a life. Send a message. Or just raise an arm and pull a trigger. But he had also flirted with death and survived.

His elation at his survival vanished when he thought of the mistake he had made with Erik. Persuaded by the neediness of the man, he forgot that the Germans paid well for information. 'My family is suffering . . .' Erik spun the story. Stinking of tobacco, his overalls threadbare, the man was obviously in trouble. 'Look at what the Germans are doing to us. I want to do something for Denmark.' It had been bad judgement on Felix's part.

Freya had left a couple of books with the food. Wincing, he picked up one – an edition of *Niels Lyhne* by Jens Peter Jacobsen, a Danish classic. Keeping his injured arm tight against his body, he managed to flip the book open at random and read:

> Something had given way in him, the night his child died. He had lost faith in himself, lost his belief in the power of human beings to bear the life they had to live . . .

He put it aside. He had to bear his life, here and now. There was no one else to help him.

He returned to the chest and stepped onto it. Outside, in the near distance, the lake glittered around the island in its centre. Beyond the lake stretched fields of arable land, dotted with a few cottages and clumps of trees. A couple of song thrushes sat in the tree to his right.

Directly beneath him was a terrace, paved with limestone flags. Various seats were positioned to catch the best view of the lake.

Voices sounded and Freya came into view below him. A pair of dogs pattered behind her. She was remonstrating with a tall, fair man whom he took to be her husband. They remained talking on the terrace for some time. Once, she laid a hand on his arm and he moved away. They continued to talk but at a distance.

Once or twice, Freya glanced up towards the window. She couldn't have known that Felix was watching. All the same, it made him feel stronger.

Around noon, he manhandled the case out of the chest. What he was doing was out of order. He was putting the house in danger. But it had to be. Those were the choices in war.

Setting it up took an age. The aerial refused to obey him,

the wire coils were unruly and he had trouble adjusting the dials.

As a result, he was a few minutes late for his sked. Placing his finger on the transmitter key, he began a stumbling transmission.

Afterwards, slumped down on the makeshift bed, he told himself that he should not have done that.

Chapter Twenty-one

In København, Hannah asked Tanne to accompany her to a meeting. 'I can't tell you what it's about. Will you come?'

'I can't,' replied Tanne. 'We've guests coming to stay tonight. My mother has . . . what I mean is, I have to help out.'

A German general was staying overnight at Rosenlund and Tanne's presence had been requested.

'I see.' Hannah fixed scornful eyes on Tanne. 'Are you sure you want to run about after your mother? Don't you think you need to be here, with us?' She thrust a pamphlet at Tanne. 'Take it home. Read it. Think.'

> When Denmark was defeated by the Prussians in 1864, the country mourned its lost territories like lost children. To many, the country was terminally weakened. Its rulers were left fractured and indecisive, a state of mind they attempted to mask by burying themselves on their estates.

Tanne winced on reading that sentence. It was close to home.

> It was a stance which underlined their refusal to face the realities. But today's younger generation refuses to accept the oppressor and will dedicate themselves to the fight. We will mount a vigil. We will take down our arms and use them. Only one path leads to freedom and **that is the path of action**.

It was signed: Nerthus, goddess of peace and fertility.

Back at Rosenlund, Birgit had spent the day taking down the damask curtains in the hall and re-hanging the antique lace summer drapes. Tanne stopped to admire the lace waterfall spilling over the newly waxed floor.

Up on the stair landing, she looked out of the window. Had she let Hannah down? Hannah thought so.

At this time of the year the outlines of the landscape were softening fast and sunlight traced gorgeous dancing patterns on the water.

Always . . . always . . . she loved the moment when new foliage unfurled and the spikes of wild narcissi and crocuses broke cover under the hedgerows and trees. They seemed almost unbearably green and vivid and this year, too, for some reason, she felt more aware of her surroundings, her eyes sharper. Her skin was more receptive to the texture of her clothes – the green wool skirt and tweed jacket that she favoured flowing coolly over her contours. Everything about her was mysteriously more sensitive to stimuli.

The sun was hitting the island. Apparently, in warm weather, Princess Sophia-Maria loved to be rowed out there, and in later years generations of Eberstern children had also made themselves master of its enchantments with picnics, games and sleepovers.

Presiding over the staircase, Sophia-Maria's portrait awaited its annual dusting. Her father would fuss. Her mother would fuss. Everyone would fuss. 'She's only a minor royal,' Tanne teased her father, more than once. 'Couldn't we have done better?'

Minor or not, Sophia-Maria – so splendid in her sumptuous court dress which, since Napoleon was ravaging Europe, was prudently embroidered with the imperial bees – held sway over this family. She had bestowed not only her ormolu clocks, jewels, furniture and china on future Ebersterns but also the constituents of her blood and her genes. In return, she apparently demanded from these innocent descendants an acknowledgement of the almost mystical link with Germany.

In her bedroom, Tanne closed the door and leaned back. Genuflecting to a past was no longer valid.

Instead, she thought of Felix.

Who was he? In one sense, the answer was easy. A man who carried a gun, transmitted messages clandestinely and disguised himself, was a spy or a soldier. But what sort of spy or soldier, and what sort of man?

Birgit knocked and entered. She had pressed Tanne's new blue dress and handed it over. '*Fru* Eberstern says you are to look your best.'

The German general and his wife were due to arrive at Rosenlund during the afternoon and to stay overnight with them. Everyone, including her mother, was tense.

Her mother . . .

Freya?

The English mother . . . with her strange quirks, such as her insistence on taking tea in the afternoons and her refusal to fight the cold in the Danish way – it had taken Kay years to accept that wearing two pairs of socks in winter boots was an efficient method of keeping the feet warm, just to cite one example. If she was honest, in her crueller moments Tanne enjoyed her mother's discomfort when she clashed against her children's innate Danishness and Danish sense of family.

Tanne hung up the frock in the cupboard, the wooden hangers on the rail clacking together. Then she checked herself. A sixth sense commanded her: *Hide Hannah's pamphlet.* Placing it in a cardboard shoe box, she stowed it at the back of the cupboard.

Her mother was nowhere to be found in the house. After a search, Tanne discovered her in the stable yard backing Loki into the shafts of the pony trap which was loaded with blankets and bottles of water.

'What on earth are you doing?'

Loki's hooves clicked on the stones. Her mother checked the harness. 'Thought I'd give Loki some exercise. He's like a buttered bun.'

'Have you got time before the exciting general arrives?'

'Would I be doing it otherwise?' said her mother.

Tanne smelled a large rat: 'I'll come with you.'

'If you want to go out, keep your father company, darling. He's driving into Køge for fertilizer, if he can get it.'

'I'm coming with you.'

'Tanne, I would like to be on my own for a bit.' Her mother threw the reins over Loki's head and hauled herself up into the trap.

Tanne looked up at her. 'The truth.'

Loki was proving skittish and her mother concentrated on controlling him. 'Tanne, you're meddling and you've no idea of . . . well, what you're doing.'

'Maybe. But try me.'

'Keep a hold on Loki.' Her mother put on her gloves and gathered up the reins.

Tanne grabbed at Loki's bridle and brought him to a standstill. 'No more evasion.' No more of the unspoken. 'I know and you know you're up to something.' She tightened her grasp on Loki. 'I'm not letting you go, *Mor*.' She paused for maximum effect. 'Or should I say *Freya*?'

'Stop it.' A tiny bead of sweat stood out on her mother's upper lip. 'Tanne, you and Nils are dearer than life,' she said. 'This is no game and I have no time. Go away, Tanne. *Go away*.'

'Move over.' So saying, Tanne swung herself up beside her mother. 'Why are you sweating?'

The reply was impassioned. 'Listen to me, Tanne. I brought you into this world, and my great responsibility in life is to you. I have to protect you, not lead you into danger.'

'Isn't it a bit late for all that?'

Her mother made a noise between a sob and a laugh.

Tanne reached over and kidnapped the reins from her mother. 'Walk on, Loki.' Loki moved forward. 'I'm learning that life is precarious . . .'

'You're too young, Tanne.'

'. . . Learning it fast, too. This war is dangerous. Therefore we can't avoid danger. Where are we going?'

Her mother sounded desperate. 'But you haven't lived yet, or even seen the world.'

Cunning and sophistry were what Tanne needed – certainly for the new kind of morality she was discovering. 'I was born to find my own feet.'

'Go back to the house. Please. I couldn't bear it if you were involved.'

Tanne shot her a look. She understood . . . or thought she did . . . that, for a parent, to work alone was much easier because it would be unendurable to watch a child suffer.

'You have done your job, *Mor*.' Tanne pressed home her point. 'We can share this.'

'God help me,' she murmured.

It flashed across Tanne's mind that the balance of power between parent and child was never meant to remain constant and this was the moment when it shifted.

'Where to?'

Her mother stared ahead.

'Where to?'

Again the noise between a sob and a laugh. 'The steps to my office and then on to Ove's cottage. It's been empty since he left for Germany.'

'Listen to me,' said Tanne, as she concentrated on turning the trap round. 'I've no idea what you're doing but I can help and I *should* help. I know every building, every path, every fox and chicken here. Every pig. Every rut in the road. And I know them better than you.' Her mother's eyes glistened with sudden tears. 'You need me. I let you baby me, *Mor*. For too long, perhaps. But it's time to be realistic. Isn't it?' Her mother wiped a hand across her eyes. 'Isn't it?'

Her mother sighed raggedly and gave in. 'It is, Tanne.'

The die was cast.

'So what's happening?'

On viewing Felix, his arm swollen, slumped against the wall in the attic, Tanne was afraid. He looked dreadful: pallid, bruised under the eyes and unsteady on his feet. The pair of them took turns to keep watch and thus it was a slow, agonizing process to manhandle him down the steps and into the dog cart.

'Get the case, darling . . .' Her mother was hauling on the reins and Tanne gasped at its weight as she stowed it beside Felix.

Tanne took charge of the driving. 'Go, go, Loki.' She urged him into a brisk trot and followed the cart track around the perimeter of the lake. From time to time they hit a rut and Felix groaned. Tanne ached to hold him . . . help him . . . do anything.

Ove's cottage came into view. It was half a mile or so from any of the other cottages and partly hidden by trees. It had been a clever choice. Versed in Rosenlund's schedules, Tanne knew that changeover day for tenants was 1 November or 1 May so the cottage would remain empty until November.

If it was secluded, it was without running water or electricity. But Tanne was confident that, thanks to her father's insistence on a roster of building maintenance for the cottages, it would be in reasonable condition.

But for a table and a bench, it was empty of furniture. There was not even a bed. They coaxed a by-now-semi-conscious Felix inside and laid him in the downstairs area on the floor.

Tanne fussed with a rug. 'He needs a doctor.'

'Not safe.' Her mother cut her off.

Tanne was almost breathless at the thought of Felix's discomfort. 'But he *needs* one. Look at him,' she pleaded. 'Let me fetch Dr Hansen.'

'Too risky. We don't know what Hansen thinks.'

Fear sharpened Tanne's tongue. '*You* don't, *Mor*. We do. His family have worked with our family forever and he's known us all our lives. We live in the same community.'

Felix was muttering unintelligibly.

'Hand me the other rug, will you?' Her mother wrapped it round a restless Felix.

Tanne watched her. 'I know we could trust Hansen.'

Hustling her into a corner, her mother hissed into Tanne's ear: 'You said you wanted to grow up. Yes?' Her tone softened, and she caressed Tanne's cheek. 'I believe you. But have you any idea what war does to people? It's good that you have such faith, really good. But even the best can act completely out of character and do terrible things when they or their loved ones are threatened.'

'Doctors don't take sides,' Tanne said, stubborn and unconvinced.

'I am afraid we've no option.'

Her mother returned to Felix. Tanne watched as she gently inserted a third rug under his wounded arm to make him more comfortable and made him drink a mouthful of water.

Her terror was that he would die – of wounds, or infection, or exhaustion.

But this wasn't the time or place to get emotional. A flush spread over Tanne's face, a shamed one. She and her mother had to deal with the situation and, despite never having had to face such a challenge in her privileged life before, she must rise to it.

Felix drank gratefully. 'Do you think you can work the set?'

Her mother nodded. 'Just.'

'Listen carefully. "Fish, stream, light, shine and kiss".'

'Got them,' she said.

'Repeat.'

Her mother recited them almost gaily. 'See! It'll be fine, Felix.'

The sight of Felix trying to concentrate affected Tanne and she was forced to look away.

'This is against every rule in the book but it's yours now . . .'

He had to pause between words. 'The poem they come from was handed to me by a bloody genius in London who would shoot me if he knew what I was doing. Use it until we organize something else, until I can get word to London.' He moved his head restlessly. 'But not from here. The listeners will have clocked the location. Do it somewhere else. Understand? Not here.'

'You're not to talk any more.'

'Tell them we're going off air for the time being.'

He looked so ill.

Her mother looked at her watch. Time to go. 'I'm going to hide the wireless,' she said. 'Stay here with him.'

Ten minutes later she reappeared. 'Done.'

They left Felix wrapped in the blanket.

'The general will be here in an hour,' said her mother as she steered Loki into the stable yard. 'Tanne . . . I've got to get ready.'

They looked at each other – two women with traces of blood on their hands and clothing. Tanne's throat constricted. Why hadn't she ever seen that she and her mother were cut from the same cloth?

'Go and change,' she said, her mind rapidly sorting out options. 'I'll see to things. Tell them you'd made a mistake about me and I had been invited out to a dinner in Køge all along which I could not get out of. I'll take food and aspirin over to him.'

Her mother raised a sceptical eyebrow.

'*Mor*, I'm in this now.'

Maybe she could make up for the fact that so far she had shamefully ignored the reach and compass of this war?

Her mother seized Tanne's hand. 'Lives depend on this. Yours, his, mine.'

An hour later Tanne cycled up Køge's main street and dismounted outside the chemist.

There was a queue for his services. On a normal day, Tanne enjoyed watching the pharmacist deploy his dark blue medicine bottles and count out the pills.

The queue shuffled forward.

Eventually, the pharmacist turned to Tanne and she requested aspirin and antiseptic powder, explaining that the friend with whom she was having supper had cut her hand chopping the beetroot.

'It could be nasty,' she said.

The pharmacist listened to Tanne carefully. 'Could be *nasty*, *Frøken* Eberstern?' It was a marked emphasis. He paused. 'It's important you bathe the wound in boiled water, disinfect it and apply a sterile dressing.' Tanne piled the packages into her basket and he added, 'And *Frøken* Eberstern, if your friend is running a temperature, she must take aspirin every four hours.'

Startled, she looked up from her basket but the pharmacist was busy pouring out cough syrup for the next customer.

Mor, I do know these people.

Finding Dr Hansen was not easy. Tanne was forced to cycle several miles around the town, chasing his progress from patient to patient. She caught up with him on the outskirts of Køge.

He was getting into his car.

'Dr Hansen!'

He turned. Dapper as always with his bow tie, he was clearly exhausted with his work load yet, on seeing Tanne, he gave a little bow. Their friendship had been forged over chicken pox and split knees, not to mention the episode when, furious at a reprimand from her mother, she had climbed up the haystack and fallen out of it. '*Frøken* Tanne?'

'Dr Hansen, could you come and look at someone?'

'What's the matter with them?'

She glanced over her shoulder. 'It's urgent.'

He didn't reply at once but leaned up against the car.

'Dr Hansen?'

'It had better be urgent,' he said.

'It is. I'll cycle ahead.'

At the north entrance to the Rosenlund estate, she motioned for him to stop and wind down the window. 'I'm afraid you'll have to walk from here. I'll put your case in my bicycle basket.'

Dr Hansen fingered his bow tie. 'What is this?'

Suddenly, she was uneasy.

You don't know people in war.

'I thought you understood.'

'No,' he said flatly. 'I don't.'

'*Please.*'

'What makes you think I'm willing to participate in whatever this is? What makes you presume? I thought you must have a friend in trouble, drunk or something, who was anxious their parents weren't involved.'

She made an effort to open the car door. 'Dr Hansen, someone is in trouble.'

He prevented her. 'I'm a doctor and I can't take risks.'

'You're a doctor.'

'*Frøken* Tanne, you are very naive.'

'Not too naive to know when to help.'

Finally, white with rage, he got out of the car. 'You've put me in an impossible position. I'll ask no questions, and you will not talk to me except to tell me what is essential. And I don't want to know where I'm going. Understood?' He wrenched off the bow tie and fashioned a blindfold.

'If that's what you wish.' Tanne grabbed his doctor's bag, took him by the arm and led him through the trees.

The room in Ove's cottage was frowsy with the smell of infection but Felix was awake, if feverish. She helped him to take off his shirt and held his hand.

Dr Hansen worked in silence, examining and probing, and did not look at Felix in the face. Finally, he asked Tanne to pass him the scissors from his bag. 'This will hurt.'

As he cut the flesh away from around the bullet's entry and exit wounds, Felix's fingers crunched down on Tanne's.

She made herself watch.

Once he cried out.

'Look at me,' she commanded him, smiling, smiling. 'Keep looking at me.'

Dr Hansen addressed the floor. 'The wound's infected but I think the bone's intact. I'll stitch you up.'

He poured surgical spirit over his handiwork, stood up and turned his back. 'You're lucky. Your arm functions will be fine. But you'll need to rest it for a month. You're likely to have a temperature for a day or two, then you should be fine. *Frøken* Tanne, scrub your hands in disinfectant and dress the wounds every twenty-four hours until the scars begin to turn pink. Then allow the air to get to them as much as possible.'

He packed his bag fast and furiously. 'Take me back to the car. I don't wish to hear from you again.'

'Dr Hansen?' This man was as removed from the pleasant, kind doctor from her childhood as it was possible to be. 'Dr Hansen?'

At the doorway, he stopped and put on the blindfold. 'You have been very stupid, *Frøken* Tanne.'

'Shush, he'll hear.' She pulled the doctor outside.

He hissed into her ear: 'There's only one doctor in this area and that's me. What happens if I go?'

Was he right? Was he wrong?

Her stomach lurched but the iron was creeping into her soul. 'I'm taking you back now,' she said and he would not mistake her contempt. 'There's no need for us to speak to each other again.'

On her return, Felix fixed his eyes on her. 'Get out of here.' 'Don't talk.'

She fetched a bottle of lemonade that she had bought in Køge and made him drink it down with two aspirins. 'You're to take two every four hours. It's not much, but something.'

He managed to smile through lips cracked with thirst. 'Do you know what I would love?'

She bent over him. 'Tell me.'

'A banana.'

Was he delirious? 'I'm going to leave you now to fetch food and drink.' She tucked the blanket back over him. 'You must stay quiet.'

As she promised him, she returned in the early evening, creeping into the cottage. Felix was asleep and the blanket had slipped to reveal the smooth, brown flesh of his uninjured shoulder.

She wanted badly to touch that smooth, brown flesh but she contented herself with kneeling down beside him and tucking the blanket around him. He was burning up. His eyes flicked open.

'It's only me.'

'Miss Only-Me,' he muttered. 'But you shouldn't be here.'

She had brought bread, cheese, a small pot of honey and some early strawberries. She shook out two aspirin and propped him up so he could swallow them. 'You need food. Sorry I took so long,' she added. 'My parents are giving dinner to a German general and his wife. I have to be careful. I should be up there entertaining him.'

'Oh, good,' he murmured. 'You can crack a joke, then.'

Carefully, she eased him up against the wall and fed him little hunks of bread and cheese, followed by the strawberries which she dipped in the honey. 'The honey should give you strength.'

'Thank you.' He tried to sit up but failed.

A little later he asked, 'Are you leaving me?'

'No,' she said. 'I'm staying.'

This was her vigil. For Denmark. For her call to arms.

For Felix.

During the night, his fever worsened. Tanne forced him to swallow more aspirin but he vomited them up almost immediately. At intervals, she bathed his face and wrists while he twitched and groaned. Once, he demanded her name. 'But not your real name.'

When she went outside to the water butt to refill the jug, an almost full moon dominated a star-filled sky and there was a beautiful velvety feel to the air. On a second trip, she gave herself a bad fright imagining that she heard footsteps moving through the undergrowth. Jug in her hand, she remained rooted to the spot. *Do not faint.* With a struggle she brought herself under control.

Back inside, she saw that Felix had woken up.

'Don't look,' she said as she took off her trousers and rolled them up to make a pillow for him.

She lay down beside him.

'Talk to me, Miss Only-Me, but nothing personal.'

How's that possible? she wanted to say. *Every single thing is linked. Me, you, my mother, the war. my father, Rosenlund.*

'The other day a pig was due to be killed,' she began. 'The butcher called in was sworn to silence. He was so skilled the pig barely squealed. Everyone was concerned that someone would hear and tell the authorities. As you know, all pigs are supposed to go to the Germans.'

'I feel sorry for the pig.'

'But he died painlessly and he was useful. He was turned into hams, sausages and salami, and his blood was used for black pudding. Bits of him were salted and made into brawn. And soap. You've no idea how exciting that was. You boil the skin in the copper for several hours, and eventually it turns into liquid soap perfect for washing floors.'

Beside her Felix was shaking. Concerned, she propped herself up on an elbow. 'Are you feeling worse?'

He turned a drained face to hers. To her astonishment, he was laughing. 'What stuff to entertain a wounded man! Most women would have gone on about fluffy rabbits and Erik the Viking.'

After that, he seemed more comfortable and fell asleep

again. His chin was stubbled and his lips fever dry – even so he appeared younger than when he was awake.

Tanne lay with her head turned towards him. She knew for a certainty that this was a precious night, a moment which she would wish to be stamped on her memory, and she refused to waste it in sleep. Her previous terrors had dissipated. She was young, and becoming increasingly bold, and the unknown and amazing adventure of life beckoned.

Carefully, so as not to disturb Felix, she fitted her body along the length of his, to prevent him from rolling onto his injured arm. Occasionally, she put out a hand to restrain him, permitting herself to let it rest on his torso . . . shoulder . . . hip.

Before she fell out of love with Aage, she had spent a night with him so she was not innocent. This wasn't the same. The interlude with Aage had been fun, very physical and transient. This . . . this guarding of Felix possessed an intimacy, almost a spiritual significance, and his weakness moved her profoundly.

She shifted position. A familiar pain lodged in her lower abdomen and dug in. Tanne grimaced. With immaculate timing, her period had arrived.

The pain growled. Illness. Doctors.

Dr Hansen?

Had she been stupid?

Despite her intentions, Tanne fell asleep. When she awoke, at dawn, she was stiff and exhausted. The floor smelled of pine and, for a second, she imagined it was the Christmas log burning at Rosenlund.

Then she realized she was the only one occupying the rug and she jerked upright. 'Are you all right?'

Incredibly, Felix had heaved himself over to the window and was keeping watch. 'I thought it best to let you sleep.'

He eased round and leaned against the wall.

Brushing back her hair, she reached for her trousers, and shielding her underwear as best she could she wriggled into them.

'Thank you for getting me through the night.'

She fastened her waistband. 'I wanted to make you as comfortable as I could.'

Scrambling up, she walked over to him and laid a hand on his forehead. He was still feverish. 'You must lie down again. You need to rest.'

He let her help him down to the floor and pull the blankets over him, then he swallowed the aspirins she gave him with a mug of water.

Tanne picked up her basket. 'I'm glad the doctor saw to you.'

'So am I. Thank you.'

'But I'm worried. I'm not sure he's on our side.'

Felix got it at once. 'So he might talk?'

'He might. I don't know. He wasn't pleased. Look, you might as well know. I had to bully him.'

If she expected anger she had got Felix wrong. 'It happens,' he said. 'More than you think.'

'I was so sure Dr Hansen was a friend. But now I'm not. I'm sorry.' The confession was pathetic, and she hated the sound of herself making it.

Felix moved restlessly and, crouching over, Tanne tried to still him. 'Is the pain bad?'

'Yes . . . yes . . .' He clutched at her hand. 'But that's not the point. We have to get out.' He closed his eyes. He was gathering his forces. 'We've got to get out. *Now*. Do you understand?'

'Shush . . .' She stroked his cheek. 'Shush.'

He gazed up at her with fever-bright eyes. 'You don't understand. We can't stay here any longer.'

'*We?*'

Felix tested the injured arm, stretching it out and clenching his fingers. 'If you're right, you're compromised.' He winced. 'We'll have to get out and lie low.'

Tanne thought of the stories she had heard from her friends. Flight. Hiding. Capture. She shivered. The finger of war was now pointing at her.

Chapter Twenty-two

Leaving Tanne in the stable yard, Kay had got herself up to the bedroom to change.

Punctual to the minute, the Gottfrieds arrived at Rosenlund and Kay gave them tea on the terrace. It was warm, the new foliage on the trees looked radiant and the birds were nesting. Afterwards, Kay took them on the promised tour of the house and the gardens.

The general studied the portrait of Sophia-Maria and turned to Bror. 'The Führer would appreciate the brotherhood between us.'

Down at the lakeside, Ingrid pointed over the bright sun patterns on the water to the island. 'It's like something out of a fairy tale,' she said.

As the party strolled back to the house, a car crunched over the gravel in the drive.

'Are you expecting more visitors?' asked the general.

'My cousin Anton,' replied Bror. 'He heard you were coming to dinner and we were delighted to ask him to join us. He's probably bringing over flowers . . . his are quite famous. He likes to supervise their arrangement.'

Bror sounded the genial host but, in fact, he had been livid. At the last minute, Kay told him that Anton had invited himself to the dinner, explaining that Anton was friendly with the general, too. In fact, she had rung Anton and given him the tip-off.

'You want him here, Kay? Is that it?'

It wasn't Anton who waited for them by the front steps but Sergeant Wulf, Constable Juncker and an unknown SS officer.

Had they found him?

Tanne? How could she protect her?

What if they searched the house?

More than anything, she wanted to hold Bror's hand and to feel safe once more.

Instead she masked her tumult with a serene smile. Stick to Felix's rules.

Be brief. Be boring. Speak pleasantly and say nothing.

If Constable Juncker was a youth on a self-declared sacred mission to heal Denmark, the shinily booted SS officer looked a far more serious proposition. He and General Gottfried exchanged the barest of unenthusiastic greetings. Kay took notice. She had been right: the Nazis fought each other.

Sergeant Wulf did his best with the introductions. 'May I introduce *Hauptsturmführer* Buch. He's joined us from København.'

Hauptsturmführer Buch inclined his head.

Whey-faced, a little shifty, Sergeant Wulf looked a wreck, and his uniform needed a press. It was noticeable that, having lost so much weight, his leather belt had been hitched in by several notches.

'*Hr* Eberstern, *Fru* Eberstern,' he began. 'Can you tell us where your daughter is?'

'Our daughter? Has something happened?' Kay needed to be astonished – and was.

'She's not here,' Bror replied. 'Although it's none of your business.'

Constable Juncker cut across Sergeant Wulf. 'Who with?'

Kay noted the *Hauptsturmführer* covertly observing the general.

Grab a few seconds to think. Kay patted her hair. 'She's with her cousins. But, really, our daughter is an adult and doesn't account to us for her movements.'

The general's gaze settled on Kay's face.

She willed herself not flush. She willed her heart to behave itself so she could remain cool and think quickly on her feet.

This was what fear felt like. Primal fear. The dry mouth. A skipping heartbeat.

'Your reasons for this visit?' Bror was asking.

Hauptsturmführer Buch was polite. 'There has been a report that someone answering her description has been aiding a terrorist.'

'How outrageous,' Kay went to stand beside Bror.

Bror said, more or less pleasantly: 'I must ask you to leave.'

Ingrid turned to her husband. 'Franz, should we go in and change for dinner?'

'General, Ingrid, I apologize for this intrusion,' said Kay.

'Just a minute.' The general drew *Hauptsturmführer* Buch aside and the two men conferred. The evening sun slanted onto the braid and brass of the uniforms. In the trees, the birds were beginning to roost. The scene possessed a dreamy, shimmery, peaceful quality which Kay had seen a thousand times.

Bror shoved his hands into his pockets.

She thought of the evening ahead – and of the huge effort it was going to take to behave normally.

But do it she would.

Hauptsturmführer Buch broke away from the general and said, '*Hr* Eberstern, you will forgive us for disturbing you. The General has persuaded us that we must have made a mistake.'

The general's eyes rested thoughtfully on Kay.

Dressed in the lace dinner gown and the family pearls, Kay took a long look in the mirror to assess the results. Good enough to please a German general? Good enough to deceive Bror?

Reflected in the mirror, the bed caught her eye. It gave her painful pause. These days she was its only occupant. A half-occupied bed was, as she had discovered, full of ghosts.

Bror knocked, entered and went straight to the point. 'What's going on?'

Kay sprayed her neck with scent. 'A stupid mistake. It happens all the time, I imagine.'

'Is there something you're not telling me?'

She lifted her shoulders in a tiny shrug. 'Of course not.' She twisted round to look at him and fiddled with the hairbrush, which had not been touched by Bror for weeks. 'I wish we didn't have to entertain.'

'You mean entertain Germans.'

She allowed herself to say, 'No, I mean I wish we had the evening to ourselves.'

Bror's face softened momentarily. Did he remember that, in the old days, they often went out together into the evening sunlight? Very often he would make her laugh. She would take his arm.

She curled an escaped tendril of hair round her finger, tucked it into her chignon and searched for her evening handkerchief in the drawer. Mundane actions steadied her.

'So, where is Tanne?'

Where?

'I forgot to tell you. Mai Federspiel rang up. They're having a *fester-cousine* party and wanted Tanne. I told her to go. Tanne didn't want to have dinner with a stuffy general.' Kay stood upright and brushed down her dress.

'Why is Anton here?'

She didn't reply.

'He's here for you, isn't he?'

Still, she said nothing.

'Christ, Kay . . .'

Under her long gown, one of her knees trembled with the enormity of what she was doing. She folded up the evening handkerchief and tucked it into her sleeve. 'If you want to believe that, do.'

'Kay, I'm not prepared to go on like this.'

She would have done almost anything to avoid causing the

pain in that blue, storm-filled gaze. She focused on his shoulder. 'Not now, Bror. I have the guests to see to. Your guests.'

He turned on his heel. 'You're right. I want to say that I'm aware that the Gottfrieds being here is the last thing you want to cope with, but I'm grateful.'

Bror was never less than generous.

'It's my job,' she replied. 'And it's Birgit's and that of the others who do the cleaning and iron the bed linen.'

He banged the door shut behind him.

She waited before following him. Fists scrunched. Pressing her nails hard into the fleshy part of her thumb. Summoning anger to conquer fear.

As dapper as ever, Anton arrived. Kissing Ingrid's and Kay's hands, he presented them each with a bouquet of peonies and roses. During drinks on the terrace, he drew the general aside and they talked intently.

When the party moved into the dining room, Kay managed to manoeuvre Anton aside. 'We might have a problem.' She outlined the situation and Anton's eyes narrowed.

They sat down at the table. With Birgit occupied in the kitchen, Else had been drafted in to serve. Nerves and inexperience made her clumsy and the pea soup that she was offering to the general slopped over the tureen. Kay took pity, rescued Else and offered it to the general herself. He wasn't at all put out.

'That was kind, *Fru* Eberstern.' He spooned up the soup. 'But I suspect you are a kind person.' He smiled most charmingly. 'Were you the sort of child who nursed wounded animals?'

'General, you're very sweet.'

Anton, Bror and Ingrid being deep in a hunting conversation, the general was free to turn his full attention onto Kay. As she had noted, he was an elegant eater with good manners and he apologized for the earlier visit of the police. 'I hope my colleagues didn't appear too heavy-handed.'

'They were doing their job,' said Kay. 'You can't blame them for that.'

'I was right. You are a kind person.'

It was almost amusing. The general – 'Why don't you call me Franz?' – shamelessly picked her brains about Britain. Did most people have a wireless set in their homes? Was it true that the iron railings in the cities had been smelted down to make weapons? Kay replied that he was probably better informed than she was.

The general picked up his wine glass. 'Perhaps.'

He talked a little of Germany and, reluctantly, of his childhood, saying: 'My upbringing was not what you might expect.'

'Have you seen any more of this country since we last met, General . . . er, Franz?'

She disliked using his Christian name.

'I've been to Randers and Aarhus. As you will know, we have a headquarters in Aarhus.'

'Oh, surely the headquarters is in København?'

'We have bases in a lot of places. As I mentioned before, we're not loved and it's necessary to have a full complement of staff in many places.'

Why was he giving her this information?

But he was and Kay listened carefully. 'Aarhus University is a good place for our archives . . . and that's no secret, by the way.' He smiled at Kay. 'No doubt terrorists will target it but I should say at once that, given the high calibre of our men, any resistance in the area is pretty much doomed.'

Else had better luck serving the beef medallions and the general helped himself to several pieces. Kay picked at hers while he talked in glowing terms about his unit. 'I have a pedigree team with hard soldiering and specialist training behind them. Unlike the cynical and sceptical reservists, they're committed.' He went on to say that reservists were a big problem for the crack units such as his.

So, she thought, the general was relying on reserves, which suggested there was a shortage of troops.

'It's not straightforward,' he continued. 'We're trying to pin down enemy agents who we know are operating on Zealand and elsewhere.'

Bror had been listening and cut in: 'We're too busy trying to keep the farms going for that sort of thing here.'

Ingrid looked uncomfortable and she laid down her knife and fork.

Kay pressed the general. 'How can you track the terrorists?'

He clearly enjoyed the technical aspects of the work. 'An agent gets hold of a wireless transmitting set. He, or she, is given a call sign, say, ABC, and a frequency on which to transmit. They are instructed to transmit four or five times a week but it takes them over five minutes to do that, which means we can get a fix on where they are holed up . . .'

What were the general's motives for coming to Rosenlund? Curiosity? He knew she was British and almost certainly held conflicting loyalties. It was possible he held intelligence on the Ebersterns. However, a simple explanation was also possible. Simple explanations should never be overlooked. Was it that, for some reason – perhaps the upbringing he had been reluctant to talk about – the general and his wife felt they were outsiders and warmed to Bror and herself, also the outsider?

At his end of the table, Anton kept a weather eye on them both.

'And if you capture an enemy terrorist?'

'As I believe I mentioned before when we spoke about this at the theatre,' he said, 'in Signals and Intelligence we never waste good material.' A finger tapped gently on the table. 'Most people have a price. It's a question of finding out what. How we do it is up for debate. But we had – we have – a captured terrorist who . . . er, has decided to cooperate, which means we can talk to each other as adult to adult. I have a different approach from my colleagues in the SS, who are more draconian.' He shot Kay a look – cunning, rueful, slightly apologetic. 'That's not to say we're soft.'

Kay touched her lips with her napkin.

A captured terrorist who decided to cooperate. Kay combed over her meagre stockpile of information. Who could it be? Besides Vinegar were there other wireless transmitters operating in Zealand? She didn't know for sure. But she did know that Felix had been trying to find out where he was.

'Kay . . . ?' The general wanted to know if she needed her water glass filled.

'Thank you . . . no.'

She imagined one of those brutal concrete buildings in which the Gestapo operated, the rooms filled with those who did not cooperate – and those who did but who almost certainly ended up the same.

Under the table, she clenched her napkin between fingers that felt numb.

'Human beings are predictable, wouldn't you say? Whatever their philosophy or religion,' continued the general, 'they have an inbuilt desire to please. It's a question of finding the trigger. If you can convince an enemy agent that it would be better for the world, for their family, for them, if they cooperate, you can usually get results.'

'A sophisticated approach, General.'

She caught Anton's eye.

'We often know where an agent is operating but we don't bring them in because we like to watch them. If you're too quick, the network scatters, which is no use.'

Kay couldn't bear it any longer. 'Heavens,' she said, lightly. 'I'll have to be careful when I'm on the phone. Just in case your men are listening in.'

'I apologize. I have been talking shop.' He was all charm. 'Did you know I have been in touch with your son?'

'Nils! How did that happen?'

Anton intervened. 'I was in a position to help,' he said. 'I took Franz to see him.'

Anton. How dare he? How could he? Kay shot him a furious look. In reply, he raised an eyebrow. *Trust me.*

She pulled herself together. 'I hope Nils behaved himself.'

'Politeness itself. He agreed to help us.'

Very carefully, Kay placed her crumpled napkin on the table. 'Did he have any option, Franz?'

'We are not complete bullies, Kay. He's a very interesting, extremely brilliant young man, a credit to his parents.'

'Are you interested in mathematics?' she asked.

'Let us say only in its applications,' he replied.

'I knew it, Franz . . .' Kay sent him a sweet, but treacherous, smile. 'You are a Renaissance man.'

The phone rang in the hall. It was for the general.

'I'm so sorry,' he said on his return into the room, 'but I've been summoned to Berlin. I'm afraid Ingrid and I will have to leave before dawn. A plane has been sent to København.'

The evening continued – a slow and heavy endurance test. Eventually, Anton kissed Ingrid's hand in the most charming fashion, complimented the general on his knowledge of wine and said goodnight to Bror. Kay accompanied him to the front door.

'Why introduce Nils to him?' she hissed. 'What are you doing?'

He pressed her hand meaningfully. 'I've cut the telephone line,' he said, kissing her cheek.

A little while later Kay and Bror escorted their guests to their bedroom. The Gottfrieds were effusive in their thanks. 'There's no need to wake you in the morning,' said Ingrid. 'Franz and I are quite used to early morning getaways.'

Kay led the way back down the corridor.

'Goodnight,' said Bror outside the bedroom. He glanced at his shoes, polished to mirror brightness. 'Thank you.'

'Goodnight, Bror.' She watched him walk away.

*

Kay awoke with a start. Downstairs there were noises signalling departure, followed by a car moving carefully down the drive. She peered at her clock. It was five a.m. and she sank into exhausted sleep.

Again, she was pulled abruptly back into consciousness. Someone was in the room, searching in her drawers.

'Tanne!'

Tanne whirled round. 'Sorry, *Mor*. Didn't mean to give you a fright. I need some underwear.' She frowned. 'You will know why . . . so inconvenient. I've taken some of your things. I thought I shouldn't risk going to my room if the general was in the guest room.'

'He's gone. Thank heavens.' In a flash, Kay was out of bed. 'Listen, darling, you can't be here. The police and an SS officer came looking for you yesterday.' She searched Tanne's face. 'Someone –'

'Dr Hansen . . .' Tanne sat down heavily on the bed. 'I knew it.' She clutched her stomach as she confessed what she had done. 'How stupid I've been. How –'

'No time for that now . . . Listen to me. Think. Did Hansen know which cottage?'

Tanne exhaled with an audible hiss. 'Not really. He may have an idea but he was blindfolded. But he didn't want to know, *Mor*. That's why I thought we would get away with it.'

Think.

'Dr Hansen . . . if it was him . . . will have told them it's one of the cottages on the estate but won't know which one. That buys time. An hour or so, three at the most, to get Felix up and running. Get back to the cottage and stay there until I can work out how to get you away.' She glanced at the clock. 'Birgit and Else will be here soon to make breakfast. No one must see you. Understand? I've told them you were with cousins and explained to your father that you went to stay with the Feder-spiels at the last minute. Let's get you some food.'

So saying, Kay flung on a pair of trousers and a jersey and they made for the back stairs. In the kitchen, she stoked up the stove, put the kettle on and packed a basket with bread and cheese.

The kettle boiled and Kay made Tanne drink some tea.

Don't ever pass up the opportunity to eat or drink.

Tanne had never seemed so beautiful. Or so focused. Or so alive. Or so beloved.

Kay refilled the cup and, pressing Tanne to eat a slice of bread and honey, watched her like a hawk as she did so.

How did resistance work?

Intelligence.

Surprise.

Attack and get out. Never hang around to defend.

'Tanne, can you memorize this and tell Felix?' She ran over the conversations with the general – captured agents, the Aarhus archive . . . 'The RAF might want to bomb it. Tell Felix, too, that they may have Vinegar. Can you remember that?'

Tanne burst out laughing. '*Mor*, never in my wildest dreams did I imagine you and I would be doing this.'

'Don't make a noise.' She pulled Tanne to her and kissed the tousled head. 'You must take care, my darling daughter. You'll have to live differently now. Be watchful. Ultra careful and discreet. Get yourself to the Federspiels. They'll look after you. Promise.'

Tanne held up a hand. 'Listen,' she whispered.

Vehicles were rolling up the drive.

Kay edged over to the window. This time there was the black car plus a couple of military vehicles. They parked. The doors were opened to release a posse of soldiers with dogs.

A dreadful certainty hardened.

'You're blown, Tanne. Leave – now! Never, ever, come back here until the war is over. Get out of Denmark. Go to Sweden. Do you understand?'

Tanne dropped the slice of bread she was holding. 'It's my fault.'

Down the passage, Sif and Thor began to howl.

'*Do you understand?*'

Tanne had gone chalk white.

'Tanne, concentrate.'

'*Mor*, forgive me.'

Think, Kay.

Wireless set.

'Tell Felix I'll deal with the wireless set. Don't take it with you.'

Were there any traces of Felix in the attic room?

'Forgive me . . .'

'Go,' Kay hissed. 'Get out the side door. Leave the cottage. Felix will know what to do.'

'*Mor* . . .'

'Of course I forgive you.'

Tanne ran.

Kay slipped up the back stairs and into her bedroom, ripped off the trousers and jersey and got into bed.

She had only seconds to spare. Bror was already at the bedroom door. 'Kay, can you come downstairs?'

No need to hurry. She took her time to put on her dressing gown and to brush her hair. Descending the stairs, she was confronted by *Hauptsturmführer* Buch, Sergeant Wulf and Constable Juncker in the hall and, beyond them in the drive, the men and the dogs.

An enraged Bror was remonstrating with Buch. Looking wretched beyond belief, Sergeant Wulf had distanced himself from the Germans. Bror looked round. 'There you are. Darling, these men want to search the house.'

The morning sunlight threatened to dazzle every wit Kay possessed. Sif and Thor surged into the hall followed by a goblin-eyed Else, who took one look and bolted up the stairs. Where was Birgit?

'*Search* the house?' She frowned. 'Do they have the authority?'

Outside, the tracker dogs barked and strained at the leashes.

These were dogs which lusted after their quarry. They were dogs that would run fast and fierce.

Sif and Thor joined in. Buch snapped his fingers at them and, to Kay's astonishment, they quietened. 'We won't take up too much of your time.'

'So I should hope,' said Bror. 'I've appointments on the farm, and we're short-handed.'

Buch was a man who could finesse a situation. 'For those who cooperate with us we are only too happy to supply more workers, *Hr* Eberstern.' There was a pause. 'If you are short-handed.'

'No,' said Kay sharply, immediately regretting it. *Be boring.*

'Let me explain again,' said *Hauptsturmführer* Buch. 'There has been enemy activity in the area and a terrorist is hiding in the vicinity. He's wounded and he probably can't get far. Our intelligence tells us he is on the Rosenlund estate.' He was polite. He was firm. He was – Kay thought with a touch of hysteria – taking pains to behave like a gentleman. 'The intelligence couldn't have been clearer.'

Juncker slapped his thigh with his gloves.

Buch continued, quiet and relentless: 'We have reason to believe it was your daughter who helped him.' He gave a polite, wintry smile. 'Probably out of misplaced pity.'

'No,' said Kay. 'As I told you, she's with her cousins. They live in Aarhus.'

Mistake?

'Name,' demanded Constable Juncker.

Kay gave it.

'May we use the phone?'

'If you must.'

Juncker tried it, only to report the line was dead.

'Oh Lord,' said Kay. 'It's always happening. It's the mice. They eat through the cables. We're always having to lay new ones. She appealed to them. 'Gentlemen, I assure you the reports are incorrect.'

'Tell them, Wulf,' ordered Buch.

'The doctor says otherwise.' Sergeant Wulf was reluctant.

'My daughter helping a terrorist?' Bror was incredulous.

'*Fru* Eberstern, *Hr* Eberstern,' Sergeant Wulf was almost begging them, 'I'm afraid we must search your daughter's room.' He took a look at Bror's thunderous expression. 'The sooner you allow me, the sooner this will be over.'

They all trooped upstairs to Tanne's room and discovered Else cowering inside. 'I wanted to know if *Frøken* Tanne wished for her tea.'

'But *Frøken* Tanne is away,' said Juncker.

'Oh.'

Tanne's bed, with an arched wooden bedhead and green and white quilt – green and white were Tanne's colours – dominated the room. Clothes were heaped on it. Scattered on the floor were books and the dance records that she played on her gramophone. By the window, housed in a Sèvres pot, was the tropical fern which, against the odds, Tanne managed to keep alive.

Kay explained who Else was.

'Have you seen *Frøken* Eberstern today?' Buch was brusque.

Else flushed. 'Yes, no, I mean no. No. It must have been yesterday.'

'Which?' Buch took up a position by the window.

Else endeavoured to hide her shaking hands in her apron.

'Please stop,' said Kay. 'At once. This is bullying.'

Hauptsturmführer Buch signalled to Constable Juncker. 'Take her down to the station.'

'No!' Else's scream of terror shocked the listeners. 'Please.'

'Let me talk to her,' said Kay. Turning her back on the men, she snatched up one of Else's hands. 'Did you see *Frøken* Tanne this morning?'

She pressed down on the clammy fingers.

Else, still a child really, struggled to speak. Her nose was running and Kay offered her a handkerchief.

Else blew into it. 'I can't remember.' The words were barely audible.

'We can make you remember,' said Juncker.

Buch pointed to the chest. 'Would you mind opening this drawer?'

Kay looked to Bror for back-up. '*Hauptsturmführer* Buch, that's private to my daughter.'

It was useless.

Opening the drawer to reveal Tanne's delicate lacy things was one of the hardest things she had ever done. Sergeant Wulf endeavoured to calm a hysterical Else. Buch and Juncker searched the room.

Kay was stiff with hatred in a way she never imagined she would ever feel.

Intent on impressing, Juncker exhibited rodent cunning. He opened Tanne's wardrobe, shuffled the clothes on their hangers and poked at the rows of shoes on the floor. Then, at the back of the cupboard, he unearthed the shoe box and removed the lid. 'Sir?'

Triumphant, he carried it over to the desk and displayed the contents.

Buch held up the pamphlet. If anything his voice had grown softer. 'An explanation, please.'

Naturally, Buch didn't believe Kay when she improvised and told him that they used any old pieces of paper to stuff into wet shoes. 'Shoes are often wet out here.'

Bror was silent.

She could almost read his thoughts: *My wife. My daughter.*

'This is seditious, dangerous rubbish. Why didn't your daughter burn it?'

'It's wartime. Probably she found it somewhere and didn't want to waste valuable paper.'

Constable Juncker spoke into *Hauptsturmführer* Buch's ear. Buch turned to Bror. 'I am afraid this confirms we must search the estate.' He picked up one of Tanne's sweaters which had been on the bed. 'I will use this. The dogs will need the scent.'

'I haven't given you permission.'

'I think you will,' replied Buch.

Wulf, Buch and Juncker returned downstairs. Orders were issued and the dogs set up renewed barking.

Bror hustled Kay into her bedroom. 'Where *is* Tanne?'

'I told you. In Aarhus,' she replied. 'Let me get dressed.'

'Don't lie to me.' He was almost too angry to speak. He paced the room. 'Is Tanne mixed up in something? She is. I sense it. What have *you* done? There must be a reason that some idiotic, but clearly dangerous, German turns up and suggests our daughter is a terrorist, and I think the reason must be you.'

'This is war. It happens.'

'Or Anton.'

'Stop it.'

'And what has Anton done to the telephone? It was him.'

Anton bought Tanne some time.

'Where could Tanne have got hold of that leaflet?'

'Maybe she's got views of her own.'

Bror grabbed Kay by the arm. It was a rough, angry gesture and introduced a brand-new element into their relations: hostility. 'What *are* you?'

'And what are you, Bror?'

'You know who I am. You've always known.'

'Aren't you disgusted by what's happening to Denmark? Disgusted by the newspapers, the industrialists and businessmen all falling over themselves to accept the German mark? How we collaborate with an occupying force?' His fingers dug hard into her flesh but she continued. 'How we entertain German generals?'

'Tell me what is going on.'

Kay's resolve wavered. On her back rested the burden of bringing suspicion down onto the house and those that lived in it.

'Go and get dressed, Bror.'

'I'm going into Køge to try to sort this out.'

'Listen to me, Bror,' she said, fierce and impassioned. 'Whatever you think you *must* act normally, as if there is nothing to worry about. We will have breakfast as we always do.'

For a second or two, she thought the appeal had failed. Then he said: 'If I find out that it's you who's put Tanne in danger by involving her in something unwise, I'll never forgive you.'

That was nothing.

It was impossible to tell Bror that Kay would never forgive herself.

A little while later they were in the dining room making a pretence of eating. From the lakeside, the barking of the dogs increased to maddened frenzy.

She glanced at Bror. As she had instructed, he was eating steadily, but with a heightened colour.

Thank God the Gottfrieds had gone. With piercing gratitude she thought again of Anton's forethought. No telephone meant they would be out of contact.

The barking reached a crescendo, followed by gunshots.

'Oh my God.' Kay couldn't help herself.

She closed her eyes and felt the blood drain from her face. When she opened them, Bror was staring at her.

'Are you all right?'

She shrugged. 'You know I never like to hear guns going off.'

'This is a manhunt, Kay,' said Bror – and she detected a menace which she had not heard before. 'Think about it.'

Silence fell. Bror had lit up his post-breakfast cigarette when Sergeant Wulf shuffled into the dining room.

'I'm so sorry . . . I'm so sorry . . .'

A drumming mounted in Kay's ears, and her head swam.

Bror rose to his feet. 'What is it, Wulf?'

Wulf had gone a pale green colour. 'Your dogs,' he said. 'They've been shot. By mistake.'

Bror was on his feet roaring with anguish and anger. 'My dogs . . . my dogs.'

Chapter Twenty-three

Refer pain on. Or divert it.

Had those STS instructors ever experienced pain? Of course they had. Some of them were tough to the point of inhumanity, and a couple had worked in the East in tough conditions. No, the answer was that you, the sufferer, had to find your own individual way through pain.

He had dealt with it.

He seemed to have been dreaming a great deal, especially in the cottage. Colourful fantasies which he imagined were the result of his fever. At a point when he felt as if his body was melting with heat, he dreamed a woman was bathing his face. Freya? Then he realized he was being tended to by a younger version.

'Name?' he'd muttered. 'But not your real name.'

'What would you like it to be?'

Man and woman . . . Adam and Eve . . .

'Eva,' he said.

She pushed back a mane of hair. 'Eva, it is.'

It was Eva bathing his face and lying beside him. Or was that a dream, too? One memory was clear enough. It was of Eva sitting bolt upright, with her hair tumbling over her shoulders. She had taken off her trousers and put them under his head as a pillow. Underneath she wore wide-legged knickers and he caught sight of the top of her thigh, a red stain and a suggestion of blonde hair. The sight worked powerfully on him but not in the way he would have expected. It had made him feel unbearably, awkwardly tender – and protective.

Perhaps it was lust, which Felix welcomed. Despite the state he was in, he wanted to feel lust, satiation, hope – all the things that proved you were alive.

Eva had brought him food and water, but he wasn't sure when. A strawberry? Honey? He recollected her telling him that her parents were giving dinner to a German general and his wife, and that she was supposed to be up at the house entertaining them.

At first, he had reckoned she was joking.

The night was a terrible one. Very early, he had managed to manoeuvre himself upright and move over to the window to keep watch. Eva was sleeping, curled gracefully on one side.

Tousled blonde hair, a strong chin, long limbs . . . it was a sight to make him feel better. When she woke, she rolled over, looked up at Felix in a puzzled way and reached for her trousers. When she was dressed, she felt his forehead and made him take more painkillers and drink a mug of water.

It was then she'd confessed her misgivings about Dr Hansen.

Someone was shaking Felix and he awoke with a groan.

It was Eva. 'Get up. The police and the SS have arrived at the house. They're hunting you, and want to talk to me.'

In a flash, he was on his feet. Pain sliced through his arm, followed by a wave of nausea. The blood drained from his head. He swayed and fell against the wall. Eva pushed his head down on his chest. He gagged, and bile and saliva dripped onto his shirt.

At last he managed to ask: 'Do they know who they're looking for exactly?'

'A man with an injured arm.'

'The doctor?'

'Stop talking, Felix. Freya . . . Freya says to leave the wireless set.'

Christ. *The wireless*. His head felt as if someone had taken an axe to it and his mouth was as rough as a quarry. 'Have they got dogs?'

'Yes.'

Fieldcraft. The hunters would use something of Eva's for the scent.

'Is there a river or a ditch near here?'

'Yes.'

All at once, he felt steadier. Propping himself against the wall, he said, 'You're in it now, Eva. Be prepared. We'll have to get out of Denmark. We must get ourselves to the harbour at Gilleleje and make contact with Sven. If we pay him enough he'll take us across to Helsingborg.'

Eva was moving around the room, smoothing away signs of recent occupation. She attempted a joke: 'So that's easy, then.'

'Not quite. The Germans have laid minefields in the Sound and the Allies have dropped magnetic mines. Between them, they are giving the fishermen grief. So he might not be too keen. But he might be persuaded to transfer us to a boat just inside Swedish waters. Could be tricky, boarding in a bad sea. You'd have to climb a ladder.'

'Do I look as though I can't?' She sounded almost offended. 'Well, I've heard the Swedes are opening up the bonded warehouses and whoever goes in can help themselves. Everyone gets disgustingly drunk.' She picked up the bottle of water and handed it to him. 'Meanwhile, here's an alternative.'

She bundled up the blankets. There was nowhere to store them and she looked questioningly at Felix.

'They'll have our scent on them — we'll have to take them with us and get rid of them somewhere.'

Together, they left the cottage and headed for the tree cover.

It was hard going. The nausea came and went and his legs felt like putty. The adrenalin should kick in eventually but, until then, he concentrated on placing one foot in front of the other.

Press the heel down, follow it with the toe.

Have we forgotten anything? There is something missing . . .

Don't think about the arm.

Referred pain.

At the road, he made Eva stop while still under the tree cover. 'Which way?'

She pointed to a large field in the distance. 'Big drainage ditch at one end. With a drainage pipe.'

'We'll make for that.'

The drainage pipe was only just big enough, but they crawled into it. The bottom was an inch or so deep in water but they had no choice other than to lie in it.

'Could be worse,' said Eva.

Quiet.

Stay absolutely quiet.

Some time later Felix checked his watch but the dial swam in and out of focus.

'Eva, how long have we been in here?'

Her voice sifted back to him. 'A couple of hours?'

Freya may be in danger.

'You know you can't go back?'

She took her time to answer. 'I know.'

'I meant you cannot go back to the house.'

'I know. I'm coming with you to Sweden.'

There was a lilt in her voice, an excitement. Unbelievably, their hiding place was filled with a wildly inappropriate gaiety that tore at his conscience. Eva was Freya's daughter, a responsibility that he had never envisaged and did not want. Yet here she was, jammed into a drainage pipe with her head up against his feet.

They were silent. After a while, she asked, 'Felix, how are you feeling?'

'Terrific,' he answered. 'I love having a shot-up arm.'

He heard her laugh.

'There's a message from my mother which I must tell you in case we split up.' There was a pause. 'I must this get this right. This General Gottfried is Abwehr and commands the signals unit but *Mor* thinks he's got a long finger in Intelligence, too. Does that make sense?'

'Yes, it does.'

'Listen, resistance in the Aarhus area is getting torn up by the Gestapo, who are using the university as a headquarters. There're reports that Gestapo archives are being stored there. She says to tell London that the archives need to be destroyed.'

'Simple,' he murmured. 'I'll get on the phone to the British RAF.'

'Can you remember that?' She nudged his foot gently. 'I'll remember it for you, if not. Oh, I almost forgot – she said something about vinegar, but I didn't understand what she meant.'

Felix dropped his head onto his good arm. Jumbled images chased through his mind . . .

The containers from the drop. Are they still sitting in the wood? Who checked?

I must manage my arm.

Messages? How to contact London?

Freya says that a general may be running one of our wireless sets.

Mustard is wiped off plate.

Kill him. Kill Erik, too.

Their blood is on my hands.

Vinegar? Were they running him?

Organize. Talk to the communists. Talk to the nationalists. Stockpile arms and explosives. Fashion an underground army out of a population who prefer it to be quieter.

Which wireless is being run?

Stop talking.

Do something.

I wish I didn't feel so sick.

Crazy, it's all crazy . . .

He dozed.

Prodded awake by the cold and damp, he realized that important political and military considerations required his attention. Item: how was Denmark going to manoeuvre itself out of the reach of the Third Reich? Item: were the communists going to be the ones who called the shots? Item: when would the Allies come? Item: how was he going to survive?

The war was too big. How could a bunch of resisters possibly imagine they could create a running sore in Hitler's hide? Certainly not he – powerless and wounded – a Dane dreaming of victory but only running on the spot.

Denmark. What was it doing to itself?

'Eva, you're in danger.'

'So?' She actually chuckled.

'Are you very wet?'

'Soaking. But I've never felt better.' Her hand rested on his ankle, an infinitely comforting contact.

He licked his bottom lip and squared up to his weakness. 'I don't think I'll make Gilleleje at the moment. So, change of plan. We'll head for the rubbish dump at Amager harbour. We can get a boat from there.'

'Amager! That's in the middle of København.'

'That's the point,' said Felix with a touch of smugness. 'Under the nose of the enemy. They would never expect it so they wouldn't look for it. You'd be surprised. Quite a lot of people traffic goes in and out. We'll have to hide up in København while we make the contacts.'

'And you get your strength back.'

'That, too.' He gave her the address of a safe house, and made her repeat it twice.

Eventually, Eva said: 'I can't hear any dogs. I'm going to get help.'

He felt a deep reluctance to let her go, fearing the absence of her physical warmth in their inhospitable lair. More worryingly, at this moment of profound frailty, he didn't want to be alone.

The training had taught him that weaknesses would surface at just this point and he had been warned of their insidious effects.

But you put your head down, sonny, and tread on through.

He concentrated on planning the next move.

Yet again, he fell into a doze, and woke to find Eva crouched down by the entrance to the pipe. 'Felix, get up. I've got Arne with the pony trap. He's going to take us to the station at Vallø. We're too well known at Køge.'

He snapped into wariness. 'Who's Arne?'

'I trust him with my life. *Come on.*'

He emerged to find that she had changed into trousers and a jacket. A bag was slung over her shoulder and her hair was brushed, her mouth lipsticked. She held out a pair of workman's overalls. 'I'm going to help you into these.'

He was stiff from his incarceration and his arm was awkward. 'How long have you been gone?'

'An hour or so. They seem to have given up and driven back into town.'

'They'll be watching. You went back to the house?'

'If I can't get back into Rosenlund without anyone noticing,' she was helping to fasten the overalls, 'then I don't deserve to inherit it. We needed clothes and money, and I needed to look tidier.'

She was right.

He remembered something important. '*Lort!* The pistol.'

Every bloody rule of training . . . broken.

'Aren't we better without it? If we are caught with it . . . ?'

He summoned his energies. 'That's one way of looking at it.'

Arne was waiting with the trap on the road. Felix gave him the once-over. A big man with greying hair, he had the air of someone accustomed to taking charge. Prudently, he avoided looking at Felix.

'You're to lie down in the back,' said Eva. 'Oh, wait.' She produced a bottle of schnapps out of the bag, unscrewed the top and sprinkled him with it. 'Just so you know, you're drunk. Try to act it.'

Slumped in the back, he spent the journey nursing his arm.

At one point, he overheard Eva say, 'Tell my mother I'm fine. Tell her not to worry.'

There was the bass note of Arne's reply that Felix could not make out. Eva replied, 'How can I thank you?'

Just before Vallø, they ran into a roadblock, manned by a couple of Danish policemen. Arne brought the cart to a halt.

The younger-looking, more nervous-looking one of the pair stepped forward. The weapon in his belt had a dull gleam. 'Where are you going?'

'Taking this man home,' replied Eva. 'He's supposed to have been working for us but has proved . . . unreliable.'

'Where?'

'Slotskro. His wife is waiting.' Eva was deliciously charming and polite. The policeman's eyes travelled from Eva to Felix.

Eva looked at her watch. 'I'm going to be late.'

A hint of steel crept into her voice which Felix could only admire: it suggested that she was not used to obstacles being put in her way.

It worked.

The policeman stood back and they were on their way. The castle, surrounded by cobblestone streets and houses painted in yellows and ochres, came into view. Beyond these lay the station and, once there, he knew the watching and the waiting would begin in earnest.

He was frightened and hated to admit it. Yet he was determined to savour these last moments of fresh air and to fight his weakness. Remember, remember the point of what they were doing – which was to get his country out of its mess. As they trotted past the gardens rustling with trees and plants, the message written in his fear and pain was: We must not fail.

So be it if he died.

They travelled in separate train compartments and in København Felix went on ahead. Check right, left. Don't hurry. Stay upright. It was strange, but he felt safer in the city, even in a debilitated state.

The safe house which he made for had been a doctor's surgery before the war and the doctor's brass plaque was still screwed into the gate. Inside, it was similar to many of the abandoned houses, with an air of despair and neglect. In this one, though, there was evidence the doctor had prospered for there were several pieces of good antique furniture and a handsome eighteenth-century French clock.

He was tempted to wind it up. It would have seemed right – a gesture of defiance.

Not long afterwards, Eva arrived. She dumped packages on the kitchen table. 'Bread, butter and milk. Couldn't get any cheese, but I got hold of some sausage. The milk looks terrible. All watered down.'

'A banquet.' There was a pause. 'Eva, I'm sorry but I'm going to have to send you out to make contact with the man with the boat.'

'Of course.' She looked around for a place to stow the milk. 'Is there anything else?'

'Nothing for you.'

She was pale and there was a suggestion of sweat glistening on her upper lip which made him feel extremely guilty. He gave her the instructions.

When she had gone, he eased aside the net curtain at the window. The street was less busy than he expected. Not for the first time, he realized that something had happened to the Danish. They walked around with their heads down. A German motor convoy eased down the street. No one paid it much attention.

He massaged his arm. A river of pain flowed up and down it.

Would they get out? Had Arne given the message to Freya?

Flexing and bending, his trigger finger needed exercise.

Could they still rely on the fact that the Germans – who were quartered there, for God's sake – apparently never noticed

Danish boats slipping in and alongside the rubbish dump on Amager island?

Was the contact trustworthy?

Go deep inside yourself. There are deep places on which to call, sonny.

The net curtain dropped back into place.

He set himself to wait.

Later, having got themselves through København, Eva and Felix were met by a man dressed in a thick fisherman's jersey and rubber boots at the entrance to the harbour. 'Call me Jens.' He hustled them into the shadow thrown by the old fort which dominated the harbour. 'Listen, we have a hitch. There's a U-boat on the other side of the harbour. Turned up out of the blue. It's either damaged, or it's resting up from an operation. Either way, we didn't get the intelligence in time to warn you. We can't do it. It's too dangerous. You must go back.'

Eva gave a little gasp.

Felix looked at her. In the darkness of the summer night, fractured by the searchlights and the lights strung along the quays, she appeared insubstantial.

Denmark's ghosts were sleeping, hidden beneath a passive, cowed, splintered nation. He was going to do his best to wake them. He had also to look after Freya's daughter.

With his good hand, Felix grasped at Jens's jersey. 'We're going.'

'Take your hands off me.' Jens stepped back. He scuffed his rubber boot along the stones. After a moment, he said, 'It'll cost you.'

'Fine,' said Felix. 'But we're going. Do you understand?'

The tactic worked. Jens nodded, and handed over two navy wool balaclavas. 'Put them on.'

An ominous breeze tugged at the pennants and Felix prayed it wouldn't get any stronger.

Surefooted and silent, Jens led them through the network of crates, bales and canvas bags that littered the quay and halted by a couple of trolleys stacked with boxes. 'Sit behind those until we get the signal.'

The three of them crouched down.

The wind battered at the rigging, and the sea slapped against the stone quay.

Felix backed himself against a hawser coiled up by one of the trolleys, which gave him some support.

Jens licked his finger and held it up to the wind. 'Stay here. Don't move or say anything. Wait for the signal then make for the *Ulla Baden* over there.'

He padded back down the quay and they were alone.

Eva took hold of Felix's good hand and placed her mouth against his ear. 'There's the *Ulla Baden*.' She pointed to a fishing vessel moored almost directly in front of them. It was a no-nonsense-looking vessel which, no doubt, had done sturdy service.

Her breath filtered through the balaclava onto his cheek, and the fingers resting in his were damp. He held them fast. '*Lort!* She's small.'

'Bad sailor?'

'Fraid so.'

'You're no Dane.'

He managed a grin. 'Hit a man when he's down.'

Again, he heard her chuckle. She consulted her watch. 'Two and a half minutes between each sweep of the searchlight. Is that going to be enough for you?'

'Like I said, hit a man when he's down.'

After an hour or so, the wind backed around and its full force hit them. Felix's balaclava tasted of salt and the wool was stiff with it. Despite the late hour, it was still just light enough to make out the shapes of the boats in the harbour. Eva was pressed up close to him. 'Storm,' he said into her ear. 'Just our luck.'

They sat out the waiting, listening to the waves rolling beside the quay, water slapping against fenders, the sighing and creaking of the pontoons as they bobbed up and down.

The searchlight swept the quays. Round, dip, round . . .

It was after midnight when their contact zigzagged silently towards them. Stopping beside the trolleys, Jens pretended to check over a pile of fishing tackle close by. 'Listen up. When a light shows on the *Ulla*, you run to her one at a time and the captain will hide you in the hold where the catch is put. He'll pile the nets on top of you. A warning: it's small.'

He dumped the tackle on top of the hawsers and vanished into the murk.

Crouching, tensed, they readied themselves. One minute. Two minutes. Five, six . . . 'Get on with it,' Felix growled. The searchlight directed its blinding arc down onto the quay and away, leaving pitch black behind.

At last, a pinpoint of light glowed on the *Ulla Baden*, and Eva was up and away.

Felix poised on the balls of his feet.

Again, the signal. He launched himself across the slippery stones, up the gangplank and onto the boat. His good elbow was seized and he was pushed down into the hold.

It was tiny, barely ten foot square, smelling of – oh God – rotten guts, fish and blood. This was no joke. Above their heads, a man issued a rapid command. Within seconds, the nets were piled on top and the hatch battened down.

The water slapped at the side of the boat. Felix retched noisily.

'You can't be sick yet,' said Eva.

'Yes, I can.'

Suddenly, there was noise: booted feet slapping onto the stones and running up the gangplank. Felix grabbed Eva's arm.

Footsteps trampled the deck above them. These were followed by the skitter and patter of dogs' paws.

Felix closed his eyes: *This is it, then.* Tension replaced his nausea. Eva clung to his good hand. He pulled her to him, buried his face in her neck and smelled flowers and spring and sun. All the things to live for.

Try to keep silent for forty-eight hours if taken.

'If they get you, feed them as little as you can manage,' he whispered, passing on the STS advice. 'Tell them that I abducted you.'

But the dogs didn't bark. Instead, they appeared to be running around in circles. Orders were issued. A bucket banged down. The wind sang through the ship's rigging. There was a babble of male voices, orders in German.

Eva's body moved within his clasp. He felt the curve of her waist and the slight swell of her hip. He felt that she belonged there and, even more curious, that he knew her, through and through. For the first time in his life, he experienced terror for someone other than himself, someone he wanted to protect.

If Eva was taken? How would she have any idea of the protocols of interrogation? The games played by the interrogator? The techniques? Their objectives? The methodical deconstruction of an agent's mind and body? Starvation. Darkness. Freezing temperatures. All the persuasive methods which were oh-so-creative.

He shuddered.

Eva pressed closer.

More orders in German. Again, a symphony of heavy boots. A voice screamed, 'Go, go!' to the dogs. The dogs whimpered and whined.

'What are you doing?' barked a voice with a German accent. 'Who is he?'

There was a mutter. A scuffle. An oath.

'Get off me, you bastard,' screamed someone in Danish.

'Your papers,' roared the German voice. 'Open the lockers.'

The skipper shouted in Danish: 'This is my ship.'

'Open the hatches.'

Eva's nails dug into his hand. The lid was removed from the hatch above them. A tiny streak of light percolated down through the nets as something prodded at them.

Felix and Eva shrank back against the walls.

Jab.

Jab.

The dogs' paws clicked on the wooden deck.

There was a whimper. A second. Then, nothing more.

The lid was shoved back onto the hatch.

To Felix's astonishment, the only voices they could now hear were not German.

Engines wheezed into life. Orders were now being issued in Danish. 'Cast off.'

The boat slipped its moorings and nosed out of the harbour. Immediately, a swell caught it up, slamming them from side to side.

'This is hell.' Felix tried not to groan as he retched into a tin he'd found rolling on the floor. 'Don't you dare laugh.'

'Would I?'

At the best of times a smallish fishing boat on the Kattegat or Øresund was a hostage to fortune. With a wind, it was Thor's plaything.

Felix spent the next hour or so heaving up his guts. Fetid already, the air in the tiny space turned rancid, but he was past caring. After a while, Eva prised the tin out of his grip and held it for him. That took something. Every so often she dabbed at his face with a handkerchief. That took something, too, given that he stank of vomit and infected wound.

'Felix?' Her voice was almost drowned out by the sea. 'I've decided. When we get to Sweden, I'm coming with you to London.'

With difficulty, he raised his head. 'No, you aren't.'

'I'm going to offer to work like you do.'

'It's too dangerous,' he said.

'That's for me to decide.'

His thoughts were moving slowly. 'You don't know the half of it.'

'I know enough,' she said urgently. 'I know that we have to do something. It took me a bit of time, but I've got there in the end.'

She was whispering this into his ear and he longed to gather her up. 'It's too big a risk. Stay quietly in Sweden until it's all over. Then you can go back to your family.'

'I'm ashamed that my mother got there first.'

Another spasm hit him. He was being dragged down into overwhelming weakness and despair.

Arms went round him. 'Lean on me.'

'I'm too disgusting.'

'You *must*.'

Her cheek was against his, like a gentle pillow.

Do not go into death without remembering the things that matter. Do not go brutalized.

Memories he would never forget: Eva cradling him in the cottage; her semi-nakedness and the snatched, intimate glimpse of her femininity; her laughter in the drainage pipe; her embrace amidst the stink and offal; this moment.

No, he would not go brutalized.

She was his saviour, the other half of his soul. Greek philosophers wrote about that, the *eros* and *agape*. Sacred and divine.

He was gasping for air and for some respite.

'Felix, this is my fault,' Eva said. 'You must forgive me.'

'I want you to live,' he said. '*Please*.'

The second's silence which elapsed felt breathless.

'And you, too, Felix.'

At last, the hatch was opened and he found himself downing great lungfuls of fresh air.

The skipper, a great bear of a man, stuck his head inside. 'We've been blown off course and shipped water. Get up here and start bailing.'

'How far are we from Swedish waters?'

'Close. But there's a minefield.'

Shivering, Felix wedged himself into the bow and bailed like there was no tomorrow. The water hissed past them and, every so often, he was drenched by a wave. Eva was up there with him. Soaked to the skin, her hair plastered over her shoulders, she looked like a fallen angel and bailed like a navvy.

Jabbing a thumb in the direction of the hold, she grinned broadly. He understood her exhilaration and the pleasure of release because he felt it, too.

An ancient beret crammed down on his head, the mate was busy in the chart room. Every so often he poked out his head to take a look at the stars. On deck, the lookouts clung to the rails, scanning the waters.

'Mine to port,' screamed one. 'Now.'

The skipper swung the wheel and the boat lurched to starboard.

There was an agonizing wait. Eva had dropped her bailer and hung over the side.

'Get back,' he yelled.

She straightened up. 'Phew! That was close. The mine was this far away.' She held up her hands and, incredibly, she was grinning.

Felix liked that, too. 'Idiot,' he said.

The *Ulla Baden* swung about and headed north, weaving and tacking as the lookouts called out warnings. An hour or so later the wind dropped to a breeze. Then it was gone. A faint, shadowy line of land appeared on the horizon. Out of the clear dawn sky, a couple of enemy planes rose like gulls.

The sight of them triggered hot anger in Felix. He hadn't survived the fish hold just to die from a German fighter's strafe.

'Get down below,' he called to Eva.

But she stopped, frozen, mid-deck.

The skipper shouted: 'Run up the German ensign.'

On board there was a collective intake of breath before a frantic burst of activity got the ensign flapping at the top of the mast. The planes roared towards them, dipped their wings in salute and flew by.

Felix lurched over to Eva, who had sunk down onto the

deck. 'In future, do as you're told.' Fury and fright made him extra brusque.

She huddled over and dropped her face onto her bent knees. Her shoulders tensed.

'Eva . . .'

'This is my fault.' She lifted a pale, tear-stained face. 'I thought I knew my country, but I didn't. *Mor* warned me people did strange things in war. But a doctor . . .'

He sat down beside her and used his good thumb to blot a tear. 'I'm grateful, and your regrets are touching. But you're not going to help by getting killed. Nor by going over and over what happened. That's one of the things to learn. Regrets waste energy.'

'But think of the people I've put in danger. My mother.'

'You're having a reaction to having been in danger,' he said.

She wasn't listening. 'Maybe Arne. Maybe other people I don't know about, and who don't know me. Or you.'

'That's war.'

'Is that all you've got to say?'

'That's all there is to say.'

'War absolves one from blame, then?' She inched closer to him. 'Are you so sure about *that*?' Felix didn't bother to answer. 'Where do you come from, Felix? Is there anyone you're worrying about? Or maybe you don't mind.'

'Best that way.'

'But *anyone*, Felix? A mother? A girlfriend. A wife?'

He shrugged, and immediately regretted the gesture which sent pain shooting down his back. 'One day, maybe, I can tell you.'

'One day? I'll keep you to that.'

The nausea was again gaining a hold over him and he pulled himself upright and retched over the side.

Behind him, Eva continued talking, but more to herself than to him. 'Whatever you say, I was stupid.'

With an effort, he raised his head from the rail. 'You can't think like that or you'll go mad,' he said flatly. 'So don't.'

That silenced her.

By the time the *Ulla Baden* steamed into the harbour at Malmø, Felix wanted only to die. As they helped him down the gangplank and onto shore, Eva cornered the skipper: 'How did you stop the dogs finding us?'

The skipper's tense, salt-flayed features relaxed a trifle. 'We throw a mixture of rabbit's blood and cocaine over the deck. It numbs their noses.' His huge shoulders shook. 'They can't smell a thing and they're off their heads.'

For the first time in weeks, Felix laughed properly.

'Hurry,' said the skipper. 'We're running guns back and we need to make the tides and outwit that out there.' He pointed out to sea.

Felix looked. To his amazement a belt of fog had appeared from nowhere to blot out the horizon. 'You're going back in that?'

'What else?'

'My God, I admire you.'

The last thing Felix managed to do before he passed out was to write the promissory note for their fare. 'There's a contract at the Danish Treasury,' he said. 'It will be repaid once the war is over.'

Chapter Twenty-four

At the first opportunity, Kay went up to the attic room to check it over.

The quilt was tangled on the floor beside a bloodied piece of rag. Looking at this evidence, Kay let out a long breath of there-but-for-the-grace-of-God.

Tanne, darling . . . where are you?

She picked up the quilt and jumped when something clattered to the floor.

The pistol.

They didn't even have that.

She pushed it into her pocket. Folding the quilt, she knelt by the chest and stowed it inside. A stale lavender aroma wafted up from the interior of the chest. She leaned over and a hard object pressed into her knee. It was a child's marble . . . which had probably belonged to Nils, or possibly to the small, tousle-headed Bror she had been shown in Eberstern family photographs.

Sitting back on her heels, she balanced the marble on her palm and asked it: What now?

The greens and blues to be found in Rosenlund's lake exploded at its frozen heart. Gazing into it, she knew that, if she could never argue that her previous existence had been monochrome, her life had now taken on different colours.

The marble rolled back and forth in her cupped palm, and the colours appeared to melt into one brilliant medley – just like the fusion of politics, action and emotion into which she had pitched herself.

Should she give it all up? Retrieve what peace of mind there was to be had by becoming a spectator?

Dropping the marble into the chest, she closed the lid and went downstairs to hide the pistol in her office.

Later in the morning she fetched her jacket and outdoor shoes and automatically whistled for Sif and Thor.

She was forgetting.

There were no answering barks. No clicking of paws over the black and white tiles.

Sif and Thor were dead. Shot in the melée. Apparently Sif had taken her time to die, which Kay could not bear to think about. But when she did think about it, she had the oddest notion that her heart was physically hardening.

It was nearing the end of May before Kay considered it prudent to travel up to København.

If she took a walk on the estate, she glimpsed figures flitting between the trees. Driving to Køge, a black saloon frequently nudged into her sightline in the mirror. Strange clicks could be heard on the telephone.

They were watching for Tanne.

How much of this surveillance fell under Buch's remit, and how much it was the decidedly more amateur operation of Sergeant Wulf she had, as yet, to work out.

Whoever it was, it was vital to establish in their eyes that she frequently visited København.

Checking into the Damehotellet in København, she phoned Anton in his office.

At half-past seven precisely, dressed for dinner in a long dress and light cape, she arrived at the Hotel d'Angleterre to find him already waiting at the hotel bar.

'We're in the lion's den,' she said, eyes flicking in the direction of a group of German officers who were at the other end of the bar.

'Hidden in plain sight,' he replied.

She glanced down at her feet. 'Anton, I'm still angry with you. Very. You should never have involved Nils.'

'He'll be fine, so stop it.' Anton placed a finger under her chin and tilted it up towards him. 'Now come and sit down.'

He ordered cocktails. Taking a sip of hers, she found herself shivering uncontrollably.

He slid his arm round her. 'Tell.'

Kay knew he knew about events at Rosenlund. 'I'm worried sick about Tanne. Most of the time, I cope. But sometimes . . . I don't.'

'I can't help you. I wish I could.'

'It feels far worse because she wouldn't have got into it but for me.'

'She might have done. Tanne is an adult. She makes up her own mind.'

'Tanne didn't make up her mind to be shot at or –' Kay could not bring herself to say what. 'You know what they do to prisoners?'

'As a matter of fact, I do,' Anton replied calmly. 'Tucked up in Sweden, she's probably worrying about you, too.'

She looked down at her glass. 'I've had my life. Tanne is only just beginning hers.'

'An irritating remark, darling. You've had *part* of your life. There's plenty more to come.'

'You haven't had children.'

There was a silence.

'Kay, almost certainly, Tanne is in Sweden and there's no safer place for her.'

'Thank you for cutting the telephone line. It gave them a breathing space. I was able to say with perfect truth that mice had got at the cables. They do, from time to time.'

'It's a basic rule. Cut off the enemy's communications.'

Kay sipped her martini. 'That bloody doctor. I've trusted him all these years.'

Anton brushed her cheek with a finger. His expression was grim. 'He should be shot. I could arrange it.'

'Don't joke.'

'I'm not.'

She looked up into Anton's face. 'Help me find her.'

He removed his arm. 'No. And you must not look for her either. Kay, you have to stay in control. Otherwise we all go down. It's absolutely imperative we do nothing except look normal. They will be watching. The telephones will have been humming between Køge and here. Probably somebody's watching us at this moment.'

She glanced at the barman who was polishing the glasses. Him? 'Bror suspects I've put the family and the house in danger.'

'Have you considered that, if the Nazis lose the war, Bror will have placed you in just as much danger? His name is writ large all over the place.'

Kay fingered her frosted glass. 'Anton, Bror isn't corrupt. He isn't a fascist either. He wants what's best.'

'The road to hell, and so on.'

'Unfair.'

'Forgive me if I smile, darling. But are you sure you know Bror?'

'As sure as I am that I know you, Anton.'

'That's my point.'

So it was. 'Could I have another martini, please?'

Anton motioned to the waiter. 'You know, darling Kay, things might be about to get worse. The Jews . . . While he's in charge of Denmark, General Best reckons it's in his interest to keep the Danes sweet. But we've heard tell that his SS friends are keen to go over Best's head. That will be a problem for the Jews.'

'How likely is it?'

'We've taken soundings in Berlin. It's on the cards.'

How had Anton got hold of the intelligence from Berlin? 'The Nazis can't do a France or Poland on us, surely?'

'They can.'

'Over our dead bodies.'

'That might not be a joke.'

Kay thought it over. 'Do you have to see a lot of General Best?'

'I make sure I do. It's my safety net.' Anton ate his olive.

'Be careful.' She felt for his hand. 'Anton . . . you will be careful?'

Anton glanced down. 'I like the hand-holding.'

'Listen to me. Bror might be in trouble but you might be, too. The army isn't popular either. Most people don't like it for supporting the government.'

'Keep your voice down, darling.' Anton shrugged. 'There's not much the Danish army can do publicly except resign our commissions. Not so clever because it draws attention to us for no good purpose. However, I do know that interested parties are slowly coming together.'

'Oh?'

A lot of talk. A lot of jostling. A lot of fractious, opposing interests. But was it possible?

Anton continued. 'Think of one united underground army.'

'I will.' She retrieved her hand. 'You must take care.'

'I make it my business to look after myself. It's not much good being dead.'

She nodded. 'About Bror and Tanne –'

'Forget Bror.' Anton cut her short in a voice she rarely heard. 'He has made his bed.'

The martini arrived, chilly and strong enough to pucker the insides of her mouth.

Anton pinched her olive. 'You say Tanne's with Felix. He trained in Britain so there's a good chance they'll make for London. The embassy would take care of her there. She won't starve, she could find a job, and sit the war out. It might be the very thing for her. She might meet an English duke or an earl. Wouldn't that cheer you up?' He became serious. 'What happens to you and Bror is another matter.'

The bar was filing up with well-dressed, animated men and

women in evening dress and uniforms. The waiters clinked glasses, rattled the cocktail shaker, clattered ice. There was an agreeable hum of civilized conversation and laughter. It was a scene with which she was totally familiar, and yet from which she was estranged. Without realizing it, Kay had moved on from this kind of life, exchanging it for one in which she was out in the dark and the unknown, running the gauntlet.

What did they need in this new life? Guns. Explosives. Money.

She leaned over towards him. 'Listen . . .' she said very softly, 'I've an idea for a drop zone. The lake at Rosenlund. Not now maybe, but when things have died down.'

She had taken him completely by surprise. 'Have you gone mad?'

'Think about it. It's reasonably remote, has one good road, plenty of back ones, and would be recognizable from the air.'

Good: she had captured his attention.

'Attach a buoy to the containers, organize rowers to collect them and hide the stuff on the estate until it can be distributed. But not in winter, of course.'

'Wouldn't it take too long to get the stuff out of the water?'

'If it's done properly I am pretty sure we could get it out before any vehicle from Køge could get there. Anyway, we could probably leave one or two buoys in the lake. The odds are no one would notice them because they wouldn't be looking for them.'

Anton stared into his martini. 'High summer means light nights and the RAF won't fly. Sitting ducks. Obviously, winter is out. But we still have a few weeks in the early autumn or spring. What about Bror? Won't you be throwing him to the lions?'

'Plenty of planes fly over the house. It would be nothing new.'

'Wouldn't Bror notice if his dear wife wasn't in bed with him?'

She allowed the pause to drift on until it became a silence.

He cocked an eyebrow at her. 'Oh, he's not in your bed?'

'Actually . . . at the moment, he's sleeping on the other side of the house.'

'I see.' Naturally, this private information amused him.

'No, you don't see, Anton.'

'All right. I don't see.'

'I gave him to think that you and I were having an affair. It made it easier.' She glanced down at her ring. 'Estrangement is easier.'

The glint in his eye was less amused. 'Poor old Bror. What crosses he has to bear.'

Anton ordered a third martini for himself.

Kay waited until it arrived. 'Shall I get the drop zone coordinates to London?' She mimed playing the piano.

He nodded. 'They'll need to send over a reconnaissance plane and check it out before anything can be arranged.' He watched her over the rim of the glass. 'Kay, if you're ever in trouble, I can't help.'

Anton made such a meal of this. 'So you've said.'

'If you are in trouble, go to Café Amadeus on the Bredgade and ask for Oskar. Remember that.'

She nodded.

He edged closer and she tried to ward him off, but he said, 'We're having an affair, remember?' His mouth was close to hers. 'Anything else to report?'

'London still has to send over the crystals for the new wireless transmitters. Felix thought they would be ready very soon.'

'Let's hope so. Never has anything been so keenly anticipated.' Anton raised Kay's hand to his lips. 'For the time being, I suggest you mend a few fences with farmer Bror. Keep on good terms.'

Another silence.

'Darling, you can swear that I'm a cad and it was my fault. Say whatever you like – you can think of something – but, if I know my cousin, he will fall over himself to give you the benefit of the doubt. Keeping him sweet gives you room for manoeuvre.'

Her hand remained in his both for comfort and for security. She needed to reassure herself that she could handle what was coming.

She phoned Bror from the Damehotellet to tell him she would be arriving at Køge the following day on the two o'clock train.

She slept fitfully, breakfasted on *ymer* sprinkled with brown sugar and drank two cups of bitter coffee. Checking out of the hotel, she took a taxi to the Gothersgade, where she bought a hat from a favourite milliner. It was a straw one, sufficiently frivolous to be diverting.

Leaving the milliner's, she flagged down a second taxi and instructed the driver to take her to the university. As she paid him, she glanced towards the university entrance and she almost dropped her purse.

Clutching a sheaf of papers, and accompanied by General Gottfried and a lower-ranking officer, Nils emerged out of the main doorway into the street, where the three men conducted an animated conversation. At one point, Nils stabbed his finger down on a paper. The general nodded. Finally, they shook hands and the Germans got into a car which drove off. Nils transferred his papers from one hand to the other, took the steps back up to the entrance two at a time and disappeared into the building.

The taxi driver's finger tapped on the wheel and the look on his face was unmistakable. *Stikker*.

Kay snapped her bag shut. That Nils was cooperating was unthinkable. Yet it *was* thinkable, for Nils had his own way of going about things. He lived by his own logic, and saw the world differently. That much was true.

One day there would be retribution. Glancing at the taxi

driver's grim visage, she had a disturbing vision of post-war Denmark split by additional hatreds and vendettas.

Leaning forward, she instructed him to continue to the station. As he drove off, she did not allow herself to look back.

The road to Køge ran parallel to the railway track for a good portion of the way. Apparently there had been an explosion on it and, while the train did its customary crawl, Kay watched armoured German vehicles speeding to the scene.

Sabotage? She hoped so.

She pressed a finger against the pane. Who would be responsible for it? The communists? The nationalists? The strange organization that she was working for? Felix would be pleased. 'Sabotage would put Denmark on the map and get London to sit up,' he had told her once.

She caught a glimpse of her pale, drawn face in the train window. Could Tanne send word? Had Felix got out? She was pretty sure he would head for Sweden if he had. Surely Tanne would have gone with him?

Shockingly, she felt dislike – revulsion almost – for Rosenlund creep over her: its night silence; its petrified winter forests; the obligations that came with its occupancy; the grip of its past. Bror's obsession with it.

They were approaching the outskirts of Køge and Kay collected herself.

The train was late. Behind a checkpoint manned by soldiers in German *feldgrau* uniforms was Bror, cigarette in hand. Pulling on her pale green gloves, she adjusted the frivolous straw hat. There was no rule to say that one shouldn't deal with the enemy well dressed. Trusting to fate that none of them recognized her from the roadblock incident with Arne, she walked towards them and joined the queue.

The train blew its whistle – a desolate sound, she thought – and clunked slowly out of the station.

The wait was tedious. The soldiers were perfectly well aware of this but made no effort to hurry over the searches and papers. A woman carrying a sick-looking child was ordered to empty her basket. Kay offered to hold the child while the mother was searched.

The man in front of Kay wore a long gaberdine mackintosh. He was given the once-over: inevitable, perhaps, because he looked Jewish.

'No, no . . .' A screech of terror rose from the man. '*No.*'

Two of the soldiers stepped forward, hooked their arms under his elbows and dragged him off, his knees buckling. 'Help me . . . help me . . .' he called.

No one moved.

The trio vanished out of sight.

She could hear the thoughts of the silent onlookers. *Bloody communist. Bloody Jew. Had it coming. Daren't do anything. Hate them . . .* A spectrum of unvoiced responses.

When it was Kay's turn, she handed over her papers. The younger German examined them and conferred with his officer.

'Open your suitcase,' ordered the officer in bad Danish.

Kay lifted it onto the table and watched the men go through it. One silk nightdress. A tin of cold cream. Underwear. Her black dress.

'Unlock this box, please.'

Kay took off her gloves and complied, opening the box which contained her pearl necklace and earrings.

From his position by the barrier, Bror was keeping a close eye on proceedings.

'Are you satisfied, gentlemen?' she asked eventually, in German.

'Not quite. Where have you been?' She explained and was asked to repeat herself. 'Are you sure?'

'Quite sure.'

'Take off your coat,' ordered the officer.

They searched the coat's pockets and patted the seams and hem.

Nothing.

'Take off your hat.'

Her hair snagged on the hat pin and she was forced to work it free. The German snatched it away and ran a finger around the headband.

Nothing.

He handed it back.

'You may go.'

She couldn't bear to put the hat back on. Stiff with hatred, she picked up her gloves and the case and made her way towards Bror. He made no move to kiss her, but handed her into the car and they drove mostly in silence to Rosenlund, where he parked by the front door.

Reluctant to make the first move, reluctant to break the deep ice, they both lingered by the car in the sunshine.

Bror gave in first. 'Wulf has been on the phone. He told me they pieced together some evidence. A girl answering to Tanne's description was seen catching a train to København.'

'A girl, you say. How many girls are there in Denmark? When did they see her?'

'The morning after Tanne vanished.'

'Why have they taken so long to tell us this amazing fact?'

'Because they're watching us, to see if she comes back. Kay, I want to know if you went up to København to see her?'

She calculated the odds. Would Wulf have relayed the information on? Or would an old loyalty keep him silent?

'No, I didn't.' She turned and walked towards the garden.

Tanne had probably got away. Yes? No? Yes . . .

Bror caught up with Kay. As they so often did, they walked through the garden, past the irises and blowsy-headed peonies, past the beds which later would bloom with white cosmos and brightly coloured zinnias, drawn as always down to the lake.

The water was calm and transparent and Sophia-Maria's island appeared to float on it.

For once, the light was dazzling.

Bror bent down to inspect the nesting area in the rushes. How often had she seen him do that? As he stood upright he asked, 'Have I lost you?'

Her eyes were watering because of the sun. 'I'm not sure.'

Bror unleashed some uncharacteristic bitterness. 'It's your doing that Tanne has gone.'

'No,' she contradicted. 'War did it.'

'Maybe,' he acknowledged.

When she first arrived in Denmark, Kay had no idea what was meant by a Danish winter, no idea how the landscape changed from one of greens, yellows and cobalt blue, to the uniform, freezing melancholy of Lutheran grey and dun. Some years, as the outer darkness closed in, she had caught herself falling into a matching inner darkness. Struggling to survive those episodes, she had learned that she must neither panic nor give in.

Kay picked up a stone, a grey one streaked with white. Unlike a stone from the seaside, it had a sharp edge. She heard Anton's voice in her ear: 'Keep on good terms.'

'Darling Bror, we must not be at odds.' Unfolding her hand, the stone balancing on the palm, she offered it to him. 'Can we build a bridge?'

Looking across the sparkling water, she fantasized that, one day, he and she might live together in harmony again.

'We can stay here, out of sight, and work to keep the farms as productive as possible. That can be our contribution.'

He thought about it.

Accepting the stone, he hefted it from one hand to the other before sending it skimming away over the surface of the water.

Before dinner, she went up to her office and encoded her message.

Do you wish for the peace of my kiss?

With extreme effort. Teeth clamped together. Nervous.

Remember the five words.

Indicators.

Transposition.

Double transposition.

She longed for Felix's help. For Nils's wizardry with mathematical patterns. For Johan, her Morse teacher, and his calm instructions. For a degree of competence.

Message number . . . what number had Felix got to? She grabbed one at random. Fifty. Felix couldn't have sent more than fifty?

SUGGEST NEW DZ 1004993 *stop* PLEASE CHECK IT *stop* NO MORE MESSAGES FOR FORESEEABLE FUTURE *stop* ON THE RUN *stop* MAYONNAISE

That done, she went down to dinner and talked to Bror about crop yields and the mystery illness which was plaguing a couple of the cow herds. Afterwards, she pleaded fatigue and said she was going to have an early night.

Bror was looking at her with a peculiar intensity. There was a question mark and a supplication.

Was he asking to join her in her bed?

Not now. Not now. Having calculated that the surveillance on the estate would not be so efficient at night, she had to use the night hours.

Deliberately, she turned away. 'I'll see you in the morning, Bror,' she said, cool and distant. A second elapsed before she added, 'I sleep so much better on my own. Don't you?'

It was after midnight when she crept down the steps outside her office and, the torch beam muffled with a handkerchief, made her way as fast as possible to Ove's cottage.

In the outside privy, she placed the wireless set on the wooden lavatory seat and wedged the torch into the case lid so its light fell over the dials.

What next? Ready the set. Aerial out. Dial tuned. A cool

mind. A steady hand. The normal sked time had long passed and she selected the night-time emergency crystal.

ZYA QTC1 . . .

From ZYA, I have one message for you.

Nothing.

Again, the arduous keying in: ZYA QTC1.

Somewhere, someone was patrolling the emergency frequencies.

Hurry up . . . please.

QVR.

Ah . . . she had been picked up.

A lump heaved into Kay's throat. *Home.* Home was where they knew what they thought, who they were fighting, and to whom they should listen. Not like here. Not like fractured Denmark.

She did her best. Her finger felt useless on the transmitter key. Clumsy. Slow. Sweat ran down from her armpits. My God, she was bad at it. And surely everyone within a radius of a hundred metres would catch the fizzing ether in her headphones, the tap of the key.

Somewhere out there, General Gottfried's crack unit had almost certainly latched onto the stumbling transmission. Had they fixed on it yet?

When it was over, her hands dropped into her lap.

She had gone over the drill with Felix. He had taught her that, if the emergency frequency was used, a pianist had to wait seventy minutes for a reply.

He explained what happened at the listening station when the emergency frequency was used. With someone standing by to type into the teleprinter, a cipher clerk at Home Station would decode at top speed. At headquarters top-priority systems would swing into action. A reply from the bosses would be formulated, encoded and transmitted.

The Morse began to pulse in her ears.

QTC1. *I have one message for you.*

Headphones on, she strained to hear the incoming message.

It was done. Finally. QSL. *I acknowledge receipt.* AR. *Over. Finish.*

She ticked the boxes.

Pack up methodically. Stow aerial and flex. Disconnect headphones. Remove crystal.

Where should she hide the wireless set? In the pigeon loft? Or leave it here?

Here.

She tore the outgoing message into shreds and tamped it down into the earth under the trees, folded the incoming message into a spill and tucked it into the cotton scarf round her neck.

Back in her bedroom, Kay undressed, sat down at her dressing table and began to decode the incoming message. It was laborious, mind-numbing work and she wasn't sure she was going to be able to do it.

But she did.

ABANDON AREA *stop* RETURN LONDON FOR DEBRIEF *stop* USE SWEDISH BUS *stop* CONTACT RICHARD *stop*

The message was too late to get to Felix but it helped Kay. London was looking out for him and, if Tanne was with Felix, they would take care of her.

Her gloves lay on the dressing table. With a practised movement, she wedged the decoded message into the first finger of the right-hand one and dropped it back down on the dressing table.

Bed . . . sleep . . . at last.

She was drifting . . . drowsing. The door opened and in came Bror. Casting aside his dressing gown, he lay down beside her.

She lay stiff with surprise. 'Bror . . . why are you here?' The relief that he was there. The terror that he was.

'Kay . . . darling Kay . . . this can't go on.'

He was so familiar, and yet so alien. They had travelled so far apart – and she thought her heart would break.

After a while, he put out an arm. 'This is madness. How have we let this happen?' He stroked her cheek. 'I can't lose you and Tanne.'

A bridge was being built. Fragile and shaky, it might not stand too many shocks.

It was so dark, Kay could not see him, only feel him – the length of his limbs, the flexed arm and the butterfly trails made by his fingers on her skin.

Exhaustion seeped through her. She loved Bror. Because she loved him, she could give him one thing. She could grant him some peace of mind. 'Bror, I suspect Tanne's in Sweden.'

'Suspect or know?'

'I can't tell you for sure.'

The stroking on her cheek ceased. 'I wondered. Sweden was the obvious place.'

They were whispering into the dark, moving closer.

'I know people are getting themselves over there,' he said.

'Then you'll know it's the best thing? Tanne will be safe, particularly if her politics are changing. Once the war is over, she can come back and she will have a clean sheet. She won't be –' Kay laid her hand flat against Bror's chest '– contaminated, I suppose.'

'And I am?'

'Let's not think about that now.'

He fell asleep with his head on her shoulder. She listened to his steady breathing and cradled her arm carefully round his body, holding him as if she would never let him go.

My God, that was close. That was very close.

Chapter Twenty-five

In early May, Mary received an unexpected communication.

Years ago, Mary's cousin Vera had married 'up' and left London – leaving behind Mary and an assortment of other cousins in their cramped Brixton terraces – and vanished into the roomier domain of a detached house and garden near Henford. Vera had always been the brainier one, and more determined. Since then, the family had not seen much of Vera, certainly not since the outbreak of war. Her letter inviting Mary to tea therefore came as a surprise, particularly as Mary had not been aware that Vera knew she was in the area.

The bus drove past rows of houses and bungalows with their lines of washing and scrubbed front steps, past the post boxes, telephone kiosks and scrubby vegetable patches. Once outside Henford, buildings yielded to green stubbled fields, and to ditches and hedgerows where Queen Anne's lace foamed in profusion.

Everything on this late spring day was bright and fresh – which Mary appreciated. Truly she did, and it lifted her spirits.

Yet she couldn't forget that the world was in a mess. Could the politicians do anything about it? Reposing in Mary's bag was a copy of Mr Beveridge's report on social policy. Apparently, in a new post-war Britain, poverty, disease and squalor would be given their marching orders, backed up by a new contributory scheme which would offer a safety net from the cradle to the grave.

Mary liked the sound of Mr Beveridge's thinking. If implemented, it would mean she wouldn't need to be quite so anxious about her future. She also approved the idea that she would be contributing to that future. And other's. *Mary Voss* . . . she murmured. *You matter.*

The walk from the bus stop to Vera's house turned out be half a mile or so and it was warm. Mary's one good blouse was made of Viyella and, within minutes, she was perspiring. Her not-always-successful solution to this universal problem was to sew pads into her clothing and to use plenty of talcum powder – if she could get hold of it – or bicarbonate. Praying that her perspiration wasn't too obvious, she walked up the path to Vera's front door.

'Mary . . . you're here already.'

Vera, a harassed-looking redhead with a redhead's translucent skin, had emerged from a room at the back of the house, wiping her hands on her apron. 'The bus must have been quicker than usual.' She drew Mary into the parlour. 'Let me look at you. It must be a couple of years.'

They were interrupted by the telephone ringing in the hall. An odd, worried look whisked over Vera's face. Pushing Mary into a chair, she went to answer it. Mary heard her say: 'Darling, *six* at dawn . . .'

Mary was amused to note that Vera's accent fluted in a way it never had when she was a child in Brixton.

'. . . *before* dawn? I'd better make the beds but I haven't had a chance to wash the sheets from the last lot yet. Too bad. They'll be too tired to notice. Will the new butcher give me extra bacon? I'm sure he suspects. Is he the silent type, do you think? I'll lay the table now. I've got one for this evening. The one last night broke my heart. He had a wild and haunted look . . . I was worried sick that his nerves were shot. They will look out for him, won't they? I must go. Mary's arrived for tea . . .' There was a pause before Vera said: 'Mary Voss, my cousin. You remember Mary?'

Probably not, thought Mary a touch acidly.

Vera's feet beat a rapid path down the passage. Mary went

after her and discovered Vera in the kitchen filling the kettle. At Mary's entrance, she wheeled round. 'You startled me.'

'Sorry.'

'No, no. Not at all. I'm just getting tea . . . I'm sorry to say that I'm a bit behind today, Mary. John and I have had a lot on. The hens, I'm so late with them . . . Trouble with animals is that they don't understand if they're not fed.'

'If you like, I'll do the hens.'

'Would you? That is *awfully* nice of you. I'm afraid I've got some unexpected visitors coming later.'

'Who?'

Vera shrugged. 'Just people. They're travelling here and there, you know, and John and I put them up.' She made a vague gesture. 'The war effort.'

'How mysterious.'

Vera whisked off a cloth covering a plate of sandwiches. They were curling just a touch at the edges. 'It's nice to see you, Mary.'

'How did you know where to find me?'

There was a pause. 'I think I saw you in Henford before Christmas. You were in uniform and I reckoned you were working at the big house.' Vera appeared cagey about the details. She thrust a bowl at Mary. '*Would* you?'

Mary found herself by the chicken coop scattering the grain. A hen orchestra tuned up as a cluster of hens scuttled towards the food. A tiny bantam, no more than a handful of feathers, clucked by Mary's feet and she bent over and touched it with a fingertip. The little thing was so warm and soft and, in contrast to the life Mary was now leading, real.

She straightened up. Vera *had* done well. Even if the hedges needed a trim, moles had been at work all over the lawn and the hens had churned up a great patch under the oak tree, there was a spacious and generous feel to the garden.

From one of the straggle of outhouses, pigeons were sounding. It was a good noise, especially on a lovely day like this one.

Curiosity piqued, Mary strolled over to the shed and poked her nose inside.

To her astonishment, it contained a row of large cages, several of which were inhabited by birds. On a bench in the middle were stacked leather carrier boxes, water bottles and blocks of hard feed.

Since when had Vera and John kept racing pigeons? Mary drifted over to the cages. At her approach, a couple of the birds fluttered their wings and called out.

A big buff-coloured male caught her eye. He had bright eyes and a strong-looking neck but there was a sore on his leg as if something had rubbed up against it. A piece of paper had fallen onto the floor of his cage. Mary squinted at it and experienced a small electric shock.

It was impossible not to recognize what it was.

Mary had sent and received enough signals to know that the neat columns of apparently random letters were an incoming message from the field, or perhaps an outgoing one. She had no idea which. What she did know was that this was a bad security breach . . . and Vera was obviously involved in secret work using pigeons to send messages.

Up to her neck in it, Vera was.

'Mary! What are you doing?'

Vera had come up behind her.

Mary did not look round. 'I had no idea you kept pigeons.'

'Well, we do.' Vera was very short.

Mary indicated the paper in the cage. 'Vera . . . Should you?'

Quick as a flash, Vera interposed herself between Mary and the cage. 'You've seen *nothing*, Mary. Do you understand?'

'I do.' She thought of the long hours of listening. 'Believe me.'

Vera swallowed. 'It was a mistake. Do you understand?'

Secrets. They were everywhere. The war was being fought with secrets. Big ones, negligible ones . . . ones that people died to keep. Those in the know had to keep silence and were forbidden to link up any tiny nuggets of evidence to assemble a bigger picture, however tempting.

The equation balanced. Mary knew she must not let on that she knew the pigeons in Vera's back garden were probably flying messages to and from occupied Europe. In return, Vera must be ignorant of where Mary worked.

Vera succeeded in pushing Mary out of the shed and shut the door. She leaned back against it. 'Mary, I have to trust you. Can I?'

'Yes.'

Both of them sounded very self-conscious – which made Mary want to giggle. But it wasn't a joke. 'That message . . . you must hide it.'

Vera blushed bright red. 'An oversight.'

Oh Lord, Mary thought. *I'm relishing this*. During their childhood, Vera had always been the cousin held up as an example by the adults, and the rest of them had suffered from it.

Vera scuffed a patch of earth with the toe of her shoe. 'It hasn't ever happened . . . it won't happen again.' Vera's embarrassment rose in waves and Mary couldn't help but enjoy it. Just a little.

Vera had a go at turning the conversation to normal. 'Did you feed the hens?'

'Yes, I did.'

The little bantam chose that moment to cluck across their path. 'It's so sweet,' said Mary.

With obvious relief, Vera said: 'That's Meeny. Miny and Mo are over there. I'm afraid Eeny died.' She touched Mary on the shoulder. 'Kettle's boiled and you've earned your tea.'

Her moment of triumph shelved, Mary sought to break the tension. 'It's quite a haven here.'

Vera gave a strained laugh. 'Rabbits, squirrels, some frogs . . .'

'We have bluebottles in the canteen which we can't get rid of and one of the girls swears she's also spotted fleas.'

'The real enemy.'

The cousins' eyes met in a glancing exchange. How strange war was, how very strange. Its reach was like leaking water which appeared in surprising places and a long way from its original source.

After a lull, traffic was hotting up at Station 53d and Signalmaster Noble was in a bad temper. Having shouted at Nancy for inattention, he left the room to deliver the latest messages to the decoders.

'*Men!*' Nancy dropped her head into her hands and tugged at her hair.

'Men have two feet, two hands and, sometimes, two women, but never more than one shilling or one idea at the same time,' Mary sat down and checked over her pencils.

Nancy raised her head. 'Not *bad*,' she said admiringly. She raised her voice. 'Here, Beryl! Listen to what Mary's just come up with.'

Mary wasn't displeased. Quite the opposite. The girls' reaction, and her satisfaction in it, was very pleasing.

'You're doing a lot of extra shifts.' Nancy's head was back in her hands.

'So are you,' Mary replied.

'I'm doing it for the extra pay.'

Pleasing though it was to bank, the extra pay wasn't the main reason Mary took on the additional shifts. Disciplined and seasoned as she was, the work flowed through her fingers. By her own efforts, she had turned herself into one of the most reliable of operators. She loved that and the reward in doing something well. Yet it was the bond with 'her' agents which was always at the back of Mary's mind. That bond – whose demands and imperatives pushed her into flights of feeling that could take her breath away.

Now the days were getting longer, Mary reckoned that the agents would be freer to move around and to plan operations. Not that she had any concrete evidence. Maybe – and she hoped they would – they would take pleasure and gain some respite and relief from the sight of wheeling swallows, meadows sweet with hay, sheep at pasture, from the arrival of fresh vegetables and fruit, the warmth of city streets . . .

'Voss!' Signalmaster Noble had returned. 'You have ten minutes before your next sked. Get me a cup of tea. Smartish.'

He was out of order. Mary knew it and he knew it. The difference: he could get away with it.

Ten minutes meant ten minutes. Taking the quickest route to the canteen, Mary had to pass a small office at the top of the stairs. The door to this office was ajar. A raised male voice sounded from inside.

'The situation is a mess.' The speaker was clearly exasperated. 'According to Mayonnaise, Copenhagen is stuffed with informers. He also reported that one of the agents on Jutland had to be eliminated and the last drop was a disaster. Everyone's furious. The RAF bods are threatening to withhold planes. Only Vinegar is up and running.'

'And uncompromised?'

'As far as we know'

Vinegar. Mayonnaise. On hearing these names, Mary's heart quickened.

Her footsteps on the wooden floor gave away her presence and the door slammed shut.

'Spies Are Everywhere' ran the legend on the latest warning poster in the canteen. Well, she wasn't a spy but, in a short space of time, she had stumbled across two pieces of interesting information.

Copenhagen.

Was it possible that Vinegar and Mayonnaise were operating in Denmark?

At the next opportunity, she visited the local library and scoured the papers for any hints of relevant activity, puzzling over the references to Sweden and 'flows of information'. At first, she took this to mean radio traffic. Having consulted a map, and read one or two articles which dropped broad hints, she revised her opinion. 'Flows of information' looked more likely to be the result of fishing boats slipping away from the Danish coast into the Øresund, or stealing around the minefields in the Kattegat, and making their way to Sweden.

How did intelligence work? Mary was groping towards understanding how important it was to possess the ability to sift random facts and to make sense of them. The ratchets in her mind clicked onwards. For example: Vera was keeping messenger pigeons, and was almost certainly involved in war work. She was also entertaining 'visitors' who might, or might not, be engaged in secret work, too. Was it possible it had been Vera who had recommended Mary for Morse training? Vera knew about her father.

During the second week in May, Mary realized she had lost Mayonnaise. Or rather, he had gone silent.

'Sir,' she reported to Signalmaster Noble. 'Mayonnaise has missed two skeds.'

He frowned. 'Right, then. We'll get that logged.'

Mary's frustration was intense at not being able to ask why Mayonnaise had gone silent – at not being able to make any kind of comment.

She was allocated another agent. Different call sign, different fist. 'Just do your best, Voss, and don't say anything.' Signalmaster Noble smiled sardonically. 'It's not your place.'

Mayonnaise's silence affected Mary badly. She was terrified he was captured or on the run without a wireless set.

Where did you hide in a country that, she knew from her research, was uniformly flat? Surely there had to be woods, even a forest? And there must be places to hide along the coastline?

The pain she felt at losing an agent took even her by surprise. It got to her in many ways. Music . . . she found herself unable to listen to Beethoven's Fifth on the radio, for example, or Schubert's Quintet, or even Vera Lynn, without choking up.

Appetite . . . she had to force herself to eat. Sleep . . . that was a subject best left, so bad were her sleep patterns.

Thank God, Vinegar still observed his skeds to the second. Please, she sent him a silent message, keep to the rules. Keep your mouth tight shut and cover your traces and tracks.

In idle moments, Mary fleshed him out. Her mental construct was of a man who was not particularly tall or good-looking, but someone who was generous, physically adept and clever. From time to time, the details altered but one thing was for sure: he was nothing like the men with whom she worked. Vinegar wouldn't be wearing uniform and there would be none of that strutting that went with it.

This, she knew, was to create a soft-focus image. Yet now that she could picture him in her mind, the moments of loss and despair, experienced so often by Mary, began to dissolve. Thus, she arrived at the beginning of another life.

All thoughts of anything else were driven from her head when, during one shift towards the end of May, Mary was making a routine patrol of the emergency frequency and Mayonnaise came back on the air.

Thank God. Thank God.

Every sense straining, she took down the Morse. The signal was good, the best she had heard it for some time. Then, quite suddenly, Mary's stomach lurched.

This wasn't Mayonnaise. Halting, uneven, and with none of his characteristic confidence.

This fist was quite, quite different.

Chapter Twenty-six

Ruby's frustration was growing. As far as she could make out, nothing was being done about the problems of the poem code.

She had learned one thing. Even an organization like The Firm became clotted with systems and bureaucracy, however much it protested that it was different.

'How does anything ever get done anywhere?' she demanded of Peter.

'By patience,' he replied. 'Cunning. Guile.'

'For God's sake', she whipped back, sharp and sarcastic. 'Changing the agents' coding practice isn't caprice. It isn't bloody-mindedness.'

Patience. Cunning. Guile.

First off: employ mathematical principles to clarify the position, define the problem and improve the reasoning.

Shifting onto the moral ground, she asked the question: Why rank knowledge that would save lives below obedience?

Thirdly . . . thirdly . . . it was more than the sum of those two. Weren't they – and by that Ruby meant all of them who worked in The Firm – collectively responsible? On to their consciences would be stamped the pain and the terror of the agents.

If the agents were prepared to take risks, those on the home front were morally obliged to do so, too. Anyway, it would give her a great deal of satisfaction to force all those arrogant, blinkered males to look at the problems again.

Knowing all too well that if she was caught, or made a mistake, her life would disappear into a black hole, Ruby worked out a plan.

*

The timing was crucial. Calculating that, after a fiendish early morning start, the galley slaves in Intelligence would be gasping for tea and their guards would be down, she phoned at eleven o'clock precisely and requested all the Danish back traffic since 1942.

'Permission?' said the male voice at the end of the phone.

'Major Martin.' She was amazed how the lie tripped off her tongue. 'I can bring up a tray of tea.'

Pause.

Please do not ask for a signed memo.

'Not strictly allowed,' said the voice at the other end. 'But I'll give you an hour and a desk.' He laughed. 'We like visits from a cipherine.'

'Good.' She did not add, *you patronizing bugger.*

Having got herself there, Ruby was faced by a desk, her two sharpened pencils, her notebook and a pile of messages. Now she had to get on with it, and she was terrified.

But she had her wits. Her sharp, twitching wits.

Compared to other sections, Danish back traffic turned out to be pitifully sparse. With regard to the agents and any intelligence it revealed that nothing much had flourished in Denmark until early 1943. It appeared that there had been four wireless sets in total operating for The Firm. Two had gone silent in the summer of 1942. The two pianists who remained, Mayonnaise (call sign ZYA) and Vinegar (call sign XRT), had been operating since the autumn of 1942.

Flexing her fingers, Ruby detailed the procedures and protocols in her head.

All agents were issued with two security checks which came in the form of deliberate mistakes – for example, they would make a mistake with every sixteenth letter. The first of these was a bluff security check which, if necessary, they could give to the enemy if they were captured and tortured. The second was the real security check which they should try to keep back.

Stacked in date order, the messages were criss-crossed in blue crayon by Intelligence.

Message Number: 8
25 November 1942
REGRET TO INFORM TABLE LEAF CAUGHT AT RADIO BACK IN JUNE *stop* DIED BY OWN HAND *stop* SET CAPTURED *stop* MAYONNAISE

Both security checks included. One mistake in transmission which the signal clerk had corrected.

Message Number: 9
4 December 1942
URGENT NEED FOR RADIOS *stop* TOO DANGEROUS TO MOVE SETS AROUND *stop* RECRUITING GOING WELL *stop* MAYONNAISE

Both security checks in place.
And so on through a sequence of numbered messages.

Message Number: 38
27 April 1943
MUSTARD HAS BEEN WIPED OFF PLATE *stop* MAYONNAISE

Both security checks were present. Message had several coding mistakes.

Message Number: 39
2 May 1943
DROP PARTIAL SUCCESS *stop* LYING LOW *stop* INJURED *stop* NON LIFE THREATENING *stop* HAVE WIRELESS *stop* MAYONNAISE

Neither security checks were present.

Message Number: 50

50? Ruby noted the leap in numbering.

SUGGEST NEW DZ 1004993 *stop* PLEASE CHECK IT *stop* NO MORE MESSAGES FOR FORESEEABLE FUTURE *stop* ON THE RUN *stop* MAYONNAISE

This one was a mess. No security checks were present. There were seven coding mistakes and five mistakes in transmission. Intelligence had noted the omissions.

Ruby glanced at her watch. Her pencils were wearing down and the minutes were ticking by. From time to time, some of the clerks sent her a curious glance. Sweat sprouted under her arms but she pressed on.

She turned her attention to Vinegar, who had sent forty-five messages, many of them quite short. Having taken the precaution of looking at Vinegar's test coding exercises, she checked over a few of the more typical messages. She realized that something did not quite add up. Was it the content of the messages?

Vinegar's traffic suggested that, to all extents and purposes, he was having an easy time. He was almost lyrical about the smooth running of his network, repeatedly requesting an arms drop and money. He fed in snippets of information about train and troop movements – although nothing very substantial, Ruby noted. However, when he was requested to return to London for briefing, he refused on the grounds that it would compromise the circuit.

Of Mayonnaise's messages three were indecipherables – which was about the norm for agents in the field – and the final one was, frankly, a puzzle which would have to be investigated. Apart from the last two, both the bluff and real security checks were always present and correct.

A rapid check of Vinegar's back traffic revealed that both bluff and real security checks were always in place. Furthermore, in direct contrast to Mayonnaise, *there had not been one single coding mistake in the transmissions.*

This was highly unusual.

How would an agent never make a coding mistake, unless they were a demigod? Good question.

Another odd thing was that very often in the later transmissions Vinegar always spelled 'stop' incorrectly: *stip, stap, stup.* Why was that? Given his exactitude, it was uncharacteristic and odd. Atmospherics?

She ran a second check. None of the earlier transmissions showed this mistake.

Stubbornly, to the last second, Ruby continued to comb back through the traffic. What was nagging at her? What was she failing to see?

Time up.

Knees like jelly, she made her way back to her own desk and dropped her head into her hands.

Her mind was full of images . . . choking . . . fearful . . .

Shots. An agent fleeing. The darkness of a prison cell. Dying on the run. An agent dropping out of the sky while the enemy waited below. A broken leg being twisted round as a preliminary . . .

The air in the office was stale, almost stifling. Ruby sprang to her feet. 'I need some exercise,' she told Gussie.

'Is that what they call it?' Gussie did not raise her head.

Ruby paced up and down the corridor. Restricted, stuffy, dim and dingy the office may have been, but at least it was in the free world.

Think.

What was eluding her? What had she not understood?

What do agents do under pressure? How do agents behave under pressure?

She remembered that during one of their many meetings Peter had told her: 'No agent in the field is ever perfect, particularly if he has a variable training record.'

Use her knowledge. What did she know for sure? She recollected Eloise, so anxious and unsure and frightened that she would not match up to the task.

Human beings tended to plump for easy options at the best of times, let alone when their confidence was low. Eloise had taught Ruby that lesson. Under pressure, agents were almost certain to choose: a) the shortest words, b) the easiest to spell, c) the words which held emotional meaning whether they were aware of it or not.

Above all, they made mistakes.

On the way back to her office, she stopped off in Stationery and requested typing paper.

'You need a docket,' said the clerk, a youth in badly fitting khakis. He was not only spotty but looked the obstinate type.

'Tell you what,' said Ruby. 'I'll take you out for a drink.'

She got the paper.

The hours came and went and Ruby typed on late into the evening.

As she did so, conclusions fell into place.

Eventually, the night duty officer, a bouncy type who always set her teeth on edge, sidled up to her desk. 'Time for the off, miss.'

Frowning she looked up. 'Two minutes.'

He gave Ruby the once-over. She could read his thoughts: *Double agent and/or conducting an affair with one of the top brass still in conference upstairs?*

Rumour had it that a major and a FANY lovely had been found *in flagrante* on a desk.

Had this charmer been the one who found them?

'Righty-ho,' he said, which meant: *Which one is going to get his hand up her skirt?*

At nine o'clock the following morning, she put in a request to see Peter in his office and was allocated ten minutes. Gussie shut Peter's diary with an emphatic click. 'And not one second longer.'

She stepped into his office. It was dusty, smoky and stacked with files marked 'Top Secret'.

'You could do with a cleaner,' she said.

Peter was writing rapidly with a fountain pen. He held up a finger. The sight of the thick dark hair brushed back hard against his head stirred up feelings which Ruby had no wish to deal with at this moment.

Gussie stuck her head round the door. 'Sir, I'm booting her out in ten minutes.'

Ruby looked over to the map on the wall which was covered with different-coloured pins. Agents? Several clusters in France. Far fewer in Greece and Albania. A couple in Italy. One in Germany – how did anyone survive there? Not enough to constitute a cluster in Denmark.

This war had gone on for so long. Could anyone remember houses with lights shining through windows at night? Or a city without rubble? Although the situation had taken a turn for the better with Monty's progress in North Africa and with Italy's surrender, there didn't seem to be much comfort on the home front. Could the unsubstantiated, but persistent, hints of atrocities in Eastern Europe be true? Other than Peter, the one or two people with whom she had discussed it had been adamant that such things were not possible.

Surely they were possible. But probable?

'Ruby?' Peter looked up with a smile that said: *I'm glad you're here.*

She placed her typewritten report in front of him. 'Read this.'

He rifled through. The smile switched off. 'Christ Almighty, where did you get this information?'

She was perfectly straight with him. Peter leaped to his feet. 'They hang people for less.'

'So?'

He swung round to face her. 'I don't think you understand. Quite apart from the position this places you in, complete and

341

utter secrecy between departments is crucial. If the wall is breached, the trust is gone.'

'The agents trust us.'

A shadow passed over Peter's features.

'Listen to me, Peter.'

Ruby extracted Vinegar's test coding exercises from a file and spread them out over the desk. 'We have to entertain the possibility that the Germans are playing back one of our radios. Vinegar's training records told us he is a reasonable wireless operator but a bad coder and decoder.' She stabbed a finger down on a training paper. 'Tell me honestly. How likely is it he will have improved in the field?'

'Not very likely.'

'We don't have a record of his fist so we can't make comparisons. I think . . . I think there is more than a possibility that the enemy have tortured the poem code and the security checks out of Vinegar and are making him transmit their messages.'

For a second, Peter was stricken and she experienced an untidy mix of triumph and apprehension. He glanced at the data and his face darkened. 'You should have consulted me, Ruby.'

She was shocked by his fury, and the old resentments erupted. 'Because you're senior? Because you're a man? I've done important work for you. Good analysis. You should be pleased.'

'For God's sake.'

They glared at each other.

She couldn't help it. '*Is* it because I'm a woman?'

'Shut up.'

Peter was right. Her sex was irrelevant and she must think strategically. 'There *is* something wrong. You must see it there. Furthermore, I think he was trying to tell us something.' She banged her hand down on the papers.

Stip, stap, stup . . .

'That's not proof,' said Peter.

'There's a pattern. Patterns are what we look for.'

'I don't know what to say to you.'

The cold and objective part of her thought: *He's a fool like other men.*

'You could say that I have a point. You could say that I'm right,' she said.

'You haven't proved it.'

'That's the point. I'm trying to show it to you but, because we deal in the shadows and with unknowns, I can't give it to you all wrapped in birthday ribbon. You, of all people, understand that.'

The dark eyes trained on her were bitterly angry.

'Go,' ordered Gussie, who had walked into the office. 'He's due at the meeting.'

'Can I come back?' she asked.

He was as icy as she was. 'No.'

Without another word, Ruby left.

That evening, she sat in the tin bath in her digs. The trains rattling past the house shook the bathroom window. She washed between her toes and legs and considered the theory of the unconscious. According to the psychologists, all humans possessed one, and it drove their inner and outer lives. An upheaval was taking place in Ruby's, but she couldn't force whatever it was to the surface.

She towelled herself dry, hoiked out the knickers with the braid edging, put on the one good frock she possessed, with three-quarter sleeves and a pretty neckline, and piled her hair on top of her head. Salt-of-the-earth Janet was in London on twelve-hour leave, and they were going to make an evening of it.

'Not bad, girl,' she informed the reflection in the small mirror.

At the Berkeley Hotel, Janet leaped to her feet when she saw Ruby at the entrance to the bar. 'Good to see you. We've got the drinks.' She manhandled Ruby to the table where, to her surprise, haughty-as-a-duchess Frances was also seated.

Frances had been staring glumly into her glass but looked up. 'Nice to see you, Ruby.'

'And you,' said Ruby, and she meant it.

Looking back, Ruby reckoned it must have been something to do with the Joe Loss band pumping out its music, or the warm and spiced summer evening, but the spiky feelings took a back seat and Ruby relaxed.

Janet pushed a glass over to her. 'Down the hatch.'

'Let's make the evening one in the eye for Hitler.'

Several cocktails later they were picked up by three RAF pilots on 'bloody well-earned' twenty-four-hour leave.

The men were drunk and very tired, but more or less in control. 'Dance with us, girls,' said the tallest, a recent burn mark visible on his cheek. His name was Tony. 'Do your bit for the war.'

'War means sacrifice,' Ruby teased, 'but I never realized how much.'

She took to the floor with him while Janet and Frances were swept up by Robin and Hal. Dancing with Tony was far from unpleasant.

Getting to London had been a nightmare, Tony murmured in her ear, but he and the boys had been hell-bent on it. 'Because I end up dancing with someone like you. Just what the doctor ordered.'

Ruby laughed. It was fun. Tony was fun. And she could tell that he wanted her. Well, not *her* precisely but a female body. She certainly wasn't offended. Such a big deal was made about sex. Such a hum and furore and hypocrisy when, in fact, it was as straightforward as enjoying good food.

The band slowed the tempo. Out of the corner of her eye, she spotted Janet entangled with Hal. Frances was moving dreamily across the floor with Rob. You could tell she had had dancing lessons and the two of them looked good together, the kind of good which money bought.

Tony pulled her closer. 'Funny old life, isn't it?'

She touched his uniformed chest. 'At least we have this,' she said.

'Meaning?'

'Sensations. Music. Dancing. Drink.'

'You should try flying. It's euphoria like you can never experience on earth. A feeling of total liberty.'

'I'd like to. I've never done it.'

'Get yourself transferred to a bomber station. You could have a new boyfriend every night and someone would be sure to take you up. Be prepared for tears, though. We come and . . . go.'

The lightly uttered words touched her. Having never flown, she didn't *know* what Tony was really talking about but she could grasp that the pilots and the WAAFs lived close to the edge.

At the end of the evening Tony tucked a hand under her elbow and steered her onto the dance floor for the final dance. 'Come to the hotel with me, Ruby? I'm flying tomorrow, and I would like it very much.'

An ache for Peter took her by surprise. Then she recollected the cold hostility with which they had parted.

Tony was smiling down at her. Oh God, he might die in the next few days and he knew it. 'Yes, I'll come.'

They said their goodnights to the others. Their bright lipstick now smudged, the girls exchanged complicit glances. One day they might share confidences about the evening and its various finales . . . Taxis. Awkward admissions into a hotel. Whisky in tooth mugs. Even more awkward, or drunken, moments in the hotel bed.

Halfway through their love-making, Ruby knew that this wasn't so much a mistake as a lapse in taste. Not that she wasn't enjoying it. Tony was nice, he made love with vigour and panache, and they had fun. And, understanding the neediness of a man about to fly into battle, she strove to give him what he wanted. But she sensed he craved more and she couldn't give it to him. Although her pity was powerful it was not as elemental as true desire.

Afterwards, she got up and went into the bathroom to sponge herself down. The water was tepid and she shivered with the late-night chill, and with a misery that she did her best to ignore.

She had used sex as revenge, and the experience turned out to be sour. And – she smiled wryly at herself in the mirror as she dried herself, her limbs pale in the dim light – how very old-fashioned the revenge lay was, too.

Hands behind his head, Tony watched her as she got dressed. 'Shall we meet again, oh Ruby?'

She smiled down at him. 'I think not. I don't make a habit of this, and there is someone else.'

He frowned. 'Heavens. An unvirtuous woman. And I had imagined you had succumbed to my charms. Didn't think most women did that sort of thing.' He beat the flat of his hand on the mattress. 'I thought . . . I had an idea . . . but never mind.' He looked up at her. 'Most girls I know aren't as cool.'

She sat down on the edge of the bed and took his hand. 'I liked you very much.'

'But it was just the sex. Or the champagne?'

'Or wartime?'

'How very honest, Ruby.' The remark didn't sound like a compliment. 'Money well spent, then.' He dropped her hand. 'You're an unusual woman.'

She picked at a thread on her handbag strap. 'Most women would think more like me if they had a chance.'

'Would they now?'

She left with Tony's derision in her ears.

She had her come-uppance. It was so late that the last bus back to her digs had gone and she was forced to pick her way through the darkness and the bomb-pocked streets in her evening dress.

When she got back to her room, she shut the door, leaned against it and cried.

The next few days saw lockdown at the office. There was either a big push on, or an emergency, and endless meetings took place behind closed doors in smoke-filled rooms where the chiefs gathered.

Eventually, Peter returned to his office and asked for Ruby. He looked as though he had eaten nothing much for days and the black circles were back under his eyes.

'You look awful,' she said.

'A forty-eight-hour special. You'd have enjoyed it.'

Ruby said nothing and waited.

Peter propped his chin in his hand. 'Are we going to speak to each other?'

What had she done? The answer was nothing, and everything. She had never admired conventional mores. If she wished to sleep with a man, she would. All the same, she wished she hadn't done so with Tony.

'I searched for you the other night,' he said gently. 'I couldn't find you.'

'And?'

'I wanted to ask if you were still angry.'

She felt thwarted by his sweetness, and maddened. Her instincts had been right all along. Love, even sex, was too complicated a subject on which to waste time. The guilt, jealousy, despair, bewilderment were neither interesting nor *worth* it.

'I was. I think I still am,' she replied. 'I know dinosaurs roam these corridors, but we're here to think laterally. Isn't that our point? And when we try to do something that needs doing . . .' She didn't finish the sentence.

'Try to understand, Ruby.' The tension was ratcheting up between them again. 'This outfit's improvised. Nothing like us has existed before. We've no experience to draw on, no manuals.'

'I've heard enough.' She had her hand on the door handle.

He added: 'There have to be rules and, if you or I were found out, we could be keel-hauled.'

Despite everything, she felt a squeak of triumph. Peter was engaged. His comment revealed that he was thinking about it.

She turned round. 'We agree the agents trust us. We instruct them to have faith . . . in *us*. We have to justify that.'

Agents were melting into enemy territory with only hope and trust and a bit of fieldcraft to get them through.

Peter got to his feet and came over to Ruby. 'Where were you the other night? Tell me.'

In that moment her feelings did an infuriating volte-face. If she told Peter the truth, she knew, *she knew*, he would disappear. She couldn't let that happen. His dark eyes, his sweetness, his clever and subtle mind, his slight elegant body were hers.

'I went home to my digs,' she said.

She was compromised. Everything was compromised.

'Is that the truth?'

She didn't believe in lying and this one was one of the hardest lies she had ever told. 'Yes.'

He stared down into her face. He didn't believe her and she felt his hurt and distaste as if they were her own. 'I thought we trusted each other.'

The old intemperate demon got the upper hand. 'Then go to hell, Peter.'

Yet Ruby wasn't giving up.

The agents had no one else to trust.

Chapter Twenty-seven

Mary was summoned by Signalmaster Falks. 'Our lords and masters have been playing silly buggers again.'

For once, she had to make an effort to concentrate. 'Oh?'

Signalmaster Falks was not an organized man and it took him several searches through his overflowing in-tray to produce the piece of paper he wanted. 'Yup. That's it.' He scanned the typewritten page. 'From now on, each agent is to produce a crib sheet of their fist before they go in. We're to keep copies here as reference. You're to refer to them at all times.'

'I don't need one,' she protested. 'I know them like the back of my hand.'

'*You* might not need one, Voss. But some of the fluffy bunnies that I'm unfortunate enough to have on my watch might.'

Mary wasn't having that. 'Sir, they do a good job.'

He eyed her up as if to say: *Not you, too.* 'As I said, our lords and masters like to stick a finger in where it don't belong and they've instructed us to keep physical records of all our agents. And we are to –' he peered at the paper '– *consult* them.'

'If it keeps them happy, sir.'

Signalmaster Falks stood up. 'You're a good worker, Voss. I have put in a recommendation to headquarters. It was the least I could do.' He cocked an eyebrow. 'Never know where it might lead.'

Her astonishment was so great that words almost deserted her. 'Thank you, sir.'

Falks returned to the chaos of his in-tray. 'Don't stand about, Voss. Get on with it.'

Several days later she was ordered by the duty sergeant to report to the room at the end of the corridor. *Pronto, Voss.*

The corridor was bustling with uniformed personnel, all of them seemingly focused and in a hurry.

Wearing a lieutenant's insignia, the FANY who was waiting for Mary sat behind the cheap-looking desk on a chair which had seen better days. An equally battered one had been placed in front of the desk. She held out her hand. 'I'm Ingram. But I don't hold much with all that formality. Please call me Ruby.'

Ruby was a good fifteen years younger than Mary, with large eyes, dark hair and enviably clear skin. Her mouth could have been termed generous except for a pinched, almost angry, set at the corners, but she was vivid and arresting.

Pointing to the second chair, she said, 'And I don't hold with standing either. Please sit.'

The two women faced each other across the desk.

To Mary's surprise, Ruby smiled. 'I've been told that apparently you lot are the signal-ritas and my lot are cipherines.'

'Could be worse,' said Mary.

Ruby was amused and then turned serious. 'The reports are that you're the best in the group, so I've been sent down here to brief you and to pick your brains.'

'Well, that must be a first.' The words flashed from Mary before she could stop them.

Ruby's interest in Mary seemed to quicken. 'You've been informed about the crib sheets for the agents?'

'Yes.'

'And?'

'It's a good precaution,' Mary replied. 'And, for the new, er, signal-rita, invaluable. But, for the old hands, probably unnecessary.'

Ruby looked puzzled. 'Please explain.'

'We just know our agents.'

'Ah, the Morse-trained ear?'

'We know the characteristics that are always evident, whatever the conditions they are sent under.'

'Even when there's a problem with the signal?'

Mary had never been so sure of anything in her life. 'Yes.'

'And when they're frightened, or under pressure. Or exhausted?'

'Especially then,' said Mary. 'Because –' She stopped herself.

'Because?' Ruby leaned forward, sniffing up facts, rooting out doubts. 'Be honest. Be precise, if you can.'

Mary shed her diffidence. 'Because I . . . and the others . . . care about each and every one, personally. I . . . we . . . watch over them.'

There was a second's uncomprehending silence.

'Because you care about them.' Ruby was sceptical to the point of offence.

Mary took up the gauntlet. 'It sounds mad, but it's true. Unless you understand them, you can't read them. Or take the message properly.'

'That's irrational and unreliable.' Ruby sat back and stared at Mary, challenging her.

Mary folded her hands in her lap and said nothing.

'I don't believe in the irrational. I believe in evidence and careful analysis,' continued Ruby.

Mary heard herself say, 'Everything has its place.'

'Of course, you have no idea who they are.'

'None.'

Ruby shrugged. 'It's unusual. Or, put it this way, your approach is not the kind of analysis that the average man would accept.'

'Maybe not,' said Mary. 'But, as I say, it has its place. I know it does.'

Suddenly, Ruby grinned. 'I'm anxious, always, to debunk the average man.'

In the adjacent room, a telephone was ringing. On and on it went.

'Someone answer it.' Ruby rolled her eyes. 'Please.'

Someone did, and there was peace.

Ruby produced a file from the briefcase at her feet. 'These

are the latest crib sheets we've taken from agents. These show us the basic characteristics of how an agent transmits, which never change, whatever the conditions.'

Mary nodded.

'These are from the newer agents, obviously. We've no records for the ones who were already in the field when the decision was taken to keep these crib sheets. But most of your section is here. I want you to check them before we put them on file. Take a look at this one.'

Mary looked at the sheet Ruby put on the table in front of her. What she saw was an in-depth exercise on square-rule paper of every single letter of the alphabet in Morse. She only needed to study it for a few seconds. 'Agent with the call sign DEV,' she said.

'And this one?'

'YEW.'

Methodically, Ruby took her through the next two pages and Mary supplied the information without any problem.

'Who else do you have who we don't have records for?'

'XRT,' said Mary. 'Vinegar.'

Ruby's chair scraped along the floor, and she got to her feet. Mary couldn't help noticing how thin she was. 'Tell me about Vinegar.'

Mary clicked back through her mental file. 'I was assigned him . . . in early November 1942. Last year.'

Ruby checked the list. 'Correct.'

'He transmits like clockwork. There's never much trouble with the signal. In fact, he's been remarkably consistent.'

There was a tiny pause. Suggestive? A cloud appeared on Mary's horizon.

'Think. Have there ever been any problems?'

'Only with his first transmissions,' she replied. 'He was nervous. I could tell by the rhythm and he was all over the place. In fact, on the very first one he muddled the sign-off and his frequency. But I didn't have to worry because, after his first four skeds, he was trouble free.'

Mary looked at Ruby. Something was up. The cloud on the horizon grew darker, and a worm twisted and turned in her chest.

'So after that Vinegar never seemed under pressure? Or frightened? Or to be transmitting in difficult conditions?'

'No,' Mary replied. 'It's quite unusual. You could trust him for a perfect message each time. Is he in trouble?'

Ruby ignored the question. 'Anything else?'

'Occasionally, his messages are shorter than most agents'.'

'Right,' said Ruby in such a way that Mary knew that the information had been important. 'Anyone else?'

'ZYA . . . Mayonnaise.' There was a catch in her throat. 'He went dark a few weeks ago and missed a couple of skeds, but I continued to search for him. Then he came back on the emergency frequency. Once. But his last message, number fifty, was odd. I reported it to the signalmaster and asked if the security checks were used.'

'What sort of odd?'

'His fist was almost unrecognizable . . . It could have been someone else transmitting. For example, Mayonnaise's H is always very dashing: full of energy and life. On that last message, the H was configured differently.' Her fingers twisted together. 'I'd like to know what's happened to him.'

Did Ruby understand how she felt? Peering at her, Mary rather thought that, despite the brisk manner, she did. At any rate, a little.

'You know I can't answer that. Even if I knew.' Her gaze was shrewd and – indeed – not unsympathetic. 'He or she is the one you care about?'

Mary stared at her. 'One of them,' she admitted.

Pushing her vacated chair tidily back under the desk, Ruby said carefully, 'Shall we just say there was an explanation for Mayonnaise?'

It was a small drop of information. But manna to Mary.

She looked down at her hands. 'I see.'

'You mustn't get involved, you know. Otherwise how do we fight the war? If you care too much then it becomes impossible.' She slotted her papers back into the briefcase.

Was Ruby giving this piece of advice to herself as much as to her? *Pot and kettle*, Mary said to herself.

'Are you quite sure you don't get muddled between them all?' Ruby shot the question at Mary.

'Muddled! No. *Never.*'

That appeared to satisfy Ruby. 'My orders are to tell you that, if you ever suspect anything, you ask to talk to Major Martin. Understood?'

'Yes.'

Before she left, Ruby gave Mary a piece of paper with a telephone number on it. 'You and I know,' she said, 'who runs the shop and, if you ever need to get hold of me, use this. But don't let anyone else see it. Or tell anyone about it.'

Finish. End of session.

On the way back to her station, Mary glanced out of a window and spotted Ruby. Briefcase parked by her feet, she was leaning up against a wall and smoking what was probably one of those popular Turkish ciggies the girls fought over. One foot was tucked up behind her for balance and her skirt had ridden up above her knee. She smoked quickly and appreciatively, looking like a woman in charge of her life.

Mary glanced up at the clock. Two minutes. Her headphones hissed and fluted.

The minute hand reached twelve.

Where was Vinegar?

He was a few minutes late for his sked but, eventually, he checked in. She took up her pencil. At the end of the message, Vinegar signed off as usual . . . *I have nothing further for you.*

Her pencil faltered. Had she got that correct? There was a

change in the rhythm of Q, which should have been dash dash dot dash. Instead she transcribed: dash dot dash dot. The letter C.

It was followed by A instead of R.

Instead of reading QRU it read CAU.

He had done it again. It was exactly as had happened on his first transmission. Not only that, he also muddled the frequency.

After putting the message into the basket, Mary made a note in her notebook: 'QRU reading CAU'.

Checking twice to see if she had made a mistake, something she dreaded, she then made another comment in her notebook: 'Frequency change from LMS to GHT.'

What was eluding her? No one was supposed to read the messages. Indeed, she couldn't. But the Q system was a universal language which the girls had got to know. Any fool could.

Mary rubbed her tired eyes. She thought about her agents, about where they might be. Was Mayonnaise moving around a city where everyone watched everyone else? How tough it must be, unable to trust anyone. Perhaps he was hidden, perched in a barn, or shivering in an open field, or high up in a mountain?

Vinegar? Why would he change frequency?

Between skeds, she searched out the duty signalmaster. It was, unfortunately, Signalmaster Noble.

'I'd like to request that you get in touch with Major Martin.'

He frowned. 'And why, may I ask?'

She held his gaze. 'I'm afraid I can't say.'

'I won't do anything unless you tell me what is going on.'

'I'm sorry, sir. I can't.'

This was a face-off. Noble opted for the usual tactic to resolve it. 'Get back to your bench, Voss.'

'Sir, this might be important.'

'I don't care if it's an invitation to Hitler's bloody birthday party. Get back to your station.'

It was a double-shift day and Mary spent the period between them at a table in the canteen with a cup of stewed tea in front of her, trying to work out what to do. After that, she took a walk in the grounds. These were extensive and had once housed a noteworthy rose garden but, since the house had been commandeered, the signal bods had stuck aerials everywhere, even among the flowerbeds. Lately, these had multiplied over the lawns, finally destroying what remained of the garden's elegance.

She wished she had someone with whom to talk things over and longed to be able to ask advice as to how to behave when she was so sure something was wrong.

She had always been obedient as a child, then as a daughter and an employee. Not unusual for a woman. Her mother had seen to that, drumming that way of being into Mary.

Clocking off, she walked into town. It was four o'clock and the afternoon sun was shifting over the town's market square and settling on the window of the Currant Bun café. There was a scurry of schoolchildren and shoppers. The butcher was about to close down his stall for the day, and the man on the hardware stall was packing up his tin bowls and clothes pegs. She made her way to the post office and queued for twenty minutes until the phone box was free.

She dialled, waited for the call to be answered and inserted the coins. 'Lieutenant Ingram, please.'

'Who is this?' demanded a female voice.

She explained.

'And who gave you this number?'

'Lieutenant Ingram. She asked me to contact her if I thought I should.'

There was a long pause. Mary raised her eyes to the ceiling. She had only three minutes and at least one had elapsed.

'You're not supposed to have this number. You could be in serious trouble.'

Something snapped in Mary. 'I insist you give my message to Lieutenant Ingram.'

356

She had said it. *Insist.*

Afterwards, she took her time to walk back to Mrs Cotton. Her sense of relief was overwhelming.

There wasn't long to wait before the repercussions began.

Signalmaster Noble was standing by her station when she appeared for her next shift the following afternoon. 'I'll have your guts for garters, Voss.'

She held her gaze steady. 'Could I sit down, please?'

His grip on her arm was vicious. 'Not so fast. You're wanted in room thirteen.'

'My shift?'

'Don't you worry your head about that.' Fury made his Adam's apple seem more pronounced than usual.

'I'll come back as soon as possible.'

'If I have anything to do with it you won't.'

Room 13 was tiny. Mary squeezed through the door and saw Ruby leaning against the windowsill.

'Hello, Mary. I came as quickly as I could.'

'Thank you.' Opening her notebook, Mary passed it over to Ruby. 'Whatever else, this is definitely not like Vinegar.'

Ruby scrutinized Mary's note about the sign-off that read CAU instead of QRU, and the later note about the change in frequency.

'He did that once before. On his first transmission,' Mary said. 'But it's not like him.'

Ruby reached for the pencil and paper on the desk and began to take her own notes from Mary's.

'Vinegar knows the Q system backwards,' Mary pointed out. 'He's never made a mistake and could transmit it in his sleep. And why the frequency change?'

Ruby tapped her teeth with her pencil. 'I don't know.'

'Do you think he's in trouble?'

Ruby said: 'I want to thank you, Mary. You've been very helpful. You can go back to work.'

As her mother would have said: 'In for a penny, in for a

pound.' Mary's hands clenched. 'Ruby, I'm afraid you'll have to sort it out with Signalmaster Noble. He told me that I'd lose my job.'

'I assure you that you won't.' Ruby gathered up her papers. 'I'll ask Major Martin to phone at once.'

Mary remained where she was and Ruby raised her eyebrows. 'Anything else?'

'Can you tell me *anything*?'

'No.' Ruby was regretful. 'I wish I could.'

'It's hard.' Mary couldn't prevent herself.

'I can imagine. But it's for their sake as well as yours.'

Mary nodded and left the room. Halfway along the corridor, she spotted Signalmaster Noble. Arms folded, he was clearly looking for trouble, but so was she. Squaring her shoulders, she walked past him and into the signals room, where her desk was waiting. She sat down and picked up the headphones.

'The old bully was swearing about you,' said Nancy.

'Let him.'

Nancy shot her a look

Mary sat down and prepared herself for work. Anxiety and doubt were like lumps of coal in her chest.

Chapter Twenty-eight

In the late afternoon, Kay rowed back across the lake from Sophia-Maria's island. She had been doing a reconnaissance of its jetty and checking over the summer house.

Would the island be adequate as a hiding place? Could they camouflage the material? How much time would be needed to get there and back? The water tumbled over the blades, making lovely watery sounds, and she ran through the sequence of a drop until she was fact-perfect. Preparation was everything . . . She didn't know how likely this was but, if and when London ever gave the go-ahead to use the lake as a drop zone, she would be ready.

Anton promised to make contact with London. 'If Felix made it, he will have been debriefed pretty thoroughly. They will have a good idea of the situation here.'

Kay felt her new isolation, both mental and physical. With Felix gone and Rosenlund under surveillance, all activities had ground to a halt, a state which Kay had imagined she would relish. She didn't, which went to prove how contrary human beings were. Lying low and keeping quiet made their own demands. Yes . . . yes . . . she was grateful for having got away with it and for her sudden peace and the chance to enjoy the summer weather. But, if she was truthful, she also found herself yearning for the adrenalin rush and the comradeship between unlikely people. Resistance, she realized, had become a state of mind.

Shortly after Tanne fled, Juncker had been sent on a course to København, which left Sergeant Wulf to pursue the enquiries. For a couple of weeks after Tanne vanished, he drove up to Rosenlund every few days to ask about her. Either Bror or Kay would report that she was still staying with the cousins and Sergeant Wulf would solemnly note it down.

It seemed that Sergeant Wulf's old loyalties had held.

Kay missed Tanne badly and often lay awake picturing the worst.

Please be in Sweden.

Allied night-time bombers had taken to flying over the area in large numbers on their way to bombing missions in Germany. Their noise broke into her already fragile sleep and she wasn't sleeping well.

But that was good. The noise was the excuse she used to Bror to keep him out of her bed. 'I can't sleep,' she told him. 'And it's worse if you're there, too.'

He didn't like it and it meant that the patching up of their relationship was additionally uneasy and, sometimes, fraught. The bridge that had been built was still shaky. But, for the moment, that was the way it must be.

The political landscape was changing. Incidents of sabotage in shipyards and factories all over the country had been stepped up, and the newspapers were full of reports of resistance activity. 'Railway line blown up,' said one. 'Factory demolished,' said another. A series of strikes had been rolled out. To no one's surprise, the Nazis did not like the behaviour of their so-called reliable Nordic brothers.

Talk in the Køge bread queues was of little else. Rumours solidified and circulated. Rumours of torture, of *stikker* going into hiding . . . of people being shot in the streets. It was said that the Allies would invade through Denmark. It was also said that Werner Best and his crew were planning to round up the Jews, which would put the Danish government in an untenable position.

Is Tanne safe?
Of course she is.
No, she isn't.

*

Kay rowed on, the boat slipping easily through the shiny water.

There was sunshine and a deep blue sky to enjoy. There was Nils to consider. He had not been home for some time.

And Bror?

She peered down into the lake.

In. Out . . .

After the bad nights, exercise made her feel better.

In. Out . . .

Nosing the boat up to the jetty, she was surprised to find Bror waiting by the mooring post.

He made no move to help her and, hauling herself up onto the jetty, she slipped and fell. Struggling upright, she peeled a tacky mess of wet and blackened silver foil strips away from her leg. Whatever these were, they seemed to arrive in the wake of the bombers. She held up one. 'What are these for?'

'Ask your British-loving friends, Kay.'

Don't get angry. Don't despair. 'Good idea.' She smiled to take away the sting from the exchange.

'Want to know the news?'

She tied up the painter. 'I'm listening.'

'The Allies have landed in Sicily.'

'Thank God.' She closed her eyes.

'I knew you would be pleased.'

But Bror wouldn't be. Or, might he be? Not possessing a way into his thoughts any longer, she did not know.

There was a flurry and a clatter of wings.

'Look!'

A flight of duck rose from the rushes and looped above the golden landscape.

'Are you going shooting this year, Bror?'

Bror did not even glance at the duck. 'Not until Tanne is safely back.'

The water was so still that the trees were perfectly reflected in it. Such soft colours, she thought.

The boat knocked gently against the jetty.

'Kay, you would tell me if you heard from Tanne?'

'How could you imagine I wouldn't tell you?'

'Very easily,' he said and that shocked her.

Later, after they had eaten supper, Bror picked up his book. 'I'm going to have an early night.'

'Sleep well, then.'

He had brushed his hair back and it gleamed like an otter's coat. Looking at him, it occurred to Kay that he had never looked so well, or to such advantage.

It was no good thinking about the future. Or, at any rate, it was no good thinking of it without a degree of fatalism. The war had done its worst. Given the context, theirs was only a small tragedy but a bitter one. Like so many others were bitter and cruel. The odds were that they could never restore their true, honest marriage, and the sense of bereavement was all the heavier because she had been the one who had brought it about.

'Bror, will you kiss me goodnight?'

Without waiting for an answer, she reached up and kissed him. After a moment, he stroked her hair.

Up in her office, she closed the door, drew the curtains and crouched down by the radio to listen to the banned BBC.

'Josephine loves her grandmother.'

'The rabbit arrived this morning.'

'The river is flooding over the meadows.'

She knew enough to know that some of the messages were instructions to someone in the field. On hearing the relevant one, a team would swing into action and prepare to receive the arms and explosives descending from the belly of a plane.

For some reason she felt uneasy tonight. True, she was no longer actively involved. Nevertheless, she could not shake off a sense that danger lurked everywhere these days and the result was to sharpen in her an urge to corral her possessions, neaten her arrangements, order her affairs – it was a feeling she remembered well from the hours before going into labour with the children. Perhaps it wasn't surprising. Birth and death were allies.

She sat up late making a list. Bring accounts up to date. Burn letters. Make will.

Afterwards, restless and disinclined to go to bed, she sat at her desk. It grew chilly and she reached for the wrap that she kept on the back of the chair. Pulling aside the curtain, she looked out. It was a clear night and the summer constellations lit up the sky.

There was a noise on the steps outside, a shuffle and scrape of feet.

In a flash, she had extracted the pistol from the desk and rammed it into her pocket.

A soft tap, then a voice whispered: '*Fru* Eberstern.'

One hand on the pistol, Kay opened the door. 'Arne.'

'*Fru* Eberstern, we need medicines and bandages.'

She didn't require an explanation. 'Bad?'

'Very.'

She was already on her knees by the cupboard, handing supplies to Arne, including bandages, a small bottle of brandy, scissors and a suture kit which she had bought from the vet.

'Where?'

'Jacob's place. I have the bicycles ready. We'll go by the back road to dodge the curfew.'

It was approaching midnight by the time she and Arne wheeled their bicycles around the back of Jacob's cottage.

Jacob was waiting to let them in and she was struck by the difference in him. No longer the pale, gawky youth he had been when she and he first encountered each other, Jacob had grown into a bulkier, confident figure. 'Thank God,' he said.

As Arne parked the bicycles he warned, '*Fru* Eberstern, what you're going to see is not good.'

She girded herself. 'I know.'

The room into which Jacob conducted her was small,

sparsely furnished and lit by one medium-sized oil lamp. At its centre, a man lay across a couple of chairs which had been pushed together as an improvised bed. A newspaper was spread out underneath to catch the blood which streamed from a slash on his chest. Its smell was sickening.

At her entrance, he turned his head and she battled with herself not to run out of the room. He was covered in sores, as thin as a rake and his face was almost pulp.

She swallowed. 'Danish police?'

'Gestapo.'

'How did he get here?'

'We had a tip-off that prisoners were being transferred from Aarhus to København. An ambush was arranged.'

'Where are the others?'

Jacob shrugged. 'Round and about.'

Kay bent over the wounded man. 'I'll try to help you.'

Drawing her aside, Jacob said, 'He can't talk . . . but we think the Germans have had him for some time, which would suggest he's important to them.' His voice was husky with exhaustion. 'Maybe they've finished with him. Or they were going to kill him off. The plan was to get him and the others out to Sweden.' He gestured to the injured man. 'But I don't think so.'

She knelt down beside him. 'Name?' she asked.

The man was conscious but since his jaw was at an odd angle, he struggled to respond intelligibly. The effort, and the smashed jaw, proved too much.

Was he one of Felix's men?

After a moment, Kay laid a hand gently, oh so gently, on his shoulder. 'Don't try any more.'

She examined him as best she could – biting down on her lip when he cried out. 'He's been beaten all over,' she said at last. 'Systematically and brutally.' Except for his hands. They appeared to be untouched, although Kay couldn't be absolutely sure about that because he was filthy. Underlying the more recent wounds, including the one on his chest, were older yellow and purple scars and contusions. His shoulders were raw – that was recent. Some of his injuries indicated cigarette burns, or small knife slashes, and they oozed pus.

Clinically, Kay noted the tally of violence: the bruises, the rotting flesh, the attempt to destroy his face.

What good were a couple of aspirin in this situation? Angry and helpless, she sponged the man down with water from the bucket Jacob had fetched, and dabbed at the worst of the wounds with disinfectant.

As she worked, her anger intensified. If she had ever doubted her refusal to tolerate evil and cruelty, this was no longer the case. If she had ever had doubts about being involved, they vanished.

Jacob and Arne watched.

'I was warned about this,' she said. 'If he's British-trained, which is possible, the Abwehr would have tried to use him and get as much out of him as possible without killing him. Afterwards, the Gestapo probably took over.' She straightened up. 'His jaw's smashed. He's got a head injury and the socket of his right eye is possibly broken. He needs to be in hospital.'

'Our contact at the hospital says they can hide him in the isolation ward. But not until tomorrow,' said Jacob.

'Right.'

But it wasn't all right.

The bleeding from the chest wound needed to be dealt with. At least Kay could do something about that. She pulled the suture kit out of her pocket. 'I'll have to stitch it.' After scrubbing her hands with disinfectant, she sterilized the needle by dipping it into the flame of the oil lamp, then threaded it. 'Could one of you get some brandy down him?'

Jacob did his best but not that successfully.

'Bring in the lamp as close as you can,' she instructed Arne. 'And Jacob, please hold him.'

Her hand shook only marginally. Thank God for that. Arne

held the lamp up and Jacob pressed down on the man's raw shoulders. Grasping the edges of the wound, she pulled them together. *Pop.* The needle pushed into the flesh with an unexpectedly loud sound.

She had no idea that human skin was so tough.

The wounded man whimpered.

How far can humans go? When do you stop fearing pain?

Questions that Kay could not answer.

Pop.

Too far gone, he barely made a sound after that.

She sewed on, knotting the thread, snipping it, then pressing a dressing onto the wound until the bleeding slowed.

The man made one last-ditch effort to speak but only a gurgling, glottal noise issued from the battered mouth. She bent over and strained to make sense of it.

But it was useless.

Before she left, Kay handed the Browning to Arne. 'You might need it tomorrow morning.'

He accepted it reluctantly.

The wounded man never made it to the hospital. When Arne appeared at Rosenlund the following afternoon, he told Kay that he had died during the night. He and Jacob hid the body in a cart under piles of old sacks and buried it in the woods.

Kay wept.

It was another warm and sun-filled day. The sky was cerulean blue, the wisteria on the terrace bloomed uninhibitedly, bright greens stippled in the woods. The air was so still that Kay felt as if the universe was holding its breath.

After dinner, she and Bror were drinking their coffee when Birgit appeared. She was sobbing incoherently.

Kay got to her feet. 'Birgit, what on earth's the matter?'

'Arne's been arrested.'

Kay put her arm round the other woman. 'Tell us.'

'They've taken him to the police station.'

'Who have?'

Birgit merely shook her head.

Bror said wearily, 'The usual nonsense. I'll phone Sergeant Wulf.' He rested a hand on Birgit's shoulder. 'Don't worry.'

He vanished into the hall.

Kay led Birgit through the French windows and made her sit down in the drawing room. She crouched down beside her. 'Shall I get you some coffee? Or brandy?'

'*Fru* Eberstern . . .' Birgit was having difficulty speaking. 'Arne had this.' To Kay's horror, she produced the pistol from her pocket. 'He was trying to hide it when they came.'

Without a second's hesitation, Kay whipped it out of Birgit's hand and stuffed it into her sewing bag, which she kept on the floor beside her chair. She raised a finger to her lips to indicate silence.

In the hall, Bror could be heard saying, 'The accusations are ridiculous.'

Birgit clawed at Kay's arm. 'Arne told me to tell you . . .'

Kay took both of Birgit's hands in hers. 'Speak softly. What did Arne tell you to tell me?'

The look Birgit flashed Kay was one of dislike and suspicion of Kay – the Birgit whom Kay had known for so long. 'He said to tell you that someone at the hospital talked.'

They heard Bror say, 'Good. That's settled.'

Kay held up a finger. 'Listen. What did my husband tell you? He has sorted it out.'

Birgit refused to look at Kay.

Bror came back into the room. 'Birgit, Sergeant Wulf says he's very sorry. There's been a mix-up. Arne will be home shortly.'

'I'm going to drive you home,' insisted Kay. 'No argument.' She turned to Bror. 'We have the petrol?'

When Kay bought the car to a halt outside the cottage, a dishevelled, exhausted-looking Arne emerged from the front door. Birgit choked up with fresh tears and threw herself out of the car.

Arne hugged Birgit hard. Then he pushed her inside.

Kay rolled down the window. 'They didn't hurt you, did they?' She could tell he was badly shaken.

'*Fru* Eberstern, you must leave the area. There's too much talk.' One of his big square hands rested on the door handle.

He was speaking rapidly, far too rapidly. Kay understood.

'You *are* all right?'

'I've known most of them at the station since they were babies. I just had to remind them that, after the war, they had to live here.' He added, '*Hr* Eberstern helped, too. Please thank him.'

Kay glanced through the cottage window. Birgit was feeding logs into the stove.

'Birgit has given me the pistol. You don't need to worry about that.'

'I would have buried it.'

'She was frightened for you, Arne. We all were.'

Arne moved his hand and she registered the age spots which mottled the skin.

'The family is at risk, *Fru* Eberstern. You, especially. They gossip about you.' He bent down until his face was on a level with hers. 'Køge isn't safe any more. Go and hide until the war is over. You and the master. I'll take care of Rosenlund.'

A sixth sense told Kay to abandon the car at the end of the drive and to approach the house with caution. For a moment she stood still, absorbing the colours and scents which she loved.

Moving as noiselessly as she could, she zigzagged through the trees which lined the drive until the house came into sight.

Parked by the front door was the black car.

Turning, Kay tracked around the side of the house and let

herself in through the kitchen entrance. Kicking off her shoes, she padded down to the drawing room and peered through the crack between the door and its frame.

Hauptsturmführer Buch and Constable Juncker occupied the space in the middle of the room. From her restricted viewpoint she had a good view of Juncker, but Buch was partially hidden.

'I've no idea what you're talking about,' Bror was saying. 'I don't care what your informant says. My wife couldn't possibly have been planning to smuggle a terrorist into the hospital without me knowing.'

Constable Juncker honed in on the miniature tortoiseshell clock which was on the table beside her chair. Kay squeezed her eyes shut. *No.* With a booted toe, Juncker nudged over the sewing bag. Picking it up, he shoved his hand inside. 'Sir.' He held out the pistol.

One small second can contain an eternity. In it, Kay travelled from debilitating craven fear to ice-cold resolve, from the bitter, bitter sorrow of farewell to the explosive excitement that, at last, things were happening.

'What on earth –?'

No one could mistake Bror's genuine surprise.

Buch's response was instant. '*Hr* Eberstern, that particular gun is known to be a terrorist weapon.'

'My wife –'

Bror was struggling. That was good. His unfeigned, unmistakable astonishment was his best defence.

'Where's your wife?' *Hauptsturmführer* Buch was, as always, calm and polite.

There was nothing Kay could do except leave Bror to his ignorance. That was all she could do for him.

She fled up the back stairs to her office, where she had everything ready on stand-by. The rucksack by the door had been packed: underwear, dried raisins, bandages and a bundle of bank notes. She snatched up the jacket and, pausing only to take a final look at a photograph of Tanne and Nils and to touch the larger photograph of Bror with a fingertip, she let herself out onto the outside steps.

Then she was away through the trees and running like the wind.

Chapter Twenty-nine

Tanne and Felix were flown in from Stockholm hidden in the bomb bay of a Mosquito, then driven up to London. They were met by a businesslike FANY who issued them with some badly fitting civilian clothes and money, and conducted them to a hotel near High Street Kensington. For the time being, she explained, they were to lie low and were forbidden to contact any relatives or friends.

There could have been few drearier places in which to hole up than the hotel but they made the best of it by exploring the streets and walking in Kensington Gardens. They spent a lot of time in a local pub, which was a fairly jolly, rowdy, sawdust-strewn place.

Having visited with her mother several times, Tanne was familiar with the pre-war city. What amazed both her and Felix was the variety of uniforms now visible in the streets: Americans and Free French, Poles, Italians and some Greeks. Anyone, they noted wryly, but the Danish.

On their walks they saw severed gas pipes and burst water mains. Here and there they came across pockets of escaped gas, and there was the constant hazard of live electric wires. Many streets and terraces were in ruins. Wherever Tanne looked, there was hardship. London was shabby and fatigued, with the look of a person pushed almost too far – but not enough to give up. It wasn't fair but its grimy dereliction contrasted badly with København's solid stone buildings and the jewelled colours of the houses and farms of the countryside.

Tanne had not wavered in her determination to join Felix in his work. 'Your mother would never forgive me,' he repeated, more than once.

And, more than once, it crossed Tanne's mind that Felix referred frequently to her mother . . . Freya's courage, her willingness to adapt, her physical endurance. *Did he love her?* Knowing enough to know that love could arrive in many forms, the question, nevertheless, troubled her and she struggled not to think about it.

She needed to be clever to win the argument about entering the fight and she banked on the fact that Felix was not a sentimental man but a patriotic one. 'Who do you put first? Your country or my mother?'

It did the trick. Tanne found herself attending interviews in anonymous-looking buildings where she was questioned – ruthlessly, minutely – on her background and motivation, and put through some searching personality tests. Eventually, she was commissioned into the FANYs as a cover, as most of the women agents were. She was issued with a temporary British passport, given details of the bank account opened in her name for her pay and informed that she was to be sent away for training. Her number was D42 and her training name was 'Pia'.

On a Monday morning, she and Felix caught the ten-twenty train from Paddington, with orders to alight at the third stop after Northampton. She was surprised by the instruction – until she realized that station names were blacked out, which meant that strangers would have no idea where they were.

The train was crammed and they ended up standing in the corridor. She and Felix smoked, and tried to ignore the small horror of the lavatory beside them.

'English plumbing. It's dreadful,' she said.

Such was the crush, her head was practically jammed into Felix's chest. To avoid pressing into his injured arm, she adjusted her position, only to find that her pelvis was pressing into his hip.

'You'll get used to it.'

Tanne was dealing with new and powerful feelings. Had they been stirred up by Felix's weakness, which she had kept watch over that night in Ove's cottage? Or perhaps on the journey on the *Ulla Baden*, during which she and Felix had seen things of each other, in each other, which in peacetime might have taken them a lifetime to discover. For those hours, they had been so physically close – closer than she had ever experienced with anyone – and they had left in her a desire to protect, to hold . . . and . . . to love?

'Will we be seeing each other where we're going?'

'Probably not,' he said. 'And we won't be working together. We know too much about each other. Security.'

She knew that he was aware of the position of her pelvis on his hip.

'We don't know *everything*.'

He squinted down at her. 'Are you being funny or crude?'

Exhilarated and almost breathless from the changes in her life, she said, 'Both,' and had the satisfaction of hearing him laugh.

It was drizzling when they alighted at the station to be met by a uniformed sergeant from the Buffs – a regiment which played host to the Danish fighters who fetched up in Great Britain. The sergeant was Danish and a man of few words. 'You'll be walking. Leave your luggage.' He issued them with a map and coordinates. 'Two hours,' he said. 'If you don't make it on the dot, you'll miss the meal.'

Two hours later, almost to the minute, having negotiated fields, stiles and streams in her flimsy lace-up shoes, Tanne stumbled with Felix up the drive of an old manor house. She knew, she just knew, that it would be cold inside and badly plumbed.

It was.

At the end of the promised meal, the students – as they were referred to – were told to get some sleep. As Felix got up from the table he sent her a look: *Goodbye, Eva.*

Nine students assembled the following morning. Information about the others was, for security reasons, limited, but she gathered that 'Lars' had escaped the previous winter by skiing over the frozen sound to Helsingborg, 'Otto' had flown in the same way as they had and two of the others had arrived by fishing boat. The rest had either been living in England or made their way from Europe via Spain to offer their services.

They were thrown in at the deep end.

Run six or so miles before breakfast.

Morning lessons. Morse code. Map-reading. Fieldcraft.

Lunch. In general, this proved marginally better than breakfast.

Afternoon lessons. The group was conveyed by a covered ten-ton truck to an unknown location and abandoned there with only a compass each. 'Find your own way back,' was the order. Each day the route grew harder.

Dinner. Sometimes Tanne was too exhausted to eat. Afterwards, drinks were dispensed from the plentiful drinks cabinet. Then bed.

Where was Felix?

Without him, she felt desolate – as if an element vital to her life had been sucked away. Enquiring after him was a mistake and she was brusquely informed it was none of her business.

'It's curious how angry you can become when you test your limits,' she confided to Major Petersen, who was mentoring her. 'Why?'

'Because you fail, usually at the beginning. Failure is important. So, too, is finding the anger that will drive you on. Both failure and anger have to be mastered.'

Morning lessons during the second week: how to handle a pistol, machine gun, Sten gun, tommy gun and rifle.

This is the breech. This, the cocking lever. This, the selector button. Get to know them as well as your face. Most of you have never handled a gun.

She thought of the early morning mist wreathing over the Rosenlund marshes. The shining lake. Gleaming, virgin snow and the squat, black shadows cast by the trees. She thought of how in that past life, with a shotgun in hand, she and her father waited for the ducks to skim over the marsh. Finally, she thought of how she had pulled the trigger without a second thought.

Tanne pointed to the Sten. 'A savage weapon.'

Major Petersen, who, as ever, was on hand, ran his finger along the skeleton butt. 'Savage times.' His voice was flat. 'But this isn't too bad for something so improvised. It's adaptable and deadly.'

He was issuing a challenge: *This is serious. Killing.*

Tanne had to consider the possibility. She must think about the smack of bullet on bone, of flesh torn into ribbons, of bubbling breath and of pain which could be inflicted by her.

Petersen continued: 'The magazine is inserted horizontally into the left-hand side of the gun, which means you can use it lying flat. But don't use more than twenty-eight cartridges in the mag, otherwise the automatic feed can jam.'

A mysterious alteration was taking place in her muscles, bones and blood. Leaner, fitter, more physically adept, she thrived on the exhilaration of prolonged exercise.

Who am I doing this for? Denmark?

Yes. Of course I am.

Not entirely.

As for her thoughts, these were changing, too. The old assumptions shared by Aage, Erika and others at university were fast fading. They were too facile, too unsophisticated. Discussing the situation with her fellow fighters, she unearthed in herself stronger political and patriotic allegiances than the easy passions of her student days.

The weather that summer was soft and equable. Whenever she had a moment, Tanne seized the chance to walk through the parkland and gardens, enjoying the vistas of oak trees, sheep, a bowling green, and a peaceful little Saxon chapel tucked into a corner of the park.

Once, homesick and low, she looked across the lawn to the

trees which fringed it and saw someone walking towards her. *Felix.* Tears sprang into Tanne's eyes and a joy lit her up. She hurried forward to meet him, but it was only Otto.

They had been warned that not all of the intake would survive to the next stage. Late one evening Tanne and four others arrived back from exercise to discover the mother of all rows emanating from the cellar. On investigation, they discovered the rest of the group, half-slaughtered on English beer, shooting pistols at a caricature of Hitler.

They had all passed.

The following morning the groggy group were summoned by Major Petersen. He briefed them that they would be embarking for Special Training School 45. 'You'll be allowed out only one day a week and you're banned from shopping or eating at restaurants within a five-mile radius of the school.'

STS45 turned out to be a castle somewhere in Gloucestershire – a name Tanne had trouble pronouncing – with a staggering number of windows and chimneys. In the grounds there was a shot-down German plane, complete with a swastika and a gaping hole in its fuselage.

Tanne regarded it thoughtfully. Men had probably died a horrible death in there.

A Major Spooner waited to interview the group. One by one, a sergeant marched them into his office.

Major Spooner immediately made plain his dislike of women. 'You're quite irregular for this section,' was his opener. 'We don't have to deal with many females.' He leaned as far back in his chair as possible and took off his glasses as if to blur the awful sight.

By now, Tanne had worked out that Denmark was low on the British agenda. Could the reason be that a dinosaur, masquerading as a man, had been allocated to run this section?

The major hooked the arms of his glasses round his ears. 'You realize that, at best, you have a ten per cent chance of survival?'

'Yes, sir.'

'Think about it. If it's too much for you, you have a duty to tell us.'

'Sir, do you ask the men the same question? Just out of interest.'

There was a silence. 'I do. And that is a stupid question.'

'You want to know about my nerves and my endurance. So do I. That's what I'm here for.'

He observed Tanne over the glasses. 'Be careful, number forty-two. You don't know the half of it.'

Curiously, she felt at home at STS45. There were big fire-places and big furniture, if badly arranged, and the pictures and displays of china reminded her of Rosenlund. The canteen produced good meals and, in the library, there was a selection of Danish papers and magazines.

The lessons resumed.

Their group joined a number of Danes who, because there had been so few operations scheduled for Denmark, had been kicking their heels at STS45 for anything up to a year. The new-comers had to work hard to catch up with them. Arithmetic. Map-reading. Reconnaissance. Morse. Using German, Finnish and Swedish weapons. Demolition. Every kind of sabotage known to man, including scuttling ships. Burgling. Writing let-ters in invisible ink. The use of pigeons.

'Apart from anything else, gentlemen and, er, miss, you will be going home to set up what you might call a sabotage univer-sity,' they were told. 'You'll be holding little workshops all over the place. In the fields. In sheds. In piggeries. Got it?'

Also featuring on the curriculum were Unarmed Combat and Silent Killing. Here, she was initiated into various methods, including the Bronco kick: take a flying leap at your opponent then disable him by driving both heels into his body. Or there was the Bone Crusher. Or Mouth Slitting: if you are in some-one's grip, you can stick your thumb in the corner of his mouth and split his cheek.

Would she ever be able to bring herself to put these methods into practice? And what if she died in the attempt?

In Danish mythology, a heroine who lost her life was spirited away by the goddess Freya to her domain in Asgard, and all was well. How useful myth was. How it tidied and sanitized. In contrast, Tanne was being taught to see that death could be agonizing, violent, often inflicted without justice or due process. She didn't like to imagine her mother's grief, and the silence into which her father would retreat, if she were to meet hers.

Their instructor watched over them like babies. 'Those who fail the exam will have to go right back to the beginning again,' he warned. 'Now, you don't want that, gentlemen and, er, miss. Do you?'

Assassin, spy, saboteur. Tanne was adding to her list of accomplishments.

Her next assignment was STS 51 and Parachute School.

The journey from STS 45 took all day. A student in the know told them the names of the stations as they steamed past the blacked-out names.

Tanne sat with Lars and Otto, a couple of Poles and a Norwegian. Soon after the train pulled out of the station before their final stop the compartment door slid open. She looked up from her newspaper – and the blaze of light was there for real.

Felix.

He looked a new man. Plus his British officer's uniform suited him. He jerked a thumb towards the corridor and Tanne leaped to her feet.

'Whoa,' said Otto. 'Do I detect love's young dream?'

'Shut up,' said Tanne.

She and Felix leaned against the rail and regarded the passing English countryside. Tanne couldn't stop herself smiling. She turned her head towards him and thought she would die of happiness.

'I shouldn't be here,' he said, touching her arm. 'But there are always exceptions to be made.'

'Good.'

'How did it go?' He peered at her. 'You look different, Eva. Which is what happens, I suppose.'

'I am different, but so pleased you are here. Really, really so happy, Felix.'

'Don't look at me like that,' he said. But he moved closer. 'I wanted to see you before . . . well, before. I have much to thank you for.'

For a second she was panicked. Was it only gratitude that made him seek her out?

Their faces were very close together. His eyes seemed to pierce her through and through. In the old days she might have ducked her head away from such a truth-seeking scrutiny. But she was beyond the restraints of her previous existence. She knew how important this moment was. She knew, too, that he had risked the wrath of the instructors to talk to her.

'I couldn't go without this . . .' He placed a finger on her lips.

'You mean it?'

'Yes.'

'It's not my mother?' She took a breath. 'I have sometimes wondered.'

Felix understood what Tanne was asking. 'She's special . . .'

Tanne thought of her blonde, beautiful, scented mother. How could she match up?

'But no.'

Tanne smiled.

'So, you've survived what those sadists have thrown at you?' She grinned. 'Ask me about the Bone Crusher!'

'Ah, the Bone Crusher. An old friend.'

'Your arm?' She could see that he was holding it a little stiffly.

'Good as new.' Felix wasn't being quite truthful. 'Are you ready for the parachuting?'

She grimaced. 'I dread it.'

The compartment door was open and, eavesdropping unashamedly, Lars and Otto were being vastly entertained.

Lars leaned over and said in a stage whisper: 'You should know there are multilingual psychologists on the train monitoring our conversations. You two will be for the chop.'

'Don't look at me,' said one of the Poles in a thick accent.

To the sound of ribald laughter, Felix reached out and shut the compartment door.

As the train approached their station, Felix said: 'This really is goodbye, Eva.'

'So soon.' She heard her voice falter. 'I thought you might be coming with us.'

'I'm brushing up on a few things for a couple of days.'

'But when do you go?'

He shook his head.

She stole a look at his face. She didn't know anything about Felix and perhaps she never would. She didn't know his name, or where he came from, or what he did. But she knew what mattered to her: the way he slept, the way in which he dealt with pain and discomfort. His courage.

Those were enough.

'Do you mean *på gensyn* or *farvel*?'

So long. Or goodbye for good?

'Your choice,' he said. 'Which do you prefer?'

He was asking her if she wanted him.

Conscious that they were being watched, she placed her hand on his uniformed chest, imagining she could feel his heartbeat. 'Not *farvel*, Felix.'

After a moment he nodded. '*På gensyn* it is, then.'

The sign greeting the group on their arrival at STS 51 read: 'You Are No Bloody Hero'.

She pondered this welcome as she lay sleepless and longing in her bed that night.

Who were they all?

Who was Felix? Where was her faith that they would meet again?

She was far from Rosenlund, chilly and homesick. No, love-sick. Eventually, she got up and pulled on a thick jumper over her pyjamas.

She imagined Felix in bed. Probably in one of the dark, narrow, attic rooms that were crammed with ancient iron bedsteads. She willed him to steal downstairs to her. *Please.* Forbidden, of course. Should she find him? Did the English always forbid sex in a crisis? Lars had told her that the whole nation had a peculiar relationship with it. How did he know?

Felix *was* going back into the field. He had made that clear. Would he see her mother? Despite their conversation, the thought of Felix with her mother introduced the tiniest speck of grit into her happiness.

Would he see Rosenlund?

She wished she could go with him.

When she got up the next morning, she felt in her bones that Felix had left.

The pace of the training ratcheted up to the relentless.

During this stage, the instructors paid no attention to the fact that she was a woman. They just made her run harder and tote a twenty-five-pound load on her back that much further.

'Keep your bloody feet together, number forty-two,' yelled the sergeant who was instructing them. 'It doesn't matter if the plane is burning. It doesn't matter if you are being popped at by Gerry. It doesn't matter if you're surrounded by the entire Luftwaffe. Keep your fucking legs together . . .'

The practice parachute drops were hell. With a parachute pack on her back, Tanne jumped twelve feet from a specially built wooden construction and practised jumping through a mocked-up Joe Hole. Next up, was a proper jump from a Hali-fax, which had sounded so easy when the instructors had outlined the procedure.

But when she sat on the edge of the hole, with the roar of

the Halifax's engines ringing in her ears, fear reduced her to jelly. She couldn't do this. She would rather crawl to Denmark than do this.

The dispatcher stood over her with a raised arm. His arm fell and he shouted, 'Go,' and Tanne discovered there wasn't any choice.

There was a terrific rush, a savage jerk through her body, then a joyous silence and she found herself floating through the air, wishing she could stay there peacefully for a long time. For those few seconds, she ruled the world.

She landed perfectly. Feet together. The hardest part was battling to undo the straps and to keep the deflated parachute under control in the teeth of a stiff breeze.

The sergeant loped towards her. 'Well done, number forty-two.' He ran an expert eye over her. 'If I didn't know better, I'd say you were one of the chaps.'

She grinned.

'Listen, I have a pretty little ditty for you. I keep it for my favourites. Learn it.'

> If you don't keep your feet together, you will hit the
>   Joe hole as you go out.
> If you don't keep your feet together, you will land on
>   one leg and break it.
> If you don't keep your head up, you will somersault
>   and land head first.

'It *is* a pretty ditty,' she said.

Finally, they endured another punishing train journey across England to Finishing School: STS35.

Waking on the first morning in a bungalow with a view across the sea to the Isle of Wight, she heard aircraft haring out across the English Channel. They had disappeared by the time she had drawn back the curtains.

'Today,' said their new instructor, 'we'll teach you the different German uniforms, ranks, regiments and so on. You'll also learn how to concoct an alibi when you're embarking on an operation.' He paused, milking the drama. 'I can't impress on you enough that it's the detail that counts.' A smile crossed his mouth. 'But tonight you are allowed to go into town. Eat, drink, enjoy yourselves.'

After an excellent night out in Bournemouth, and a little drunk, Tanne returned with the others. A dogfight was going on over the sea. She watched and wished she hadn't. Engines screamed and black smoke obscured the moon as one of the planes corkscrewed towards the water.

Halfway through the night, she woke with a start. A torch shone in her face.

'Get up.' The order was in German.

Three men in SS officer uniform had their guns trained on her. Groggy with sleep and beer, she moved slowly. Two of the men frogmarched her down to a small, fetid cellar lit by a spotlight. Lars was already there, tied to a chair. They did not look at each other.

The harsh light was directed onto their faces.

'*Sprechen Sie Deutsch?*' demanded one of the SS officers, his accent immaculate.

The SS uniforms looked authentic, too. Where did they get them from? Dead Germans?

Irrelevant thought. *Concentrate.*

She felt outrage beating below the surface of her calm exterior and a slight nausea from the evening's excesses.

'Answer.'

She thought rapidly. Her German was almost perfect but if she asked for an interpreter it would give her an extra few seconds to think.

'No.'

One of them, groomed and pale, switched into English.

'Where were you yesterday evening?'

'I went into town.'

Never give too much detail.

'How?'

'On the bus.'

'What did you do there?'

Be dull.

'I went to the cinema and ate fish and chips . . .'

'How many uncles do you have?'

Cunning. Slipped in.

'What time was the film?'

The interrogation lasted for hours. Her hands remained tied painfully behind her back and she wasn't allowed to move.

At first, she thought with a slight contempt: *I can cope with this. It's a lie.* But, as her discomfort increased, doubt insinuated itself. Was it going to be as easy to hold on as she had imagined?

Lars had been taken away to another room and she could hear sounds as if he was being beaten up. Would they really beat him up? Would he get through?

She could not be sure and she discovered that not being sure was almost as bad as the discomfort.

'I need to go to the lavatory.'

'Tell her to go in her knickers,' one of them ordered her interrogator in German.

Urine ran down her legs and she ground her teeth at the humiliation. It soaked her clothes, too, and very soon the tender places between her legs began to smart.

Again, she told herself that it was not real. It was a lie.

They shoved a map under her nose. 'Give us the detail of where you went.'

She obliged and they threw the same questions at her over and over again.

'What did the conductor look like?'

'Who served you the fish and chips?'

As the hours wore on, her body grew stiff with tension and ached from the strain of holding out. To her alarm, she felt herself weakening. What on earth was she doing in this strange organization? What did they want from her? How far would they go?

She told herself: *There is no point. Give up.*

Cancel all knowledge of the instructors and the techniques and mental tools which they had so carefully taught her. Cancel thoughts of the family. Cancel thoughts of Denmark and what was happening there. This exercise was pointless.

She smelled of urine.

She thought of walking through the streets of Køge. She thought of Felix.

Surrender?

She lifted her eyes and encountered those of the pale German-speaking officer. He didn't bat an eyelid. Getting to his feet, he walked over to Tanne and slapped her hard on the face.

Her mind was swept clean of everything except anger. If she had to die, she wouldn't give him the satisfaction of making a noise, or giving a reaction.

Her cheek burned with shock and the impact of his hateful hand on her flesh. Bending her head, she looked down at her lap and her jaw tightened. This was the moment she would summon her resistance to bullying, violence and a dictatorship of souls – plus, she was damned if she would let them know how much she hated them. She must strip away her feelings. Concentrate on being the operative – hard, unsentimental, clever.

She lifted her head.

It was late morning when, without a backward glance, the officers got to their feet and filed out, leaving Tanne, still tied to the chair, alone in the cellar for another couple of hours.

Exhausted, she permitted her head to slump over her chest.

This was only the beginning. From this moment on, Tanne knew she was required to dig into her reserves of body and spirit, to peel away the layers that made up who she was, and to step out of the skin of the girl she had been – that girl who had so blithely gone to fetch a doctor. She must understand what people did in war.

Never more, never again, would she whistle to the dogs at Rosenlund and set off with them, light and innocent of heart.

All gone.

These were the bitter lessons of this charade.

Later the instructors went over their respective responses piecemeal. 'You were inconsistent here . . . You were unconvincing there . . .'

Even later, discussing the 'interrogation' with Lars, who had been as shaken as she had been, they speculated about the real identity of the 'SS' officers. Lars thought they were agents probably destined for active service in Germany, but no one could be sure.

That idea was enough for Tanne to forgive them. But only just.

Chapter Thirty

The day before he went back into the field in early September 1943, Felix was summoned to The Firm's London headquarters for a briefing with Colonel Marsh, head of the Danish section, and Major Iversen, a recently appointed senior Intelligence officer. Both looked unfit and had the waxen pallor of those who spent too much time indoors.

The colonel went straight to the point. 'We don't really know how the mass of the population thinks. But we have had some pointers. The general strike in August, being one. However, for us the balance is tricky. Significant resistance activity in Denmark will keep Jerry busy and preoccupied, which will give our Russian friends some relief on the Eastern front and is desirable. On the other hand, we don't want a mass uprising before . . .'

Felix helped him out. 'Before the Allies invade?'

'Something like that.'

Major Iversen moved restlessly around the room. He had large feet and his shoes creaked.

'So, you're telling me that the Allies might invade through Denmark?'

The two men exchanged glances. 'Who knows?' said the major.

Felix leaned over the desk. 'I don't believe you. You know, and I know, that it's highly unlikely. You're just giving me that to keep up the smokescreen about the invasion.'

The colonel's expression was as blank as a virgin blackboard. 'We rule nothing in and we rule nothing out. Whatever the scenario, it's vital that you, and we, keep control of all resistance activities. Otherwise advantages may be lost and our grip weakened. But it is true . . . one of the things we want is for you to spread the idea that the Allies may invade through Denmark, which hopefully will result in large numbers of German troops being tied up there.'

'But I'm not to know the real situation.'

The colonel shrugged as if to say: *Don't be so naive.*

'Many Danes don't relish the idea of being directed from London,' Felix was very dry.

'Make 'em,' said Major Iversen from his position by the window.

Felix said, 'Throwing dust in our eyes is not always the best way.'

He was curt and dismissive and, in response, Iversen emitted a gusty sigh. 'You must remember that Denmark's official policy of neutrality gives us problems. But we must concentrate on the positives. Getting this organization up and running has taken a bit of effort. We've made mistakes. We have had to feel our way. But the time for heroic amateurism is over.' With a creak of shoes, he turned round to face Felix. 'We've done a good job so far. What we need now is a tough, professional fight using whatever means, however unconventional, to bring Germany to its knees. Your task is to coordinate and support that struggle.'

'Through the British?'

The two men looked at Felix. 'Well, if you're sitting here, it would suggest that's the case,' said the colonel.

There was a chilly silence eventually broken by Felix. 'Then bring me up to speed. I'm out of touch.'

The colonel coughed, a phlegmy unhealthy rasp. 'You probably know that on the twenty-ninth of August martial law was declared, the Danish government resigned and Danish military personnel were interned . . .' He laid out some facts, placing them in a narrative as carefully as if they were the pieces of a jigsaw puzzle. 'Intelligence reports suggest that the German defeat at Stalingrad has given new heart to the resistance in Europe.'

Felix nodded.

'We welcome the increase in the Danish resistance but that balance I spoke of is crucial.' Was there a touch of impatience? Hostility, even? Felix couldn't be sure. 'We don't want it to become so big that a mass uprising takes place which would sting the enemy into a complete lockdown. That's why we are so keen to control the resistance activity from London. But we're happy with sabotage directed against shipyards and factories producing materials for the enemy.'

Felix drummed his fingers on the desk. 'So far you have sent a total of four wireless operators into Denmark, two of whom have been taken out. Thirteen sabotage instructors, of whom one had to be eliminated. And thirty-two containers have been dropped in various locations. Hardly huge.'

The colonel sent Felix a long, cool look. 'We are doing our best.'

There was more discussion, and then Felix said: 'It's agreed, then, that I operate on Zealand and build up the circuit from København. My task is to bring together the resistance factions and weld them together. Until I get radio contact up and running, I will send messages to Sweden, via our fishermen friends. I understand other agents will shortly be sent into Jutland and they will make contact with Vinegar and use him.'

'That's about it,' said the colonel. 'The agents are being trained at the moment.'

'You are sure Vinegar is up and running?'

There was another silence. Three minds were working around tricky questions to which there were no sure answers.

The colonel asked sharply: 'Any reason why you are querying it?'

'The silence. A feeling.'

'He's transmitting.' The colonel sounded just a touch patronizing. 'I understand how hard it must be not to become too paranoid in the field.'

You bugger, thought Felix.

Iversen intervened. 'Can you retrieve your wireless sets?'

Felix nodded. 'With a bit of luck. My first one's hidden up in København. The second I had to leave with Freya. I'm sure it will still be there.'

As Felix left the room, Colonel Marsh called out, 'Felix . . .'

Felix turned back. 'Yes?'

'*Tak.*'

Thank you.

Felix returned to Denmark with a couple of other Joes via a complicated route similar to the one he and Eva had taken to escape. They endured being stuffed into the back-end of a bomber that flew them to Stockholm, a train journey to the coast and a nightmare few hours in a fishing boat.

When the boat nosed discreetly into Rødvig harbour, he staggered ashore and breathed in the stink of fish, salt and seaweed. It was good to be back.

He and the Joes sat out the rest of the night under cover of the woods outside the town. Near dawn, a German vehicle appeared from nowhere, cruising down the road. The three men flung themselves flat in the undergrowth. The car halted. A searchlight beamed out of its back window. Felix's fingers clawed into the earth, digging deep into bark and pine needles. Digging into Denmark.

He was not fucking well going to be captured within a couple of hours of arriving.

The car moved on.

In the distance, dogs barked.

Once the sun was up, they filed down to the stream and shaved as best they could, taking turns with the razor. They dampened their hair and rubbed their shoes before separately making for the station, where they bought tickets to different destinations. They were all aboard their trains before the German guard turned up at seven-thirty for duty.

It was back to life on the move, never sleeping more than a

couple of nights in the same place. No two days were the same, and he tackled this lack of routine by treating every move calmly, as if it was the most banal of activities. He became a master at scanning every face for clues. Who were they? Them or us?

In København, he tapped up his contacts and 'sleepers' and made plans to meet each one. Activating a funding arrangement that had been organized with the bank by London, he set about building necessary bridges with other resistance groups.

It was Jacob who told him Freya was on the run and moving between safe houses in Nørrebro, one of the districts of København and he sent a message to her. After that, he contacted Odin and asked for soundings on the state of the Danish army. Was it with the resistance or not?

Late one afternoon, he and Odin rendezvoused near the Torvegade bridge. Fog wisped over the water and there was an autumn chill in the air.

They walked along the waterfront.

Odin was as persuasive as ever. 'London's making a mistake by not taking us into their confidence. My contacts don't like it and the lack of trust compromises our relationships. Some of my army colleagues, very senior ones, were forced to do a runner to Sweden the other day.' Odin came to a halt. A tug was chugging slowly downstream and its hooter echoed across the flat grey water. 'Someone betrayed them. The interesting question is: who? Some idiot in London? Or in Sweden, which is even leakier? Or was it here?' He was twisting a packet of German cigarettes between his fingers. 'Your guess is as good as mine.'

Odin had changed. There was an edginess, a bitterness, which Felix had not seen before and it made him wary. It was true, he didn't know Odin . . . or what drove him . . . and, in this game, no one ever really knew what the other was up to. For that, you had to be led by instinct, your experience and your 'nose'. Plus, questions had to be asked. All the time.

He listened to Odin carefully – sorting out the details, storing away information, searching for the weak spots.

German intelligence-gathering had become highly efficient, in particular the Direction-Finding Signals Unit, Odin reported. But, as far as he knew, he was still trusted by his contacts in the Abwehr. Occasionally, General Gottfried shared operational details with him and some of it was useful, including the intelligence that parachute drops in the Aarhus area were almost all ending in disaster for the agents.

'Betrayed?'

'What do you think?'

Felix considered. 'The Aarhus area, you say? It's possible.'

Vinegar?

'There are limits to what I can find out.' Odin's gaze travelled thoughtfully up and down the waterfront. 'What's happening with the new wireless sets?'

'Nothing to report.'

Not true but Odin didn't have to know that. On his return, one of the good pieces of news to greet Felix had been that Johan and his team had, after several bad setbacks, which included a raid on their underground workshop, almost completed the task to manufacture the smaller, lighter wireless transmitter.

'I dare say London won't be happy about the new wireless sets.'

'They took some persuasion,' Felix replied. 'The British like to think they're the best at everything.'

'Crystals? Transmission schedules? Codes? What about those?'

Again the evasion. 'We'll know in good time.'

'Pig shit,' said Odin. 'We don't have time.'

The fog was deepening over the waterfront. Water slapped monotonously against the moorings.

A group of students were walking towards them and Odin gestured that he and Felix should turn aside.

'I have a proposition. Our ever-tidy German cousins have decided to marry the archives in the German Chamber of Commerce here with those in Aarhus. It's planned for next Thursday. We should snaffle it before it's locked away in a Nazi stronghold.'

Again, they fell into step.

'We don't need the archive.'

'You're a fool, Felix. It's a treasure trove. It'll tell us who's cooperating and for how much.' He tapped Felix's shoulder. 'Think of the blackmail opportunities.' He flashed Felix an unpleasant grin. 'Get stuff on your enemy. I might even check up on the family and see what I can get on them.'

The joke was not funny and almost painful.

Yet Odin was right.

'One more thing,' Odin added. 'You should know that the word is the Nazis plan to round up the Jews quite soon.'

At the junction with Hans Christian Andersen Boulevard they parted. 'Get the archive,' were Odin's parting words.

Felix watched his retreating figure. The instructors on his refresher course had been emphatic.

Question every friend or foe. Especially every friend. Trust only very sparingly. Question motives thoroughly. Avoid a direct answer.

At three o'clock the following day, Felix entered the Café Amadeus and took a seat under a portrait of the young Mozart. He had dusted talcum powder onto his hair, parted it on a different side, and stuffed his cheeks with torn-up bits of sponge.

Seeing Freya would be a boon, and good for him, but it was her younger version – the wild-haired, bold, tender companion of his flight – who preoccupied him.

Felix's appearance was bad enough but when Freya slid onto the banquette beside him, he was shocked.

The long blonde hair had been replaced by a page-boy bob with a fringe. Worse, it had been dyed red-brown although, here and there, a few blonde streaks stood out from the brown.

A pair of large, unflattering, dark-rimmed spectacles could not disguise that she had lost her healthy glow.

She wouldn't have it any other way, Freya assured Felix. Life had become difficult at Rosenlund. Impossible, even. She recounted the story of the dying tortured man – 'He haunts me,' she said – and told him what happened with the Gottfrieds, with Arne, her subsequent escape and life on the run. 'War has freed me,' she said.

That struck Felix forcibly. Maybe it was true for all of them. Maybe, in its subversion of ordinary life, war was liberating.

'And your husband?'

The grey eyes narrowed with distress. 'You always have to pay something, don't you?'

Freya was someone else now. Johan had procured forged papers identifying her as Lise Lillelund, infant school teacher. Born on Funen. Widowed. Currently recovering from a bout of TB that required frequent journeys into the country for recuperation.

'Tell me about the man who died. Was there any clue to his identity?'

Their table hugged the wall and there was no one within earshot but she moved closer. 'I *think* he was one of us. But who he was working for I don't know. He was being transferred from Aarhus to København.'

'Aarhus!'

'He was brave, Felix. They'd tortured him for a long time.'

'Anything that would give us a clue. Anything?'

'Despite being beaten up, his hands hadn't been touched. It struck me as odd. Don't they usually go for the fingernails?'

Piecing together intelligence required lateral thinking . . . the sixth sense which pounced on a tiny detail, the scantiest of hints, perceived its import and set it beside another tiny detail.

'Some of his injuries were months old,' Freya continued. 'I wondered whether it might have been Vinegar.'

During the silence that followed, Felix looked around the café. To an onlooker, this was such a normal scene. The white coffee cups. The half-full ashtray. Waiters. Chatter. A man and a woman huddled together on a café bench.

He felt a sickening thud as he groped towards a conclusion.

'It's possible,' he said at last. 'Especially if the prisoners were being transferred from Aarhus. Vinegar operated there.'

He ran back over the events of that first drop. That funny, air-sick, brave little man. Vinegar going in first. Disappearing. The *stikker* on the loose. The rapid dispersal. If the Germans *had* captured Vinegar it would have been easy to run him. Why would the enemy not do so? Running an agent was a useful method with which to capture other agents and equipment, to snaffle up information and to transmit misleading intelligence back to London.

He added: 'If Vinegar had been picked up by Danes working for the Germans when he first came in, he could have been fooled into thinking he was among friends and cooperated.'

At STS they had been warned about how this might happen.

They begin with friendly talk, good treatment, promises. They progress to maltreatment. Use everything you have to avoid third-degree interrogation. Weakened resistance can cause you to reveal all sorts of things.

Freya asked: 'But London should have realized. Why didn't they?'

'You tell me.' Felix knew his anger to be irrational, for it was easier said than done. 'They assured me they had checked up on Vinegar.'

Freya helped herself to one of his cigarettes. 'Why keep Vinegar alive?'

'Possibly because they thought London would know his fist. They would assume that Vinegar's records would be kept and consulted. They wouldn't have wanted London taking fright and closing the transmitter down. In that way, they got information, masterminded any drops . . . you name it.'

He spoke bitterly and she laid a hand on his. 'Don't waste your energy on anger.'

'I am angry. Precisely at the waste.'

'Felix . . .' Her grip on his hand tightened. After a moment, she continued: 'What I can't bear is that he died more or less alone. I would have held his hand.'

Her expression reflected a kind of terror, which Felix understood – and shared. It was the fear of the void, the one where nothing was known or certain and an agent was abandoned by everyone to the misery, terror and torment of its nothingness. Warned to expect periods when it would attack him, he had found its corrosiveness shocking and enfeebling. So too . . . by the look of her . . . had Freya.

Regrets and sentiments were useless. 'Freya . . . don't.' He got back to business. 'The wireless transmitter?'

Freya lowered her voice. 'The cottage. I used it to send one message after you left. Told them you were going dark.'

'London got the message.'

She breathed out a sigh of relief. 'That's something.'

'Freya?'

She knew and he knew they needed the wireless transmitter. No question. A trace of colour crept back into Freya's cheeks as she weighed and measured the decision. 'I'll bring it to København.'

'Freya, why do you do this? You of all people.'

Cigarette smoke curled between them. She tamped down the butt end of hers with a finger and a tiny fleck of tobacco clung to it. 'Many complicated reasons. But, in the end, it's simple, really. If I don't, who will?'

Jacob slid into the café and the three of them sat under Mozart's portrait, smoking and drinking beer and coffee.

Jacob reported on the twenty-four hours of intensive reconnaissance which had been mounted on the German Chamber of Commerce. 'The concierge is one of us . . .' he said, nicotine-stained fingers curled around his glass. 'But we have to rough him up and lock him in. He's terrified his family will suffer. He knocks off at about six. So far, a night watchman hasn't been posted. He let me take a look at the room.' He downed a swig. 'Full of stuff.'

It was good to be thinking of practical matters. 'Right,' Felix said. 'Two vans and all the Stens and ammo we've got. We need lookouts, cover outside the building, plus a rifle with telescopic sights for the sniper. The weapons must be hidden in the area a couple of days ahead.'

Jacob tackled a second beer. Two days ago he had been on Funen, instructing a group in sabotage, and his voice was hoarse from the shouting. He didn't approve of this operation. 'What are we doing wasting lives on this one?'

A speck of foam clung to his upper lip and Freya leaned over and wiped it away. 'Beer moustache.' It was a fleeting moment of camaraderie and affection.

'Better by far to blow up the railways and stop Fritz using Denmark as a transport hub,' he said.

Felix ignored him. He found a pencil and paper and drew a diagram. 'Opposite the annex, is the commercial college. We need a couple of machine guns to cover that as well.'

'You don't ask much,' said Jacob.

They settled on the time of operation, and the routes, lookouts and the getaway.

The sceptical Jacob repeated: 'What's the point of getting killed or wounded for a load of papers when we could be blowing up a bridge?'

Felix grinned at Jacob. 'Your moment in the sun is coming. London has instructed us to step up the sabotage.'

Jacob snorted.

Before she left, Freya whispered, 'Do something for me, Felix. If you can.'

'If I can . . .'

Her mouth twisted painfully. 'If you see a file on Eberstern – on my husband – will you destroy it?'

Four days later.

6.00 p.m.

The sky was a uniform grey and darkening. At the north end of the Saxogade three men in dark clothing drifted into the doorways and took up positions.

6.05 p.m.

Chatting and smoking, ten men wearing loose overcoats strolled into the street from the Matthåusgade and spread out along the road. A large grey van drew up behind them.

More men appeared.

Sitting in the cab beside the driver, a raw-boned giant from the docks, was Felix, balaclava pulled down over his face. He counted up the men. He was expecting seventeen. All there. Good.

6.07 p.m.

In a headscarf and nondescript mackintosh, Freya walked down the street towards the annex. Outside, she stopped and retied the scarf under her chin. Then she bent down to fasten her shoelace.

It was the signal that it was clear.

6.09 p.m.

One of the men sprinted up the steps into the annex building, ran through the door and took up position at a first-floor window.

6.10 p.m.

The men who had waited in the doorways now approached from the other end of the street and covered the commercial college with the guns that they pulled from under their overcoats.

6.13 p.m.

A second grey van rounded the corner and parked by the entrance to the Chamber of Commerce. The men took out their weapons and trained them on the street.

6.15 p.m.

Felix leaped down from the van. Freya, Jacob and six others materialized from doorways and followed him, one of them peeling off to deal with the caretaker. The rest ran with him up to the first-floor archive room, where the leading man shot out the lock of the double doors. Guns levelled, they advanced into a room where boxes were stacked in rows, neatly labelled in German script.

Jacob whistled. 'There's too much.'

Felix checked over the nearest boxes. 'Form a chain. Take the Roneo as well.'

They worked in silence and at top speed. Felix had calculated on half an hour, max.

6.45 p.m.

A siren sounded in the distance.

'Time to go,' said Felix. 'Now.'

He watched as the final box was hefted into the back of the van and the doors banged shut. The second van ground its gears. Tyres spun. Freya and the team melted away up the street.

Felix swung himself up into the first van. The driver drove cautiously along the street and headed south over the Langebro bridge. In the distance, sirens screamed. Felix turned round to take a look. So far, so good.

The driver drove fast but competently. He seemed an unflappable sort. 'What are you going to do with this lot?'

'Hide it. After the war we'll send it to the official archives,' said Felix.

Once over the river, they drove down the Amager Boulevard before turning right into a network of streets. They were heading for a gateway that led into a yard with a warehouse on one side. As they approached, the doors opened and the vans drove straight into the warehouse, one after the other. The doors smacked shut. The driver gave a thumbs-up to Felix. 'That was good.'

The warehouse was stacked with barrels, boxes and sacks of

concrete. Six men, who had been waiting for their arrival, threw away their cigarettes and got to work.

Two of them changed the number plates on the vans and sprayed the words 'Kraft's Electricians' on the sides. The remainder of the men concentrated on unloading and stacking the boxes behind the barrels.

Felix gave the vans the once-over. 'Fine,' he said.

Within a short time, the drivers had backed them out of the warehouse and were away.

The final box stowed, the men dispersed with instructions to take different routes back to the city centre.

Felix's balaclava was sodden with his sweat but he waited until the last man had left before removing it. All was quiet, the place stank of paint, but he allowed himself a moment's satisfaction at the success of the operation.

Picking up the nearest box file to hand, he rifled through it.

Immaculate. If this was the calibre and organization of the intelligence then it would be a big, creamy piece of cake to piece together a trail of information. He read on. German nationals living in Denmark were sending streams of business intelligence to Berlin – so far, so predictable. More surprising was the tally – and it was a sizeable tally – of Danish firms who were falling over each other to be appointed suppliers to Germany. Letters from them, plus letters from young men volunteering to undertake unpaid work in Germany in order to prepare for 'the new post-war Europe', letters begging for preference . . . They were all present in file after file.

Felix hunted on and unearthed a card index, which he set down on a box. Brushing a finger over the cards, he watched them waterfall forwards and backwards, revealing a fulsome *dramatis personae* of businessmen, bankers, landowners and farmers, together with the numbers of their files. Then, as he knew he would do because of Freya . . . because of Eva . . . he tamped down on the letter E.

Eberstern. Green file 257.

Time was short. Why should he bother? What on earth was it to him?

Shuffling through the boxes marked E, he retrieved file number 257. Stapled into it was the Declaration which bore the signature of Bror Eberstern.

He skimmed over it. Now he understood what Freya wanted.

War had taught him about . . . oh, hatred, vendetta, but also about the surprising modesty of some, and the heroism of others who were prepared to lose everything. Its uncertainties and violence had also taught him friendship – his friendship with Freya – which was why he was now going to take possession of this incriminating document.

Folding the certificate into a square, he slipped it down inside one of his socks and stowed the file back in the box.

War had made him love his country. It had also caused him to burn with longing for . . . Eva . . . who had held him fast in the fish hold of a bucking ship. It had given him intense emotional experiences. In its aftermath . . . if . . . *if* . . . he survived, he would give thanks for such inner grace.

Time to go.

At the far end of the warehouse there was movement in the shadows.

A *stikker?* One of his men come back to check up?

Felix reached for his pistol and ducked behind the boxes.

Don't blink. Wait.

'Felix?' Odin materialized out of the shadow. He was dressed in a suit, with a light cashmere overcoat, shoes of the best quality and a hat pulled low over his face.

He had been right. This man didn't entirely add up.

'How did you get here?' Felix was curt.

'I followed the convoy and waited.'

'A word of advice.' Felix put the pistol away. 'Don't creep up on me. I shoot first.'

Odin shoved his hands into his pockets. 'What were you looking for, Felix?'

'None of your business.'

Odin pointed to the squat shape of the card index. 'That's what I've been sent for. Our chaps will keep it safely hidden.'

Was he after something else?

Odin moved closer and Felix caught a blast of alcohol. 'Motives are not always straightforward. They may be the right motives but they are not straightforward.'

'Since you're here,' said Felix, 'help me drag the tarpaulins over the boxes. This lot would be better hidden.'

Odin glanced down at his expensive clothes and sighed. 'In war it's necessary to make sacrifices.'

With some difficulty, they manoeuvred the tarpaulins into place. Spotting a half-empty bag of concrete power, Felix took a fistful and scattered it over the tarpaulins.

Good. They looked as though they had been there, untouched, for months.

Odin brushed down his lapel. Then, without warning, he reached over and patted Felix's pockets.

In reply, Felix's hands clamped down on Odin's. 'What the hell do you think you're doing?'

'Have you been snaffling information?'

'Fuck off, Odin.'

'You know as well as I do that everyone's in it for themselves.'

Felix increased the pressure of his grip. 'While we are asking questions, are you here to "check up on the family", as you put it?'

Odin looked down at Felix's hands. 'Get off me.'

Felix pushed him away.

Wiping his hands on a handkerchief, Odin said, 'Let's do a deal, Felix. You let me have half an hour here and I'll do my best to see that the dogs are called off Freya.'

Felix whipped out the pistol from his pocket. 'Get out.'

'You're missing a trick, Felix.'

Who could one trust? Did it matter any more?

Felix calculated. He didn't want trouble which would draw attention to the warehouse. Also, Odin was an important link and it would be cleverer, more constructive, to let him have his head and to keep an eye on him.

'Maybe.' Felix dropped the pistol back into his pocket.

Odin hefted up the card index and slotted it under his arm. 'Don't bother with trying to protect the fat cats in here. It will come out in the end.'

To punch him or not? Felix was sorely tempted. 'We're not going through this war just to return to how things were. You won't be giving the orders.'

'Someone always gives the orders,' said Odin, pulling his hat down over his eyes. 'But maybe you're right and it's over for people like me. Rest in peace, the ruling class.' He peered through the gloom. 'For some reason we Danes see ourselves as one big, happy, democratic family, and maybe that will happen.'

At the door, he turned round. 'By the way, where is Freya?'

'Shut up.'

'I've seen the way you look at her. You should be careful.'

'Shut up.'

'Or is it the daughter that's taken your fancy? I'm told she's disappeared.'

Felix actually laughed. He adjusted the torch beam so it blazed onto Odin's face. 'Get out of here.'

'Aren't you forgetting that we are on the same side?' Odin patted the card index. 'My informant tells me that this little sweetie is kept bang up to date. Which is good for us, don't you think?' He raised a hand and waved. 'So sorry I can't give you a lift.'

It was after nine o'clock. Time was catching up with him.

Felix hurried through the streets, always conscious that there might be something gaining on his back. His steps quickened. Hurry. *Hurry*. But don't look too hurried.

Making his way through the back gardens to avoid the curfew, Felix got himself to the safe flat near the Vesterbrogade.

Had he been followed? *Check*.

Escape route out of the house? *Check*.

The routines had been laid down in his brain like neural pathways.

He slid in through the door. At his entrance, a figure reared up at him in the darkness. His hand flew to his pistol.

'Easy!' Freya said. 'Easy.'

'What are you doing here?'

'I wanted to see you.'

He put the pistol away and placed his hands on her shoulders, 'Idiot.' Odin's words came back to him: 'I've seen the way you look at her.'

He moved away.

'Have you got a cigarette?' she was asking.

He chucked her a packet.

She smoked it in quick, nervous bursts. Watching her, Felix thought how lonely she looked. He understood perfectly. This life turned you into a solitary person and a solitary spirit. Spending nights alone in a room, a gun to hand, hardly remembering which name it was you had today, twitching at every sound, yet prepared to go out with weapons blazing – it changed you.

Looking at this room, who wouldn't feel depressed? In one corner a dispirited plant struggled for survival and the overstuffed furniture was upholstered in a dingy brown.

'Freya, what do you want?'

'Is there any news of my daughter and husband?'

'You know I can't tell you.'

'*Please.*'

Felix crossed to the window to check the street outside. Vulnerability was not permitted in an agent's arsenal. Yet who was he to deny Freya what she needed to know? 'All I can tell you is that she got to Sweden safely.' He turned round to face Freya. 'That's it.'

'I'm sorry to harass you.' She stubbed out the cigarette. 'One day, you might understand. When you have children. Loving them is the most powerful thing.'

Once she had been glossy and perfumed. Now she was thin, crop-haired and her clothes smelled, but the pair of them understood danger, exhaustion and lowness of spirit. Intimately. They had shared it. What existed between them now went beyond mere description and beyond measuring.

'Felix . . .' Freya laid a hand on his chest. 'If anything should happen to me, will you look after my daughter, who I think – I'm sure, whatever you say or don't say – is out there somewhere? Or will be, knowing her. For the war, I mean. Bror can't.'

He squinted down at her. 'You know I can't make a promise like that. No one can.'

She pretended she hadn't heard. 'I know she would be safe with you.'

'You don't know anything about me.'

'I do.' She lit up a second cigarette. 'Don't ask me how. I know you're the sort of person who always prefers to work on his own. Yes?' She chuckled – and at the sound a lump climbed shamefully into Felix's throat. 'I imagine you as an only child, playing on the beach, haring about on a bicycle, being taken to a pantomime at Christmas and sitting uncomfortably between your parents. Am I right?'

'Maybe.'

'I may not know your name but I understand the important things. That's why I'm asking you.'

Felix was sharp: 'Don't invite death by entertaining it.'

Her eyes narrowed in triumph. 'My point, Felix. That's exactly what someone who doesn't have children says. But for those who do, they *have* to think about it.'

Outside in the street, a car slowed down. Felix pulled the curtains shut, dowsed the light then snatched the cigarette from her and stamped on it.

'There's a way out of the window and over the wall into someone's back garden,' he said.

'So will you?' Her whisper seemed to echo in the dark.

'I can't make promises.'

A faint sigh emitted from Freya.

He knew he had disappointed her.

They pressed back against the wall by the window. He edged close to her. Closer. Their shoulders collided and he said, 'Your daughter is pretty extraordinary.'

Again, the chuckle that tore at his heart. 'Tell me something I don't know.'

'I have something for you.' He reached down to his sock, pulled out the certificate and pressed it into her hand.

'What is it?'

He told her.

Cradling it between her hands as if it was one of the jewels that she had once worn, she said: 'You got it for me?'

Their faces were almost touching. 'Do what you will with it.'

He barely heard the whisper. 'I cannot thank you enough.'

Felix slid his arm round her shoulders. 'I'm not going to ask questions. Nor am I ever going to talk about what it contains.'

A sliver of light from the car's headlights poked through the slit in the curtain and he saw that tears were running down her cheeks.

'I'm frightened,' she said.

He took his time . . . the images running hither and thither in his head.

'So am I.'

'Not of this . . .' She gestured into the darkened room. 'But of not coming up to the mark. Failing when it matters.'

Felix leaned over and kissed Freya on the cheek. 'Shush.'

He was tender. He was loving. Those were the things he had been anxious that he would lose.

Twenty minutes or so later they agreed to turn the lights back on. Freya slid the paper into the lining of her jacket and tied on a headscarf. 'I'll go.'

'It's after curfew. You'll have to stay here.'

'I was forgetting.' She pulled off the headscarf. 'How I long for a deep, hot bath,' she remarked. 'A scented one. Sometimes I dream of being back in the bathroom in Rosenlund.'

So saying, she almost broke Felix's heart.

Chapter Thirty-one

Jacob sent a message from Køge: 'Lie low. SS Schalburg Corps in area for next two weeks playing war games. Currently north of Rosenlund.'

'Whoa,' said Felix. 'We keep away.'

There was no question of retrieving the wireless set. Instead, Felix sent Kay with a message to the group leader in Roskilde. Having delivered it, Kay criss-crossed the town, doubling back more than once on her path, and finally she boarded the København train.

The carriages were crowded and she was pressed up against the window.

The landscape was familiar, plunging Kay into nostalgia for her former Danish life. Then she reached further back into memory, to the little English girl she had once been who had waved a Union Jack at the British King and Queen as they drove through her town.

Her mother would think of her often. Of that, Kay was sure. As for her sisters? They would be too busy with their families to spare her more than a passing recollection.

Bror would be thinking of her, too, inevitably with anger. Perhaps he was astonished at how twenty-five years of a good marriage could turn on a sixpence into ... bitterness and absence.

She missed him with a painful, scratchy emotion and yearned to see him, knowing perfectly well that the best thing to hope for was that, as with all desires, it would fade with time.

Kay's instructions were to avoid Køge and the areas of København where she was known. She did her best to follow them and to observe the things Felix had taught her about the undercover life before he had fled to Sweden. Tips on where to sleep, how to walk, what to say. The art of deception. The art of subterfuge.

Living undercover was an intense and overwhelming experience, and she was working on how to handle it.

Items to be carried in a bag, or to be worn on top of one another: one vest, two pairs of underwear, two pairs of socks.

She wore a long-sleeved blouse, pleated skirt and a beige mackintosh which she tried to keep immaculate. More than once, she had been forced to wear wet clothes because it hadn't been possible to dry them overnight.

Obedient to Felix's diktats, she never stayed more than two nights in the same place. Her sleep was fitful. Plus, her stomach responded badly to being on the move and frequently played up. After a life of plenty, infrequent meals had taken some getting used to. Felix allocated her what he could but obtaining money was difficult, and she was forced to eke out every kroner. Unsure where the next meal would come from, she dreamed unsettling dreams of roast pork, cherry flans and the best bread and butter.

A mile or so outside Hedehusene, the train ground to a halt. Kay's hand tightened on her basket. They were at a standstill in a steep-sided cutting, which meant it would be impossible to escape.

The sturdy woman opposite, who looked like a farmer's wife, peered at Kay. She willed herself not to shift in her seat.

Who could you trust? Who couldn't you trust?

A dog barked. Kay tensed. *Gestapomen* searching the trains with dogs were a regular occurrence.

Remain on it or not? Instinct told her to run but, before she could decide, the train moved off. The barking faded into the distance. Even so, she decided to get off.

At Hedehusene station, Kay dropped lightly down onto the platform.

Walk as if everything is perfectly normal. Look neither right nor left. Do not hurry out of the exit.

At the taxi rank, she asked to be driven back to Roskilde's main square. There she paid the taxi driver, further reducing her ever-diminishing stash of kroner, walked to the library and enquired if Pernille was available.

A woman emerged from an interior office. She was short, anxious and underweight. 'Yes?' She wasn't welcoming.

'Would it be possible to take a parcel of cabbages?' Kay asked.

Behind the spectacles, Pernille's eyes widened. 'I'll organize someone to deal with them.'

Half an hour later Kay was being driven towards Køben-havn in a taxi which had appeared at the back entrance of the library. Approaching the suburbs, she felt a relief. City streets and crowds provided cover and in them she could be safer. Anonymous.

The taxi driver deposited her behind the main station in the Colbjørnsensgade. He refused to take any money but said that she should come back to Roskilde after the war and pay him then. 'You trust me?' she asked.

'Yes,' he said and drove off without looking back.

A good Dane.

Walking towards the town square, she noted the uneasy atmosphere. Unusually, huddles of people were gathered at the street corners. 'Is anything happening?' she asked a woman at the bus stop. The woman was carrying a tiny boy with a green woollen hat and refused to look at Kay. 'I don't want to say anything.'

'Whisper it,' said Kay. 'Please.'

Reluctantly, she muttered, 'Extra German SS have arrived in the city. And Nazi police.'

'Do you know why?'

The woman shook her head.

Locating a public phone, she dialled Anton's office. His sec-retary answered but was unwilling to put Kay through until Kay gave her name.

'All right,' Kay conceded. 'Tell him that Princess Sophia-Maria wishes to see him.'

Back came the message to meet at the Café Tivoli in an hour's time.

The Café Tivoli was to be found down one of the smaller streets in the Frederiksstaden district and five minutes or so from the military headquarters. Kay knew it. Expensive and discreet about the meetings and liaisons which took place in it, and with a reputation for the best hot chocolate in København, it was the sort of place Anton would favour.

He was already seated at a table at the back of the café, nurs-ing a brandy. The lighting was dim and the table was set apart from the others. At her appearance he looked up. She sensed him recoil. 'You look terrible,' he said.

'Hello, Anton.'

'What on earth possessed you to contact me?'

She took in the uniform and the handsome face. 'Aren't you glad to see me?'

'Of course.' He looked her up and down and it was clear he wasn't.

In a flash, Kay understood she was no longer useful to Anton.

'You've caused a lot of trouble. General Gottfried was beside himself. It's taken me a lot of sweet-talking to keep in his good books. I suspect that he's worried he let you into his confi-dence. Did he?'

'Nothing you don't know already.'

'You've made an enemy of the enemy. A personal one, dar-ling. Always a bad move. Fouled the nest. The bore is that the general isn't so keen to take my advice any more. You've tainted me and I'm having to work at it.' The corners of his mouth turned down. 'Paddling hard like a swan.'

The waiter placed coffee in front of Kay.

'And Bror?' She had difficulty saying Bror's name.

'If I didn't know him better, I would say Farmer Bror was grieving. But the old boy was always gloomy at the best of times. Not that I see much of him.' He added, 'I'm told he's been up and down to København since you vanished. He sees Nils. How they must enjoy each other's company.'

'Nils! How do you know?'

Since she last saw him, Anton's laugh had turned chesty. He was smoking too much but Kay couldn't blame him. 'Don't be naive, darling.'

So Bror was being followed.

'I would suspect –' Anton did not disguise his amusement '– that Farmer Bror thinks you and Tanne have made a fool of him and Nils is the only one left with any sense.'

The coffee was wonderful. It tasted of times long ago, of money and of luxury. Ravenous for it, she drank it down. 'Order me another one, please.'

Anton obeyed.

'Why the extra Gestapo and the Nazi police drafted in, Anton?'

He positioned his cigarette case carefully on the table. 'Politics. In-fighting. It's an open secret. Hitler makes sure that he keeps his top brass on tenterhooks over their positions.' His smile was not reassuring. 'As you once said, darling, they fight like rats in a sack. It's always a winning tactic.' He seized Kay's hand, turned it over and ran a finger along the blue vein at the wrist. She felt a familiar tug of sexual attraction, but it was a discordant, disturbing feeling.

'Something must be happening. You must know what.'

He released her arm and spoke in a low voice. 'In the past few days, two German ships have docked here,' he admitted.

'Despite denials, our contacts tells us that Werner Best and General von Hanneken have been ordered to obey the directive from Berlin to round up all Danish Jews onto the ships and take them to Theresienstadt concentration camp.'

Kay forced herself to make the second cup of coffee last. Bitter. Black. Hot. And badly needed.

The brandy glass was empty.

'What are you going to do, Anton?'

'There's nothing I can do.'

She met his eye. 'Yes, there is. You *must* do something.'

'Don't look at me like that.'

She gathered her wits. 'What we do now determines our future. This is the moment when Danes can show who they are.'

'Spare me.'

He wasn't interested.

'You do have a choice,' she persisted. 'You can warn the Jews and make arrangements to hide them.'

Anton transferred his attention to the waiter.

'Anton, *Anton*. Think.'

'Shut up, darling.'

'How many Jews are there in Denmark?'

'Six or seven thousand. I don't know the precise number.'

'It must be possible to get a good few out to Sweden. Some could hide in the more remote areas.'

The waiter was approaching. Anton raised a finger. 'Another brandy.'

She recalled their relationship over the years – the teasing, the oblique flirting and the efforts to keep him and Bror on good terms whenever they met. 'Has the general, with his highly efficient signals units, corrupted you?'

'If you must joke, make it more subtle.'

She nursed her coffee. 'It's early to be drinking brandy.'

He shrugged. 'It isn't easy keeping afloat. In fact, it's quite a strain. Do you know how many of my brother officers have been interned?' Anton contemplated the refilled glass. 'War isn't black and white, tempting though it is to think it is.' He pinged a fingernail against the glass and it gave off a haunted, watery echo. 'For instance, sometimes you have to surrender information in order to keep credible. How black or white is that?'

Kay cut off the echo with a finger. 'Losing faith?'

He shrugged again – it was becoming a familiar gesture. 'In the long run, it's probably irrelevant who wins or loses. The imperative is survival. I took the view the Reich wasn't going to survive. Empires are tricky to achieve. And America is too powerful. Plus, in my way, I'm a patriot.'

Something pushed its way to the surface of her mind. Doubt? She peered at Anton and realized she had been reading him wrong all these months. 'Anton, you're on the right side, but for the wrong reasons.'

'Survival is the best reason. Think about it.'

Kay ran her fingers through her hair, stiff and dry from the cheap dye. 'Perhaps we never understood each other.'

Anton's jaw tightened. 'Melodrama doesn't suit you.' He pointed to her hair. 'I long to have back the pretty, witty woman I used to know. You look terrible.' When she sighed impatiently, he added: 'You realize you can't go back to Rosenlund? Or to Bror.'

'That's between him and me.'

'You're on the wanted list.' Anton smiled grimly. 'Mind you, Bror will be, too, at the end of the war.'

'So be it.' She got to her feet. 'I never knew what went wrong between you.'

Anton swallowed down the brandy. 'Went wrong between us? We don't like each other, that's all.' But something slipped from him . . . an envy, a longing, regret. 'And it's true my brooding country cousin had everything I wanted. Rosenlund. A wife like you.'

'You could have married.'

He caught up her hand in the old way – and, once again, she was the perfumed Kay Eberstern wearing Parisian couture. 'Tell me honestly, darling. Were you happy with Farmer Bror?'

'Yes. I was. Very.'

'But you like me, too?'

She braced herself. 'Yes, I liked you, too.'

Anton digested the past tense. 'What a pity it's all in the past and we can't go back. Are you frightened?'

She thought of the stories about bodies being taken apart piecemeal, the shootings, the incarcerations, the tortured man in Jacob's cottage. She thought of what the Jews must be experiencing. She thought of the fragmentation which had taken place within herself. 'Yes.'

'Keep away from Rosenlund.'

She breathed in sharply. *Home.*

'Kay . . .' Anton picked up his cigarette case and got to his feet.

'Ssh, that's not my name.'

'Get out of here. *Please.* Go to Sweden. Sit it out until the war's over.' Then, as once before, he pulled her to him and kissed her.

His kiss was a reminder. Of what? Of being desired? Or of the time when she knew who she was and her days had been sweetly prescribed and bounded by innocent sleep. He murmured into her ear. 'Go to Sweden. Bror will never have you back.' His hand tightened on her shoulder.

No one could be trusted. Nothing remained the same. Nothing was normal. Her affection and fascination for Anton was turning into dislike. War had done that. She now saw that Anton was a profoundly cynical man – and cynicism was a fatal weakness.

The lie left her lips. 'Perhaps you're right. We'll meet after the war. Make sure you survive till then, Anton.'

'I have every intention of doing so.'

She detached herself. 'Goodbye, Anton.'

'Where are you going?'

Kay raised an eyebrow. 'You don't expect me to tell you, do you?'

Dates no longer meant much to Kay but everyone else knew the first days in October were important.

Anton had predicted correctly. On 1 October the long-suspected edict went out to round up the Jews.

In her shabby skirt and coat, Kay slipped here and there through the streets of København with Felix's messages, moving through the crowds of grey-looking people – heads down, shuffling, depressed – her appearance as nondescript as theirs. No doubt, if she'd looked, she would also have found the usual quota of flourishing black marketeers, *stikker* and criminals.

Yet sniff the air, as Kay did, and it was obvious something had changed. A mysterious trigger had been pulled.

Reports filtered in from their underground contacts all over the country.

Overnight, many of the Jews disappeared. They had been secreted in barns, outhouses, attics, cellars and churches, and a huge effort had been mounted to smuggle out to Sweden as many as possible.

She and Felix worked frantically. Planning. Coordinating. Alerting.

On 4 October, Felix instructed Kay to get herself down to Dragør, eight miles south of København.

By six o'clock that evening she was ensconced in a café on the harbour front. The tide was on the turn, and it was change-over time for the fishing shifts. The port bustled with craft pushing in and out through the wind and rain.

She scanned the quay for one in particular. Eventually, a small shabby boat eased alongside and moored.

Kay left the café, picked her way over rain-slippery cobbles to a house with a blue door and knocked.

'Dr Muus?'

Almost immediately the doctor emerged into the street carrying a black bag. She beckoned and he followed her to a house several streets back from the harbour where they were greeted by 'Bent', middle-aged and short-sighted, and one of the most successful and reliable of their men.

'They're traumatized,' said Bent, leading Kay and the doctor upstairs into a bedroom. 'You'll need to handle them carefully. Her name is Miriam.'

A young woman, still almost a girl, a small boy and a baby were huddled on the bed. The woman's hair was hidden under a scarf, accentuating a complexion as pale as whey. The children were dirty and the toddler was tear-stained.

Kay recollected her own pampered babies. The funny little sounds they made when feeding, hands batting her breast, the soft wool around their tended bodies, their yeasty smell.

She hunkered down beside the girl. 'Try not to worry, Miriam.'

'I-I'll be all right.' She was having difficulty speaking. 'I'm getting over the shock, that's all. Everything . . . we had to leave everything.'

'Your husband?'

'We didn't have enough money to pay for the fare for all of us. He's trying to borrow more so he can come, too. He promised we would meet in Sweden.'

'Have you eaten?'

'Bent has been so kind and given us bread and cheese.'

'We're going to get you on board and this is what's going to happen.' Kay outlined the plan. 'I'm sorry, but we must do it now.'

Miriam clasped her baby tighter to her. 'You're sure it's safe?'

The doctor unlocked his bag. 'As safe as I can make it.'

He drew out a hypodermic needle and prepared it.

'That needle looks so big.' She swallowed back her tears. 'It will hurt them.'

'Yes, it will,' said the doctor. 'But you must be brave.'

'Hurry,' said Kay.

As she rolled up her son's sleeve, revealing his little arm, so white and fragile, Miriam whispered, 'We're playing a funny game, Erik. Look into my eyes and tell me what you see.'

The doctor acted swiftly, sticking in the needle and depressing the plunger. The child screamed once, short and sharp, then his eyes rolled back into his head and he fell forward onto his mother's knees.

The baby girl took a little longer and screamed harder, but eventually she was silent, too.

Miriam held them both and sobbed.

The doctor picked up his bag. 'The drug will wear off after several hours. They might be sick when they wake up.' His hand hovered over the heads of the unconscious children. 'Good luck.'

Kay carried the boy down the stairs. Miriam followed, cradling the baby. As they slipped and slid over the cobbles towards the harbour, salty rain lashed their faces.

When they reached the harbour, Kay was alarmed by the frenetic activity on the quays. A queue of taxis by the moored boats was disgorging passengers, all bowed down with bags and suitcases. Figures ran here and there.

She grabbed one of the sailors unloading his catch. 'What's happened?'

He didn't look up from his task. 'Word got around that the Jews could get boats out of here.' He moved away.

Someone shouted, 'Save my family.'

Shut up, she prayed. You never knew who would pick up the phone to the German commandant.

She turned to Miriam. 'See the light on that boat? We are going to make for it as fast as you can manage.'

Her arms wrapped round her daughter, Miriam ran. So did Kay, terrified one or other of them would fall over with their burdens as gusts of wind threatened to topple them.

Kay was running, running, feet fighting for anchorage, struggling to keep upright, the boy a dead weight in her arms. She felt the muscles in her back and arms take the strain. Pressed up against the child's body, she felt the beat of her own heart.

At the boat, she hustled them up the gangplank. Miriam was sobbing with fear, with sorrow, with relief. She turned to look at Kay and her mouth moved but Kay couldn't hear what she said. On board, other hands reached out and took charge of them. Kay relinquished her burden and the trio vanished into the bowels of the boat.

She turned and fled back into the shadow of a house. Here she waited until the putter of the engine and the visibly widening gap of black water between the fishing boat and the harbour reassured her they were on their way.

When she returned to Bent, he served her heated-up soup and slices of bread, then sat quietly while she ate and drank. Afterwards he ushered her to the room which had been occupied by Miriam and her children. Opening the window, he showed her an escape route over the roofs.

A rope had been slung up as a handrail between two chimneys – but it looked precarious.

'Which way should I go?'

'It's possible to get over the roofs of the two houses to our right, there is a walkway for the repair men, but be especially careful over the second. I'm not sure what their politics are. A fire escape leads down into a garden.'

Bent wished her good night. Kay stretched out on the bed, fully dressed, nerves thrumming. Rain beat against the window and the wind rattled the frame, and she prayed the fishing boat was well under way.

She awoke with a start.

Bent was pounding on the door. 'Cars everywhere. Probably German. Stay on the roof. Don't try to escape.'

She ran to the window which overlooked the harbour. A fleet of cars was driving at full speed towards the waterfront, followed by a bus. To the north of the harbour, there was gunfire.

Whirling round, she flung open the escape window to rid the room of any telltale warmth from her occupation, smoothed over the coverlet and grabbed her shoes.

Then she was up and over the sill.

Her bare feet made contact with the tiles outside with an unpleasant smack. Reaching up, she closed the window as quietly as possible. Within seconds, she was shaking with the cold. Not good for balance. She made the calculation. Take thirty seconds or so to put on the shoes which would aid her flight? Or go?

Think.

Who or what were the Germans after? Someone might have given them a tip-off about her. More likely, they were putting a stop to the escape of the Jews in the harbour.

Stay put, therefore.

Inching across the roofs, clinging to the rope for dear life, she reached the shelter of a chimney and, with the utmost care, lowered herself behind it.

Shouts.

Screams.

Vehicles stopping with a screech of brakes.

The dogs. Always the dogs.

The shouts in German and Danish.

Craning round the chimney, she caught the tail end of a searchlight moving in a huge arc. A whistle blew. There was more shouting. Feet raced over the cobbles in the street, apparently coming closer.

She clung to that rope. How was she going to get out of this one? The rain stung her face and seeped through her clothes. What she would have given for Felix's training: the toughening, no-mercy-shown, stripping-down-to-the-essence preparation that he had described. At the very least, she would have been better at negotiating rooftops.

If you're caught you must hold out for forty-eight hours. That will give us enough time to disperse.

Forty-eight hours to discover one's limits and to experience real fear. Except for childbirth, she had no real acquaintance-ship with pain. But she was becoming intimate with fear. Fear was a companion and, if not exactly a friend, a counsellor which taught her wisdom, although sometimes it also drew her down to a debilitating place.

More shots.

Shooting.

Ducks rising over the salt marshes, winging over the lake.

Bror.

Her children.

Up here, on this roof, she must not think about them. Those thoughts only made her vulnerable.

Her hold on the slippery roof was increasingly in doubt and Kay felt herself slipping. She wound the rope round her arms. Steady.

Better, much better, to think . . . of the Germans surrender-ing in North Africa, of the Allies landing in Sicily, of Mussolini being deposed. Inch by inch, *inch by gory inch*, the war was chang-ing. Over there, in the heat and the mud and the blood . . . And here in Denmark, too, where the grey spumy sea lashed the shores.

Still, by the time the hubbub had died away she was almost at the end of her physical tether. Bent appeared at the window. 'Come.' He helped her back in, supporting her because her legs wouldn't obey. He had brought up a hot milk drink and an extra blanket. She had never been so glad of anything, *anything*, in her life before.

Kay shook as Bent spooned the hot milk up to her lips. 'Some bastard *stikker* gave the commandant a tip-off. A busload of soldiers arrived just as the Jews were boarding the ships. Dozens of them have been arrested.'

Thin and chalky as it was, the milk was blessedly reviving. 'We should be out there, helping.'

'Too dangerous and you should rest for a while.' He offered her a cloth to wipe her mouth. 'Drink up, Freya. You might need it.'

'You're a good man, Bent.'

He blinked short-sightedly. 'It's my duty.'

Impulsively, she reached over and kissed him. He smelled of onions and fish.

A little after midnight, when Kay was trying to sleep, an explosion tore through Dragør. She leaped to the window. Out in the Sound, a ship was on fire, flames tearing into the sky.

Ambulances raced towards the quays.

Within minutes, she and Bent were running down to the port. Already a crowd had gathered. Someone shouted that a Danish ship had hit a German mine.

She and Bent fought their way through the onlookers to the edge of the harbour. On the quayside, a doctor was organizing medical help for the wounded sailors being rowed ashore. Some were screaming. Others lay charred and silent on the stretchers. The doctor worked on stabilizing the worst injured before they were loaded into the back of the ambulances.

'Take him.' The doctor gave the signal for a badly burned sailor to be put into the ambulance. 'Come.' As cool as a cucumber, the doctor beckoned to a couple clutching bundles who had shrunk back out of the spotlights. They hesitated and he repeated: 'Come.' So saying, he packed them into the ambulance along with the stretchers.

The whole thing happened very fast.

Kay whispered, 'Bent, he's loading up the Jews with the injured.'

More ambulances raced to a halt and formed a queue. One by one, the stretchered sailors were dealt with by the doctor, and men, women and children were plucked from the shocked, huddled mass and shovelled in alongside them.

No one said anything.

No one in that shifting, disturbed crowd.

But they knew.

Good Danes.

How admirable the doctor was. In the end, Kay thought, most . . . the majority . . . of people were good and acted justly. Kay's throat tightened. It was important to know that truth. It was important to see it. Here was a man who seized a chance to defy evil. A man who acted.

Shouts. Sirens. German cars were racing along the road. Recking of fuel, smoke from the blazing ship drifted inland, folding over the watchers. To Kay, it seemed to summon up all that was dreadful about the conflict – a hell, both real and metaphorical.

The rowers on the lifeboats strained to reach the port. The craft banged against the jetties. Yet more injured were landed.

'Who's the doctor?' she asked Bent.

'Dr Dich. He's one of us.'

One of us.

Kay gathered her wits. *What would the trained agent do?* What anyone would do in this case, was the answer.

Working their way around the crowd, she and Bent pushed to the front those who they reckoned were on the run. Bent peeled off to collect any who might be wandering the side streets or sheltering in the local cafés.

'Don't be afraid. Look straight at the doctor,' Kay instructed those she helped. 'Get close to the ambulances.'

Some were dazed. Some wept hopelessly. Others were defiant.

A fourth and fifth ambulance manoeuvred into the increasingly crowded area. More Jews were pushed inside them. The doctor fastened the doors. 'The hospital,' he ordered the drivers. 'Next.'

Sirens blazing, lights flashing, they raced off. Kay watched. Eventually, all the injured sailors had been dealt with and the crowd had begun to thin out. Now it was imperative to scoop up any Jews who hadn't made it.

Bent clutched at Kay's arm. 'It's a good night's work for us Danes,' he said. 'Wouldn't you say?'

Us Danes.

Chapter Thirty-two

Twenty-four hours later Kay returned to København from Dragør with two teenage boys in tow. Separated in the melee from their parents, they had been wandering around the harbour, clutching satchels full of their school books, when Kay found them. They were almost speechless with shock.

'Pretend I'm your mother,' she instructed, snatching up the youngest one's hand.

It lay in hers, icy with its owner's desolation.

Where to hide them in the city while she arranged a safe passage out of the country? She took a decision to make for the Mueller house, only to catch sight of SS cars in the street. Aborting, she hurried them away down a street which ran parallel. It was sullenly empty, with only a few bicycles chained to the lamp posts.

What next? Where to go, whom to trust? The answer arrived — and it drove the breath from her chest. Nils. *Nils* . . . ?

A black car nosed down the street. Hustling the boys ahead of her, she rounded the corner and cut down a side street.

Could she trust her son?

A little later Kay led the boys across the university courtyard and up the stairwell leading to Nils's room. Instructing the boys to stay quiet outside, she entered without knocking.

The usual sight greeted her. The light from the desk lamp revealed piles of dusty books, the sparse furniture, and paper stacked into wire baskets. Nils was at the desk, transcribing formulae onto a piece of squared paper.

Her son.

The characteristics she knew so well were all on display . . .

clothes in need of a press, shaggy hair, threadbare tie. Familiar things which she so loved, and so hated, in him.

None of that mattered, of course, only that he was there. He looked well and busy and she loved him beyond words.

'What the –?' He looked up but it took a good few seconds before he recognized her. 'Good God!'

She held a finger up to her lips. 'Say nothing. I'm Lise, an infant school teacher you met on holiday.'

Shock slowed him. But he got to his feet and made his way over to her. 'Where've you been? We've been out of our minds with worry.'

Tears came into her eyes. She dug her hands hard into her pockets. 'Don't make me cry.'

'Nor me.' He brushed the palm of a hand across his eyes – touching Kay to the quick. It was as loving a gesture as Nils would ever make. She longed, *longed*, to kiss him but knew he probably wouldn't tolerate it.

Did he look well? Yes, he did. Why hadn't he had a haircut? On balance, though, longer hair suited him. Precious, precious pieces of information on which to catch up, and to mull over, later.

'*Mor, why* are you here?'

'I need to hide some people and I thought of you. Please don't ask questions, Nils. Will you let me?'

He stuffed a hand into a pocket. 'I always ask questions, *Mor*. I'm not doing anything unless you explain to me.' He added, 'Sensibly.'

He meant without emotion.

'Who are they?'

'Jews,' she answered.

Nils started.

'Will you do this? Not for me but for them.'

He gave a drawn-out whistle.

'Nils, you can't let this happen. You can't have listened to the rubbish that's being said about Jews? They're herding them up like animals.'

Nils smoothed his hand across the network of symbols and figures on the papers in front of him.

She hissed, 'There's very little time. There are two boys out in the corridor who don't know what's happening to them. They're terrified and they have no idea where their parents are. Or what's going to happen to them.'

He reached for his pencil and turned it round and round between his fingers.

Her beloved son was not a monster . . . no, never that . . . but, as she knew so well, he looked at things from a different angle to most people.

'I can't leave them in the corridor.' If she had to beg, beg she would. '*Please.*'

Nils put down the pencil.

'You have the chance to be part of something . . . big. Worthwhile. More importantly, Nils, something right.'

He frowned.

'Nils?' One last attempt. 'It *is* the right thing to do. The moral thing.' She searched for the words to which he might respond. 'I wouldn't ask you . . . I wouldn't put you in this position except I don't know where else to go.'

He looked up. 'All right.'

Love for Nils broke in a wave over her head. 'Pretend they're pupils and you're giving them extra tuition but the session ran over and they found themselves trapped by the curfew. Keep them here. It'll only be for one night while their passage is arranged.'

She ushered the boys into Nils's room. 'You're being given tuition in applied mathematics,' she briefed them. 'Tomorrow morning I'll take you to Gilleleje where I'll get you a boat to take you to Sweden. Until then, you have to be quiet. Very quiet. And very patient.'

The boys' dark eyes registered their bewilderment.

'No need to look like that,' said Nils. 'I'm not going to eat you.' He pointed to the bedroom. 'In you go.'

Nils's no-nonsense approach appeared to cheer them. The older one flashed a reluctant grin. 'Where will you be?'

'Right here, working. So you'll have to shut up.'

He closed the door on the boys and retreated with Kay to his study, where she thrust a paper into his hands. 'Read it and then get rid of it.'

He glanced at the headline: 'The Danish Freedom Council sharply condemns the pogroms the Germans have set in motion against the Jews in our country'. Nils slotted it into the paper pile in a wire basket. 'What happens if you don't turn up for them tomorrow?'

'Get them to Rosenlund and Arne.'

'Arne!'

'Yes, Arne. He knows what to do.'

Nils's expression was a master study of shock. In a different time, in a different situation, she might have laughed. 'Nils, darling.'

He retreated behind his desk. '*Mor*, I'm only doing this once. Have you got that? The thing is . . .' He scratched his head. 'The Germans visit me. Regularly.'

The skin on her arms goosefleshed. With alarm. With dislike.

'Don't look like that, *Mor*. They come here to discuss mathematical problems. What do you expect me to do? If I tell them to get lost I'll be put on a list, or thrown into the Vestre. Anyway, it's the mathematical problems we're interested in.'

Memories of Nils as a tiny boy. He and his German cousins were romping around a hay meadow near Munich. It was a scene full of sunlight, fragrance, happiness.

What *did* she expect him to do?

'I saw you with General Gottfried.'

'Did you now?'

'I was in a taxi on my way to see you but I left when I saw who you were entertaining.'

'He wants to pick my brains. I allow him to up to a point. But only up to a point.' He shrugged. 'Self-preservation, *Mor*.'

'I knew you couldn't really support what the Germans are doing.'

He turned away. 'It's tedious when people take sides. I don't approve of people who don't think for themselves, that's all.'

'But supporting them?'

'I don't support them. I tolerate them.'

The difficulties of understanding her son's thought patterns were never going to lessen. 'How's your father?'

'Completely at sea. He can't believe what you've done.'

Unable to stop herself, she reached over and caressed his cheek. 'I'm sorry, Nils, but I'm not sorry. Can you understand?'

'That you've placed us all in danger? That you've gone?'

The harshness was mitigated by Nils slipping his arm round her shoulders. With that unexpected, and rare, sign of affection he was telling her that, perhaps, there was some point of convergence, some level of complicity.

After a moment he said: 'Do you think you were spotted coming here?'

'Possibly. I was desperate. But you take quite a few students, don't you? I thought I could take the risk.'

It was a bad night, holed up in the boiler room of a hostel near the river.

She went over and over what she should do. What could go wrong? Everything. What was her plan? Get the boys to the station. The risk? Being caught on the train. She must coach them on behaviour. Find more money.

In the discomfort of the boiler room she felt her will to keep going under attack and her resolution splinter.

Up early, Kay adjusted her clothes, tied a different headscarf under her chin and went out into the street.

Everything was grey. Sky, streets, people . . . her forebodings. She walked quickly, but not too quickly. One day, the grey would lift and they would all be normal again.

Watch. Check.

Shortly after eight-thirty, she let herself into Nils's rooms. A sweep of the room revealed he was not at his desk and the door to the bedroom was shut.

But someone was standing at the window which overlooked the courtyard. Hands in pockets. Worsted suit. Fair hair swept back. A man whom she knew through and through.

She tried to back out into the corridor.

Too late.

He turned. 'What —?' There was a second's shocked silence. 'Kay!'

Bror grabbed her and kicked the door shut. 'What are you doing here? Are you mad? But you're safe, you're safe.' He pulled off her scarf. 'Oh my God! What have you done to yourself?' He cradled her face between his hands. 'Your beautiful, beautiful hair.'

She clung to Bror's suit lapels – as if she could tap into his strength. She had dreaded this meeting. She had longed for it. During those frequently claustrophobic hours hidden up in a lair somewhere she had been riddled with hate for Bror, and shame for his rotten politics.

To see him in the flesh was different. 'Hello.'

'Is that all you have to say?'

The material under her fingers was so familiar, the best quality, totally reliable. She grasped it tighter. 'Are you going to give me away?'

'What do you think?'

They looked at each other.

Dane and Briton. The husband and the wife. The landowner and the terrorist.

Bror put his arms round her. 'There's a price on your dyed,

obstinate, stupid head.' She looked up to see unfathomable sadness reflected in the blue eyes. 'I'm so glad to see you, Kay.'

'And I you.'

His chin rested on the top of her head. 'Each day I wake up and my first thought is of you. But today it was different. Perhaps it was the unfamiliar hotel room? Or perhaps it was because I'm seeing the bank manager?'

'Is that a joke?'

'I haven't made a joke for – oh, months. Yet something pushed me to see Nils . . . and I find you. Do you think I knew without knowing?'

She smiled. 'That's a nice idea.'

Rain began to lash against the windowpanes.

'Where is he?'

Bror released her. 'Sleeping. At least, so I presume.' He paused. 'Do you know what you've done?'

'I do.'

'Did you hate me that much, Kay?'

'It's not a question of hate, or love.' She gave a small smile. 'But, yes, at times I did hate you.'

'I see.' Bror's right hand had a half-healed cut on a knuckle. How many times had she dealt with his bashed-up fingers? 'Come back, Kay.'

'You know I can't.'

'I know,' he said. 'It's hopeless but I thought I'd say it. Despite everything, I dream that you've come back. I imagine I can hear you whistling to the . . . the dogs and we walk down to the lake together.'

There was no time for this.

Kay took in a deep breath of Bror's Berlin cologne. 'Bror, I can't explain but, if I promise to meet you, will you leave now?'

Too late. A tousled, blinking, but fully clothed Nils appeared at the bedroom door. '*Far?* Here again? Why?'

'To see how you were. Is that so odd?'

Kay made to close the bedroom door, but not fast enough. It swung back to reveal the boys sleeping face to toe on the floor.

Bror looked from Kay to Nils. 'What's going on?'

'None of your business,' she said.

Bror reached inside his jacket for his cigarette case and lit up. 'Have you any idea how dangerous this is? The authorities are searching everywhere for the Jews.' He gestured to the untidy human heap on the floor. 'I presume . . . ?'

'Shush.' The boys stirred and Kay closed the door to the bedroom. 'They've enough to put up with. Don't make them more frightened than they already are. Please.'

Nils sat down at the desk and pulled the papers sitting on its top towards him. 'Don't start, you two.'

'Do you think I'm a monster, Kay?'

He was sad, desperately so. She knew the signs.

'No, I don't. But do you know what's going on? Bror, *do* you know?'

'Of course.' He sounded more like his old self. 'Anton rang. God knows why. I didn't ask him to. His excuse was that he wanted to know how things were at Rosenlund. He couldn't wait to tell me about the round-ups and arrests. But at the hotel last night the talk was that most of the Jews have got away.'

'Yes,' said Kay. 'People did the right thing.'

'They did.' Bror wandered over to Nils's desk and flicked ash into the ashtray. 'Which makes one proud.' He looked up from the ashtray, meeting Kay's gaze. 'Don't you think?'

'Thank God . . .' Kay felt almost happy with relief. 'Thank God you feel like that. I didn't know . . . I dreaded that . . .'

Bror looked as though he had received a punch in the guts. 'You dreaded that I would agree with people being rounded up?'

'No, no . . . of course not.'

'Christ,' he said.

This was the moment and she took a gamble. 'Bror, I'm going to ask you to do something. Have you got the car? Take me to Gilleleje. Please. We can't have these boys' blood on our hands.'

'*Mor*,' Nils rattled the papers. 'What are you doing?'

Bror said, 'I'm not a murderer, Kay, either. Of course we can't have their blood on our hands.'

She stood before Bror – and she knew that she had become a travesty of the woman he had married. 'Help me, then.'

Bror picked up his hat and turned it round between his fingers. Outside, in the quad, a clock struck the hour.

Every second of delay was dangerous.

'*Please*, Bror.'

Bror held out his hand to Kay. With a sense that she had come home, she took it.

The boys were woken, briefed and hustled out into the corridor. At the door, Kay hesitated. Then she turned and ran back to Nils. 'I'm going to kiss you goodbye.' Cradling his head between her hands – in the way she had so often done when he was small – she did so. He smelled of sleep and beer and benign neglect. 'Please, please take care of yourself.'

'*Mor* . . .' To her surprise and delight, Nils kissed her back.

She swallowed.

Then she was gone.

Arm in arm, Kay and Bror crossed the quadrangle, the boys tagging behind them as if they were an ordinary Danish family. Ten minutes or so later they were packed into the car. Kay was in the front and the boys were in the back with a rug tucked around them.

They headed north out of København.

Kay sank back in the seat – and it was to sink back into a past she almost couldn't remember. A past in which the rich veneer of a walnut dashboard and the smell of leather seats – so luxurious and pleasing – were taken for granted.

Bror kept his eyes on the road. 'What do you want me to do?'

'Just get us there. Please.'

They were leaving the outskirts of København behind. The

road was more or less clear. A few cars and vans chugged along and some wet cyclists battled the wind. Driving past the last ribbon of housing, it was clear that some of the houses were unoccupied. People were disappearing so fast . . . families were disappearing. The Jews had gone.

She thought about Køge. The place where she had spent most of her life was a mishmash if ever there was one. Nazi lovers and supporters lived there and shopped in the market place. As did realists and waverers and the frightened. There were the Birgits who lived in a state of high anxiety and didn't know which way to think, and there were the Jacobs and the Arnes who did know what they thought and acted on it. As ever, it came as a shock to Kay to know that she was part of that group.

What could be said in the final analysis? Resistance was always a matter of principle and politics? Or was it that some human beings were intrinsically bloody-minded? Or did resistance achieve that almost impossible synthesis by marrying both at the same time?

Who knew? Who knew?

Rain lashed down and the windscreen wipers gave off a customary screech. She laughed. 'You've never got them fixed.'

'There were other things to think about.'

Bror went first. 'Tanne?'

She had to tell the truth. 'She got to Sweden,' she said.

A nerve twitched at Bror's temple. 'But she's safe, you think?'

There was a long pause. 'If she's in Sweden . . . but I can't know for sure if she's safe, Bror.'

'At least that's honest.'

She flinched.

At this section of the road the surface grew unreliable and Bror dropped his speed. He spoke with a rare intensity. 'I can't let you go again, Kay. For one thing, I can't stand the not knowing and . . .'

'And?'

'I can't bear to hate you.'

'We don't have to hate each other,' she replied. 'Not now.'

He glanced at her. 'The old life has gone and we can't have it back. That's the one sure thing in all this. You can accuse me of wickedness, or short-sightedness, and some of it would be true.'

The exhilaration at seeing Bror was draining away to be replaced by a numbing exhaustion.

'But will you believe me when I say I didn't know the extent of the Nazis' brutality . . . None of us understood at the beginning of the war what was going to happen. Even you. In Denmark there *was* an argument for the practical. For being a pragmatist.'

'No one thinks of arguments in the aftermath,' she said sadly. 'You are either the winner or the loser.'

'But you must understand why I chose the side I did.'

'Do you regret it?'

His gloved hands tightened on the wheel. 'I can't regret what is part of me. I'm not English or American. I'm Danish and some of my roots are in Germany.'

It hurt her to reply: 'But aren't these decisions moral ones?'

He nodded. 'That was my mistake.'

She checked on the boys. They were dozing. One of them whimpered in his sleep. 'Bror, let's not talk about it. Let's just drive.' She crouched forward on the seat, willing him to push on faster.

For a fleeting moment his hand lay on her thigh and the car picked up speed. After a while, he said, 'I've moved back into our bedroom. It has your things, your scent. I like that. I like to look out to the lake as you always did.'

Kay's first thought was that Bror was more likely to hear the plane if they made a drop. Her second was: *I can't bear it*. Followed by: *I have to bear it*.

'Kay . . . I know you understand what you have done.' There was a hint of bitterness. 'But I want you to know that *I* understand why you did it.'

435

The generous Bror. 'It was gradual thing,' she found herself confessing. 'A growing conviction. I got sucked into it so I can't claim a road to Damascus conversion. It was a little resistance here, then there . . . and suddenly . . .'

'Look at me, darling.' Reluctantly, she obeyed and when she encountered the blue eyes she knew that what had anchored them together was still there.

Suddenly Bror checked himself. 'Kay . . . roadblock.'

It was a hundred metres or so up ahead. Bror cut the car's speed and drew up in front of it. Kay ran an expert eye over the soldiers standing miserably in the rain. 'Danish,' she hissed. 'Not German.'

'I'll do the talking, Kay. Do you trust me?'

Did she?

'Trust me, Kay.'

It was an order.

She gave a quick nod. He smiled for a second. 'Good.'

She turned round to the boys in the back. 'Not a word. Do you understand?'

The youngest looked half dead with misery. The older one had bitten his lower lip almost raw.

Bror tipped his hat down further over his face and wound down the window. Wind and rain blasted into the car as he conducted a polite, respectful conversation. Yes, he was taking his family north to visit relations. They had all been ill with some strange germ. His friend, General Gottfried, had advised him that the family needed a bit of a holiday and some good Danish dairy food.

The Danish soldier, wet and miserable, stamped his feet. Rain glistened on his youthful face, boredom registering in the downturn of his mouth. His companion, older and tougher, took a bit more persuasion.

'General Gottfried is going to join us,' said Bror. 'We plan to walk a little before the bad weather sets in.'

They were nodded through.

Bror started up the engine and they were away.

Kay stared at the windscreen and her eyes filled.

'Don't cry, darling Kay.'

'I'm sorry, Bror. Very sorry. But I would do exactly the same if it happened all over again.'

'So would I,' he said. 'Given what I am.'

'Bror,' she whispered. 'I . . .'

'Shush, Kay. None of our differences matter now. I love you. That hasn't changed and I want you alive. Do you understand?'

The car gathered speed. A familiar landscape unrolled. Ahead lay a grey sea and a passage to Sweden. Safety?

The poor boys. She turned round. Hands clasped, they had fallen back into a twitchy sleep. God willing their parents were still alive. They must be mad with anxiety. How she ached to give their children back to them. If she couldn't do that, at the very least she had to try to save their lives.

A short while later they drove into Gilleleje.

They kept the boys in the car while they entered into negotiations. The sum of money which Sven demanded for the fare over the Øresund was more than Kay possessed and it was Bror who paid up. Sven pocketed it. 'You think I'm overcharging,' he said. 'But consider the risks I'm taking.'

They left the boys hidden in his harbour boathouse, Sven having promised that he would ferry them over at the turn of the tide. Huddled on a bench, the boys barely managed a goodbye.

They returned to the car. Bror started up the engine and drove along the sea road out of Gilleleje for a kilometre or so. 'We came here one summer with the children. Remember?'

'I do.'

'What do you remember?'

She laughed. 'The wind. Trying to get a barbecue going on the beach. A lot of beer.'

A small, sandy bay came into sight and he braked. 'Do you think it might have been here?'

'I'm not sure.'

'I am.' He stopped the engine, got out of the car and walked around to the passenger door. 'Come.'

'I can't. You must get me to the train at Helsinger.'

'Come, Kay.'

It flashed across her mind that he might be planning to kill her – and she shuddered inwardly. This was to become too habituated to a life of distrust.

'Why?'

'Gilleleje is a tiny place. We will have been noticed. The car will have been noticed. Don't you think we should make a show of being lovers?'

Again she laughed and looked up into his face. 'The ironies . . .' she murmured.

The wind caught them in a hard grip and they slithered down the sandy slope of the dune onto the beach. Bror put his arm round Kay and placed his mouth against her ear. 'Make for the beach hut over there.'

It looked familiar and she had a dim recollection of walking past it with the children. But, from the state of it, no one had bothered with it for years. A bleached, salty and cracking hulk, its wooden clapboards were rotting and the lock on the door was broken.

Inside, it smelled of tar, fish and brine. Abandoned coils of fishing twine and rope, stiff with age and mould, were strewn across the floor. Draughts knifed between the cracks.

Kay pulled off her headscarf.

'Kay.'

She turned round to face Bror. 'Yes.'

He leaned against the flimsily fastened door and reached for a cigarette. 'I want to know . . .'

'What?'

'About what you've been doing?'

Trust no one.

He made no move to touch her.

'You owe it to me, don't you think?'

Tell no one.

She told him about running through the woods, of her limited wardrobe. Of carrying her possessions on her back and of eating one meal a day. Of how one becomes an itinerant in spirit with such a regime. Almost addicted to it? She described clinging precariously to a roof. She told him of the sad little Jewish family she helped to put on the boat to safety. But she didn't tell him about Felix or Arne, or the meetings and the plans and the wireless set. She didn't tell him, either, about London and the activities of the strange outfit for whom she was working. Nor of the struggle of the resistance to convince London that they mattered.

Telling Bror. Not telling him.

'You were too busy to miss me.'

'Oh, I missed you.' She tapped her chest. 'In there, deep down. Always.'

They could have been in their bed at Rosenlund, their bodies fitting together under the duck down. Talking.

Bror opened the door and threw the cigarette stub outside. Then he was beside her. 'Is this the truth?'

'Yes. Yes.'

'We have really got to the truth . . . between you and me?'

'Yes.'

He placed his hands on her shoulders in such a way that they cradled the curve of them. She drew in a breath. 'Bror?'

His hand sought under the much-worn, nondescript blouse and found her breast. 'Do you know how much I have missed you?'

Oh my God, she thought. Here she was . . . dirty, dyed, thin . . . and here he was, pulling up her clothes . . . and, now, pushing her to the ground . . . like an impatient teenager.

'Do you remember that time at Rosenlund? In the lace dress?'

'I don't want to think of the past.'

'I know,' she said. 'But I can't help it.'

He didn't answer but pushed her legs apart. 'And Anton is part of you?'

It so often led back to Anton.

No more lies.

'I missed him, too.' Kay wanted to be truthful. 'But the old Anton. He was never anything, Bror. He was part of a life in which we didn't take things too seriously.'

Bror hesitated. 'So you used him to put me off the scent?'

'I did.'

'Christ, Kay,' said Bror. 'Do you know what you did to me? Do you know what it's like to lie awake imagining . . . Do you know what jealousy does? What it is? It's cruel. It's bitter. It's murderous.'

'I'm sorry.'

Bror bore down on her with his full weight. Deliberately crushing and exerting what power he possessed. 'Are you really sorry . . . ?'

She spread her arms out wide, her half-opened blouse revealing her breasts. 'I am here.' Stirring deep in her body was an excitement, a sharp – almost too sharp to bear – desire and the longing for resolution.

Tar, brine, old wood . . . the smells would be forever associated with this moment.

After that, they were mostly silent. Her rucked-up clothing made a dent in her back as Bror took out on her both his anger and his love – and she permitted him to do so.

A little later he asked: 'So he's no longer in your head?'

'He never has been.'

There was a long pause. 'You hurt me, Kay.' Then he bent over and kissed her hard on the mouth.

Afterwards, he lay spent on top of her, his face pressed into her shoulder. She turned her head and the grain of the wood walls seemed monstrously enlarged. If permitted, jealousy became stronger than love and the urge to forgive.

'Forget Anton, Bror. Forget him.'

'Tell me you love me . . .'

Bror had never asked that of Kay before. 'I do.' She breathed in a shuddery breath. 'I do.'

Their marriage? After all these years, this is where they were. Almost broken by war, battered, with vast areas of darkness, irrevocably altered . . . but still living, still breathing.

In the silence, they heard the beat of rain on the roof.

It was time to go.

Kay wriggled out from under Bror and tried to tidy herself up. 'I know I look awful. I'm sorry.'

Bror touched her mouth with a finger. 'You look terrible. You look wonderful.'

Outside, the wind was stronger and a sleety rain slanted over the beach. Leaving the beach hut to its debris and decay, they headed for the car.

They drove in silence until Bror said, 'I don't feel right abandoning you, Kay.'

'You must.' Deliberately, she hardened her tone. 'You *have* to.'

'I want you to live more than anything.'

'As it happens, so do I.'

'I don't know what's going to happen. Or whether or not we will be here by the end of this mess. And it isn't a question of forgiveness because there's nothing to forgive.' He negotiated a corner.

Bror's sweetness made her cry. 'Actually, I wanted to thank you.'

'But I'm not stupid. I realize nothing will be the same,' he continued. 'Can it?'

'No.' She groped towards the answer. 'I can't give up now, Bror. I have to go back to what I am doing and you must go back to Rosenlund.' She raised her hands. 'I don't feel there's any choice.'

His hand searched for hers. 'Was it the adventure that kept you going? I sometimes thought you were restless . . .'

Had she been drawn to the fire because something hidden in her demanded it? Whipped her on?

'Perhaps. Among other things. Among other important things.' She took a deep breath. 'Bror, I am so sorry for what I've done to you and what I've done to the family. I'm sorry. I'm sorry.'

The wind rattled the car windows.

She began searching in her pockets. 'Oh God, I need a brush or a comb. My hair. I can't look a mess.'

Bror stopped the car, reached over to the glove compartment and extracted the comb which had always been kept there for Kay. 'Here. Sit still.'

They were back to long ago.

Carefully, tenderly, Bror combed Kay's ruined hair. What was he telling her – the terrorist wife?

The slow, gentle strokes told her that he loved her. In the turmoil and confusion of loyalties and politics and violence, that was still true.

'There must be something I can do to help, Kay?'

She looked down at her hands clasped in her lap and considered the answer which had been hovering. To keep whole in the face of fear was a colossal demand on anyone. Fear splintered the resolution and muddled the objective. It made one craven. Of all things, Kay continued to fear her fear, however hard she battled against it.

'There is one thing.' With a sense of profound relief, she leaned over and kissed his cheek. Bror let the comb fall to the car floor. Kay kissed the corner of his eye where the lines were being etched, then his chin, then his mouth. 'Promise me something?'

Bror dropped Kay at Rungsted station and drove on to Rosenlund.

At the station, she sat down on a bench next to a man who was reading the daily paper. He looked nondescript enough – but you never knew. The paper's headlines were visible from where she sat. The mass escape of the Jews provided the main subject.

The man looked up as he turned the page – and, for a tense second, Kay thought she was in trouble. 'Holger awakes,' he murmured. 'Holger awakes.'

Holger Dansk . . . the legendary Danish hero. A symbol of resistance.

She sighed with relief.

Communists, freedom fighters, the new Freedom Council . . . how and where these factions would unite into one effective force depended on people like Felix, Jacob and those such as herself.

What had brought them together? The question would never cease to fascinate her.

In København, Kay made for the safe house on the Ny Kongensgade. On the way she stopped at a couple of shops, and with the money Bror had stuffed into her pocket she purchased a comb, soap and cold cream, bread, and also sausage and a bottle of watery, greyish milk. At the hairdresser's, she asked for dark-brown hair dye. 'For my mother,' she explained to the assistant. 'She so hates being grey.'

At the safe house, she applied the dye and waited patiently for it to dry. Framed by the atrocious haircut, the face which looked back at her belonged to a stranger.

She ran a bath. Undressing, she discovered that her period had arrived unexpectedly and she had not made provision for it. The stains on her clothes were going to take time and trouble to remove.

In the bath, she regarded her newly thinned-out body. Was her system trying to recapture the days of marriage and maternity? Perhaps it had been love-making with Bror? The inconveniences of being female and on the run struck her as both funny and sad. How she ached to talk to Tanne about it and to ask her how she was coping with being female.

The water was only lukewarm but better than nothing. Kay made herself sit there for as long as possible. In this new existence, being clean was not always possible.

Lying back, she closed her eyes.

Bror?

She cupped her hand and trickled water over her chest. Grains of sand sifted out into the water and sank to the bottom of the bath.

Bror?

Think of his cattle and pigs in the fields, the mounds of cheese and pitchers of cream. Think of fresh bread. Of the jewels she used to wear. Remember always the fresh colours and scents of new growth in the Rosenlund woods, the smell of paper-white narcissi in the garden, the duck-down quilts on the beds, Bror's silk dressing gown. And always, always, the mesmeric moods and reflections of the lake. Its dreamy summer sparkle. Its frozen secrets in winter.

Chapter Thirty-three

Ruby and Peter hadn't spoken properly for months – and it was now October. And, no, she hadn't counted the weeks.

In August, Peter disappeared. He had been seconded to The Firm's headquarters in Cairo and wasn't scheduled to reappear in the office until late September.

Ruby lectured herself that she didn't mind his absence. Nor was she bothered that they had clashed so bitterly. There were other, much bigger, worries as the war lurched on.

Quite apart from anything else, she was half dead with fatigue. The agent traffic was building. With Peter absent, she had to cope with the situation on her own, which often meant working around the clock for days on end. Every brain cell had been squeezed dry.

But from time to time, she would raise her head from her desk and . . . there he would be, a ghostly Peter hunched over the desk in his office. She despised herself for it, for she didn't wish to see him either as an apparition or in reality . . . but he was there. Ever wayward, even obstinate, her psyche disagreed.

Peter returned on a bright autumn morning, reclaiming his office with a slam of the door and a shout to Gussie. He was tanned but painfully thin as a result of a bout of dysentery.

Ruby sat at her desk and didn't move.

Gussie enquired if he had fully recovered.

'I was banged up in hospital with a lot of pretty nurses,' he replied.

She offered him a cup of stewed tea. 'Here's a reward for all that deprivation.'

The routines slotted back into place. First, Peter and Gussie tackled the backlog. Only then was Ruby summoned.

She walked into his office, closed the door and leaned back against it. Despite her fine intentions, her heart beat faster.

'Things seem under control here,' he said, shuffling through papers. 'It's to your credit that you and Gussie managed so well.'

'Isn't it amazing?' said Ruby.

'Just one or two things that need to be corrected.'

The old irritation stirred. Gussie and she had got on fine without him. 'I know,' she replied. 'Gussie and I often said: "We need Peter to put us right."'

She had succeeded in gaining his full attention.

'Oh Lord . . .'

'Oh Lord?'

'Don't look like that, Ruby. It spoils it.'

She looked down at her feet shod in regulation lace-up shoes. 'Spoils what?'

'The image that kept me going in hospital. When my insides were threatening to dissolve and I couldn't sleep, and it was painful, I thought of you.'

'Why?'

'Because when you smile, the sun, er . . . comes out.'

Ruby frowned. 'And?'

'Because I reasoned that, if I thought of someone as obstinate and bloody-minded and angry as you, then I couldn't possibly give in.'

'Fair enough.'

He got to his feet. 'Can we start again?' A pause. 'Ingram?' The last was said tenderly, like the private joke it was. The dark eyes raked over her face. 'Now. Quickly.'

Were they . . . were they going to begin all over again?

She kept her voice brisk and professional. 'I've thought of a way of trying to prove how unsafe the poem-code method is and it involves Vinegar.'

Peter sat down again. 'Right,' he said coolly and steepled his hands. 'You think Vinegar is being run by the Germans.'

They stared at each other.

She began: 'As you know, I went through his back traffic and there are several things to consider about him. Or her. We know Vinegar is no good at coding and yet he has produced impeccably coded messages. At the very least, should this not be questioned?' She shot a look at Peter. He was listening. 'But we can do it, Peter. To test Vinegar, we could send a deliberate indecipherable to him. Not too difficult for a trained German cipher clerk to cope with, but too difficult for Vinegar. If he asks for it to be retransmitted, we can conclude that he's still at liberty because, bad at codes as he is, he won't be able to decode it. On the other hand, if he replies, we'll know that an expert has worked on it.' She paused. 'And the expert is likely to be German.'

Break open a hypothesis and deconstruct it against every possible eventuality and consequence.

That was what she had been taught at Cambridge. That was what Peter would be doing. He needed time to examine the idea. Rightly so.

Eventually, after a long week, Gussie jerked her head in the direction of his office. 'Sir wants you. But, for God's sake, keep him sweet this time. He's been like a bear with a sore head.'

At Ruby's entrance, Peter got to his feet, a courtesy which touched her.

He went straight to the point. 'The idea's a good one,' he said. 'Suicidal but a good one. We just need to find a way to work it.'

Ruby hadn't realized how strange she had been feeling – as if she had been holding her breath for weeks.

Moving a little stiffly, Peter sat down.

What was she going to do about her feelings for him?

He's still very thin. He needs care. Her guts twisted painfully and the question forced its way out of her: 'Did you work through the night?'

447

His expression lightened. With relief? 'Are you worrying about me? And the answer is yes, I did.' The old, wry Peter – and the old, sparky Ruby – were back and they welcomed each other with a big smile.

Enough. To the problem.

'You realize the security protocols are draconian,' he said. 'Every message is logged and checked, both here and in the signals office. If one goes missing, or someone tries to send one that isn't authorized, there's an immediate witch-hunt. How we get our message transmitted is going to take some thought.'

'In any defence, there's always a weakness.'

'True. But it's bloody small in this case. But we agree, Ruby?'

'We agree.'

'Meanwhile . . .' He pushed the message he was holding over to her. 'Could you take this to the signals office? The night squad broke an indecipherable. It took over ten thousand attempts. I want to teleprint them my thanks.'

She looked down at the piece of paper. Running and fetching for Peter?

'Please?' His eyes danced. 'I wouldn't ask you normally, but there's a war on and you look useful.'

'Bugger off.' She found herself stiffening.

'Has nobody ever teased you, oh lovely Ruby? They should, you know.'

She glanced at it. Automatically, she began working away to disinter the words hidden among the letter groups – a Michelangelo chipping away at the block of marble to reveal the figure in its depths.

Oh, habit.

Up in the signals office, Ruby hovered by a signals clerk. He was young, frazzled and looked extremely anxious. He barely glanced at Ruby when she handed over Peter's message. 'Put it with the rest.'

Something prompted her to ask, 'Are you having trouble?'

'I'm not sure what to do,' he confessed as he rifled through a stack of paper. 'Can you advise?' He held up one of them. 'There are new procedures for cancelling messages. I've orders to cancel this one but I'm not sure how to proceed. It's message number sixty for Vinegar.'

The signals clerk could be in for bad trouble if she did this – but Ruby didn't hesitate. 'Give it to me,' she said. 'I can deal with it for you.'

Inside, she was shaking.

Later she and Peter faced each other across the desk in his office. Message number sixty to Vinegar – in reply to message number fifty-nine – lay on the desk between them. It had taken them an easy fifteen minutes to decode.

STAND BY FOR DROP ON TWENTIETH *stop* DZ AS SPECIFIED BY US NOT YOU *stop* LETTER K REPEAT K SIGNAL *stop* BBC MESSAGE CANUTE GETS HIS FEET WET *stop* ACKNOWLEDGE AND PLAY BACK BBC MESSAGE *stop*

'Why have they cancelled this?' Ruby asked.

'Maybe the section heads want to add something, but need to break it up as it is a long message.'

It made sense.

'Let's go over this.' With each point, Peter tapped a finger on the table. 'What do we know about Vinegar? He's a rotten coder but turns out impeccably coded messages. He is also a highly reliable wireless transmitter operator. He keeps asking for money and more agents. He's also been very specific about drop zones and won't take London's suggestions. Finally, despite requests, he omits to give details to London of any of the agents he says he's recruited. But his bluff and real security checks are in place.'

'Our argument, therefore, is that London is being played by the Germans, who are operating Vinegar's set,' said Ruby. 'That is why he is never keen to answer their questions. It also means that it is possible that any agents and equipment dropped at

Vinegar's request have been delivered straight into German hands. If that has happened, it would only be because Vinegar's poem code has been tortured out of him.'

If ever a man looked at breaking point, Peter did then.

He had held off smoking until now but gave in. 'Question: why haven't our other agents noticed? Answer: there're only two of our wireless operators in Denmark at the moment. One is Vinegar, who was allocated to Aarhus on Jutland. Mayonnaise, who is operating on Zealand, reported that Vinegar was missing from the initial drop when they all went in. But, when checked out, it appeared Vinegar was sending traffic regularly. London discussed it, dismissed the problem and informed Mayonnaise that all was well.'

'This would be because the Germans had got the bluff and real security checks out of Vinegar and so all seemed to be normal?'

Peter twisted a pencil round and round.

'But why didn't Mayonnaise check up on Vinegar?' asked Ruby.

Peter leaped to his feet and consulted the map on the wall. 'Getting between Jutland and Zealand is not a doddle. Probably impossible at times. The Germans will have mounted watches on ferries and sea traffic.'

'Couldn't they get messages to and from? The couriers?'

'Who knows?' said Peter. 'London is relaxed about it because the chiefs are convinced that their coding methods are foolproof and that the enemy can't possibly be reading our traffic.'

Ruby raised her eyes to his. 'So . . . we go back to the initial proposition. We arrange for this message to be sent, but this time we encode it in such a way that only a very experienced cryptographer could read it. If Vinegar replies, it suggests very powerfully that an expert, who almost certainly won't be Vinegar and is probably a German, is working on the decoding. We can present this as evidence to your chiefs.'

'But *if* Vinegar isn't in German hands, he'll reply asking for a retransmission and then the balloon will go up, and we'll be found out.'

Ruby was feeling sick enough as it was. 'What would they do with us?'

Peter raised an eyebrow. 'I gather there's a cooler in the remotest part of Scotland. Odds and sods are sent there. If they don't kill us, that is.'

He opened his drawer and produced a piece of paper. 'Vinegar's poem. Taken from "Helge",' he read. 'Vinegar insisted on a poem he knew from childhood, which doesn't help one bit. Oehlenschläger is the national poet and everyone knows his poems.'

She trembled inwardly.

'Are you ready?' he asked. '. . . Ingram?'

They chose 'late', 'heart', 'night', 'more' and 'begin', and wrote them out with a couple of spelling mistakes, since tired cipher clerks were sometimes guilty of that, and numbered the letters sequentially underneath. Next they made the first transposition with four of the columns in the wrong order: hatting, as it was known in the trade, and chicken feed to an expert cryptographer to correct.

They argued – almost pleasurably – over the deviations in the second transposition.

'Final question,' said Ruby. 'If it's an indecipherable won't they just ask us to repeat it?'

'Fritz won't want to hold up a drop. It's rich pickings.'

'And if it is Vinegar who's transmitting all along?'

'Trust you like haggis and turnips?'

As she left the room with the message, he said, 'Ruby . . .'

She turned back.

'Ruby . . .'

Her heart jumped and fluttered.

He looked at her with love. Oh God. And with tenderness. And openness. Ruby returned his look but her previous treachery – so lightly done – felt as heavy as lead.

If Peter ever found out it would hurt him, and hurt him deeply. Equally, her discovery that her strongly held beliefs on sexual liberty lacked staying power troubled Ruby not a little. The payback from the Tony episode was to realize that she would be haunted by it for a long time – and that was stupid, time-wasting and ran against her grain.

But she loved Peter.

And that was the price.

Handing over the message to a different signals clerk, she lied: 'The chief encoded it himself.'

Twenty-four hours later Peter sent Ruby a note: 'He's missed a sked.'

Another day crawled past.

They met in the corridor and whispered to each other.

'Would it be an idea to talk to Signals Clerk Voss while we wait?' she asked.

A third day.

Nothing.

For much of the time, Ruby couldn't eat. She relied instead on cups of stewed tea which turned the inside of her mouth to cotton wool.

Eventually, Gussie took a telephone call. She tossed her head. 'There's a car outside and the orders are that you are to join His Majesty. You're going down to the listening station. Bring writing materials.'

Listening Station 53d looked picture-postcard perfect as they swept into its drive. The trees were just beginning to turn and the unspoiled areas of the garden were full of shrubs and creepers.

'Ready?' asked Peter.

Ruby ran her tongue around her mouth, wishing she could brush her teeth, and that she didn't feel so nauseous.

She nodded. 'As I'll ever be.'

After Security had done their bit, they were shown into the

signals room and found Signals Clerk Voss, headphones on, at her station.

'Sir.' She acknowledged Peter by pushing back one ear of the headphones but kept the other in place.

Save for the necessary equipment of sharpened pencils and sheets of paper, her station was immaculate. Propped up against the transmitter was an encoded message from London, ready to go.

Peter checked the skeds pinned up on the wall. 'Mayonnaise, when is he due?'

'Tomorrow. He went dark for some weeks but he's back.'

Ruby was quick to pick up that she sounded strained.

Encountering Mary Voss for the third time, Ruby paid more attention to her, taking on board the slight lilt to her voice and her passionate involvement in her job. Almost a possessiveness. Ruby resisted fiercely the temptation to categorize women by their looks, but on further scrutiny Mary Voss was blessed with a lovely skin and kind eyes. Unshowy and modest, she looked like the type of Englishwoman who, having never been encouraged to consider her looks, didn't.

'I gather Vinegar missed two skeds?'

This was confirmed by Signals Clerk Voss, but with obvious anxiety. She was about to add something when Peter cut her off.

'Tell me what you told Lieutenant Ingram here about Vinegar's fist?'

Mary had been waiting for the question. 'He was nervous in his early transmissions. I could tell. His C and M dotted about a bit. Agents are like that sometimes. Then they settle down . . . more or less. But they can be quite changeable. Some days they'll be that nervous and one can understand it. Other days they're smooth and confident. But they settle into an acceptable pattern. It was different with Vinegar because his improvement was so marked.'

Ruby shifted closer to Mary. 'In what way? Can you give Major Martin every detail?'

Mary Voss looked up at her. 'Vinegar is always assured. Smooth. Easy.'

'Anything else? Anything at all about him?'

Mary took her time. She was very careful. And precise. 'As I told you, in the first message he transmitted QRU as CAU. After that, he used the normal QRU sign-off.'

'That suggests he relaxed a bit,' said Peter.

'*Relaxed?*' exclaimed Ruby.

Mary looked at Ruby, who nodded encouragement. 'There was another thing,' said Mary. 'He got his frequency wrong.'

'Could be nothing,' said Peter.

'Except,' said Mary, 'he's made both mistakes a second time. I've got the note here with the date and time.'

She handed it over to Ruby.

'Did you inform the signalmaster when you first noticed the variations?' Peter asked.

'I reported it to Signalmaster Noble.'

'And what did he say?'

'To get on with the job.' Suddenly she held up a hand. 'It's one of mine, sir.' Her expression looked as if dawn had broken after a long, freezing night. Replacing her headphones, she took up her pencil and began to take down the Morse. Everything about her was pure concentration and Ruby was startled by its fierceness.

A furious Peter went to find the signalmaster to give him one of his typically quiet, but deadly, dressing-downs.

Letters streamed from Signal Clerk Voss's pencil onto the message paper.

There was a pause. Then she tapped out a short phrase. She explained: 'That's AK/R. I'm acknowledging receipt. Now, I'll give him QTC1 which means I have one message for him.'

As she watched the message being dispatched as easily and professionally as the one received, Ruby's guts told her that Vinegar was definitely being run by the Germans.

'Mary, it's vital to say nothing to anyone else about our

investigations. But, if there is anything else you can think of, however tiny, please will you contact me or Major Martin?'

She was apprehensive and troubled. 'Not through the signal-master?'

'No.'

Mary's lips curved in an enigmatic little smile.

Although the FANY chauffeur would be subject to the Official Secrets Act, it was a security rule never to discuss matters in the car. As they approached Regent's Park, Peter ordered the driver to pull up. 'Out,' he said to Ruby. 'We need to walk.'

They set off at a lick through the cherry trees. Barrage balloons swayed in the sky. An ambulance's bell sounded in the distance. Fallen leaves lay scattered over the grass.

'Ruby . . .' Peter was sounding a warning. 'Ruby –'

She knew without being told what he was going to say and swung round to face him. 'Vinegar has replied confirming arrangements for the drop in Jutland. Why didn't you tell me?'

'Because I wanted your mind clear when you made your judgements after talking to Voss.'

'Oh God, oh God, I was right.' Despite herself, Ruby let Peter take her hands in his.

'You were right.'

His grip on her hands began to drive the circulation from her fingers.

'Thoughts?' demanded Peter.

'We begin with this and use it to construct the case.'

How does a captured agent try to warn Home Station?

What do you do if Home Station is blind and deaf to your warnings?

'Peter, what if the security checks have been tortured out of him and he's been trying to tell us a different way? Say, you are made to transmit with the Germans watching you. There's no chance of leaving out the real check. Is there?'

A man came up behind them and Peter released her. Ruby rubbed her fingers while she waited for the man to move out of earshot.

She continued in the same impassioned undertone: 'They keep him alive for as long as he is useful and make him do the transmitting, because they know we know his fist, but they read, compose and code the messages.'

Peter nodded. 'It could happen.'

Stip, stap, stup . . .

'Was Vinegar trying to tell us way back when he misspelled "stop"?' She grabbed his arm. 'I now think he was. I think it was his way of telling us and we weren't listening.'

Picture it: captured, roughed up. Tortured? Alone, so alone, but your every move watched.

'My God, Peter.'

Picture his despair, or rage, or both. Did he think: They have not kept their promises?

'Then the Germans are very clever. Having studied his fist, they gradually take over the actual transmissions and get rid of him when they have no more use for him.'

Did she or he die thinking: They did not listen to me?

'It's possible.' Peter searched Ruby's face. Thinking, probing, assessing.

'Right, Ruby, we have to go and deal with this.'

'To the Danish section?'

He paced up and down. 'If there's going to be a major row, and there will be, it should be with the top bosses.'

'If there was a drop planned, it should be stopped.'

They faced each other. 'Trust me,' he said. 'I know how it works.'

She shoved the strap of her handbag further up her shoulder. 'You're thinking bad, aren't you?'

'Very bad.'

'So am I.'

She reached out her hand and he took it. A simple enough gesture, but she sensed it was a life-changing one. He stroked her fingers. 'Are you ready?'

Dizzy with love and fear, Ruby inhaled a shaky breath. 'I think so. Yes.'

It happened quickly. Within an hour of their return to the office, Ruby was summoned.

'Busy little bee,' Gussie did not look up from her typing. 'Buzzing about.'

The hours the two of them underwent being grilled by the head of intelligence, head of signals, chief code master and Colonel Marsh, head of the Danish section, were not ones she would look back on with affection.

The lamp on the desk shone very brightly as the assembled men conducted their interrogation.

Why . . . what . . . how?

How did you get hold of this material?

The gravest indiscipline.

Courts martial . . .

The heat from the light caused beads of sweat to spring onto her upper lip.

'Sir –' it was easier to focus on one face and she chose Colonel Marsh's '– the probability was that our assumptions were wrong about Vinegar. I decided to investigate.'

These men were baffled and furious. More than that, she sensed they were also frightened: frightened because their systems and intelligence had failed them.

'You realize,' said the head of signals, 'that you used one of my staff who could have been accused and put in the dock?'

'I would have taken the blame, of course,' said Peter.

The head of intelligence was livid. As he talked, spittle flew. 'You bloody fool, Martin.'

Peter stood his ground. 'Perhaps. But how do we explain why Vinegar has never mis-numbered his transposition key, or misspelled a word or made any of the coding mistakes which are perfectly normal in other agents?'

The head of intelligence folded his fingers together. 'They've been trained well.'

'What about the "stip", "stap", "stup"? Wasn't he trying to tell us something?'

A look of utter contempt was directed at Ruby.

'How many times did the misspelling occur?'

Ruby told them.

'Out of how many messages?'

'In approximately a quarter of his transmissions. There was a cluster early this year.'

'So why didn't he continue to use that device?'

Peter said: 'It's possible that he was being monitored extra closely. Perhaps he was weaker, more brutalized, less willing to take the risk. Perhaps the Germans took over the transmissions rather than dictating them to him. We don't know what is happening, or happened, to Vinegar. Will probably never know.'

The head of signals said: 'It's a just a tic. Other agents have them.'

Ruby thought: *No.*

Colonel Marsh had a Welsh lilt to his voice that dropped into a softer and softer register. 'This has been an outrageous breech,' he pronounced.

Peter was firm: 'But justifiable. It's my considered view that, as from today, Vinegar should be considered suspect and any drops arranged with him should be diverted elsewhere in Denmark. Plus, we *must* revisit the arguments for dropping the poem code.'

'You could have bloody jeopardized the whole set-up, Martin.'

The truth was that no one knew the truth. It was one step forward, one step back. As far as they were concerned, Europe was shrouded in darkness. There was no clear, luminous, steady light to shed understanding on what was really happening. No clarity.

'What to do?' Colonel Marsh posed the question delicately into the smoke-laden atmosphere.

'What's best,' answered Ruby. 'What's logical. We must consider the worst.'

The heads of intelligence and signals could barely bring themselves to look at Ruby.

The subtler Colonel Marsh reflected for a moment. Then he nodded. 'Yes,' he agreed. 'Let's begin.'

Towards the end of the exhausting session, while searching for further proof, Ruby rifled through the report worked up from the notes she had taken during the conversations with Mary Voss. Then . . . then . . . something obvious, so *blindingly* obvious, struck her.

'Sir,' she addressed Colonel Marsh. 'Sir, look at this.' She added angrily, 'I insist.'

Grudgingly, he cast a look at where her finger rested. It was on a section of the notes dated July 1943. His colour changed as he read out: '"Variations in signalling: QRU reading CAU. Plus: Frequency change from LMS to GHT."'

The head of signals shoved his chair back with a screech.

Colonel Marsh lifted a now-ashen face. 'That spells CAUGHT.'

The balloon went up.

When Ruby returned to the office, she sank down onto her chair.

'For the record, Gussie, bees die once they've stung somebody.'

Gussie sniggered.

'My last request is that you give me a good funeral.'

Chapter Thirty-four

So many things for Tanne to remember. So much information to store in an impregnable place in her mind until it was embedded and the lies sprang naturally onto her tongue.

Today you shoot with your left hand.

Today you shoot in the dark.

This light will dazzle you but you must keep shooting.

Concentrate.

Describe your drop zone in detail. Remember you will have no map.

The addresses of your contacts. Who are they? What do they do?

You will pretend that I am Jens Borch of number forty-five Algarde, København. What do you say to me?

'Good day, Mr Borch. My aunt Karen sends her greetings. She says to tell you that she remembers the wonderful saddle-of-mutton dinner you shared before Christmas. She hopes that your wife has recovered from her miscarriage.'

You are to be dropped into the Aarhus region. Stand by.

'Are you ready to go?' asked her dispatching officer. 'Do you understand what's required of you?'

Had her mind notched up a level? Did she understand that, *from now on*, nothing would be straightforward? Everything should be, would be, viewed obliquely and familiar things, places and people would have a question mark over them.

'Do you understand that your life may be at risk?'

She remembered running through the fields, stubble whipping at her ankles. Dogs baying.

Just as well to get used to it.

She glanced up at the sky which looked infuriatingly blue and settled – she wouldn't have minded if the drop was called off today. She hadn't been sleeping so well and needed to catch up on rest. Was the insomnia a way of telling her she was frightened?

They filed into the large drawing room. Calm and serious, the dispatching officer waited in front of the fire. 'Operation Table d'Hôte is on. You will be fed at four o'clock, and this is your lucky day, with wine.'

Before that came the fuss of the last-minute details. Hair? Tanne's had been cut short and dyed raven black. The result was awful. Spectacles? With great difficulty a Danish pair with heavy black rims had been obtained and plain glass lenses inserted. Clothes? Had a Danish label been sewn onto the waistband of the serge skirt? Correct laces in shoes? Check for London bus tickets, cigarette butts, the wrong kind of face powder – oh, for God's sake . . .

My code name is Serviette. My field name is Eva. My alias is Else Steen. I was born in Randers and came to study in København but decided studying was not for me. I am currently a waitress in the Casablanca Café in Aarhus. I have lodgings at number two . . .

Ready to go.

Nerves strung. Bowels twinging.

Then . . . phones started ringing. All over the house. There was a flurry of activity, the sound of rapid footsteps going in and out of rooms. Eventually, the briefing officer appeared. 'This is the final briefing and there is a last-minute alteration,' he instructed. 'The drop zone is shifted to Zealand. Jutland is out.'

Tanne started.

'Something has come up and the section heads have decided not to take any risks. You must deal with this as best you can and take evasive action.'

The briefing combed over the details.

Later a car with blinkered headlights nudged around the perimeter of a secret airbase heading towards a couple of buildings. It stopped outside what looked like a cowshed.

Appearances were deceptive. Inside, a fire burned, one

uniformed officer checked over racks of equipment and a couple of others played poker in the corner. They smiled and nodded in their direction as Tanne and the others filed in.

'Hello, again.' A captain she recognized from STS 51 greeted them. 'I've been allocated as your dispatching officer.' His expression was of kindly concern. 'Hope you don't mind,' he continued, 'but I thought I'd see you off.'

It was good to see a familiar face. Tanne waited quietly while he handed out equipment to each of them: overalls, overshoes, gloves, a small flask of rum, a rubber crash helmet, a tin of sandwiches and five thousand kroner in used ten-kroner notes.

The flying suit was far too big, and she struggled to pull up the sleeves. The captain assisted her.

'Knife, dagger or pistol?' he asked.

'Pistol.'

Of the unpleasant, not to say awful, options they suggested, killing or wounding someone from a distance was distinctly better than one-to-one combat.

He handed it to her, plus ammunition. The butt fitted into the curve of her hand. *My lifeline*, she thought.

The captain must have noted the slight tremor of her hand. 'Rumour has it that one of the agents, nameless of course, hid a dog in these overalls and it jumped with him. He argued that a man with a dog who answered to its name was not likely to be suspected by the Germans as a parachutist. The man was a genius but God knows what the dog thought.'

The diversionary tactic worked and Tanne smiled.

'And this –' he held out his hand, palm uppermost '– is your cyanide pill.'

She had never, ever imagined that death would sit in a palm of the hand: a rubber-encased capsule.

'Use it if necessary.'

To die for the honour of her country? So that her soul would be snatched up by the goddess and borne away to Asgard?

'Thank you.' She stowed it carefully and tried to defuse

the atmosphere with a joke. 'The helmet makes one look dreadful.'

The captain rested his hand briefly on her shoulder.

Leaving the barn, she turned to take a last look. The shelves of equipment. The men playing cards. The slightly fevered expressions. The map on the wall. The fire – a symbol of sanity and comfort. The captain lifting a hand in farewell.

Having climbed into the belly of the Hudson, she crawled into place. The others followed.

'I feel like a suppository.' Lars was squashed up against her. 'Eh?'

The roar of the plane's engines intensified as it began a lumbering progress down the runway, finally lifting up and over a ridge which hid the airfield from the village.

Very soon, the last of the land disappeared from view. She forgot about England – and it vanished into the past.

Lars looked almost as bad in his helmet as she did in hers. He shouted up to her. 'Denmark very soon.'

Was she being heroic?

She trusted that some part of her was.

Be truthful, Tanne. Be truthful, *Eva*. Heroism, she had learned, was almost certainly diluted by other impulses and desires that had been only briefly touched on at the training schools. In her case, if she was honest, she was eaten up with a love for Felix and it was quite, quite different from anything she had ever felt before.

She closed her eyes.

Concentrate on the immediate. The noise of the aircraft. The smell of the fuel. The tea sloshing around her stomach. The infuriating need to pee.

Tanne dozed.

Much later the red light glowed, and the dispatching sergeant snapped to attention. Within seconds she was positioned by the Joe Hole. Tanne glanced down. God Almighty . . . she was going down there? Terror gripped at her guts and her heart beat in a chest which felt as tight as a drum. *Go on, Tanne.* Trying not to flinch, she made herself look down again. Moving across her vision was a magic lantern of moonlit fields. Occasionally, among the dark, dense patches of woodland, there was the fractured glint of water.

Home.

The sergeant tapped her on the shoulder, pointed up to the static line to show he had attached it properly and gave her the thumbs-up.

The light switched to green.

'Go.'

Terror. Abject terror.

No time left to think . . . and there she was, suspended in the sharp, thin air, a shape billowing down to the moonlit field below, with four others above and beside her.

The earth reared up: a big flat plate that tilted alarmingly.

Keep your bloody legs together.

Tighter than a nun's.

For a couple of seconds she lay winded on the ground, smelling home: a mixture of turf and grass and the tiniest suggestion of salt. Feet ran towards her.

The wind tugged at the deflated parachute and she scrabbled for purchase by digging her fingers into the turf.

'Eva!'

Home.

No longer Tanne, she was Eva.

'Get up, Eva.'

Grinning broadly she got to her feet and held out her hand. '*Hej!*'

Two weeks later, keeping under cover as much as possible, Tanne hiked cautiously up the road from Køge in the direction of Rosenlund. Autumn's dropping temperatures were colouring the tree foliage and the silver birch and beech presented a fire dance of yellows and oranges shot through with sparks of red.

Stop.

Engines in the distance?

Dodging back among the trees, she dropped down flat into the undergrowth. A minute or so afterwards a convoy of Danish army trucks drove past in the Køge direction. Head down, she counted the number of trucks and staff cars. An entire unit? Furthermore, the fact that it was using this back road suggested their orders were to be inconspicuous.

She waited until the last vehicle was well out of sight and gave herself a few more minutes.

She thought of the other Joes who had come in with her. There had been no time for proper goodbyes, just farewell pecks on iced cheeks – before they were spirited away to separate locations. She had been driven to København where, as Else Steen, she had been given a room above a café and worked as a waitress. 'Wait for your orders,' was the instruction. When they came earlier that afternoon, Tanne felt the shock waves.

She checked her watch. Five p.m. Approximately an hour and a half until dark. She set off again. Her speed was good and she held it steady, enjoying the exhilaration that came with a fit body and a good pair of boots. In her backpack were bread, cheese and her pistol.

Slipping into the Rosenlund estate via the north gate, she made for Ove's cottage. The door was locked, but she swung herself up to the first floor and crept over to the window which had a faulty catch. Thank you to all the instructors at the STS. Once inside, she unlocked the door, propped herself against the wall and ate the bread and cheese.

So near to the family home . . . and yet as far away as it was possible to be. She tried not to think about her father. She knew what his distress at the absence of his daughter would be – and imagined his feelings of betrayal. No, no . . . to think of her father would be to induce weakness and that was out of the question.

Sleep when you can.

Tanne awoke with a start. Danger! Its proximity flashed through her warning systems. Groping for the pistol, her hand closed around the butt, its reassurance so welcome.

A footfall. Careful and almost noiseless. Expert.

The catch at the door moved . . . infinitesimally . . . but enough.

In a flash she rolled to one side and was up and crouching, pointing the gun with both hands. This was it. Her training had prepared her for this encounter, and this was the point when it translated into reality.

The door pushed open. Tanne took aim.

'Eva?'

'Felix.'

The pistol clattered onto the wooden floor.

She was so livid that she trembled. 'How dare you do that? Do you know what I could have done to you?'

He bent down and picked up the pistol. 'Actually, I do. Sorry.'

'Idiot, idiot, idiot.'

He grinned broadly. 'I like the temper.'

Now she was trembling not with fright or anger but from joy.

'I wanted to see you,' he said.

He was wearing a thick jersey, corduroy trousers and boots, and an ammunition belt was slung across his midriff. A Sten was tucked up under his armpit.

'Why aren't you at the rendezvous?'

'I have been.' He handed the pistol back to her. 'I came to say there's been plenty going on since my return . . . and it's going to get more intense.'

'And? Is that news?'

'The odds on us surviving shorten.'

He was matter-of-fact. Yet his words conjured a picture of them both, wrapped in the Danish flag, being rolled into a hasty grave.

It is important to understand that your life expectancy is short.

Until that moment . . . until Felix appeared in front of her,

Tanne accepted the prospect of extinction. She had been taught. She had trained. Possible death was the deal. But now everything in her that could, cried out: *I want to live.*

That was a lesson, she thought, and she cringed at the feebleness of her resolve.

'But we're going to survive, Felix,' she told him.

As he had done once before, long ago, he placed a hand over her mouth – and she knew she had come full circle. 'Don't tempt fate.'

'Superstition.' She pressed her chin against his hand. 'If we will ourselves to live then we stand a good chance.'

'Just shut up, will you?' Felix took Tanne roughly into his arms. 'But I applaud the principle.'

Tanne knew, she absolutely knew, that her life had been leading up to this point of revelation and understanding. The exhultation at having arrived rendered her speechless.

The ammunition belt was pressing painfully into her chest. 'There's no time now to say much,' he said. 'But afterwards it will be different.'

'Afterwards . . .' she murmured, and the promise danced like the reflection of the sun on Rosenlund's lake.

He ran his hand through her awful hair. 'I'll find you a good hairdresser.'

Tanne laughed. 'Go on.'

'I'll take you to a private place and we will take our time to get to know each other.' He was almost apologetic. 'Because I will want to be sure.'

She was smiling idiotically. 'Be sure of what?'

'That I have got to know every inch of you. And . . .'

That pleased her immensely. 'And?'

'I will learn about you. Properly.'

'Ah. You might have to practise a long time.'

Her feelings were new and unfamiliar. Certainly uncharted. They almost fell within the category of painful – by which she meant the depth and searing-ness of loving Felix. It's good, she thought. It's a miracle. About to go out into the dark and the danger, she had been granted this moment.

'I mean I want to know you, Eva.'

To reassure herself, she touched his face. This was real. He was solid. Felix was no dream. No.

She had no idea who he was, or where he came from. But she had no reservations about him and no reservations about what she wanted.

Holding her face between his hands, he peered at her through the gloom.

He kissed her.

She put her arms round his neck. *Remember*, she told herself. *Remember this.*

After a while he asked, 'Am I forgiven for startling you?'

'What do you think?'

After a while Felix disengaged himself and she gave a small groan of protest. 'We've just under two hours.' He laid the back of his hand against her cheek. 'There's no choice.'

It was time to be professional.

She briefed Felix on the army trucks she had spotted and he questioned her about the numbers, their direction. 'They've been around for a few weeks,' he said. 'It has held things up here.'

'I thought Rosenlund was compromised as a drop zone.'

'It is and it isn't.' Felix moved over to the window and took a look outside. 'It was Freya's idea and it ticked a lot of boxes. The RAF did a reconnaissance but we had to mothball it while the place was being watched. Then Odin sent word that the surveillance had been called off. The alternatives are few and far between, and for some reason London has suddenly banned drops in Jutland. Instructions were sent via Sweden to use this one.' He shrugged. 'We need the stuff. So . . .'

'Who's Odin?'

Felix pressed a finger against her lips. 'A mole deep in where it matters.' He didn't speak with any enthusiasm. 'But vital. He tells us when and where the Germans are likely to be busy.'

He explained the plan. Because of the last-minute switch, he had been forced to draft in men from København as well as Køge. 'We need everyone we can get hold of.'

'*C'est* on, *c'est* off . . .' she murmured, phrases she had picked up from one of the agents during training. She looked at Felix. *C'est* on. *C'est* very much on.

'There is one thing I have to ask you,' Felix said finally.

'Ask me, then.'

'The wireless set. Freya was forced to leave it here and we need it in København. It won't be any use here once this is over.' There was a long pause. 'You know what I'm asking.'

She was getting ready, checking the pistol, tying back her hair. 'Yes.'

'It's the last thing I want to ask you.'

'It's my job, Felix.'

She bent down to retie the lace on her boot. He knelt beside her and put his hands on her shoulders. 'Afterwards, Eva . . .'

'Afterwards,' she repeated.

She gazed into his face, trying to memorize every flicker of expression, everything about him.

She knew that he knew that they both knew the truth: the only thing certain was that nothing was certain.

Felix fetched the wireless set from its hiding place where Freya had left it and, moving like the trained agents they were, they went out together into the night.

Chapter Thirty-five

The sun set at approximately six-thirty but the large and brilliant moon ensured it was not totally dark. Observing their training, Felix and Tanne moved cautiously through the trees in the direction of the lake.

Felix carried the wireless transmitter. Tanne had her pistol at the ready.

The glorious autumn had dried out the undergrowth and they trod over layers of snapping, crackling leaf fall. Checking, always checking, they went carefully.

At the lakeside, Felix went ahead to rendezvous and Tanne, the wireless transmitter at her feet, kept watch under the tree cover.

Home.

But it was hard to make out the house, which was a good thing.

It was growing chilly and she was grateful for the long-sleeved woollen jumper she had on under her jacket.

Felix stole back through the trees. He reached out and took Tanne's hand. Their fingers locked.

'The others?'

'On their way,' he said.

A couple of men, in dark clothing and berets, materialized out of the undergrowth and joined them. Shortly afterwards four more followed. Finally, a tall, slender, black-clad figure in a beret crept up to the edge of the trees and crouched down.

The figure was familiar, and yet it wasn't.

Was it?

Tanne's sharply indrawn breath was audible in the hush. '*You!*'

Her mother quivered as if she had been hit.

Fury – because Felix should have warned her – mixed with relief at seeing her and gratitude that she was still alive, made Tanne clumsy and she lurched into her mother's arms.

They clung together.

The touch was the one from childhood – the touch that had anchored Tanne to her life, her family, her home.

Nuzzling Tanne's cheek as she had done so often over the years, her mother kissed her – once, twice, three times – and whispered, 'Remember that I'm Freya now . . .'

'And I'm Eva. How are you, Freya?' But she longed to say: *How are you*, Mor?

In the gloom, Tanne was able to make out that Kay was smiling. 'Better for seeing you.'

Hugging her, Tanne noted that her mother was very thin – thinner than Tanne could ever imagine – and her hair had been dyed into a dark mass. She smelled different: of unlaundered clothes and sweat and a world away from the scented, powdered, soft-bodied woman of the past.

Kay turned away and grabbed Felix. Tanne heard her say: 'Your promise, Felix –'

Felix cut her off. 'Eva has been trained. She has chosen to do this. It's her job now.'

Kay looked from one to the other. 'You've been in England?' Tanne nodded. Her mother swung round and hit Felix hard on the chest. 'You've betrayed me, Felix.'

He caught her hand. 'Freya . . .'

'It was the one thing I asked of you.'

Felix the lover had vanished. In his place was the agent. 'I'm not going to stop anyone who wants to join in the fight –'

'Freya,' Tanne intervened. 'It was my decision.'

'Shut up now,' said Felix.

He checked the time and signalled to the team to gather round. They were passing around the hip flask. One of them was finishing the tail hunk of a sausage. Another cracked such a filthy joke that his companions hushed him.

'Five minutes. Listen carefully. Army vehicles are on the move in the area. It could mean nothing, it could mean trouble. Our intelligence suggested they were moving out of the area but we can't be sure. The noise will be bad but the British bombers fly over here frequently and, with a bit of luck, Fritz will take no notice.' He paused. 'Anyone who wishes can bugger off now.'

No one moved.

'Right, then.'

Close to the shore, the lake was stippled by clusters of underwater reeds. Further out, the water was calm and gleaming under the moon and stars.

Tanne wondered what the pilot would be thinking. Had he briefed himself sufficiently? Had he written a list: fly east, turn south, look for a lake? Did he believe the intelligence that would have reassured him there were no anti-aircraft guns nearby? Had the navigator memorized the towns, rivers and forests?

Felix was now briefing them individually for the final time.

There was a noise. A footstep . . . ? It came from behind a clump of bushes.

'*Lort!*' One of the men swung round and took aim.

Nostrils flaring, they waited. Nothing. Placing a finger to her lips, her mother crept towards the bushes. The dark swallowed her up. Tanne's heartbeat quickened.

Kay returned. 'An animal, I think.'

She stood beside Tanne and drew her close. 'Promise me you won't take stupid risks,' she whispered. As she spoke, they heard the faint throb of an engine. 'Promise.' The noise increased in intensity and volume. She looked up into the sky and continued calmly, 'You have to make sure you live. For *Far*. For Nils. For me.'

Tanne said nothing.

'Eva . . . do you understand. Do you promise?'

On time. On cue. Silhouetted in the moonlight, the Halifax flew into view and her mother gasped. The Halifax could never be called a beautiful plane, yet, bathed in chalky pale moonlight, it was almost elegant, and it hung in the sky like a Chinese lantern.

Dodging flak, the Halifax had got here, the result of hours of meticulous planning. Tanne thought of the people she had never met back at The Firm: the coding experts, the instructors, the good-mannered FANYs, even the cook who had made the sandwiches to eat on board. All contributed to this moment.

Gut-churning, ear-splitting waves of sound.

The moonlight played over her mother's uplifted face. Impossible to know what Kay was thinking. Was it grief, or pride, or elation? 'Oh, well done,' she murmured. 'Well done.'

She sounded incredibly British and a lump edged into Tanne's throat. Moving closer, she made sure their shoulders touched. Whatever happened, they were in this together.

We are not going to be beaten, she wanted to shout up at the lumbering aircraft. *And you have made it possible.*

Felix knelt on the shoreline. The beam from his torch dotted and dashed the letter R.

The Halifax flew across the moon and Tanne whispered, 'We are going to be fine.'

Don't be negative.

Think of the task in hand. Go over it, piece by piece.

Outwit the enemy with your mind.

Would she have the courage to take her pill?

Five hundred feet, that was the optimum flying height, no more, no less. The Halifax took a fix, grinding around in a circle before making a low pass over the water. A hot, fuel-laden wind buffeted the watchers below. From its belly fell six parachutes. Huge, ungainly jellyfish which the wind caught, slapping hard against the silk and snapping at the straps.

His job done, the pilot circled once more. The Halifax's

wings dipped in farewell, and salute. *Look what we've managed.* Her mother gave a suppressed sob.

The plane rose, roared, set its course for home and drove on into the night sky.

The noise. The noise. It would waken the dead. An instinct made Tanne whip round and look towards the house.

Just in time. A light snapped on in her parents' bedroom.

'Felix . . .' She pointed to the house.

The group swung into action.

Six buoyancy flags bobbed in the water, each one marking a container. The first two men into the boat rowed out to the couple furthest away. Hauling the parachutes and containers on board, they rowed back to shore and unloaded. The scene was filmic, almost dream-like. The second team leaped into the boat, rowed hard and fast and picked up two more.

Once on shore, the wet parachutes were bundled up, and battens slotted through the container handles. The loads were lifted and the men disappeared in the direction of the road and the parked-up vans.

It was Kay and Tanne's turn. The oars settled like old friends into the palms of Tanne's hands – as they had so often done at the family's summer gatherings.

In the stern, her mother was positioned to catch up the containers. Reaching the first of the buoys, Tanne feathered the oars. Her mother bent over and hooked the buoy to the rope.

In the same way they netted the second container.

It was not easy. The rope was wet and tough to manipulate and Kay had to fight it. Time was passing.

Job done. Edging over to sit beside Tanne, Kay took an oar. Containers dragging behind them, they rowed as fast as they could towards the island.

The landing stage was tiny and rotten but they knew its tricks. Even so, hauling the containers onshore took all their strength. Tanne knelt and prised open the first, revealing tightly packed bundles in waterproof material. These they ferried up into their designated hiding place under the summer house.

Her mother searched for one in particular. Double-wrapped in protective material, the package was marked with a red dot. 'The crystals.'

Tanne unhooked the buoys, chucked them into the containers and stuffed the parachutes on top, piling in the stones which her mother had collected into a heap by the jetty. 'I shall dream of that lovely silk,' she said, shutting the lids down. Between them, they dragged the two containers back to the water.

How many minutes had elapsed?

'Team Eberstern?' In the boat, Kay positioned her oar. 'Are you ready?'

Water glistened on the feathering oars. Moonlight splintered onto the lake's surface. A couple of times the boat wallowed as, in their haste, they mistook their timing.

Halfway across, Tanne unhitched the rope from the containers and held each one down, waiting for the water to invade them. With a hiss they filled up and sank into the blackness, a trail of silver bubbles rising from their grave.

The two women rowed liked demons. As they neared the shore, Tanne sneaked a look at her mother. She looked pinched from the effort and her strokes were becoming uneven. The moonlight revealed an ill-fitting padded jacket and a thick fisherman's sweater underneath. Her mother would never normally wear that sort of sweater.

Tanne's eyes pricked.

At STS they had warned of the effects of adrenalin but they had not explained how an air of unreality could hover over an operation, or that feelings which should be safely buried could push and kick their way to the surface.

Forward. Pull. Feather. Forward. Their two bodies worked in unison. Voices carried across water so they didn't speak until they reached the shore, where they moored the boat and ran into the trees.

They paused for breath.

Craning her head, Tanne spotted Felix carrying the case and moving towards them through the trees. He beckoned. Tanne grabbed the package with the crystals and the women ran over to him.

But, as she picked up speed, Tanne was aware of a familiar figure hanging back by the treeline, almost out of sight. But she could spot him.

Her father.

He was staring across to Sophia-Maria's island.

Tanne ran even harder.

Parked on the road, a van was waiting. As soon as they came into sight, the driver revved the engine. Hands reached out from the back and hauled them inside. Felix swung himself and the case up beside the driver.

The back was packed with the packages and sopping parachutes and Tanne, Kay and a couple of the men were forced to cling on as best they could.

They drove for about three minutes and then screeched to a halt. Tanne squinted through a slit in the bodywork. 'We've been flagged down,' she reported. 'The driver's talking to someone.'

There was a rapid exchange and the driver swore violently. Whoever had flagged them down now leaped up beside Felix. Gunning the van at top speed down the road, the driver swung it to the left and drove for another hundred metres or so and into a farmyard.

The driver sprinted around to the back of the van and hauled open the doors. 'The Germans are onto us. Word is they waited until we were on the move because they want to get their hands on the stuff. This is Tage Seest's place but he's in hiding. There's a slurry pit here. Shove it there.'

Working silently, they tipped the packages into the slurry. The parachutes were rolled up and pushed under hay bales. Tanne scattered straw over their footsteps.

'Get in,' ordered the driver.

Clutching the crystals, Kay scrambled back into the van. Felix swung up into the front. The driver coaxed the van out of the farm and back onto the road.

Tanne was conscious of every breath.

They headed down the lane and looped back on themselves.

Where does the enemy least expect to find you? Behind him.

The van halted. 'Out,' said the driver, barely waiting for them to disembark before driving off.

They were back on the northern perimeter of the Rosenlund estate. First Felix went over the wall, climbing with loose-limbed confidence. Then Kay handed up the wireless set and followed him. Tanne took charge of the crystals, slung them around her neck and went up and over.

They dropped down onto the scrubby turf and headed for the copse to their left, where they hunkered down.

Panting, Felix leaned back against a tree trunk. 'Time?'

Tanne peered at her watch. 'Three forty-five.'

There was nothing to be done but to wait it out.

Tanne was dozing when she felt Felix grip her arm. 'What?'

He pointed. Over in the Køge direction, a finger of light cut through the night sky.

Her mother shivered. With cold? With fright? 'Listen,' she said.

Vehicles were moving down the road in their direction.

'We split.' Felix leaped to his feet. 'When it's light, make your way to the station and catch the six-thirty train to København. Or the seven o'clock. I'll wait there for you with the set and hand it over. If you don't make either of those, I'll abort. At København, look for the blue taxi in the rank outside the station. He knows a safe house. The password's *skummet melk*.'

Hefting up the case, he disappeared out of sight, skilful and almost silent.

Tanne and Kay backed further into the copse. When they

judged they were close to its centre, they dropped down into a sitting position against the tree trunks. In the silence, their breathing was audible.

Tanne's heart thudded. Easy now.

It was still very dark. Small animals were moving around in the undergrowth. *Snap.* There was a crackle in the undergrowth to their right. A rustle to their left.

Wait in silence. Listen. Silence can tell you more than noise.

Her mother's shoulders slumped. 'You're not to touch the wireless set,' she whispered. '*Understood?*'

'Shush.'

'If you won't think of me, think of *Far.*' Kay pulled Tanne to her. 'It's an order.'

Back to the nursery. Her mother's soft lap. The murmured endearments.

'How long since you've been home?' Tanne asked her.

'I left not long after you.'

'Any news of *Far?*'

'He's well. And safe.'

'Has he any idea of where you and I are?'

'It wouldn't be hard for him to work it out.' Her mother's mouth was close to her ear. 'Whatever happens I want you to remember that I love your father.'

Tanne was conscious of tiredness. Big, all-encompassing fatigue creeping right down to the soles of her feet. The cold nipped at her exposed skin.

'But is that enough?' How stupid was that? She, too, loved her father. But she, too, was sitting in a dark wood waiting to go on the run.

'If it wasn't for the war, it would have been enough. But war changes people.' Kay detached herself, took Tanne's hand. She pulled at the little finger. 'We're different now from what we were. For you, this war will affect only a small part of your life. It doesn't seem like that at the moment . . .' Tanne could tell from her voice that she was smiling. 'But it's true. You will get over what's happened.'

What to say? What to think? '*Mor*, I swear I saw *Far* earlier. I think he came down to the lake to see what was going on.'

'The plane woke him, then. I thought it might. He told me he had moved back into our bedroom.' Her voice grew urgent. 'He mustn't find us, darling. Do you understand?'

They agreed to take turns to get some sleep and Tanne insisted on keeping first watch. Her mother must have been tired, too, for she dozed.

Her mother had forbidden her to touch the wireless set.

That heavy, bulky case which was impossible to explain away if challenged. Tanne supposed a brilliant actor might pretend it was a gramophone or . . . or a dictating machine, and get away with it. She wasn't an actor, but perhaps terror would make her so. If caught with it, there would be no question what would happen. Operationally, too, it acted like a flaring beacon, pulsing Morse and attracting every direction-finding unit in the universe, trapping its pianist in its crystals, aerials and headphones.

The cold filtered through the wood. Cold always smelled, Tanne found.

After an hour, she and her mother swapped. Tanne settled herself against the tree. Her body relaxed, her legs grew heavy.

She was woken by Kay pressing a finger over her mouth. With the other hand, she pointed in the direction of the road. 'Car stopped. Someone's coming.'

Cradling the pistols, they stood upright. There was a merest crack. A shuffle. A rustle of leaves.

Fieldcraft: muddle the enemy and, if necessary, surprise him from behind.

Tanne gestured to her mother: *Go right*.

She went left, moving stealthily, cautiously.

The footstep?

It was that of the experienced hunter. Easy. Assured.

Dawn was breaking, but it was still fiendishly difficult to make out shapes with any clarity.

Tanne froze. Three metres or so in front of her hiding place, a figure padded past. Male. Tall. She could just make out that he wore a long hunter's jacket, with a hat pulled down over his face. A rifle was slung over his shoulder, probably one used for game. On reaching the place where they had holed up, he dropped down and placed the flat of his hand on the earth.

Listening.

He was familiar, achingly so. At the same time he was alien and unknown.

Tanne wanted both to run towards him and to flee. Neither was possible.

The man straightened up and walked back towards the road.

Wait until you are sure.

Kay materialized like a ghost from her hiding place. 'A *stikker?*'

'Poacher, I think. '

'That would be it.'

The two women stared at each other. Kay placed her hands on Tanne's shoulders. 'Let's both believe that.'

This was complicity as strong as the umbilical cord. Neither of them was going to acknowledge that it had been her father. Neither would ask what the other thought he had been doing. *Please, please let it be a simple explanation . . . that he was up early to shoot duck as he has done so often before.*

Kay looked shattered. Tanne seized her hands. 'You're ill. You're shaking. This is too much for you. Please will you get yourself to Sweden? And let *Far* know.'

Her mother wasn't having any of that. 'I'm shaking because I'm tired, cold and hungry. So are you. I'll be up and running once I've eaten.'

Tanne said, 'We have to go.'

'Let me look at you, Tanne. Please.'

Hearing her name was odd.

Kay placed a hand under Tanne's chin. Familiar. Loving. 'You're filthy. We'll have to go into the washrooms and clean up. We'll be mother and daughter if anyone talks to us.'

'No,' said Tanne. 'Our papers are different.'

'Of course.' Kay shrugged. 'I was forgetting.'

First light was dawning and they prepared for the off. Unwrapping the crystals which were embedded in sponge, Kay buried all traces of the packaging under a clump of bushes. Tanne checked them over for damage. They looked fine.

They lay in her palm. So mundane and squat – the gateway to the ether which pulsed to a secret poetry and to the cries and whispers of those trapped behind the lines of the Reich.

Tanne slipped them into the pouch she wore round her waist under her trousers. The bulge was masked by her jacket.

'Tanne . . .' said her mother. 'Tanne, darling. I want you to take this.' And she pressed her beret down onto Tanne's head. 'It will get cold, very cold. You'll need it.'

Snatching it off, Tanne asked, 'What about you?'

Kay took the beret back again. 'It's for you.' She pulled it down over her daughter's ears, tucking her hair under the rim. 'There.' She leaned over and kissed her cheek. A butterfly touch. 'There.'

Her mother tucking her up in the bed with a red and white quilt. Her mother stroking her face. Her mother bathing a cut on her knee . . .

'Mor?'

Again, Kay's mouth brushed Tanne's cheek. 'Go well, my beloved daughter.'

They hiked into the town together but when they reached the Sankt Nicolai Kirke, they parted.

Tanne allowed herself to watch her mother progress down the street. Dyed. Thin. Shabby. Kay did not look back once.

She set herself to walk purposefully.

Always look as though you know what you are doing.

Slipping inside a café she made for the washroom. Here she

sluiced her face and hands, combed out her hair and put on the glasses.

So what had *Far* been doing? She frowned at the face in the mirror. It hurt, it really hurt, to be questioning his motives, but she must acknowledge – she had to – that he supported the enemy. Would he . . . would he tip off the Danish police?

Of course she still loved him, but painfully, protectively, and with a new consciousness.

What secret decisions had been taken that meant she ended up here rather than in Jutland? And why? Coincidence? Fate? Bungling? Possibly all three. The more Tanne reflected on it, the more curious she found it. God knew how, but her life had been fused together with those of the war-makers, and inter-connections made for political and strategic purposes.

Pinning up her hair, she extracted the crystals from her bag and tucked them into the scarf which she tied, turban fashion, round her head.

There was still time to order milk and a roll. She paid for them up front and ate them at a table facing the door. Afterwards, via the backstreets, she made her way to the station and bought a return ticket to Holte, the station after København. She would, however, alight in København.

Felix was already at the far end of the platform. He was sitting on a bench reading a paper, the case beside him. To see him . . . just to see him . . . Tanne was truly astonished by the strength of emotion that hit her like a hammer.

Four minutes until the train.

The passengers waiting on the platform projected a grey uniformity. The war, and worry, Tanne supposed. What, where, *who* were they in this war? These were questions that people must be asking themselves over and over. When peace came, how were they all going to live with one another again?

Escape route? Tanne noted a gap in the railings which ran alongside the platform and she checked it out. The aperture was large enough to squeeze through and gave access to the area where cars and carts parked. A couple of delivery vans near to the entrance could possibly provide temporary cover if necessary.

Two minutes to go.

One minute.

A convoy of trucks roared into the station forecourt, followed by a staff car.

Tanne swung round.

Soldiers in *feldgrau* uniform surged onto the platform, followed by two German officers, plus a man in Danish uniform.

She glanced at Felix. Routine?

No.

Felix's mouth had settled into a grim line.

The soldiers fanned out and corralled the passengers waiting on the platform. A couple more blocked the exit. Tanne checked her escape route. *Lort!* A woman with a child clutching her skirt was peering through the gap, obstructing Tanne's getaway.

Lort! Lort!

Four soldiers advanced down the platform, followed by the officers. Tanne's training clicked in.

Learn to recognize the uniforms as well as you know your times tables.

The first wore the closed-collar uniform of the Waffen-SS, the second that of a high-ranking Abwehr officer. A general.

The general turned and beckoned to the Danish army officer who was lurking in the rear. Tanne stared. She knew who that was. Of course she did. It was Anton Eberstern.

On time, the train came into the station. The instincts in Tanne still untamed by her training screamed: *Flee!* With a supreme effort, she made herself walk up the platform towards Felix, timing it so she drew level with him as the train halted and its doors opened.

Check the getaway route.

At the gap in the railings, a man had joined the woman with the child. Hunter's jacket, hat pulled down and a rifle in a case slung over his shoulder. It was the man she and her mother had spotted in the wood.

Far.

It made sense. Alerted by the drop, he would have tracked the pair of them as they walked into Køge. The accomplished hunter, *Far* was perfectly capable of it.

She knew then. She knew that, in his way, he had been watching over them.

He bent down, said something to the woman and pushed her gently away from the railings. That simple gesture told Tanne he would never betray them. No, her kind, loving father would be telling the woman to go, to be safe, to save her child from possible trouble.

Far.

Tanne patted her scarf to check the crystals were still in place.

Felix rose to his feet and joined the passengers surging towards the train doors. Head down, she edged in his direction.

Hand at the ready. *Give it to me.* Felix looked straight past her but a foot nudged the case over to her. Tanne reached down . . . but before she could pick it up, the case was snatched away and a piece of paper pressed into her hand.

What? *What?*

Tanne watched in horror.

At a steady, purposeful pace, her mother walked towards the carriage nearest to the engine. She was carrying the case as easily as if it weighed very little.

There was nothing Tanne could say or do.

Felix snarled into her ear: 'Get out.'

She hesitated – an absolute violation of the training. But leave her mother? 'Help her,' she whispered.

'I'm ordering you. Get out. Lie low until I make contact.'

'Halt!' The order was shouted by the German sergeant.

Her mother continued to walk down the platform – and

with every step she was growing smaller, thinner, more insubstantial . . .

'*Halt!*'

Reckless, reckless *Mor*.

Please, please, Tanne prayed.

'Halt or we shoot . . .' The order was bellowed out but, at that precise moment, the train sounded its whistle and the first words of it were lost.

Only the word 'shoot' was audible.

One of the soldiers, a young keen one, took aim. Tanne watched his arm swing up in a rapid response, his finger adjusting on the trigger, the slight tensing of the muscles under his sleeve.

She heard the crack of the shot. Heads turned. She watched, unable to move, as her mother staggered. Blood flowered on the back of her blue jacket, spreading unevenly.

Kay stopped. She swayed, staggered, took another step forward before dropping to one knee.

The sergeant ran across and slapped her on the wounded shoulder. 'Get up.'

Tanne leaped forward. 'No.'

Felix hauled her back savagely.

'Let me go.'

His fingers dug into her arm – agonizingly, cruelly. 'No, you don't.'

'You can't leave her.'

'Yes, I can. So will you.'

A sound between a moan and a scream came from her mother as the sergeant pulled her to her feet.

The crystals were burning under Tanne's scarf. The crystals sent in for the new wireless sets that would help to win the war.

She glanced at the folded paper Kay had pushed into her hand. Written on it in her mother's writing was: 'Give to *Far*.'

She couldn't leave her. Felix must understand.

The passengers had formed a tight, frightened knot. The Waffen-SS officer walked towards Kay. His fellow officer stopped to brief one of the soldiers guarding the entrance to the platform.

She would never forgive Felix.

She hated him.

She loved him.

The war had to be won.

Her mother knew that.

Kay turned her head slowly, agonizingly slowly. Her gaze drifted towards Tanne, rested on her for an infinitesimal second and moved on.

Go well, my beloved daughter.

You can't cry, Tanne. You can't cry.

Felix jabbed a finger hard into her spine. 'Go.'

Tanne went.

Chapter Thirty-six

The sergeant in the hateful *feldgrau* uniform bellowed at Kay and she forced herself to look at him. *Who are you?*

She was growing faint. But it didn't much matter because she knew she didn't stand a chance.

The SS officer issued an order – and she knew that voice.

Her knees wouldn't hold her and she sagged between the soldiers who were holding her up. The sergeant grabbed her by the hair so she was forced to look directly at *Hauptsturmführer* Buch.

'Have you anything to say?' he asked.

She remained silent.

'We know who you are.' He articulated the words very precisely. 'This is the wanted terrorist, Kay Eberstern.' His face loomed towards hers. 'What are you carrying?'

She closed her eyes.

When she opened them again, it was to see Anton positioned behind Buch. Everything became clear. To give him credit, Anton had warned her in the København café: 'Sometimes you have to surrender information in order to keep credible.'

Anton had sold them out because, on the run, she was no longer useful to him. Or rather she was more use to him as a sacrifice. It was the perfect equation.

'Open it up.' At the order, one of the soldiers, a skinny, underfed lad, undid the clasp and swung back the lid. Dials, crystals, the coiled antenna of the wireless.

Aladdin's cave.

'What's this?' asked Buch.

'A gramophone,' she managed to get out between icy lips.

The soldiers were told to stand away and she was left swaying tipsily.

'Stand up,' he said.

Think of something to keep going, she told herself. Think
of the grasses rippling in the fields at Rosenlund.

Again, the driver sounded the whistle — a harsh, despairing
wail.

She was losing blood. It was running down her back and
pooling in the waistband of her knickers. They would be ruined
and she had only a couple of pairs.

'What is it?' he repeated.

The swimming sensation intensified. 'It's a gramophone.'

Buch pulled his pistol out of the webbing at his waist, levelled
it and calmly shot her in the knee.

She went down flat without a sound.

Then, there was nothing.

No, there was something.

'There must be something I can do to help, Kay?'

*'There is one thing.' She leans over and kisses his cheek, the corner of his
eye, then his chin, then his mouth. 'Promise me something . . . Don't let them
take me,' she says. 'Promise. You don't know what they do to you. I do.'*

'Kay . . .'

'Promise.' She rests her hand against his cheek. 'Will you?'

'It's not a promise I can make.'

She means to say all sorts of things. That she loves him.

Had Kay told him? She hoped so.

She became conscious of a singing in her ears. Through a
slit in her eyelids a ribbon of sky appeared: the big, flat, white
Danish sky at the periphery of which faces stared at her. One
of them, a man, had eyes as round and terrified as those of a
scared child in a cartoon. A woman had clapped her hand to
her mouth.

The pain began in earnest. Waves of it, each wave mounting to a higher crescendo. She tried to control it by imagining

herself in the lake at Rosenlund. Freezing water numbed sensation.

Time became elastic. Each second expanded infinitely.

General Gottfried's face swam into her vision. 'Get up.'

Why wasn't she surprised that he was here?

She focused on him. The intelligence that she had marked on first meeting him was obvious. So was anger. He was a man who knew he had been duped and didn't like it. He would kill her whatever.

Enough. Why waste time on the general?

'So,' he said. '*Fru* Eberstern. I'm sorry to see you like this.' He paused. 'I'm sorry about a lot of things.'

He would be. It was a tiny grain of comfort to think she had run rings – or a ring – round him. She looked away.

'Get up,' he repeated.

Her limbs refused to obey.

The general was speaking in German. 'You thought you'd got away with it? Yes? But you weren't clever enough. We ran your colleague for months. London seemed wilfully blind. So many little things they ignored which we were sure they would pick up on. But no. The British are very self-satisfied.'

Security checks. Double security checks.

Summoning every ounce of her strength, every wit which remained, she managed to say, 'Are you sure they weren't playing you, General?'

He frowned.

Fear threatened to sap what was left of her strength. Kay knew what lay in store. Where had they hurt her so far? Her shoulder? She tried to flex her right arm. Useless. Her left leg wouldn't work either.

I'm going to make the fear go away.

I'm not going to die riddled and rotten with it.

She was dragged to her feet again. Nausea and pain warred with faintness.

She looked up. Smoke from the train filtered across the sky. She looked down to her shoes, now splattered with blood.

The onlookers were murmuring, shifting. A child cried.

'Shame,' said a woman. 'Shame on you.'

What did the woman mean? Shame on whom?

She longed for Bror.

Painfully, she turned her head away from the general and his men. From Anton.

Was it so surprising that human beings were untrue to each other?

Concentrate on the sky instead, the same sky which stretched over England and Rosenlund.

Her chin dropped onto her chest. The sergeant yanked her head up and her gaze was jerked towards the railings.

And there he was. Bror. Dressed in his hunter's clothing with his rifle. Was he returning from the duck shoot? She ached to be there with him, ranging through the woods, matching his careful, loving progress and his delight in the land. She wanted to be beside him at the lake shore, watching the water as the sun set.

Her eyelids dropped down over her eyes.

He had kept his promise.

He had tracked them.

He was there . . . she was not alone . . . he would never abandon her.

With a monstrous effort, Kay lifted her head. Their eyes met. They had shared their lives.

Do it, Bror. Please.

I can't.

You can. You must. They will torture me until I am nothing.

I want you to live, Kay, live.

Life was sweet with you, Bror. Remember that. And I don't want to die.

She watched him position the rifle and take aim.

Nils. Tanne.

She watched the tears roll down his face.

Then she closed her eyes.

Thank you, darling Bror.

They were in the drawing room at Rosenlund playing Racing Demon. Both of them were laughing. Kay looked up and out of the window to the lake.

Chapter Thirty-seven

June, 1944

Mary battled her usual exhaustion.

The previous two shifts had been difficult, with shrieking atmospherics, and her ears were ringing.

Straightening her serge skirt, Mary glanced in the mirror. Was she dreaming it? Or was the face that looked back at her beginning to be the sort of face of which people might say: She looks good for her age? A face that looked as though its owner knew what she was doing.

She thought back to her training days – when everything had been alien and alarming.

'Speed in Morse', said the manual, 'can only be achieved when one ceases to "read" individual dots and dashes and the groups of dots and dashes which make up individual letters. With practice, all these become subliminal.'

Mary had never thought it would happen, but it had.

Nancy looked up as Mary came into the signals room. 'Okie dokie?'

She was trying out the new Americanism that was sweeping the country.

'Fine,' said Mary, and she took her seat.

'This bloody, bloody war,' said Nancy, and she regaled Mary with the story of a never-to-be-forgotten stay in a luxury hotel before the war. 'The bedroom had a bathroom attached to it, with soaps and towels. And –' Nancy's voice lowered dramatically '– there was a basket of fruit, a crystal bowl for face powder and a huge mirror over the bed.'

Another life.

Some of the girls were finding the snail's pace of the war difficult to cope with. It was all very well listening to Mr Churchill's speeches, which were designed to whip the heart into fiery resolution, but the truth was that when you were stuck into endless shifts, they had a limited impact. Patriotic and determined as the girls were, they needed encouragement sometimes.

She considered tackling her superiors and even rehearsed what she would say. 'Some acknowledgement would work miracles. And we know secrecy is crucial, but not being told anything is hard for the girls and it can grind them down. Of course, they realize they can't be told the real identity of the agents but they need to feel they're trusted by you.'

Perhaps she would say something.

For she so longed to know what had happened to her agents, where they were. She wanted to know partly because they were part of her . . . partly because she needed to compensate for what she saw as her dereliction of duty towards Vinegar. Her particular Gethsemane.

Ruby had come to see her at the station, which was very kind of her. Mary had a premonition that it wouldn't be good news.

'Do you mind if I sit down?' she'd asked Ruby.

'Be my guest.'

Ruby lit a cigarette and, as she dropped her lighter back into her briefcase, Mary noticed a wedding ring. It was then that Ruby told her about Vinegar.

It had taken a while for Mary to respond. How could she – the best listener and one who loved her agents – have failed to see that Vinegar was being run by the enemy?

She *should* have known – and the knowledge that she had failed ate into her. It was bitter bread to eat. But that was the price of this war. And it was the price of life.

What had happened to him? Vinegar was almost certainly dead . . . but did he die knowing that someone back home was listening out for him? Could he have possibly intuited that she cared for him? That the Morse whispering and bouncing over the earth's curve carried her blessings?

If so, he might just have thought – a brief, flickering comfort – that his death would not be lonely, and certainly not in vain.

'Thank you for taking the trouble to tell me,' Mary said. 'No one else would have done.'

'This is strictly out of order.' Ruby smoked thoughtfully. 'But something you said when we first met, about how you felt about your agents, affected me. You'll be pleased to know that the coding system has finally been changed to a much more secure system.'

'That's good news.'

Ruby flicked ash into the ashtray. 'You do understand that, if anybody finds out I've told you, I will be shot.'

Mary nodded. 'Understood.' She fixed on Ruby's ring. 'Forgive me, but have you just got married?'

A curious expression flitted across Ruby's face. Exasperation? Joy? 'Yes, last month.'

Later Mary wondered whether that last meeting with Ruby was linked to another encounter. A short while after Ruby's visit, on being ushered into an office at the station that she hadn't known existed, Mary was informed that after the war 'they' wanted to offer her a job. Somewhere near Pinner. 'Eastcote, actually,' her interviewer said. 'The country needs listeners like you.'

That was all she was told, but she had accepted the job nonetheless.

'Jamming's bad at the moment,' said Nancy. 'Never know where they get the sugar.'

A familiar bad joke. It helped with the exhaustion.

As usual the room was filled with benches, unwieldy wireless sets, people. Signalmaster Noble was on duty. The old joke – 'Noble he is not' – kept on running. His power complex made him far more energetic than the decent Signalmaster

Falks. Noble made a point of patrolling between the desks. Every so often he would bend over a clerk's shoulder to check her progress.

'Bloody perv.' Nancy wrinkled her nose. 'Hasn't he had enough of looking down our blouses?'

Mary swept the frequencies, meticulously checking each one as well as the skeds. She had a new agent: BTU, code name Jelly. Dead on time, a message came in from him. She handed it up to Signalmaster Noble.

Nancy was frowning at the letters written on her log paper. Some of the girls were adjusting their dials, the precise and delicate articulation at which Mary excelled. Others were slumped over their benches, gathering their energy.

The hours limped on.

Sniffs. A cough.

'Oh, my lord!' Anne on Number 14 tore off her headphones and leaped to her feet. 'Listen to this.' She began to read, her voice young and hopeful, shaking with excitement: '"*Vive la France! Vive l'Angleterre!*"'

It took fully ten seconds for the listeners to understand that the message had come in *en clair* and not in code.

'My God!' screamed Nancy. 'It's begun. Our boys must have gone in.'

The room erupted as Anne waved the piece of paper aloft and hurried off to find Signalmaster Noble.

Tears streamed down Mary's face.

She wept for the deaths, for the violence and for the darkness that had gripped humanity. Inexplicably, she wept for the pigeons who, carrying their messages and regardless of storm and flak, battled through to come home.

She wept for the sacrifice.

Nancy stood over her. 'For God's sake, Mary, the Allies have gone into France. Buck up.'

With a supreme effort, Mary wiped her face with her handkerchief and tucked it back into her sleeve.

She checked the clock. Time for the search.

Where are you?

Summoning her skill, she swept the dial.

The whisper of the sea in a shell . . .

As she checked and adjusted, the upheaval in her heart subsided for the time being.

The needle quivered. She steadied it. *The professional.* She owed her agents everything she possessed.

Time? It was time.

And . . . there he was. Mayonnaise. Tapping with his usual fluency. There they were: the upward slope of Z; the jagged pattern of Y; the simplicity of A . . .

The rush of emotion was anything but professional, but it was pure and sweet.

Do you read me?

We read you, Denmark.

I am here.

Acknowledgements

Some years ago I wrote a novel about the SOE and I was lucky enough to get to know Noreen Riols, whose friendship I treasure and whose own book on her experiences in the SOE, *The Secret Ministry of Ag. & Fish*, provided both a remarkable and poignant insight into secret wartime work and a source of inspiration. Seven other books also became bibles: Leo Marks's brilliant and haunting *Between Silk and Cyanide*, H. J. Giskes's *London Calling North Pole*, Virginia Nicholson's *Millions Like Us: Women's Lives During the Second World War*, Knud J. V. Jespersen's *No Small Achievement: SOE and the Danish Resistance, 1940–1945*, Christine Sutherland's *Monica: Heroine of the Danish Resistance*, Cyril Cunningham's *Beaulieu: The Finishing School for Secret Agents* and Flemming Muus's *The Spark and the Flame*. I have taken and made use of material and scenarios from all seven. In addition, David Lampe's *Hitler's Savage Canary*, John Oram Thomas's *The Giant Killers*, Bernard O'Connor's *RAF Tempsford* and Sinclair McKay's *The Secret Listeners* yielded riveting details with which to work.

Any errors are mine but I would like to emphasize that this is a novel and for complete factual accuracy I would refer anyone to primary sources and historical texts.

Many people are owed a thank you. First, as always, Mark Lucas, who said, 'Why don't you look at Denmark?' Anne Ponsonby, who generously told me her stories of listening during the war. Thank you to my brilliant publisher, Louise Moore, to my editors Sam Humphries and Celine Kelly, to Clare Parkinson for her skilled copy-editing – all of whom are owed a deep debt – plus the rest of the Penguin crack team. Gratitude in spades to David Wilson, who drove me to Tempsford airfield and invited me to watch Noreen being filmed in Orchard Court, to Liz Jensen, who talked to me about Denmark and opened up contacts, to Helen Dunmore who sent me valuable material, and to Isabelle Grey and Fanny Blake, who were both ever-open doors and rocks.

Thank you also to Marika Cobbold, Annabel Markova, Belinda Taylor and other friends (they know who they are) who put up with the novelist in labour, plus a big thank you to Judith Murray.

Last but not least, thank you to Benjamin, Adam and Eleanor.

Reading Group Questions

1. Kay feels loyal to both Britain and Denmark, but do you think she would have acted differently if it weren't for her British roots?

2. How did you feel towards the character of Anton? Was Kay wrong to trust him, given what was at stake?

3. Do you think that Ruby and Peter would have ended up together had it not been for the war? Would she still have had a chance to show him her strong personality?

4. What did you think Tanne's motivations for joining the resistance were?

5. How did you interpret Bror and Nils' attitude towards the conflict? Were their choices influenced by fear, loyalty to Germany or simply the desire to protect the family name and estate?

6. Do you think that Kay would have been more hesitant about joining the resistance if she had not had a life of privilege up to that point?

7. Were you surprised by anything that you didn't previously know about the Second World War?

8. How would you like to think Tanne and Felix's story ends? Would Tanne ever be able to return to her family?

9. Do you think the author was trying to tell us something about the changing relationships between men and women in Western culture throughout the novel?

10. Who, if anyone, was to blame for Kay's death?

Author Q & A

What tempted you to revisit the Second World War after seven bestselling contemporary novels?

I am always intrigued how, even if the writer has already written about it, a subject sometimes refuses to die and nags away until something is done. But then who wouldn't be fascinated by the women who worked in the Special Operations Executive (SOE) during the Second World War? My second novel, *Light of the Moon,* was about a female SOE agent operating undercover in occupied France where she discovers, like Edith Cavell, that patriotism is not enough.

Researching the SOE was addictive and I made many contacts and some cherished new friends who worked in the undercover agencies. They told me about the beautiful and fantastically brave Violette Szabo (*Carve Her Name with Pride*), the equally splendid and intriguing Christine Granville, and the extraordinary Nancy Wake, who they revered for their cool bravery and resourcefulness.

All of the agents, both the men and the women, knew that in going into the field, their life expectancy was very short, in some cases it was judged to be as little as six weeks. Many of them met gruesome ends. Several novels on, my obsession resurfaced with a splash when I was talking to Noreen Riols about her recently published memoir, *The Secret Ministry of Ag. & Fish,* which describes her work in SOE's F-section. I found myself going back into histories, biographies, memoirs and anecdotal evidence and it seemed there was no question of dodging the subject any longer. Thus, *I Can't Begin to Tell You* began to take shape.

What made you want to write about such a well-known period of history from the perspective of the Danish resistance?

Having written *Light of the Moon*, I knew that I couldn't revisit France, however much I was in love with it. It would be better to tackle the subject from another point of view. But which? Like many, I had been hooked on the television series *Borgen* and *The Killing* in which Denmark figured as an intriguing and, for me, little-known country. A light bulb lit up in my head and I began to read more about it. Denmark had been taken over by the Reich in April 1940 with the minimum of fuss. Yet, as the strategists must have asked themselves back at the SOE's headquarters, even if everyday life was relatively calm in Denmark, there must have been undercurrents and cross-currents surging beneath the surface? How could they stir them up? They had to wait until September 1943 when the order went out to round up the Jews in Denmark. It was then that the country rose to magnificence and, overnight, most of the Danish Jews were smuggled to safety.

However quiescent Denmark was in the early stages of the war, loyalties were conflicted, which triggered much suffering. Searching to find the shape of *I Can't Begin to Tell You*, I stumbled across a biography of an English woman who worked for the SOE during the war and helped the Jews to escape, while her husband tolerated the occupation. They lived in a house with a lake in front of it.

I sat down to write.

There is so much detail throughout *I Can't Begin to Tell You* – how did you begin your research? Were there any areas that were particularly tricky to find information on?

The SOE agents in the field were still as fascinating and important to me as they had always been. Yet, so too was the organization that trained them: a shadowy set-up whose component parts were slotted together with such secrecy and unorthodox thinking. How was I to make the link between the agents in the field and those working secretly on the home front? The answer was coding – the sort of stuff we know from Bletchley Park and the Enigma machine.

It's a good idea to get the heavy spadework done first and I tackled books on coding – which required concentration and several restorative cups of extra-strong espresso. Then, the magical and fun bit began as I researched the personalities who had been involved.

I dug around and discovered there were women coders and decoders – such as my character Ruby Ingram, a brilliant mathematician and angry feminist. There were the lowly signals clerks – such as my Mary Voss, who listened out day and night for the call signs of the agents. It was exhausting, often brain-numbing work. Although they had no idea of their sex or their names, the signals clerks grew to know their agents simply by becoming intimate with the agents' 'handwriting' or 'fist' as they tapped out their messages in Morse from the field. Who was to say that the coders and listeners didn't cherish – and even love – these agents? They strove to protect them and to alert their bosses if they thought an agent was under pressure or on the run.

We will probably never know exactly what went on. The Official Secrets Act was not broken lightly by those involved. Also many of the SOE files were destroyed after the war. Therein lies the challenge for the novelist!

There are some wonderful strong female characters in the novel who drive the plot forward; was this your intention when you began writing? And if so, why?

The women who worked in the shadows have always exerted a powerful draw on me. Did they make good spies? Did they lead resistance armies effectively? What made them leave their children to go into the field? The answer is that, like the men, some were superb intelligence gatherers and inspiring leaders, some less so. The point was, however, that women worked in the resistance alongside the men. Less easy to answer was the question about their children – and it is one I don't think I can answer except to say that, at the time, they felt their reasons were compelling.

Were they tougher? Take, for example, the charismatic and hugely attractive Nancy Wake who was an Australian living with her French businessman husband in Marseilles. When the war broke out, she plunged into resistance work which resulted in her having to flee from France, leaving her husband behind. He was rounded up and tortured horribly before being shot. He left a message for her. 'Tell Nancy I love her and I didn't betray her.' Filled with hatred for the Nazis, Nancy trained with the SOE and was parachuted back into France in April 1944 where she successfully led an army of *maquisard* fighters. In *The Secret Ministry of Ag. & Fish*, Noreen Riols describes how the daring and audacious Nancy admitted to taking a German officer as a lover as part of her undercover work. 'Of course, I shall have to kill him,' she was overheard saying – which did indeed happen. Nancy did not personally do the deed. Instead, she betrayed him, which led to his execution. On another occasion, Nancy had to order the death of a so-called 'Dutch' girl who had joined her Resistance group, but who turned out to be a German agent. They had been friends. As she was taken out to die, the girl spat at Nancy and a second or two before she was shot, she looked at Nancy and said 'I am patriot too.'

On the other hand, to be a young mother at home who is asked to shelter a fugitive on the run with possible dire consequences to her children poses – to me at least – a quite different problem. I know that when my son and daughter were small, if one hair on their head was threatened I would not have hesitated to defend them with any means at my disposal – and, if that included sacrificing a friend, I think I would have done it.

It's not an easy thing to admit, and I hate to do so, but I am pretty sure that I am not alone.

Thus, I gave Kay – my heroine – a family, which meant she was plunged into the kind of moral and emotional quagmire that so many must face in a war.

Were you tempted to write a happy ending for Kay and Bror?

No. I am not sure that even as deep and happy a marriage as theirs could survive such divisions. That is not to say they stopped loving each other.

What can you tell us about the next book?

At the moment the title is *The German Wife*. I am fascinated by the aftermath of something like a war. How can you become Mr and Mrs Respectable if you have seen and done terrible things in order to survive violence and battle?

Will Gus – an intelligence officer working in Berlin – and his new German wife Krista be able to make a peaceful life for themselves when he brings her home as his bride to the house on Clapham Common? His sisters and ex-fiancée are furious and intend to make Krista's life as difficult as possible. They do not want the enemy under their roof.

Krista may be young and inexperienced, but the young and inexperienced have a way of growing powerful – after all, she has survived the cataclysm of her defeated country. And now, as the family struggles to regroup and adjust to the future, she brings everything she knows about survival to ensure that she does too.

Can't wait for more?
Read on for an extract of Elizabeth Buchan's
new novel, coming soon from Michael Joseph.

This text is unedited and subject to change.

Introduction

Infected by the latest gardening fashions, they decided that nothing else would do but a new terrace. They had moved to Clapham Common by chance because it had been recommended as an area that was still affordable in London. Once there, they had fallen for the green of the common, the pleasant streets and the late Victorian and Edwardian architecture. It was an area in which they felt they could put down roots and, if all went well, have a family. If the house needed a lot of attention it had the benefit of being roomy and filled with light. Slowly, slowly, inch by inch, they were kicking it into shape. However, the basic problems such as replacing windows and gutters had first claim on their budget and it wasn't until they had been living there for well over two years that they turned their attention to the garden.

It was a long garden, with a south-west aspect fringed by two overly large trees that had been allowed to grow unchecked and, because she craved the sun, the plan was to create a seating area well beyond their almost perpetual shadow.

The digging began. Both of them enjoyed it – although she tired more quickly and had to take a couple of coffee breaks. He was mocking her lack of grit when his shovel struck an unyielding object and he bent over to take a look. When he straightened up, every iota of colour had drained from his face.

'I think we will have to call the police,' he said.

Many months and an official investigation later, the forensic pathology report detailed the bones of a female skeleton, 5' 4" – 5' 6", probably between twenty-five and thirty years of age. Her bones registered that she had suffered from osteo-malacia – bone fragility – as a result of a vitamin D deficiency. The trauma to the back of her skull was considerable and she had probably been killed by a blunt object. A poker? A gun handle? A spade?

The date of her death was placed between 1945 and 1947.

Chapter One

Krista was to remember that taxi ride from Waterloo. Not that anything was so different from the Berlin she had just escaped. Here, unpeeling before her eyes, was the same bombed-out landscape. Her city had been flattened in places, but she recognized the same gap-toothed terraces which, like tired old can-can dancers, revealed in their muck and rubble flashes of a previous life – a paraffin heater, a rotting teddy bear, a torn and grimy towel.

Yet, it was different too. The journey from the station to Gus's house was through streets where people were living like ... well ... like people, not animals, and the houses, if damaged, were still upright. To see buildings that were upright was surprisingly pleasing. In the area of Berlin in which Krista had last been she could not remember a single building which could be said to be habitable.

Gus leaned over and captured Krista's gloved hand. She still didn't like being touched much, but she had to allow him to as was his right. He was her husband.

Turning it over, he inspected Krista's wrist. 'How frail it still is,' he said.

He had bought her the gloves – at vast expense – on the black market in Brussels where the unreliable trains had forced them to stop overnight. There was no need, she had told him, she was used to the cold. 'Precisely sweetheart,' his expression reflected a kind of male protectiveness that she knew to be a sham. 'I'm going to make sure that life is the opposite of what it has been.'

Her hand moved in his and he squeezed her fingers. 'My aim is to make you fat and rosy.'

'You're very kind to me.' She was polite and, as she always did, used the formal *Sie* not *du*.

They were speaking in German. She marvelled at how good his was. It would have to be since Gus had been seconded, after the allies reached Berlin, to the team assembled to interrogate war criminals.

Gus bent over to her. 'Krista, I can never fathom what is going on in that head of yours. That funny look you have sometimes . . .'

Why should he? No one knew anything about anyone else and would it be a good idea if they did? Much of what was hidden in people's hearts was shocking.

'Does it matter?'

'Possibly not.' Gus removed his hand. 'But, if we are to have a marriage . . .'

He allowed the subject to hang between them.

Krista probed at her bottom lip, a habit she had developed which left it raw and cracked, particularly in the cold. 'Gus, should you have told your sisters about us? When they see me . . . they've had no warning.'

'It's better if we tell them face to face.' He stared out of the taxi window. 'I've become a stranger to them. Being away for so long and having the sort of experiences that one does have in war changes someone. It has to.'

'But they know nothing about me.' Again she bit her sore lip. Why did she keep doing that? 'They will not want me. They will hate me. I'm German.'

'They will get used to you. One can get used to anything. That's not to belittle you, Krista. It's just what happens.' He smiled slightly. 'They might even get to love you.'

'After a war . . .' Krista looked up at her new husband. 'Things have been learnt. I think people more often want to kill each other than to love.'

'Don't,' he said sharply.

Krista changed the subject. 'What's the time?'

That was not so adroit either. Gus frowned, for she had reminded him that in Berlin no one possessed a watch any longer. The Russians stole them wholesale. The more watches a soldier possessed, the greater his status. She remembered one underfed but cunning soldier – a sergeant, as he boasted to Krista, who understood a smattering of the language – raising his arm and there they were, a dozen or so watches stacked up over his thin wrist. Apparently, the fancier the watch, the greater the standing with his platoon, and he had taken care to point out the one where a jewel winked in the centre of its face.

A couple of minutes later he raped her. But she had been expecting that and made herself lie quiet until it was over.

'I'm going to buy you a watch,' Gus looked away and out of the window. 'Wait and see.'

This was a statement of intent and she took it as such. Gus was telling her that she had a new life. Even if she was in England, a place for which she no particular affection, this promise of a new life was better than the one she had left behind.

Not so long ago the nights had belonged to the British bombers. Or had it been days? In the end, Krista became confused. Night or day, the sky had turned a flickering, violent red and nowhere had been safe. Those still alive existed like rats in the rubble, except the rats were doing a better job of surviving.

Sometimes, only occasionally, in the aftermath of the fire and terror, she spared a thought for the British airmen who flew the planes. What did they imagine they were doing as they sent down their bombs? Most days she prayed they were rotten with fear, because down below they crawled with it. They breathed, ate, slept and excreted terror. Or, if the bombers were fearless, Krista prayed that they were rotten with conscience.

The taxi slowed and Krista found herself peering into the front garden of a house. It had a workable gate, a front door with a brass knocker, windows that were streaked with dirt and a rose bush straggling in the front garden.

How grey and drab it was and, yet, how respectable. She felt herself submerging with relief into its dreariness, its lack of imagination. Inside that house she knew that the routines did not shift and those between its walls would be telling each other: *things will go back to normal.* There would be set times for meals, for housework, for listening to the radio, for shopping. Krista gave a little sharp intake of breath: nothing was more desirable in heaven or on earth.

The taxi moved on, progressing up a high street on which so many shop fronts were either smashed or boarded up. What shops were open had queues spilling out of them.

'Nearly there, Krista . . .'

Something flickered across her consciousness that she knew all too well: the uneasy, queasy marshalling of nerve and sinew that was needed to survive.

The street opened up on to a large open green space, fringed with trees, criss-crossed with earthworks and what appeared to be vegetable patches.

The taxi driver glanced around. 'Road's a bit of a problem here, sir, so hold on.'

He wasn't joking and she was clinging to the strap as the driver drew up in front of what she assumed was Gus's house.

There was some too-ing and fro-ing with the luggage – but since they had only one small bag each that was soon done. The driver searched his leather wallet for the correct change. 'Never have enough these days,' he said, handing over a sixpence.

Krista was rooted to the path. How on earth had she got here?

Chapter Two

Someone stood at one of the long windows on the first floor looking out at them.

The presence was rendered shadowy by the lace curtain which sagged from a pole and obscured their features. But the silhouette suggested a tall woman with fair hair rolled back from her face. Her pose suggested extreme tension. One hand rested on the lace curtain, the other was clasped tight against her body.

Outside, the house itself was beautiful. Intrinsically, at least. It was one in a line in a pretty terrace, but the war had done its worst. The house to its left was more or less a ruin and the one to its right had rags stuffed in the windows and the front door was hanging on a hinge.

But, short of demolition, nothing could hide the bones of Gus' house. Good, lovely bones they were, complimented by the long sash windows. Unlike its neighbours, it had survived more or less intact.

The district's ruin recorder had done a check on it. Gus had told Krista this in one of their curious, getting-to-know-you conversations. The ruin recorder had worn a boiler suit with ribbons from the last war pinned above his council badge and had spent considerable time knocking at walls and peering out of windows. 'They check all the houses?' Krista asked, thinking: *there are no houses left in Berlin to check*. Apparently this was so. Furthermore, a tight rein was kept on anyone trying to refurbish. You were only allowed to spend £100 on paint and whatnot, Gus added, and it was a struggle to get anything smart and shipshape. Anyone caught using too much paint would be reported.

Did people really report each other for using too much paint? Yes . . . oh yes . . . Krista understood better than most. She knew all about people reporting each other.

Herr Miller leaves by his back door . . . Fraulein Best is wearing an expensive perfume . . .

Gus touched her on the shoulder: 'Come'.

The front door was painted a holly green and had a big brass knocker in the shape of a hand. Gus paused and searched in his pocket for a key, but before he found it the door swung open.

A woman was framed in the doorway – the same one who had been watching them from upstairs. She was wearing a light blue skirt and jacket and lace-up shoes that needed repairing. 'Mr Summers?' Her expression switched into one of extreme astonishment. '*Gus.* I wasn't expecting you. I was expecting Mr and Mrs Summers who were coming to be interviewed.'

Gus put down his suitcase and kissed her on the cheek and she clung to him. 'I couldn't get you a message.'

'A telephone?' She sounded very dry.

'You have no idea, old girl, how difficult things are out there.'

'Never mind,' she said with a glimmer of a smile. Turning to Krista, she asked. 'Who . . . ?'

Gus took Krista's hand in his. 'Julia, this will come as a shock, but a good one, I hope. This is Krista.' The small pause which followed seemed to expand infinitely. 'Krista and I got married while I was in Berlin.'

Married.

The word appeared to ricochet from one to the other, catching all three in its trajectory.

'Good gracious.' Julia's hands flew up to her cheeks. '*Married.*' She stepped back and her heel clicked against the skirting board. 'I don't believe it. You can't . . . there's . . . what about . . . ?' She checked herself. 'Look, this is a shock. I just need a minute or two.' She flashed a strained smile at her brother. 'You always loved surprises.' She called over her shoulder. 'Tilly! Tilly, *come.*'

Gus smiled. 'Whether you believe me or not, I refuse to stand on the doorstep of my own house and debate it.' Picking up the case, he ushered Krista though the front door.

'Your own house,' Julia murmured. 'Yes of course.'

Before Krista's eyes, she was pulling herself together. Straightening her shoulders, adjusting the cuff of her blouse. Once upon a time, in another world, Krista had read about Englishwomen in a magazine that a visitor had bought into the convent and left behind. It had been snatched up by Berta who had shared it with the girls. There was an article on the English *memsahib* who took for granted that the atlas was coloured a lovely red, stretching more or less across the globe.

The article had not been particularly kind or reflective. It seemed to Krista to have repeated received wisdom without examining it. But, looking at Julia, perhaps it had not been so wide of the mark?

By comparison, Krista was shaking with nerves which she found intriguing because it was a long time since she had felt normal emotions. Not that she knew what was normal any more.

Stepping into the hallway, a feeling instantly settled around her. Like a rug on a freezing night. Like a good and welcome coat. What precisely? This house needed people in it and it was one which could be a home. The walls and paintwork were in a bad state, and the bannister on the beautiful curving staircase needed attention, but the house itself felt solid enough.

The impressions ran through her mind within seconds. Out of dire necessity, Krista knew how to assess where she found herself: was it safe, could she be spotted, where could she hide?

Julia banged shut the door behind them and leant back against it. 'Well . . .' She brushed down her skirt and struggled with what to say.

Gus's elder sister was a good-looking woman – long and elegant of limb – but there was a tightness around her mouth that suggested she had to struggle to control her emotions. 'You could have told Tilly and me, Gus.' The emphasis deepened.

'About something so important.' She glanced down at the gold band on Krista's finger and then up at Krista. 'I'm sorry, but you will realize that it is a shock.'

'I know.'

In this situation, she knew that her accent would sound particularly marked. Her English was excellent, made even better by the translation work which Gus had given her. But it was not, as yet at least, the language of her heart, plus she was struggling with such a wall of fatigue that she felt she might faint at any minute.

Julia shifted upright. 'Are you home for good?'

'Yes, we are,' Gus replied. 'Back for good. Back to work. Back to get this house in order.'

Julia stiffened visibly. 'I have done my best with it, Gus. I think you will find it is in order. We have been at war, you know.'

He sent her one of his smiles. 'I'm very grateful, Julia. I could have trusted no one else.'

Julia seemed mollified. 'You've been away too long. It's almost harder to get things now than during the war. The rationing. But you must have been all right where you were. Berlin wasn't it? The government would have seen to that.'

Krista felt herself swaying.

Ever vigilant, Gus noticed. He tucked his hand under Krista's elbow. It was a firm, reassuring grip. 'We can discuss all that later, Julia, but at this precise moment . . .'

Julia was right. In Berlin, those employed on the post-war work were on the receiving end of government bounty. People fought to obtain those positions. Sometimes, they killed for them.

Gus was pushing Krista towards a staircase leading down from the hall into the basement. 'Julia, do you think we could have a hot drink? We've been travelling non-stop.'

'Of course. Where's Tilly?' She stood at the bottom of the curving staircase and shouted up. 'Tilly! Come down. There's news.'

But Tilly didn't appear until they were seated around a table in the kitchen drinking tea. Because it was in the basement, the kitchen did not have much natural light and the single, unshaded light bulb hanging down from the centre of the ceiling did little to make it appealing. There was no food to be seen, no shiny pots and pans, only some china stacked on the shelves. There was a large cast-iron cooking range, a wire rack for vegetables. Otherwise, it appeared meagrely stocked. No jars of spices. No onions. No dried herbs. No loaf of bread waiting to be sliced. No flitches of bacon. No sausage.

The wooden table top had been scrubbed so hard that it appeared chalk white and the china cups which Julia took down from the shelf were of such an intense blue that the tea, sheltering in them, appeared weak and beige.

Krista couldn't help comparing this dingy, sparsely stocked kitchen with the well-appointed convent one which she had known before the war began.

'Pride is a sin,' Sister Hannelore had repeated (oh, so frequently) before she died of starvation. 'But when it comes to my kitchen, well, my sisters excuse me a little of it . . .'

All that was a long time ago. Before the worst had happened. After boiling the kettle and filling the teapot, Julia took a seat opposite Krista. 'The tea isn't up to much.' She grimaced. 'We have to take as we find. There's no proper help these days either. That's why I asked Mr and Mrs Summer to come for an interview. Their references weren't marvellous, but everyone seems to have vanished. They can't all still be working in factories . . . or dead.'

'Let's hope they turn up,' said Gus. 'You can't run this house without help.'

Julia lifted her head and stared directly at Krista who, in turn, stared down at the white furrowed grain of the table top.

'If only Martin hadn't been killed,' said Julia.

'Julia . . .'

Krista did not know Gus very well, but she knew enough to know that he was warning his sister.

'Martin deserved to live,' said Julia. 'Not to end up smashed into a French field by . . .'

'*Julia* . . .'

Her craving to have something hot to drink almost over-powering, Krista did not care about the quality of the tea and gulped it down. A pool of heat settled in her stomach.

'Lord, it's Gus,' said a voice from the doorway. 'Well I never.'

'Tilly . . .' Gus rose to his feet. 'Tilly . . .' He sounded unreservedly pleased, unlike his warier greeting with Julia earlier.

Julia sighed loudly.

Tilly advanced into the kitchen in a way which suggested she had waited to make this entrance. Certainly, she staged her entrance well for three pairs of eyes swung in her direction.

Fairer than her sister's, her hair dropped loosely over her shoulders. She was clad in black from top to toe and had a slash of bright red lipstick. The overall effect was very young, louche and suggestively fatigued.

Grasping Gus by the shoulders, she kissed him, French fashion, on his cheeks. '*Bonjour* . . . Why did you not tell us you were coming back?'

Julia came and stood beside Tilly. 'Gus has some news.'

It was then that Tilly appeared to register there was someone else in the kitchen. A pair of intense blue eyes trained on Krista. 'Who . . .?'

Gus explained.

Krista got to her feet. The three women faced each other and it was noticeable that they were all approximately the same height, with Krista a fraction taller perhaps.

The surprise on Tilly's face was genuine. 'But . . . what of Nella? I mean . . . sorry.' A smile half flickered and was banished. 'Sorry. Forget that.'

Krista drained her tea.

'So where did Gus find you?'

Good question. Krista shot a look at him. In the rush to

marry, they hadn't agreed on their stories. If truth be told, they didn't *know* each other's stories.

'In a convent . . .' she began. 'I was hiding there . . . Berlin was being sacked and I had been brought up in the convent so I went to the place I knew best. I was working in the library and Gus came in.'

'Reconnaissance. We needed an office and someone suggested the convent. Krista here was trying her best to get the books and documents cleaned up.'

Why had she bothered? She had been low on energy because she had not eaten any kind of fat for weeks and there was a wavy mist in front of her eyes and she felt as if she were floating most of the time. Talking to Gus had been a release – her feelings had been bottled up for so long. If she had any left. She must have done, for after talking to Gus she began to feel human after all.

'He gave me a tin of spam.' Krista looked over to Gus. 'It was the best thing I had ever tasted.'

If she closed her eyes, she could summon up the small fat deposits casing the meat. She had taken a finger and run it around the inside of the tin, before licking it until it was almost raw.

Tilly remembered her manners. 'I must congratulate you. No, really. This is very exciting. Have you been travelling all day?' She swung round towards Julia. 'They must be tired. We should make up a bed.'

Krista said – and she sounded very, very German: 'Please let me do it. I don't want . . . no trouble.'

Julia said absolutely not and it was no trouble. But she didn't mean it.

Having led Krista up the carpetless staircase, she pushed open a door which led off the first-floor landing. 'This is Gus's room. I'll fetch sheets and towels.'

Krista hovered in the doorway. With a rush of relief, she saw that it was a nice room, large and airy with a sash window. The paintwork was blistered and peeling, but that was to be expected.

The sashes in the window overlooking the garden needed replacing and the bed in the centre of the room looked as though it sagged in the middle.

Would this room be the refuge she craved? A place where she and Gus could lay the first brick in the building of their new lives? She stepped into the room and inhaled sharply. This was the beginning. A moment etched with significance. She took a second step.

Perched on the edge of the bed, she listened to the inevitable altercation between Gus and his sisters which floated up through the open door of the sitting room below.

How could you? She's a German. We'll be a laughing stock. Her life will be misery.

'What about Nella?'

What about Nella?

Much later, lying beside Gus in the dark, she listened to the noises in the house. A brief exchange between the sisters on the stairs, the sound of a chair scraping across an uncarpeted floor, the small shriek of a bedspring, the rattle of a window.

She tried to pinch the flesh over her hipbones between finger and thumb, but there was none to spare. She was well aware that her extreme thinness was off-putting to some. Despite the rationing, the two sisters looked reasonably well fed and, beside them, she knew she must look like a figure from hell. Well, she had come from hell and there was no use tiptoeing around it.

She knew nothing about this house. Who had lived here, who cared for it. Who wanted to live here? Which of the sisters would feel usurped? Or would it be both? Then there was this person, Nella. There was an entire dimension about which she knew nothing.

Meanwhile, there was a roof over her head which she fully intended to keep. Having gathered like the high tide waiting to break, fatigue hit her, drawing her down.

Further Reading

Elizabeth Buchan Recommends:

Non-fiction

A Life in Secrets: The Story of Vera Atkins and the Lost Agents of SOE
by Sarah Helm

Isak Dinesen: The Life of Karen Blixen by Judith Thurman

A Quiet Courage by Liane Jones

Alan Turing: The Enigma by Andrew Hodges

The Spy Who Loved: The Secrets and Lives of One of Britain's Bravest Wartime Heroines by Clare Mulley

Fiction

Charlotte Gray by Sebastian Faulks

The Girl Who Fell from the Sky by Simon Mawer

Their Finest Hour and a Half by Lissa Evans

Sophie's Choice by William Styron

Hornet Flight by Ken Follett